D1040215

HIGH PRAISE FOR BONNIE VANAK!

THE TIGER & THE TOMB

"Bonnie Vanak . . . create[s] a highly entertaining, exciting, romantic read. . . . You can't go wrong when you read anything by Bonnie Vanak!"

—*Romance & Friends*

"Vanak has written a totally sensually satisfying and action-packed romantic adventure."

—*Historical Romance Writers*

THE FALCON & THE DOVE

"Bonnie Vanak touches upon a fascinating period of history with charm and panache. A wonderful first novel."

—*Heather Graham, bestselling author*

"Bonnie writes with humor and passion. She masterly weaves a stunning vista of people, place and time. I truly enjoyed this unique and compelling story."

—*Old Book Barn Gazette*

"A fast paced tale that hooks the audience . . . a riveting novel."

—*Harriet's Book Reviews*

WARRIOR OF LOVE

"Are you the one I seek?"

"If you are Ramses," Katherine replied softly.

"I am. Is there something you require of me?" His voice was a deep, low purr, a seductive lilt that brushed across her nerves, making them crackle with desire.

"Yes," she said in a breathless whisper.

"Why the need for secrecy?" His voice shifted, became lower and huskier. "Or does the service you request . . . not require my famed horses?"

Katherine's palms went clammy. "I have heard you called the warrior of love," she blurted out, thinking rapidly.

A narrow slit of light from the shuttered window spilled into the room, like a moonbeam upon the Nile. Katherine approached him from behind. With feral grace, he whirled around. The dark stranger possessed a warrior's dangerous moves.

"Do you need such a warrior?" he purred.

Sliding closer, Katherine could feel his warmth, his strength radiating like the sun's aura. "Yes."

Other *Leisure* books by Bonnie Vanak:

THE FALCON & THE DOVE

The Tiger & the Tomb

BONNIE VANAK

LEISURE BOOKS   NEW YORK CITY

A LEISURE BOOK ®

December 2003

Published by

Dorchester Publishing Co., Inc.
200 Madison Avenue
New York, NY 10016

ISBN 0-8439-5299-7

The name "Leisure Books" and the stylized "L" with design are
trademarks of Dorchester Publishing Co., Inc.

Printed in the United States of America.

Visit us on the web at www.dorchesterpub.com.

*In memory of Marcia Montague,
a talented artist who taught me to hear the music in colors;
and Eve Sama, who inspired me with her tremendous
faith, hope, and love.*

Thank you both for reminding me what's most important in life.

The Tiger & the Tomb

Chapter One

Akhetaten, Egypt, 1893

"Tomb robbers!"

The words roared throughout the immense stone chamber. Walls reverberated with the shuddering force. Ancient dust seemed to tremble before his raging might.

Nazim Ramses bin Seti Sharif glowered at the men he had surprised. Four Egyptians in long, shirtlike *thobes* and a pale Englishman looked up from unearthing an ancient papyrus. The map of the gold mine, the key to finding Rastau's tomb. For thousands of years, his ancestor's tomb, filled with priceless treasure, had remained a secret buried with time.

He was a Guardian of the Ages, a warrior who swore a sacred oath to protect royals. He ate tomb robbers for breakfast. And he was very hungry this morning.

Sliding the scimitar from its sheath, he twirled it in the air. Torchlight reflected the deadly steel's gleam.

Draping the trailing end of his indigo turban across his face, he veiled himself before his enemies. Then he touched a hand to his heart and lips in the Khamsin gesture of honor before battle.

"I am Nazim Ramses bin Seti Sharif, Khamsin Guardian of the Ages. Leave these sacred premises now!"

"What goes here?"

The commanding voice of his sheikh, Jabari bin Tarik Hassid, echoed through the tomb. Ramses spotted the English thief withdrawing a pistol as the others unsheathed their blades. Gunfire crackled. The Guardian dropped in a graceful roll, yelling for Jabari to duck. He leapt up, kicked the gunman's feet from under him and slashed. The man moaned and fell, grabbing his chest. Ramses retrieved the pistol. Jabari pressed against the wall, his face twisted with shock. Ramses's gaze roved to a bullet hole a whisper from his leader's head.

"You dare attempt to harm the one I have sworn to protect!"

Letting out an undulating cry, echoed by Jabari, he charged. One Englishman feinted, striking air as Ramses lithely sidestepped. Jabari rushed forward, engaging two as his partner concentrated on the others. Snarling with righteous power, Ramses felt the spirit of his ancestors flow through him.

"May our ancestors curse those disturbing their ancient resting places!" The words thundered like a prophecy of doom.

Suddenly, one of five blazing torches went out. The frightened men made signs against the Evil Eye.

"Tell me his name and your lives are spared,"

Ramses said, gesturing to the Englishman lying on the ground.

"B-Burrells," a thief stammered.

Ramses nodded. "Take him. I do not want his body desecrating these sacred premises."

Without another word, the tomb raiders lifted the injured Englishman and ran from the chamber.

Jabari glanced at the extinguished torch. "I could swear our ancestors did that. Or you did."

His Guardian did not answer. He tucked the ancient map into his *binish*, approached the sarcophagus and fell to one knee. Placing his sword's point on the ground, he rested his hands on the hilt. As he bowed his head, Jabari joined him. The men uttered a prayer of homage, then stood, wiping and sheathing their weapons. They left the tomb, careful to once again seal its entrance, and climbed down to the dry riverbed where their mares waited.

"I told you to stay outside," Ramses scolded his friend as they rode through the canyon. "How am I to guard your stubborn hide if you will not listen?"

The sheikh shot him a piercing stare, one that would usually turn the bravest warrior into a quivering mass. "I do not need a keeper," Jabari growled.

"You dishonor me." Ramses rolled up the right sleeve of his *binish* and underlying *kamis* shirt to his heavily muscled upper arm. He pointed to a blue-inked falcon. The mark of Jabari's clan had been tattooed on him when he became a Guardian.

"Your life I shall defend as my own, my right arm shall be always there to protect you, I will remain always at your side to safeguard your steps through life, to the point of my death. This I solemnly vow as your

Guardian of the Ages." Rolling his sleeve down, he repeated the oath taken at manhood.

Jabari's fierce scowl faded. "It is a vow I am deeply grateful for, Ramses."

"I cannot get used to that name," Ramses admitted, even though he used it for trysts with women in Cairo. For twenty-six years, he was Nazim. With his upcoming wedding, he followed ancient Guardian tradition and assumed a new name with marriage.

"You will no longer be known as Nazim when you marry and take the name of Egypt's greatest warrior pharaoh. I only wish to prepare you," Jabari said quietly.

Ramses flicked a fly off his horse's mane, wondering what his bride looked like. Distant kin. Daughter of an English earl and an Egyptian royal. Lady Katherine Smithfield had been betrothed to him upon her birth eighteen years ago. A half *samak*, a fish, as he termed the English. Skinny, pale and cold. How could he love such a woman? Silent anguish filled him.

"I marry a woman who is half English," he muttered.

"Which half do you think is English?" Jabari teased.

"The top half, I hope. English women are as frigid as their climate." Ramses shuddered.

"They start out frigid, but the warrior of love's weapon slowly heats their inner core," Jabari said slyly. He quoted an ancient Arabic proverb: " 'Patience is the key to release.' "

" 'At the end of the night you shall hear shrill cries,' " Ramses quoted back. "Patience? The secret of one hundred kisses does not suffice. It is now the secret of one thousand kisses."

"The warrior of love takes his last prowl through

Cairo next month and retires, his weapon weary, his lips as well." Jabari mocked. "Why do you bother with the English ladies?"

"Because I enjoy bedding the wives of condescending Englishmen who think we Egyptians are too stupid to run our country. The English men are all alike. Small, like their minds and other . . . organs," Ramses quipped. "They are greedy and untrustworthy."

"And what of your English father-in-law? You do not trust the English, yet you will show Lord Smithfield the map? Reveal to him the sacred tomb hidden within the gold mine?"

His friend's swift twist to his own words left him speechless. Jabari did not trust the earl, even though he had consented to partnering with him to work the gold mine. The Khamsin needed Lord Smithfield's backing to buy equipment to extract the gold and they needed the gold to educate their children. If only Ramses's ancestor had not been laid to rest in the same place.

Ramses hastened to reassure his sheikh. "He will swear silence or pay the price." he said grimly, putting a hand on his scimitar's hilt. He caught Jabari's startled look and added, "The earl consented to sign an agreement promising never to reveal our tribe's secrets. This includes the tomb."

"And your bride? Women love to talk." Jabari frowned.

"All she knows is my name is Nazim. She has no idea that her father partners with us on the mine. He promised not to tell her until just before the wedding." Ramses took a deep breath. "I trust him."

The sheikh grunted. "I do not. But I trust you, Ramses."

The words placed heavy weights on his shoulders.

Jabari had allowed Ramses to reveal a huge Khamsin secret, staking the tribe's future on the earl's partnership. But neither of them had counted on an English tomb robber discovering the priceless map. Disquiet raced through him. Instinct warned him the man named Burrells had not died. He had looked into the man's cold blue eyes and saw greed shining there like gold. Burrells would do anything to steal the map. Unlike the Khamsin warriors of the wind, he possessed no honor. Nothing would stop him.

Cairo, one month later

Lady Katherine Kalila Smithfield, descendent of generations of English lords and Egyptian royals, embarked on a mission to add a new title to her name. Thief.

Her victim was an Egyptian named Ramses who possessed a map of a gold mine hiding a treasure-filled tomb. With every ounce of strength in her tiny frame, she pressed on toward her destination. Cairo's streets bustled with the usual frenzied activity of the very rich and the very desperate. Sniffing for scraps, a rib-thin dog darted past the wheels of a *gharry*. A well-dressed English lady emerging from an antiquities shop flicked open her parasol and sidestepped the pleading palm of a blind beggar child. Katherine's sensitive heart ached for the girl. She reached into her reticule, dropped a few coins into child's tin cup. As she went to pass, a dirty hand seized her skirts. Katherine bent down to tug them free.

"Lady," the little girl said in a toneless voice, "turn away from the tomb. Beware the curse."

Her mouth went dry as dust as she stared at the orphan. "What curse?" she whispered.

"Those who enter the tomb to seek its treasures will die," she droned, her sightless eyes staring ahead.

Katherine crouched down, touched the girl's tattered sleeve. "Please, tell me more." But the little girl began singing to herself, lost in a world of her own.

Her heart skipping a few beats, Katherine stood and scurried away. The beggar girl knew nothing. She had felt the soft silk of Katherine's dress and identified her as English. English explorers and tomb raiders as numerous as Egypt's sands roamed through Cairo's streets. *She was trying to scare you.* Still, Katherine couldn't resist tossing an anxious glance over her shoulder. Her eyes sought the little girl.

She had disappeared like raindrops in the desert.

Swallowing her distress, Katherine scurried on. Curses were nothing compared to the threat hanging over her head like a sword suspended by a thin hair. If she didn't retrieve the map, Foster Burrells and his partner, Lord Estes, would frame her father and imprison him for stealing an amulet from the Giza Museum. "Things happen in Cairo's jail," Burrells had said with a mocking grin. "Men die. Do you want your dear papa to die?"

Katherine bit her lip. She wished she hadn't begged Papa to take her to the Giza Museum. He had arranged a private tour with Burrells, the curator, and Estes, the museum's patron and inspector general for the Egyptian Antiquities Service. A gold amulet of the Egyptian cat goddess had caught her father's eye. He had asked to hold it and became overwhelmed with grief because it resembled one her mother had worn. Papa swore he had put it back. She believed him.

Katherine hurried along. The stately building of the Shepheard's Hotel loomed ahead. Through a third party, she had arranged to meet Ramses, a breeder of purebred Arabians, at the hotel to inquire about breeding her mare with his stallion.

She had just enough time for daily tea with friends before her appointment with Ramses. Katherine mounted the steps to the verandah. Tourists sat in rattan chairs, sipping hot tea. Staccato chattering rattled her frayed nerves. Cigarette smoke stung her nostrils. Male heads turned as she passed. Smiles withered as they saw her face. The familiar lip curls began. Her scarred left cheek. They always stared with revulsion. Always.

Katherine covered her cheek with a trembling hand. She thought of her middle name and the ironic meaning of Kalila. No man would ever call her "beloved." Swallowing tears, she entered the lobby. Crystal chandeliers cast soft light upon the guests. Splendid columns encircled vases of fragrant flowers. She clutched the veil she had purchased in the *souks*, then fingered her dress. Egypt in her hand, England on her body. Like her two halves, they clashed. Wishing the veil could always hide her scar, Katherine ran upstairs to put it away.

When she returned and headed into the lounge, the three other members of the Ladies Pyramid Society were already seated on a red chaise. Beautiful blond English roses with peaches-and-cream skin, Katherine thought wistfully. Two passing men gave them admiring glances. Her friends did not notice. Like hungry children eyeing a pastry tray, they stared at a man across the room. Acting as normal as possible, Katherine warmly greeted the women as she pulled up a chair.

Three heads turned, issued languid "hullos" and then snapped back to the object of their fascination.

"Whom are you looking at?" she asked curiously as a waiter poured tea from a gleaming silver service.

"Someone we've heard of. Ram. He's known to assist with hysteria treatments," replied Mrs. Hunt in a vague voice.

"Hysteria treatments?" Katherine wrinkled her nose.

"You know, dear. Women's problems."

Shrugging, Katherine picked up her notebook and began reading aloud to begin their daily discussion of the pyramids.

" 'When Napoleon fought his battle before the Great Pyramid in 1798, he remarked upon its tremendous size. . . .' "

"Size," drawled Lady Fitzwilliam, a young widow. "I hear his is most impressive."

Katherine tried again. " 'Flinders Petrie mapped the inside of the Great Pyramid, using a Rigid Tripod Stand of thirty inches. . . .' "

"Definitely rigid. But thirty inches?" giggled Mrs. Simmons, whose husband was a military attaché.

"Of course not," scoffed the buxom Mrs. Hunt. "An exaggeration. Even for the warrior of love."

Katherine nibbled on a cucumber sandwich and sipped tea. Doggedly, she continued reading. " 'Mr. Petrie noted the King's Chamber's ceiling is supported by poles thrust against it . . .' "

"Thrust," said Lady Fitzwilliam dreamily.

Katherine shut her notebook. "Ladies, if you don't

Bonnie Vanak

want to discuss the pyramids, then we should touch on another topic."

"Touching is so important in the cure of hysteria, my doctor in England always said," observed Mrs. Hunt.

Doctors. At last something she could comment on. "I love medicine. Our physician in England taught me some healing arts when I nursed tenant farmers on the estate. I even helped him remove a bullet from a patient wounded during a hunting accident."

Three heads looked at her, shook, then ignored her again.

"My physician is an enthusiastic believer in Dr. George Taylor's manipulator," Mrs. Hunt said.

Katherine's eyes grew large. "What is a manipulator?"

Lady Fitzwilliam glanced her way. "A useful appliance powered by steam. Quite invigorating, but noisy. It vibrates and provides an excellent massage to a woman's regions."

"I heard Ram cures the need for a manipulator," noted Mrs. Simmons. "His patients find themselves very relaxed after his treatments. And there's no bill."

Lady Fitzwilliam smiled softly. She dropped her voice. "I could use one of Ram's massages after being atop a camel all morning. I feel quite hysterical after riding."

"Ram is quite the rider himself, they say."

All three giggled. Katherine felt a rush of heat sweep through her at their suggestive remarks. Feeling out of sorts, she mentioned her own expertise.

"I miss riding my mare, Jenny. Every morning in London I would take her to the Row for a gallop

10

around the track. So few opportunities to ride are here in Egypt." Katherine sighed.

"It depends upon the type of riding one does, dear," Mrs. Hunt said sagely.

The object of their attention turned his head, profiling his chiseled features. Katherine looked and stifled a gasp. Her heart stilled at his male perfection. "Did you say his name was Ram?" she queried, unable to stop staring.

"Ramses, actually," Lady Fitzwilliam corrected.

Ramses. The very man she had to steal the map from! Her jaw dropped in astonishment. Suddenly all the stares and giggles made sense. A man this beautiful could make ladies quiver with anticipation over hysteria treatments.

Chestnut-streaked dark curls spilled from beneath his indigo turban. A strong jawline and firm chin framed a handsome face that blended a curious mixture of European features with Egyptian. A closely trimmed beard and mustache did not hide a generous mouth that looked accustomed to laughter.

But he was too early. She must have told her contact, the gold seller in the *souks*, the wrong meeting time. Katherine thought rapidly, formed a plan. She said good-bye to the ladies and headed into the lobby.

A bony hand seized her wrist. She gasped with fright at the short, white-turbaned man grinning at her.

"Lady Katherine," he said in Arabic. "You gave me the slip earlier. I've been searching for you."

"Go away, Mohammad, or you'll ruin my plan," she whispered.

He leered at her. "I can help you if you cooperate with me." He ran a slimy tongue over yellowing teeth.

11

"I don't need your help." Katherine wrenched her arm away.

His eyes narrowed to slits. "The desert sun burns like a living hell, but it is paradise compared to what your father will suffer if you don't get the map. I'll be keeping an eye on you."

Watching him slither away, she squelched the revulsion rising in her throat, then dashed upstairs to her room.

Minutes later, she reappeared downstairs. A black veil shrouded her lower face. Long ebony hair spilled about her shoulders. Folds of a loose, black *abbaya* hid a money belt and the small knife strapped to her hip.

Katherine passed a note to a waiter to discreetly hand to Ramses. "Your appointment awaits you in the men's smoking room down the hall," she had scribbled in perfect Arabic. Then she hovered behind a potted fern to watch.

Ramses read the note and stood. Katherine's gaze roved over his body inch by perfect inch. Indigo trousers were tucked into soft leather boots. The wide-sleeved indigo coat covering his broad shoulders fell to mid-thigh. A long scimitar and dagger dangled from his belt. He exuded a powerful aura of confidence and dark danger. Hope sank faster than a stone in the Nile. So much for using her knife to demand the map. What was one small dagger compared to the wicked length of steel he carried? A shiver snaked down her spine. The fierce warrior would retaliate swiftly if he caught her. But she must risk it.

Ramses paced with catlike smoothness toward her. The warrior stole her breath away as if he had grabbed the air rising in her throat. As he neared, she saw his eyes. A dusky golden brown, as dreamy and large as a full moon. They perused the lobby with critical regard as he stopped near her hiding place. The handsome warrior's magnificent stride and burning amber eyes resembled the tiger she'd seen in childhood. But his mouth was kind. She hoped it offered laughter and not cruel words.

A spicy scent of cloves lingered as he passed. Mystical awe at his imposing presence swept through her. The warrior seemed as much a part of ancient Egypt as the map she sought. Katherine imagined Ramses's ancestry dating back that far. His broad shoulders like those of an ancient king carried an air of pride.

Katherine stiffened with resolve, then ran down the hallway toward the room. She turned the doorknob and peered inside. He stood by the tiny shuttered window, his back toward her. Meager light from a small lamp sent shadows dancing across the carpet. She drank in the sight of him, poised as if studying the window, his hands laced behind him.

Katherine slipped inside, closed the door and stole nearer. Alerted to her presence, he spoke over his shoulder. "Are you the one I seek?"

"If you are Ramses," Katherine replied softly. He spoke the Arabic of the desert tribes and she answered in kind, thankful for all her studies.

"I am. Is there something you require of me?" His voice was a deep, low purr, a seductive lilt that brushed across her nerves, making them crackle with desire.

"Yes," she said in a breathless whisper.

"The note the gold seller in the *souks* gave me said you wished to see me about stud services. Why the need for secrecy?"

13

Then his voice shifted, became lower and huskier.

"Or does the service you request . . . not require horses?"

Katherine's palms went clammy. "I have heard you called the warrior of love," she blurted out, thinking rapidly.

A narrow slit of light from the shuttered window spilled into the room, like a moonbeam upon the Nile. Katherine approached him from behind. With feral grace, he whirled around. The dark stranger possessed a warrior's dangerous moves.

Her tongue moistened dry lips as he studied her. "Do you need such a warrior?" he purred.

Sliding closer, Katherine could feel his warmth, his strength radiating like the sun's aura. "Yes," she replied softly, then fell against him as if fainting. Two strong hands caught her before she could reach for his pocket, and set her straight.

"You are most eager," he murmured. "Do not be so impatient, little one. Love should not be rushed. Nor should a kiss."

He reached for her veil. She cried out in panic. "Wait! Put out the light. You mustn't see my face."

Sharpness edged his tone. "Why?"

Katherine groped for an excuse. "I can't risk you telling anyone who I am and what we did."

Ramses grunted, crossed the room and extinguished the lamp, dimming the room to near blackness. He strode toward her with languid grace. Her heart tripled its cadence as he stood a whisper away.

"Now I have a request of you. Kiss me," he commanded.

She must go through with this, or he would suspect. Katherine removed her veil and let it fall. Hooking her hands around Ramses's lean hips, she stood on tiptoe and pressed her lips against his. Even to her, the kiss felt inexperienced. She broke their contact and felt something crinkle beneath her right palm. The map!

Ramses chuckled. "That is not a kiss," he said softly.

He cupped her chin with one strong hand and brought her face close to his. His other hand encircled her waist as he pulled Katherine against him. He sought her mouth, returning her innocent maiden's kiss with a man's passionate one.

Fear flickered down her spine, then disappeared at the hunger of his kiss. His hard body pressed against her breasts. Map forgotten, she clutched the wide breadth of his shoulders. His mouth was seeking, demanding, and she uttered a tiny moan as he forced her lips to open to him, then teased her tongue with deadly skillful thrusts. Her golden tiger captured her in his muscled embrace and attacked every raging nerve in her trembling body. Her senses roared back with life of their own.

As the warrior slid one hand up her back, his heated touch burned through the *abbaya's* covering. He massaged the nape of her neck, raked his fingers through her hair. The handsome warrior gently plundered her mouth, claiming her as his. A sandstorm of sensations engulfed Katherine like a Khamsin, Egypt's hot desert wind. Her limbs turned to liquid, her brain senseless. Then he stroked the left side of her neck, tenderly thumbing her skin, tracing her jaw, nearing her scar.

"No!" she cried out, panicked at the thought of him discovering her disfigurement. Katherine tore her lips away, jerking back as if he'd slapped her. He let go.

"Who are you?" he demanded, stepping forward, his arms outstretched as if to pull her against him once more. Her mouth felt swollen from his savage, tender possession.

"I am no one," she said in a half sob, the truth lacing her heart. Katherine backed away and then pressed a finger against the lips that had brought such sweetness into her life.

"Good-bye," she whispered, grabbing her veil and fleeing.

She raced out of the hotel toward the *souks*, deeply shaken by the power of Ramses's kiss. Surely the gold seller who arranged their meeting knew of someone else willing to steal the map for enough money. Katherine attached her veil as she ran, feeling she escaped a tiger. A tiger that enchanted her just as much as the tiger cub that had scarred her cheek, forever damning her to men's cruel sneers.

"Come back," he said in a hoarse whisper.

He was bewitched. Ramses stood still in shock for a moment, then shook off the dazed feeling and ran out to the lobby. He must find out who she was! He gazed frantically about. Like a man possessed, he searched the crowded room.

His pulse pounded. Ramses licked his mouth, still tasting her honeyed lips. His manhood throbbed and demanded release. Drawing in a ragged breath, he fought for control.

Childhood fears of the dark had surfaced when she asked him to blow out the lamp. Then Ramses realized she desired privacy. Her innocent kiss delighted him. She had plenty to learn. He grinned wickedly, savoring the idea of teaching her.

He'd thought himself fully sated from seeking pleasure in women's soft arms. As always, he forgot the women after leaving their beds. *This* woman he could not forget. This enchantress aroused him instantly to a fever pitch. Her kiss was a few droplets that barely quenched his raging thirst. Rather, it drove him mad, made his throat close up and ache. Ramses felt like a man in the desert allowed one brief sip from a shimmering oasis before the pool vanished.

He hadn't even seen what she looked like! Ramses bunched his fists. Then he remembered, and smiled. A sliver of light had spilled across her eyes. Her eyes flashed the rich fire of a rare jewel. Sapphire? Emerald?

Such a woman. Far different from the one pledged to him. Tomorrow at this very hotel, he would sign the marriage contract and further taint his progeny with English blood. The truth assassinated his pride. Ramses's grandfather had been sired by an Englishman. He didn't hate the English for their culture. He despised them because he was half-English, himself. Ramses dismissed thoughts of Lady Katherine. His mind was too besotted with the lovely stranger. No frigid Englishwoman, but an Egyptian woman as warm as sun-kissed sand.

Somehow, he would find her. Jabari once joked Ramses was as fierce and relentless as a tiger when stalking something he wanted. His friend was right. He would not let the mysterious lady slip out of his grasp. He would hunt down every single woman in Cairo. Prowl every street and alley. He burned for her, wanted her with a raging desire.

He would do anything to have her for one last night of passion before signing the marriage contract. Somehow, some way he would find her. And possess that sweet mouth once more.

Ramses spotted the waiter who had handed him the note and demanded to know if he had seen the woman.

"She—she ran out of the hotel in the direction of the *souks*," the man stammered.

Ramses left the Shepheard's. The gold seller at the Khan al Khalili who arranged their meeting would have answers. The *souks* were a few blocks away. With a determination in his gait, he headed for Cairo's exotic, open-air market.

Chapter Two

The man blocking her path would not move.

Katherine's heart pounded. Pungent odors of animal dung and rotting fruit rinds hung in the narrow alleyway that led from Khan al Khalili. Each section harbored specialities: perfumes, gold and silver, rich Persian carpets, exotic spices, clothing. Unsavory types also lurked in the dark alleys, waiting to prey upon the unwary. The shortcut had looked safe, until now.

"A woman all alone. Where are you going, pretty lady?"

"Please let me by." She tried to keep her voice even. Her nose wrinkled at the stench of fermented sweat and old wine rising from him in an invisible cloud. The tall, paunchy man clad in a *thobe* grinned, showing rotting teeth.

Katherine swallowed and stood as tall as her five feet, three inches would allow. She hated being so bloody short! Anger overrode the fear. She glared at the burly man.

"Let me pass. *Now*, you insolent piece of sheep's liver."

His narrowed look indicated her insult had angered him. Katherine felt inside her *abbaya* for the dagger.

The man stepped forward. Her palms grew clammy. She could fight him, but he was taller and stronger. No one would rescue her. Fear squeezed her heart as she envisioned him dragging her off, a hand over her mouth to cover her screams. . . .

"Let the lady pass." A deep, commanding voice, like that of a tiger's purr, caught her attention. Katherine turned with gratitude to her rescuer, stifling a gasp.

Her amber-eyed warrior stood with an air of expectation, like a fierce jungle cat sizing up prey. His broad, muscled form radiated with golden light in the dim alley. Hands on hips, he moved ahead of her. Ramses became a large barrier between her and the man. The protective gesture melted her even as panic filled her. He had followed her! But why?

"Oh, and you're going to make me?" The fat man sneered at Ramses as he narrowed the distance.

"No, not me. This." Ramses withdrew the long scimitar at his waist. He twirled the blade in a ritualistic manner and touched his hand to his heart, then to his lips. He draped his turban's trailing end across the lower part of his face.

"Care to step aside now?" Ramses sounded friendly. "Let us pretend you have honor. You can pretend, can you not?"

The man withdrew a dagger and shuffled forward. Ramses nodded at the obvious challenge. "I see you care to make the acquaintance of *Shukran*," he said, indicating the blade in his right hand. He had named his sword "thank you."

20

" 'Thank you?' " her tormentor asked in a puzzled voice.

"You are welcome," Ramses replied and lunged forward. He slashed the man's *thobe*, ripping it from waist to hem. Ramses playfully lifted the parted garment with the sword's tip.

"Care to lose anything else?" he asked meaningfully.

The man reddened and ran off. Ramses gave a formal bow. "My lady, after you."

She stood dumbstruck for a minute, then nodded her thanks, scurrying ahead. He did not recognize her. Ramses only played the gallant to assist a woman in distress. Katherine entered a bustling lane filled with merchants arguing with buyers in high-pitched protests. Turquoise, navy, crimson and yellow fabrics stretched across rods formed a colorful canopy across the alley.

Her rescuer fell into step beside her, his long legs easily keeping pace with her hurried stride. Ramses had removed his veil. Katherine felt the power of his muscular presence shield her. Calmer now, she processed this new twist of events. He seemed determined to follow her.

His voice rumbled with protective concern. "The *souks* are no place for a woman alone. Where is your escort?"

She kept her head and eyes lowered, not daring to meet his gaze. Egyptian women were humble. They did not look a man in the eyes. "I have none. But I shall be all right."

"I think not," he said arrogantly. "Cairo is filled with loathsome snakes such as that one. If you will permit, I shall escort you myself." His tone indicated he would not accept a refusal.

"I am in your debt," she murmured. "But I must admit curiosity. Why do you call your sword 'thank you'?" Katherine darted a glance out of the corner of her eye.

Golden eyes twinkled with merriment. "It sends my enemies flying into Paradise. Since they are no longer capable of expressing their gratitude, my blade's name says it for them."

She stifled a giggle. "You presume that they journey there. What if their spirits head in the opposite direction?"

"Ah, I do not think so. My mother said all the space there is reserved exclusively for me. Since no one dares to question her word, I am assured that my enemies will never join me."

Now she laughed openly. Anywhere with him, even the bowels of Hades, would be paradise. "I cannot see that happening. Surely one of your good deeds, such as rescuing a lady in distress, will merit you the joys of Paradise. Perhaps I would even petition for you."

"Perhaps," he said softly. "A woman's tender pleas can move even the coldest heart of stone."

His deep voice sent shudders of need raging through her. She felt dazed by his sheer power and large, imposing presence. The more she looked at his broad shoulders, his quiet air of controlled command, the more nervous she became. Those amber eyes held sharp intelligence. Katherine bit her lip.

"May I have the pleasure of your name? I am called Ramses."

Flustered, she put a hand to her face. "A beautiful name," she stammered. "It suits you."

"It does?" He cocked his head at her.

Katherine thought frantically. "Ramses the Great,

the warrior pharaoh. How prophetic of your father to choose it!"

He let loose a hearty, full-bodied laugh. She loved the sound, and her spirits soared on its waves. Enchanted by their easy banter, she wandered into the street without looking.

"Watch it!" he yelled as a wooden cart piled with colorful fabric careened toward her. Ramses grabbed her arms and pulled her back. His powerful hands, even through the *abbaya*, sent a tremor of desire down her spine. Katherine remembered the way he'd caressed her neck with those strong fingers.

"I see I shall have to stick by your side very closely, as you are inclined to stray into trouble," he declared.

She swallowed hard. "This marks the second time you've saved me. Thank you. Another good deed to add to your list. Perhaps your mother's influence will not hold fast and you will indeed journey to Paradise."

His warm palm suddenly enfolded her hand. Ramses caressed her fingers with slow, sensual strokes. "My experiences with women have taught me Paradise can be found here on earth," he murmured. She dared to look up. The gleaming smile he offered melted her senses. He swept a majestic bow to her, offering her the street as if it were paved with gold.

"Shall we press on? After you, my lady."

She bedazzled him like no other woman. Intuition told him he'd found his mysterious, jewel-eyed maid. Ramses examined the diminutive spitfire strolling beside him. Her black-clad shoulders bore the dignified grace of a woman of breeding. Her mouth . . . He hid a smile. She had a man's feisty spirit.

He could not place her accent, but her sultry voice

23

sang to him with its own sweet music. Her speech indicated learning. There were few things Ramses valued as much as a good education. He had learned to read and write with Jabari, as they had shared quarters and tutors in Cairo during their youth.

When he'd noticed the small, dark-garbed figure drift past with an air of regal grace, he became deeply troubled. A woman unaccompanied in the *souks* presented an easy target for vagabonds. Her dauntless courage in facing that foul cur raised his admiration for her behavior, feckless as it was.

Now, as Ramses glanced at her by his side, his naturally inquisitive nature took over. Who was she? She maintained an aloof demeanor that differentiated her from other women. Was she married? If so, her husband must be a strong one to tame such a bold creature. Jealousy shot through him. He preferred to think her a maiden.

"Where is your home? Is it far from here?" He hoped her answer would reveal something of her identity.

"I am visiting. We stay at a hotel near here."

"We," he echoed. "Your husband and you."

"My father and I. I am unmarried."

His spirits lifted as his distress grew. What manner of man would let his daughter wander the streets alone? Ramses put a hand on his sword hilt, his protective instincts rising again.

"So you strayed from the safety of your father's house? You should not be alone. A woman without a husband to defend her needs her father to guide her steps," he scolded gently. *If I were your husband, I would never let you out of my sight.*

"I have no need of a husband to defend me." She

paused and reached into her *abbaya*. He noted her dainty hands, as delicate as porcelain. She withdrew a sharp silver dagger. Her shoulders squared as she held the knife up with practiced ease.

His eyes widened as they fixated on the weapon's wicked edges. This woman stood armed and ready with a warrior's stance.

"I have my best friend here. We keep each other company as I shop."

"A handy best friend," he murmured as she sheathed the blade and they resumed walking. "Such friends may keep one from harm. But they can make trouble, especially for women."

A small, outraged sniff came from beneath the black veil. "You do not think I can defend myself because I am a woman?"

"I do not," he stated with conviction. "Certainly not against a man."

She halted and made as if to tilt her head up, then lowered it again. Suddenly Ramses wished he could see her eyes. Were they sparkling with fire and passion?

"You do not," she said in a saucy tone that had an underlining threat to it. Before he could consider a reply, something jabbed into his *binish*. Something sharp.

The woman pressed the dagger into his side. Ramses's lips curved into a huge smile of delight at her crafty, swift response. He did not see her withdraw the blade again. Truly the woman had the cunning and stealth of a man!

"Now will you admit that I can defend myself against men?"

He ran a thumb across his lower lip, as if considering her challenge. "Perhaps against a fat, weak lout such as the one back in the alley. Yes, perhaps." Ramses paused.

"But against a warrior? No." Before she had time to react, he turned and twisted, grabbing her hand and gently forcing her to release the blade. Her skin was warm and soft. Not porcelain. More like the delicate petals of a flower. A rapid, sudden feeling of desire flickered through him.

Ramses chuckled as he flipped the knife into the air and caught it by its handle. With a flourish, he handed it back to her. She uttered a pretty little sigh and tucked the knife away.

"I see your point," she said. "I shall have to continue my practice."

He halted, placing a hand on her arm. She seemed so slight, so small, like a fragile lotus blossom. This woman reminded him of the blossom's beauty, so delicate and shy, hiding below the water at night, but longing for the sun's caress every morning.

"I did not do this to hurt your feelings. But you must understand how dangerous it is to be alone in a city such as this. There are thieves and men without honor who would harm you. Women are precious jewels, little one, and should be protected, not left to fend for themselves."

"I am quite used to fending for myself," she retorted. "There are other weapons besides knives. Such as guns."

He laughed, enjoying the defiant anger in her tone. Such spirit. His desire grew.

"A woman's best weapon is her tears," he murmured. "I know few men who can fight against that defense."

"Then I am quite defenseless," she said with a haughty demeanor. "I refuse to weep and wail in front of anyone. I despise such ploys women undertake to get their way."

So did he. Ramses glanced at her, his admiration rising. "It is best to keep one's feelings concealed from others. . . ."

"To not let enemies spot one's weakness," she finished.

He stopped short as if yanked back by invisible strings. "That was exactly what I was going to say."

She halted. "We seem to speak each other's minds."

A strange, dizzying feeling came over Ramses as he regarded the lady with awe. They had crossed into a narrow, empty alley. Suddenly it was as if the world had emptied itself and only the two of them inhabited it, frozen in time and space. As if destiny had sent them colliding together like two distant stars hurling toward each other in the midnight-black sky. His breath hitched as she bent her head, hiding her face from him.

"My hotel . . . is not far from here," she said in a low, husky voice as if issuing a daring invitation.

"I shall take you there," he answered hoarsely, as if accepting.

Her voice . . . it tugged at his memory with demanding insistence. A breathless sensual whisper. Skin soft as lotus pedals. A stolen kiss in the dark

Eyes the color of a rare jewel, flashing fire.

In the gentlest of motions, Ramses reached down and cupped her chin with one strong hand. He lifted it to his eyes. Two exquisite jewels stared back. Not sapphire. Emerald.

"It is you," he said softly, overjoyed at discovering

that the two women who had so enchanted him were one and the same. "The one who kissed me at the hotel."

Her chest rose and fell rapidly and she stepped back. In the depths of those exotic emerald eyes he saw naked longing, and then . . . fear. They darted about as if he'd cornered her and she searched for escape.

Ramses stepped forward, wanting only to ease her fright. She looked at him as if he were a predator about to devour her.

"Do not be afraid," he said softly.

She stopped backing away. Putting a hand to her veiled left cheek, she stared at him with wondering eyes.

He felt the power of her gaze pull him into a vortex of wonderment, a magical place where the world spun only for them. Ramses's lips parted in memory of her honeyed lips. He reached for her. She extended her arm toward him as if offering her hand, fingers opened in total trust. She took one brave step forward. Captivated, he neared her, not caring that they were in public, he a warrior and she a maid. Not caring that anyone could see them. He ached to feel her slender body against him, to touch those lotus-soft lips with his.

Ramses slid his arms around her waist. He felt her trembling hands explore his body past waist and hips in a heated caress. Her touch made his head pound and his body burn. He needed to see her sweet mouth, to brush his lips softly against hers. Inflamed, he wanted to possess her mouth with tenderness, to gentle her before releasing his passion. She whispered "no" as he reached for her veil.

"Hush," he said softly. "I will not hurt you. Just relax."

He felt her hands stop their delightful exploring. Ramses went to unhook her veil.

"No!" she cried out. He recognized fear and panic and beneath it, an odd, choking grief.

Ramses pulled away, staring down at those beautiful green irises. "I know you want this as much as I do. I sensed it back in the hotel," he murmured, wanting to calm her fears.

"Your Highness!"

The dry, loud bark shook him from the spell. Ramses turned his head and released her as a man in a white turban and *thobe* ran toward them. His scowl and the pistol he withdrew from his pocket caused Ramses to reach for his scimitar. He felt the gentle pressure of a soft palm rest upon his hand.

"No, Ramses. It is all right. He is . . . with me."

The man smiled, a gesture that didn't reach his eyes. He nodded slowly, as if approving of her statement.

"That's right, isn't it . . . princess? I'm her bodyguard. You gave me quite the slip. It's best you return to your father."

Her proud figure crumpled under the reprimand. The woman sighed and nodded. "Yes, Mohammad."

Scorn filled the bodyguard's gaze as he regarded Ramses. "I would like it if you left us," he said to Ramses.

Not as much as I would like to send your head rolling on the ground. He could do it, too, faster than the arrogant cuss could cock that pistol and aim.

"You would? Twice I have saved this woman from danger. What type of warrior are you to let a woman roam the streets unescorted? You have failed in your duty." His voice filled with the contempt he felt.

The guard's cheeks flushed. He ignored the man and turned back to the woman. A precious jewel. A treasure more valuable than the gold secreted in the tombs of the ancient sovereigns. One that should be not left alone to be stolen by others.

"I will not release you to this man unless it is your wish. And I will not do so until . . ." He narrowed his eyes at the guard, "I have your promise to remain with him until you reach the safety of your father."

Those emerald eyes blinked and widened. Ramses smiled down gently at her to deflect his stern tone. He settled both hands on her shoulders.

"Trust me; this is for your own good, little one. You cannot wander the streets alone anymore. Do I have your word?"

"Yes," she whispered. "I promise."

He gave her shoulders a light squeeze. "Good."

"Good-bye, Ramses." Her beautiful green eyes grew luminous.

He could escort her back himself, he reasoned, making certain she remained safe. Then meet her father formally. Share coffee in tiny handleless cups. Hear her gurgling laughter once more. And dare to ask permission to court her. The dream slid to the razor's edge of his scimitar. Hung there precariously. He put his hand on the sword's hilt again.

I vow as a Guardian of the Ages to pledge myself and my undying fidelity to my betrothed. I will keep my body and spirit pure for her, giving myself only unto her. The sacred vow of commitment he was to recite sliced through the dream.

"Yes. I must leave now," he said gently. Ramses

watched her eyes grow brilliant. He ached to see her pain.

Then she gathered her dignity. Her slight figure grew rigid with pride. "I shall never forget your kindness. Thank you again," she murmured.

In a graceful move, she spun around to leave. His hand reached up, caught her shoulder, turning her toward him.

"Good-bye little treasure," he said quietly. "May God guard and protect your path."

She turned again and flinched as the bodyguard grabbed her elbow. Ramses swore under his breath. Catching the other man's arm, he lowered his voice to a threatening growl.

"Release her. Your duty is to guard her, not touch her. And do not let her out of your sight. You face the wrath of a Khamsin warrior of the wind if you do." The words rose in a rumbled warning. The man paled, but let go of her elbow.

As he watched them march off, he realized she never told him her name. A heavy weight settled on his chest. He wanted to protect her. Guard her with a possessiveness he'd never felt for a woman before. In his desire to claim her, he'd failed to protect the one thing that could lead him into danger. His heart.

He was a Guardian of the Ages. A warrior bound to sacred bonds of trust. His honor depended upon it.

Watching her walk away, something deep inside him twisted. Just weeks before his wedding, he finally did the one thing he swore he'd never do. He had given his heart over to an emerald-eyed maiden with a soft voice and lotus skin.

But honor came before all else. Even his heart. Ramses turned and left, leaving his heart behind.

A few blocks later, his mind finally cleared of the enchantment she cast over him. Something felt wrong. He stopped in mid-stride, ignoring the stream of pedestrians that flowed like water past him. The familiar scratching of river reed was gone. Ramses dug into his pocket. The map that had nestled safely there, protected by him as fiercely as he protected his sheikh, had vanished. He rubbed the heel of his hand against his forehead. The woman. Those trembling hands had explored him. Stealing the map.

Fooled by a lovely mouth and a sweet, saucy disposition. He would find her again. He would hunt her down and find her. But this time, it would not be her mouth he possessed. His body trembled with silent rage. A soft string of curses in ancient Egyptian tumbled from his lips. Ramses's hand shot to his scimitar's hilt as he quietly vowed:

"Oh, little lotus blossom, you have no idea whom you crossed. I will find you. And you will know what it is like to face the wrath of a Khamsin warrior of the wind. You will find yourself wishing you stole only a kiss. Indeed."

Chapter Three

"Did you get it?" her father asked.

Landon Burton, the eighth earl of Smithfield, looked up from his pacing. Katherine nodded. His immaculately tailored frame sagged with relief. Nearby, a dumpy-looking Egyptian stood guard, a pistol clutched in his hand. Mohammad went to join him as she shut the door to the hotel room.

Her beloved Persian cat eagerly padded over to Katherine. Osiris meowed as he twined around her legs. Her heart resumed a normal cadence as she picked him up. Egyptians revered cats as guardians of the afterlife. Surely this one guarded her against the world's pain, for he loved her unconditionally.

The earl sighed. "It's my fault, princess," he said, using her pet name. "I shouldn't have asked to see the amulet. . . ."

"Ah, the amulet," came a mocking voice from the window.

Katherine whirled and saw Foster Burrells sitting in a chair with a slender, exotic woman nestled in his lap. His shirt was unbuttoned to the waist, exposing a large bandage across his midsection. The woman began stroking the curator's chest. Burrells made an impatient sound.

"Not now, Maia," he snapped, pushing her from his lap and standing. She had dark sloe eyes and long hair, black as a raven's wing, and wore a scarlet gauze gown. Katherine saw two dusky nipples and looked away, her cheeks flaming in embarrassment. Burrells handed the woman some money.

"Fare for the train to al-Minya. This should be enough for the next few weeks."

Her red lips creased into a sultry pout. "Amarna is a dull village. Why did you bring me to Cairo just to send me back?"

Burrells cupped her cheek. "I knew you were restless, my dear. But now it's time to return home. He'll be expecting you."

Maia shrugged into a black *abbaya*, put a black scarf over her head. With sinuous moves, she floated out of the room. She had the exotic grace of a cobra. Katherine watched her leave, her suspicions rising. Why was she going to Amarna?

The blackmailer reached into his pocket, withdrew a necklace with the gold amulet of Bast from his fingers. Light shimmered in its rich emerald eyes.

"Thou shalt not covet museum antiquities, Landon. Between this and your history of stealing the Ramses mummy, I can send you to jail," he drawled, pocketing the amulet.

"I didn't steal the mummy. I bought it and gave it to authorities when I discovered it was stolen from the tomb at Deir el-Bahri. The authorities will believe my

innocence about the amulet as well," her father said
tightly.

"No one will believe you, not with Lord Estes tes-
tifying he saw you take the amulet," Burrells said flatly.
"You should have sold me the Ramses mummy, Landon. For thirteen years, I've waited for you to fall into
my hands. And now you have."

Her father's piercing blue eyes widened. "My God,
that's what this is all about then, isn't it? Revenge?"

"Lord Estes wanted a royal mummy and offered me
thousands of pounds," Burrells shot back. "I would
have been comfortable for life. But no, you wouldn't
sell it to me—you and your contemptible sense of
honor. You had to turn yourself in to authorities and
tell them about the tomb with all the royal mummies
stashed inside. They got there before I had a chance
to find it and take another mummy. You cost me, Landon. You cost me a lot."

Katherine hugged Osiris so tightly the cat gave a
protesting meow. She let the cat down, gave Burrells
the map. "Here. You have the map and another tomb
to rob. Now return the amulet and let my father go."

Her father glanced at the papyrus she handed their
blackmailer. Katherine watched him uneasily as he
raked a hand through his jet black hair. "That's what
you had her take?" He directed his question at Burrells. "You told me you wanted her to steal an artifact
from this Egyptian."

Katherine broke in. "Papa, I knew it was a map, but
he told me not to tell you. . . ."

The curator grinned. "It is a map. And an artifact."

The earl muttered almost to himself, "It can't be the
same map. . . ."

"What Papa?" she asked, her stomach knotting.

"Nothing." He shook his head and aimed a piercing scowl at Burrells. "Let her go, Burrells. Katherine has to leave. If she doesn't show up, my wife's cousin will question her absence."

Pocketing the papyrus, he looked up. "Where are you going?"

Katherine hesitated. "To al-Minya to prepare for marriage."

Their blackmailer's lips twitched. "Oh, yes, that's right. Marriage. You're getting married." His thin chest heaved as if he fought to contain hysterical laughter.

Mystified at his odd remark, she studied him with growing confusion.

"Who's your groom?" he asked.

"His name is Nazim," she reluctantly admitted.

"Right, Nazim." Now the curator burst into full-fledged laughter. *What was so funny?* Katherine exchanged glances with her father. Then, like a sudden windstorm, the laughter stopped and Burrells' mood shifted into deadly seriousness.

"You can't go. Not yet. You're both coming with me to find the tomb on that map."

"You have the map. You don't need us," she protested. Suddenly Katherine remembered the beggar girl.

"Or are you afraid of the curse?"

Blood draining from his face answered her question. The curator fingered the bandage around his torso then buttoned his shirt. "I'm not wasting time sweating in the desert looking for gold that may not exist. The tomb could have been raided centuries ago. Most of Egypt's tombs were plundered and emptied of treasure. Curses. Old wives' tales. I'm not afraid." But his flared nostrils and restless gaze told her otherwise.

"Katherine needs to study with Ahmed, her cousin's shaman. She must spend time in the desert to prepare for marriage. Return the necklace and let us go," her father quietly ordered.

The curator's gaunt face twisted with anger. "You'll go to jail if you don't do as I say!"

Her gaze shot back and forth between the two furious men, standing like gladiators facing each other. A sudden chill, as if she'd been dipped into an ice bath, goosed her flesh.

Desperate to break the stalemate, Katherine blurted out, "Maybe I'll tell Ramses what you plan. He'd be more angry at you stealing treasure than me stealing the map."

Burrells snapped around, his eyes narrowing. "If you dare mention a word, I'll . . ."

Terror seized her as he grabbed Osiris by the neck. Burrells fished a knife from his pocket and laid it against her pet's throat. Her horrified gaze shot to her father. Enraged, he lunged forward, but the Egyptian guarding him whipped out his dagger and restrained him.

Her mouth went dry with terror. The enraged cat spit and slashed out with sharp claws. She ran toward Burrells, reaching out to grab her cat.

"Please," she whimpered. "He's just a cat, please don't . . ."

His cool gaze met her terrified one as he flung Osiris at the wall. Katherine shrieked and went to her pet, lying stunned on the floor. Her shaking fingers caressed his soft white fur.

Burrells watched her, his eyes furious slits. "I have a well-placed spy who knows every move Ramses makes. You tell Ramses, or anyone else about me, your cat dies." His gaze slid over to the earl. "Along with your father."

Burrells left with the Egyptians. Katherine tried to smile as she looked at her father's paling face.

"Princess, are you all right?"

"Yes, Papa," she tried to assure him.

He knit his brows. "Don't worry about me. He's just trying to scare you. I'll make him listen to reason. But we need more time. I'll postpone the wedding by three months. When I meet with Nazim tomorrow to sign the marriage contract, I'll tell him you haven't adjusted yet to Egyptian life. You were raised in England and know nothing of the culture."

She grimaced. "Papa, why must I marry this Nazim?"

"I promised your mother on her deathbed I would honor her wish to see you married," the earl said gently.

"What does he look like?" she begged. "What's his tribe?"

Her father hesitated. "According to the marriage contract, I cannot tell you anything. Their tradition says that the less a bride knows about their people, the less likely she is to spill secrets before the wedding. Only Ahmed can be trusted with that knowledge. He'll tell you. But your mother assured me they are a good people. They raise horses, goats . . ."

"You're marrying me to a goatherd," she said flatly. Her hand tapped the scarred cheek. Sudden insight came to her.

"Mother wanted me to marry this Nazim because he won't see me until the wedding," she told him.

Her father shook his head, but guilt crossed his face.

She knew then why he was eager for this match.

His mouth felt cold as he kissed her cheek and left. Picking up Osiris, Katherine fled for her bedroom. Laying him gently on the bed, she stroked his fur. He meowed softly, reassuring her. Osiris, like Papa, loved her despite her looks. Her unknown bridegroom, Nazim, had never seen her face.

Katherine went to the mirror. Surely if Ramses had kissed her like that, she could not be truly ugly. His kiss enchanted her, made her believe the mirror could reflect beauty. She stared into the looking glass, inventorying her image. A soft Cupid's-bow mouth. High, aristocratic cheekbones. Smooth skin, tinged with the golden tint of her mother's people. Ebony curls spilled down to her waist. Her brow was stamped with intelligence and her eyes were green as river grass.

Then her gaze drifted to the scar. She touched it, remembering hot agony when the tip of the tiger cub's claw swiped her cheek. A scream echoed in her mind, pitched fever high with fright and pain. The tiger's mark ran below her left eye, a rose-pink gash the length of her pinky.

The handsome Ramses's kiss burned into her lips. He breathed beauty with every step he took. If he saw her face, he would turn in disgust. Tears rose in her throat. With a sob, she picked up her silver hairbrush and hurled it into the mirror. It shattered into tiny pieces. Just like her heart.

Chapter Four

She felt it in her bones. Danger lurked around the corner.

Sitting downstairs on the Shepheard's verandah the next day, Katherine lifted her veil and sipped a cup of good English tea. Upstairs, Papa met with Nazim in his suite. Veiled and in Egyptian dress, Katherine had hovered in the hallway to steal a peek. A thin, middle-aged Egyptian in a white turban and robes passed, saw her and smiled. He knocked at her father's door and Papa issued a hearty, "Come in!" Nazim had lived down to her every expectation. He looked like a goat-herd.

She watched the street below cautiously, abandoning the paper for Egypt's parade of nationalities. Ethiopians as dark as thick molasses passed by in colorful costumes secured by wide sashes. Turbaned Egyptians in ankle-length *thobes* walked briskly. And then a familiar indigo-robed figure walked down the street with determined purpose. Moving with a

40

hunter's natural grace, he mounted the steps and stood near her table.

Ramses. The cup froze halfway back to the table. He could not know her, for her gold-strapped sandals and crimson and yellow *kuftan* marked her as just another Egyptian woman. One hand flew to the veil hiding her scar from staring men. Katherine wished she possessed enough courage to ignore them, for she faced a greater threat than a few rude looks.

She lowered the cup and picked up the paper, hiding behind it. Held in her quivering hands, newsprint shook as if caught in a desert wind. Boot heels clicked along the terrace, paused a bare foot away. Out of the corner of her eye she saw him stop. Those fascinating liquid gold eyes narrowed as they surveyed the terrace. Katherine swallowed fear and the mouthful of tea. She buried her head further into the paper.

Boot heels passed behind her. Cold sweat prickled the back of her neck. The air shifted, pressed against her rigid spine as he stopped again. A long shadow fell over a section of chatty news about English theater. Katherine leaned closer to the black print as if suddenly affected with nearsightedness. She could feel the hulking threat of the sword-wielding warrior behind her. Then his shadow moved over the paper and slipped away.

Katherine felt the kind of trembling relief a hare feels upon avoiding a predator passing its hiding space. Closing her eyes, she took a deep, steadying breath. It turned quickly into a shocked gasp as a firm male hand seized her forearm.

* * *

Not there. Ramses felt keen disappointment as he scanned the verandah. He hesitated, knowing his prey had eluded him, knowing he should go to the earl's suite to sign the marriage contract. The Khamsin's attorney was probably already there.

At least the stolen map had been a forgery. It showed a cave where Guardians went to meditate. Ramses felt reluctant to reveal the real map until the marriage was sealed. Had his future father-in-law known anything about antiquities, he'd have seen the map's vegetable dye was too colorful, not faded by the passage of centuries. But the earl signed the confidentiality agreement and believed the map real when Ramses had shown it to him two days before, and he had agreed to sign the contract today.

Few people lingered in the midafternoon heat on the terrace. Ramses lifted his face to the sun, enjoying the heat. Small wonder his ancestors worshiped Aten, the sun god. How could anyone live without the golden globe that coaxed life out of the ground? He glanced around. Only some elderly men sipping tea occupied the wide verandah. But one woman in a silk *kuftan* read a paper at a nearby table. A cup and saucer sat before her. Ramses sniffed the air. Not strong Arabic coffee, but something milder. A woman alone, enjoying afternoon tea.

An aristocrat. A princess. With a veiled face and haunting green eyes? Ramses inhaled more air. Ah, yes. Her scent. Myrrh. He drew nearer, studying the woman as his shadow drifted across her newspaper, then onto the ground as he moved away.

He waited as the tense figure seemed to relax. Then he pounced on her arm, seizing it with rude strength.

"Excuse me," he said politely in Arabic. "Do I know you?"

"No," the soft squeak replied.

Ramses kept his grip on her arm and peeled back one corner of the paper with his other hand. Two lovely green jewels as round as her cup's saucer greeted him.

He offered a smile utterly lacking any humor. "Oh, you are much mistaken, my green-eyed princess."

A cold fist of fear wrapped around her heart with fingers as unyielding as those gripping her silk-covered arm. Such strong fingers he had. Katherine imagined them squeezing her cheeks to part her mouth, forcing truth from her lips.

"Now, princess, you will accompany me. It is an exquisite day for a stroll, and you are enjoying the sunshine so much."

She must obey, for he tugged her upward. The newspaper fell to the table, knocking over the delicate china cup. Ramses kept a firm grip on her arm as she rose. He pulled her against him, those powerful fingers lacing around her arm with a possessive grip. She smelled cloves and anger radiating from him in rich, spicy waves.

Her body went numb. Ramses pulled her along as they clambered down the steps, walking briskly through Cairo. His silence frightened her almost as much as the intensity of his grip. When they reached the same alley where he had tried to kiss her, he yanked her into the narrow recesses again.

Pressing her none-too-gently against a wall, he pinned her with his broad palms on her shoulders. Her entire body shook with fear as his beautiful amber eyes darkened with hard, cold anger. He was a fierce warrior who would not stop his quest until he claimed her very soul. Or worse.

"Who sent you? Was it the Nubian gold seller in the *souks*?"

The question startled her. She thought he'd ask for the map. Katherine glanced away from his handsome face, the penetrating eyes forcing confession from her lips.

"Look at me. Who sent you?" he demanded.

"Sent me?" She tried a little laugh. "No one sent me. I have no idea what you're talking about." She continued staring at a pile of rubbish strewn in the dark alleyway.

She felt his hand grasp her chin, turning her face toward him. Katherine stared at the slight curve of his Adam's apple. Her gaze drifted up to the close-cropped dark beard, then up to his eyes as Ramses forced her chin up. She shook with fear at the dark coldness on his face, the tight lips, narrowed eyes and flared nostrils. What did he plan to do with her?

"You stole from me. I do not tolerate anyone taking what is mine." His left fingers curled around her shoulder. "So I ask you again, who sent you to steal the map? And where is it?" he growled.

Katherine's teeth began chattering. Ramses was no gullible fool, but an intelligent man with a ruthless warrior's stubbornness for relentless pursuit. She licked her lips, deciding to stick to the barest details.

"I don't have your map." She squared her shoulders in a desperate attempt for courage and looked straight at him.

Those golden eyes glittered with anger. "I do not believe you," he growled.

She turned the pockets of her *kuftan* inside out. "I don't have it. See?"

"That proves nothing."

"I'm telling you the truth. The map's not on me. See for yourself," Katherine taunted.

His eyes took on a different cast. They glinted with dark hunger. "Perhaps I should search you to make sure."

Ramses turned her around as he hooked one muscled arm around her waist, pulling her tight against him. Her body backed into the solid wall of his body. With his free hand, Ramses began a ruthless search. The bold intimacy shocked her as much as the feelings it brought.

It wasn't the impersonal touch of a man searching for a valuable treasure map. It was the very personal caress of a man meaning to arouse every nerve in her body. Slow, deliberate strokes slid over the silk hugging her hips, up her belly, pausing just below her breasts.

Katherine swallowed a moan as he slid his warrior's callused hand over her breasts, his caress possessive and assured. It was a move stating he was in control, a man who knew exactly what made her body flame. She bit trembling lips as his warm breath tickled her ear. His voice held a light, teasing note beneath the edged steel of his tone.

"I do not . . . feel that it is anywhere on you. Should I continue my examination?"

Her answer came in a single breathless word. "Yes."

"I think not." He chuckled softly, then released her, turning her to face him again. She gazed up, feeling he lifted the caul of ugliness from her face. Surely a man who could make her body tremble with aching need possessed special powers.

"Confess, princess. Where is the map?"

Katherine looked at Ramses's shining hair, his bronzed skin, his laughing mouth pursed now in expectation. Mesmerized by his beauty, Katherine reached out and fingered one long sun-streaked lock. He initially jerked back, his brow furrowing as she slid it between thumb and forefinger, fascinated by the highlights. She stared at him, as entranced as when the caged tiger cub had enchanted her with its stunning beauty.

The steely grip on her shoulder eased as he sensed her surrender. Hunger sparked in his golden eyes as it had when he'd tried to kiss her. Instinct warned her to seize the opportunity. Ramses's grip had slackened. She remembered what the family physician taught her about where men were most vulnerable.

Katherine raised her leg. With all her might, she rammed it into his groin. *I'm sorry, Ramses. But I must do this.*

The result was instantaneous and pitiful. Ramses howled, let go and doubled over. She ran. Hands flew out, grabbed a fistful of silk *kuftan*. Katherine strained against the powerful grip hauling her back like prey into a tiger's yawning jaws. Terror fed adrenaline through her veins. She yanked and heard a thundering rip. Not pausing to see the damage, she fled. A string of loud curses followed.

Katherine fled into the street, panting for breath. She zigged and zagged, heading for the safety of the bustling *souks* as she turned to Al Azhar Street and ran to the heart of the Khan al Khalili. Pushing past chattering tourists, and customers looking at the spice stalls, she darted past the stalls of the perfume sellers, the thick, cloying scent gagging her as she gulped for air. Pausing a minute, she wriggled free of her ripped *kuftan* and tossed it aside. Beneath it she wore a shirt and silk trousers. Katherine tore her veil off and pocketed it as she lost herself in the safety of the crowd. She felt as if she ran from the sun god himself, and for a moment, was tempted to run back to the hands that had caressed her with sultry heat.

His prey had evaded capture once more.

Ignoring the now-dull throbbing in his groin, Ramses pressed through a crowd of black-robed women, chattering men and wide-eyed tourists in the *souks*. As he came to the section of gold sellers, he located the stall of the Nubian who had arranged for the meeting with the princess. Ramses's temper flared as he caught sight of the man, who sat twisting metal into a necklace. The Nubian tried to flee. Ramses vaulted over the display table and in two steps, caught him by the back of his collar. He growled deep in his throat.

"You tricked me, gold seller. There was no one interested in Khamsin stallions at the hotel, just a woman thief. Who is she and where is the map?"

"I know nothing," he said, frightened. The man shook as if affected with palsy. "Please, leave me be."

"Who set me up?" Ramses demanded, lifting him off his feet as if he weighed no more than the necklace on the table.

"Please, I cannot tell . . . I don't know . . ."

Withdrawing his scimitar while he continued to collar the vendor, Ramses passed the blade before the man's eyes. "Perhaps you need more persuasion. Is this enough to make you talk?"

In the reflection of the gleaming steel he saw the man's eyes widen with fright. Ramses turned him around, keeping the sword a mere whisper from the gold seller's throat.

"All I know is a man came through here asking all the gold sellers who would pay the best price for gold. He said the man he represented would sell me gold in the future. He would give me a bonus if I did a favor for him," he squeaked.

"What nationality was this man you saw?"

"Egyptian."

"Did he say he would get this precious gold from the Khamsin?" Ramses brought the blade closer.

"He didn't, I swear it! But some gold sellers have heard of the Khamsin gold mine. None dare to look for it, for the desert is a large, hostile area and there is a curse."

Ramses studied the gold seller, his trembling lips, huge brown eyes and the shine of sweat gleaming on his brow. He told the truth, for this simple vendor could not pull off such a sophisticated, elaborate scheme. He was merely a player. Giving him another shake, he sheathed his sword and uttered a threat.

"Know this, gold seller. I would pack your gold and go elsewhere, for if I see you again in this lifetime, I may not be as charitable as I am feeling now."

Ramses turned on his heel and headed away. As he pressed through the crowd, he recalled the lovely thief. He could squeeze a confession out of an enemy with merciless skill. But a woman? Khamsin warriors swore an oath at manhood to protect and defend women. A frustrated sigh escaped his lungs.

Had he continued his tender assault, Ramses knew he would have coaxed answers from her. She had handed him the key to unlock her secrets about why she stole the map. Only this key threatened to unlock a different cage containing the restless desire that always paced within him.

The delicious scent of myrrh, those luminous green eyes, the soft shoulders beneath his hands had made his head spin. She teased him with her luscious curves and fiery spirit. He raged for her and it unnerved him. No woman did this to him. He did it to them, made them plead and beg. Now the tables had turned. His own lust had turned into a frothing beast rattling its cage. It took all his control to keep the beast penned inside.

For now, he needed to sign the marriage contract and then return home. His sheikh needed him. Elizabeth was nine months pregnant, and Jabari was extremely anxious. He would find his little thief. And when he did, Ramses knew he must keep the beast caged, no matter how much it demanded release. Just one press of her soft lips against his would unlock the cage. Heaven help them both if that happened.

Hours later, Katherine returned to the hotel, certain she had lost Ramses. She went to her father's suite, collapsed into a chair. The earl emerged from the bedroom, papers in hand. Immediately he went and crouched down beside her.

"Princess, where were you? I told you to stay away for a few hours, not all day."

"I was playing tourist, Papa." Katherine eyed the papers in his hand and grimaced. "Is that my marriage contract?"

He folded the papers and tucked them inside his vest. "Honey, I found out something about your bridegroom's real name. I have a bad feeling the map Burrells has is . . ." Her father's jaw tensed as he glanced around the room. "I signed an agreement not to reveal any information, but perhaps I should tell you . . ."

A sharp, authoritative knock sounded at the door. The earl strode over, opened the door briskly. George Sanders, earl of Estes, came inside, accompanied by two policemen. Katherine's heart sank.

"I apologize, my lord, but the Egyptian Antiquities Service has a warrant for your arrest for thefts from the Giza Museum." The officer reading the warrant looked uncomfortable.

"I'm sorry to do this, Landon, to a fellow peer. I can assure you will be treated fairly. Come with us quietly and we won't make a fuss."

Her father's shoulders sagged. "Let me gather my things."

"They'll be collected for you," Estes said crisply.

"I'm going with you," she cried out.

Her father looked stricken. He worried about her, not himself. The earl kissed her forehead. "No, princess. Go to your cousin's house. That's an order. Ahmed will protect you. Don't worry. I'll find a way out of this."

Lord Estes and the two policemen bracketed him, marching him away. Katherine paced, frantic with worry. Minutes later, the door opened. Foster Burrells ambled in, his lanky frame encased in a brown suit, his pale hair combed back.

"What must I do to free him?" she asked dully. "You know I have to go to my cousin's in al-Minya or he'll know something's wrong."

"Already planned for that. You're going into the desert with this shaman. You'll just visit a different part of the desert for a lot longer. Four of my men will meet you at the gold mine. I'm coming after you in one month and you'd better have proof you found the gold."

"One month!" Katherine's jaw dropped. "I need more time. My cousin will expect me to spend time with him. . . . I can't just rush out. What if I can't find the tomb?"

His cold blue eyes snapped to hers. "One month, Katherine. Find a way to do it."

"Let me see the map," she demanded.

Burrells hesitated and complied. Katherine studied the map and handed it back. "It doesn't show much about the tomb's location. It could be anywhere inside the mine. You've excavated before. It'll take time to dig through that rock. With only four men, I need two months." She prayed he'd see reason.

He frowned. "All right. I'll give you two."

Relief shot through her. "And once I find the gold?"

"Lord Estes drops all charges and finds the amulet in the museum." The curator narrowed his eyes. "Don't forget. Don't tell a soul. Cairo's jail is a dangerous place. Lots of men would gladly stab a fellow prisoner for enough money. Find the gold, and your papa goes free. Tell anyone, and he dies."

Burrells grinned, his thin, knifelike lips twitching upward, and left the room as silently as he had entered.

51

Chapter Five

The screams of childbirth were deafening.

"You can do this," Ramses said in an encouraging voice.

"I simply cannot take this. Why does this have to happen?"

"It is God's will for women to suffer so. You must not question it," Ramses replied.

"I shall question what I want!"

"Look at your wife. Some example you are setting for her," Ramses admonished.

Jabari bin Tarik Hassid, the great sheikh of the Khamsin warriors of the wind, paled as another scream came from the birthing tent. The two warriors sat outside the tent, Jabari refusing to go elsewhere, the women attending Elizabeth refusing to let him in. Their fearless warrior leader, his face white with anxiety, buried his head into his hands.

"Come," Ramses said, putting a gentle hand on his sheikh's shoulder. "Let us go visit the horses. I want to spend more time with Fayla before I leave for the deep desert."

Jabari looked up, his face alight with interest. "Why?"

"I'm sending her back when Kareem returns to the southern camp so they can breed her." Ramses sighed, hating to give up his beloved mare, but knowing her bloodlines must be passed on.

They walked to the edge of the camp, Jabari tossing worried glances back at the birthing tent. "Elizabeth will be fine," Ramses reassured him. "Soon you will have a fine, healthy son."

"I should have taken her to the Cairo hospital," Jabari fretted.

Ramses's eyes widened. "Elizabeth wanted a hospital birth?"

"No, I did. She insisted on doing it here."

"That is your Elizabeth," Ramses chuckled, admiring the woman's courage and stubborn insistence on sticking to tradition. "Tribal customs all the while, learning to milk camels, make yogurt, weave cloth . . ."

A high-pitched scream sounded through the camp. Jabari turned as pale as camel's milk at the sound.

"And give birth in the black tents."

"I must go to her." Jabari turned. Ramses gently steered him back toward the direction of the animal herds.

"Your aunt and Badra are with her," Ramses said firmly.

"Elizabeth did not expect to go into labor this early. She wants her grandmother. I wish my grandfather hadn't taken Jana to visit relatives."

Last year, Elizabeth and Jabari had brought her ailing grandmother from a tuberculosis sanatorium in New York to Egypt. Jana, in the early stages of the disease, improved with the fresh air and diet. She and Nkosi, Jabari's grandfather, were spending time with Jana's relatives in the Al-Hajid tribe.

"Elizabeth will be fine. She is young and strong."

Jabari stared, grim-faced, at the ground. "She is in pain and there is nothing I can do about it!"

He squeezed his sheikh's shoulder, wishing he could do something to ease his friend's distress. Perhaps a joke. "The time to do something about it was nine months ago," he suggested, winking at him.

Jabari shot him a thunderous scowl. "Easy for you to joke. The love of your life is not suffering in agony. You do not even love your bride. Your wife will not mean half as much to you as Elizabeth means to me."

Ramses stepped back, recoiling from the verbal blow. He reminded himself Jabari was deeply upset and frantic with worry about Elizabeth. He told himself his best friend did not mean what he said.

Then he steeled himself against the hurt and offered the grin he showed the world when his insides crumbled. Only this time, it came off a little more lopsided than usual.

"Yes," he agreed. "I marry a woman I do not love. When she gives birth, I will demand to know what is taking so long."

He meant it as a joke, but bitterness laced his words. Ramses bit his tongue, regretting that he let his feelings show.

They reached the outcropping of scrub grasses where the horses grazed. A young warrior curried a mare some distance away. He lifted a hand in greeting.

Ramses waved back to Kareem and whistled for Fayla, who trotted over. He stroked her muzzle fondly, wishing that people were more like horses—loyal and faithful. And without the gift of speech.

He felt the pressure of a firm hand upon his shoulder. "Ramses," Jabari began in a tentative voice, "I am deeply sorry. I did not mean it. That was most . . . ill-mannered of me."

Ramses continued rubbing Fayla's velvet muzzle, not looking up. "Do not apologize Jabari. You stated a fact. Nothing more."

He married a woman he did not love. How he wished the pain roping his heart and squeezing it would lessen. Just a little.

"A fact that grieves me. I want you to be happy."

Ramses faced his sheikh. He lifted his shoulders in an impassive shrug. "My happiness matters less than removing the shame my father has walked with since the day your father was killed. I must restore his personal honor with this marriage."

Grief twisted his insides as he remembered how Jabari's father, Tarik, had been killed in a caravan raid. His father, Tarik's Guardian, had been in Cairo at the time. Seti had felt deep disgrace that he had failed to protect his sheikh.

Jabari sighed. "It is not Seti's fault my father died."

Ramses's chest tightened with emotion. "I know. But my father cannot forgive himself. He is eager for this marriage. He sees it as another chance to fulfill a vow he made. If I do not marry Lady Katherine, I break his oath. I must honor my father."

Jabari placed both hands on his shoulders. He looked very upset. "You already have brought honor to your father. I can think of no Khamsin warrior more honorable than you, Ramses. You are the most courageous of my men. I would fight a legion of demons if I had only one man at my side—you."

He paused, seeming to struggle with his emotions. His grip tightened. "I am proud and humbled that you are my Guardian, but the title I honor most is that of friend. A man you call friend has an honor he carries with him to the grave."

Ramses grinned, a true smile this time. "You are getting soft on me again."

"The time for me to be soft was nine months ago," Jabari shot back, his grin wider than Ramses's.

He laughed. "Knowing you, it will not take long after the baby is born for you to fill Elizabeth's belly with another."

Jabari nodded. "It is good to see you laughing again, my friend. I have been much concerned about you."

He assumed a cocky swagger as he shrugged off Jabari's hands. "Why? You have enough to occupy your mind these days."

"I know you, Ramses. Something is deeply troubling you. Something happened to you in Cairo."

Jabari, as always, could read him as easily as he read the stars in the night sky. Ramses felt torn between confessing to his best friend and the instinct to keep his mouth shut.

"It is a woman, is it not?"

He whirled about, ready to deny it when he saw how worried Jabari looked. He uttered a sigh of defeat and nodded.

"Ah, I had thought so."

"You would have wrung it from me eventually."

He beckoned to the ground and both men sat, crossing their legs. Ramses picked up a stone and began rolling it between his fingers. They sat in companionable silence for a few moments, listening to the sounds of horses snorting softly behind them and the desert wind brushing across the sand.

"I would tell you her name, except I do not know it," Ramses finally said. At Jabari's questioning look, he relayed the story. When he finished, his friend narrowed his dark eyes.

"Who do you think she works for?"

"Perhaps the Al-Hajid," Ramses ventured, locking gazes with his friend. Elizabeth's uncle headed that tribe, but despite the family ties and the peace between the people, Ramses still did not trust them. The two tribes had been longtime enemies.

Jabari rubbed his bearded chin. "I cannot see this. If it were, it must be a renegade band, for Nahid has kept tight control of his people."

"Who else could it be? No one else knows of its existence."

"Except for that tomb robber you wounded."

"I should have run him through," Ramses muttered, withdrawing his dagger. He drew in the sand with its tip.

Jabari stayed his hand. "Put your dagger and regrets away, my friend. I have a feeling you will find this clever woman again. God has strange ways of arranging one's fate."

Ramses smiled ruefully as he sheathed the blade. "Let us hope God arranges my fate in a favorable way."

They heard Kareem calling and stood, brushing dust from their *binishes*. The Khamsin warrior, barely seventeen, had been staying with them for a few months.

He lived in the southern camp, where the Khamsin bred their Arabians.

His face shining with excitement, Kareem bounded over to them. He stopped, jerked forward from his waist and muttered a respectful greeting. Then he grinned. Ramses grinned back. He liked Kareem, who followed him around like a faithful puppy and always bombarded him with questions. Ramses promised Kareem's father he would watch over the boy.

"Ramses, so good to see you again! Tell me about Cairo. Was it exciting? Did you see many great sights?"

He smiled at Kareem's enthusiasm. "I did," he admitted briefly, thinking of a beautiful, green-eyed thief.

"I hear every woman in Cairo clamors for attention from Ramses, the warrior of love. Even the ones trained to pleasure a man in every way. They do something with their toes and pomegranates."

Toes and pomegranates? Where did he get those ideas? Ramses gave Kareem the indulgent smile of a world-weary man entertaining a fascinated child.

"Ah yes, the toes-and-pomegranates women. Ramses has met a few." Jabari gave his friend a sly wink.

Ramses scowled. "Women in the city cannot compare to the beauty of our women, Kareem. A Khamsin woman is like the rays of the Aten, whereas the women in Cairo are but candlelight. You will see when it is your turn to take a bride."

Kareem looked slightly jealous, then sniffed. "I have a mistress, you know, in Amarna. Lovelier than a dawn sky. She says I am the best she has ever had."

Ramses exchanged an amused glance with Jabari

over the young man's posturing. "She sounds quite lovely, Kareem."

"What about your bride, Ramses? Is she beautiful?"

He could not even force a nod. He would not see her before the wedding. Did she have a face as ugly as a camel's butt?

Jabari must have noticed his troubled expression, for he put a protective hand on Ramses's shoulder. "I am certain his bride is very attractive."

Kareem smiled smugly. "I hear English women are tall and bony, although some are pretty. At least the tiny and delicate ones like Lady Katherine. But I suppose marrying an English woman suits you, since you are not a full-blooded Egyptian."

The insult came at him with the full force of a blow to his jaw. Ramses recoiled, dumbfounded Kareem dared mentioning his heritage. His guts twisted, as they had in childhood, when his brethren called him "half-breed." Unlike most Khamsin warriors, who married within the tribe, his family clung to an age-old tradition of marrying Guardians to distant relatives who came from various cultures, including English and Italian.

Jabari noticed his distraught expression. The sheikh bristled. "Ramses's family is descended from the greatest Khamsin warriors. His line has been Khamsin Guardians for thousands of years. Lady Katherine is from an honored family, as well. Only the best will do for my Guardian, the bravest Khamsin warrior this tribe has ever known. I will not tolerate you insulting my friend," he said in a low tone, laced with anger.

Kareem paled. "I am sorry, Ramses. I meant no insult," he stammered. He looked truly abashed.

Ramses forced a smile. "No harm meant," he said

quietly. "Why do you not go repair the tassels on my battle gear?"

Kareem nodded, wide-eyed. "It would be an honor. I will go do it straight away!" He jerked forward again and dashed off.

He watched him go, a little sadly. "Was I ever that young?" he mused.

"Once. And you were equally as annoying."

Ramses grinned. "Kareem will mature. I will visit his father when I finish my retreat in the deep desert."

Jabari frowned. "Why are you going on your retreat? Why pledge fidelity now to your bride when the marriage has been delayed?"

"Queb thinks I need more time to repent since I have so much more to repent than any other Khamsin Guardian," he joked.

In reality, he needed to pledge the oath before he lost his nerve. He was deeply troubled by the earl's news that Lady Katherine couldn't adjust to Egypt. Ramses envisioned a spoiled English woman accustomed to servants and riches. How could his bride assimilate to Khamsin life?

"I wish you would take someone with you to investigate the mine when you leave on your retreat."

"I cannot. I need solitude for my traditional Guardian period of fasting, penance, meditation and . . ."

"Celibacy." His friend's dark eyes twinkled. "To witness that, alone, would be worth the trip for me."

Ramses scowled. "You think I have no control and would violate my oath?"

"An oath you should not take for three months. I wager you cannot return without having bedded a woman at least once."

"An easy enough bet. You are certain to lose."

Ramses grinned, rubbing his hands. "What is the payment?"

Jabari lifted one eyebrow, considering. "If I lose, I will give you my best brood mare's next foal. If you lose . . ."

Ramses grew uneasy at the sly gleam in his friend's eyes as he scrutinized his hair. "No Jabari . . . Not . . ."

"Not as short as mine. But," the sheikh picked up a lock of Ramses's hair. "Just past your shoulders."

"That is barely longer than yours!" he protested.

"I know," Jabari said with a smug smile.

He sighed. "I have no fears of you winning. Only jinn live in that part of the desert."

"If I know you, my friend, and I do know you, you will find one worth bedding. And I will not lose a fine foal." Jabari winked at him, but Ramses had the uneasy feeling that maybe this time, his friend might be right.

"Ramses? Stop hovering outside and come in to greet my son."

With a quiet hesitancy, Ramses pulled aside the flap and entered the birthing tent. He had escorted Jabari back shortly after the birth.

He tiptoed inside and hung back, wishing to respect their privacy. A tired-looking but radiant Elizabeth rested upon a bed, a thin, striped blanket covering her modestly as she cuddled a tiny bundle. Jabari sat next to her, his arm draped around his wife's shoulders, gazing down with adoration at the bundle.

Jabari looked up, beckoning to him with an encouraging hand. Ramses carefully maneuvered toward him. He approached the bed, not wishing to intrude, but eager to see the baby.

Bonnie Vanak

"Look." Elizabeth opened the blanket, showing off her baby. "You are the first to see him. Jabari insisted."

Ramses felt deeply moved. Tradition dictated that privilege for Jabari's grandfather, especially for a sheikh's first child.

"Thank you," he said faintly. "This means much to me that you would honor me so."

"Would you like to hold him?" Elizabeth passed her son over to Ramses, instructing him to keep his little head upright.

The small bundle in his arms felt like air, it was so tiny and delicate. Ramses stared down in awe at the baby's reddened face, its tiny head dusted with light hair. The miracle of new life overwhelmed him. He gently touched the baby's cheek, marveling at its softness. The infant sleepily opened his eyes.

"He has your eyes," Ramses commented, grinning at Elizabeth.

"All babies have blue eyes at birth," Elizabeth said. She fingered her long blond hair. "I think he will have his father's eyes and my hair."

His smile widened. "I wonder what else he inherited from his father?" Then he set the baby upon the bed and pulled back the blanket covering him. His big hands seemed awkward compared to the delicate newborn.

"What are you doing?" Elizabeth asked in an amused tone.

"Checking to see if he is his father's son," Ramses answered mischievously. With tremendous care, he untied the baby's diaper and peered down. The object of his curiosity suddenly rose and let loose a stream of warm yellow liquid straight into his face.

Jabari and Elizabeth howled with laughter. Ramses

gave a good-natured smile. "He is his father's son, all right."

He wiped his face with the cloth Jabari offered. The sheikh then retrieved his son, skillfully tying back the diaper and holding him with ease. "He is, indeed," Jabari said proudly.

"Jabari would have it no other way," Elizabeth said, giving her husband a look of adoration as deep as the one she gave her son. "Nor would I."

The loving glances Jabari and Elizabeth exchanged further isolated Ramses. He was intruding upon their intimacy, the most memorable moment they shared—the birth of their first child.

His heart ached that he would never share that special bond with his wife. His future was carved out, a wife who did not love him.

Jabari looked at him expectantly. Ramses cleared his throat and gave a sheepish grin. "I had nearly forgotten. Forgive me, I am quite absent-minded lately."

Ramses lifted his hand and gently placed it upon the baby's brow. "Firstborn son of Jabari, as a Guardian of the Ages, I promise you my protection and the protection of my line. My progeny will defend you unto death. My son will guard your life as his own. This I solemnly vow."

He reached into his belt for his dagger and opened his palm. The cut was clean, a narrow, vertical slash. He wiped the dagger with the silk sash attached to his belt, replaced the blade and then bound his bleeding palm with the cloth.

He looked at Elizabeth's blanched face. "I am sorry Elizabeth. I forgot you are not entirely familiar with our ways. I did not mean to make you queasy. But this means I will give my life's blood for your son, just as

Bonnie Vanak

I would for his father. As well as for you. As my first-born son will after me."

She managed a shaky grin. "You have an enormous task ahead of you Ramses, as will your son, if the baby is anything like his father. Reckless, charging into danger without thinking . . ."

Jabari scowled as Ramses laughed deeply.

Bending down, he kissed Elizabeth's forehead. "Congratulations. May you have many more fine, handsome sons."

He gave Jabari a thoughtful look. "Soon I leave for the deep desert. But know this. In my absence, my father's protection extends to you and your family."

Jabari's face clouded with sudden emotion. "It is a shield I shall wear with pride," he said quietly. He stood and embraced Ramses. "Thank you, for all you do for me and my family."

Exiting the tent, Ramses looked around the camp. Many people, joyous at news of the sheikh's new son, milled about, their faces reflecting their happiness. The birth of a baby was a monumental event for any Khamsin couple, but for the sheikh it was a very special occasion. As much as Ramses loved Jabari and Elizabeth, he felt deep sadness he could never experience the joy they felt this moment. Tomorrow he swore an oath of fidelity to a woman he did not love. He doubted he ever could.

The time had come.

In a wide circle at the Khamsin's secret ceremonial site in the Arabian Desert, they gathered upon the grayish, rocky sand. Freshets of sweat rolled down Ramses's back, dampening the band of his indigo trousers. Sunshine beat upon his naked shoulders.

Standing in the circle's center, he breathed deeply. More so than the ritual that carved the mark of Jabari's clan upon his arm, he feared this ceremony. Not the physical pain, for today he would receive another tattoo. But today he would take the oath of fidelity to his bride. A woman he did not love, but was sworn to remain faithful to and protect with his life.

A stone tomb encased his heart. With the words he'd speak, the tomb would be sealed. He preferred physical discomfort to the aching agony in his chest.

Jabari, Queb, the tribal shaman, and the Majli, the council of Khamsin elders, surrounded him. No women were present at this solemn male ritual. He felt great trepidation until he caught his friend's eye. Jabari gave him a reassuring wink. Ramses suppressed a smile and relaxed.

Centering his breathing, he watched his father approach. At fifty, strength had not left his side nor had his excellent reflexes dulled. The proud nose, the chiseled jaw were all mirrors of Ramses. The rich, dark hair showed streaks of gray.

But the marked contrast was Seti's manner. Since Tarik's death, the lofty shoulders slumped. The regal bearing that echoed his namesake, a king of Egypt, vanished. His father shuffled his steps like a feeble old man.

Today, he detected a trace of the old, arrogant confidence. Ramses hoped his father would regain the dignity lost to him. He longed to see his amber eyes sparkle with life once more.

"My son, fruit of my loins, Guardian of tomorrow." Seti regarded Ramses with a quiet look of pride.

"My father, giver of life, Guardian of the past," Ramses replied back in the traditional greeting of a

Guardian to his father before the sacred ceremony began.

"Are you ready to take the betrothal vow?" Seti asked.

Ramses could not speak his assent. He nodded. Emotions rose to the surface. He slammed them down. He steeled his spine and heard the tomb door close on his heart as he recited the sacred vow of commitment before the assembled witnesses.

"I vow as a Guardian of the Ages to pledge myself and my undying fidelity to my betrothed. I will keep my body and spirit pure for her, giving myself only unto her. I will protect her unto my dying days and guard her life as my own."

Queb, the tribal shaman, stepped forward. Shaky hands rose before Ramses in a mystical gesture as he recited the time-honored blessing. "May the Udjat, the watchful Eye of Horus, fill you with his power of protection to guard your mate. For as you would fall on your scimitar to protect our honored sheikh, so you would do to defend the one to whom you pledge your heart. May the Ieb, the heart, center of all consciousness, be the center of your marriage. And may the sacred flail of Min fill you with fertility to father many sons to carry on after you."

Queb swabbed Ramses's upper left arm with a cleansing lotion. He took the ceremonial dagger, its ivory handle gleaming in the brilliant sun, and raised it skyward, muttering prayers in ancient Egyptian. The elderly shaman then handed Seti the blade. Ramses stared straight ahead and braced himself as the tattooing began. When it was finished, Queb cleansed the wound. Seti wiped the blade, handed it to Queb and stepped back.

"Today another Guardian of the Ages has taken the sacred oath and will continue the tradition for generations to come."

The assembled men let out a wild cheer. Ramses flushed with pride. He glanced down at his arm. The thick muscles now bore a mark twining the Eye of Horus with the Ieb, the heart. The two hieroglyphs had a long, spear-like line drawn through them, with tassels at its tip. Min's flail.

"My son, today you have restored honor to me and our clan. I am deeply proud of you and the fine job you have done in guarding our sheikh's life. I know you will equally embrace the task of extending the same protection to your bride."

Tremendous joy filled his aching chest. Ramses smiled. "Thank you, Father. I shall endeavor always to honor our line and hold steadfast to my duty as a Guardian of the Ages."

"As will your sons after you," Seti said. Mirth came into those aging amber eyes. "I expect you to father no less than an even dozen with that hair of yours." It was an old family joke. Seti, father of five sons, had shorter hair than his son.

"To accomplish that task, I shall need to grow it down past my knees," Ramses shot back with a grin. He hid his pain with a wide smile. *If I were to bed my emerald-eyed thief, I would gladly father sons more numerous than the stars.*

Jabari stepped forward and embraced him. "Congratulations." He lifted Ramses's arm and looked at the tattoo. "A fine job, Seti," he said. "You have a steady hand. This is as perfect a mark as when Queb tattooed the falcon upon your son."

Ramses's old spirit returned. The elderly shaman

was half-blind. "Better my father than Queb," he joked. "Or I would have a mark resembling a donkey's ass more than the Eye of Horus."

Darting a glance at the shaman, who had walked away, Jabari shot back, "Or Min's flail would be too short and limp," he said, winking. "Not a promising sign for your bride."

Your bride. He forced a smile, but his own heart ached more than the one tattooed on his arm.

"You go soon, my son, into the desert. Take all my wisdom with you," Seti said.

"And I will return it to you," Ramses answered.

"Ramses." The voice rose, filled with hesitation. "It is not an easy task before you. The sacred retreat tests the stamina and endurance of many Guardians. The oath you pledged will prepare you for your bride, a period of abstinence before marrying."

"As well as repenting before God all your past transgressions." The shaman suddenly reappeared. His rheumy eyes managed to pin Ramses down with a severe look. Ramses felt a guilty flush warm his body.

"I have not so very many of those," he muttered.

"I have heard otherwise, from your mistress to your exploits in Cairo," Queb retorted. "The women . . ."

Ramses couldn't help protesting. "I am very fond of women, as they are of me." He had bid good-bye to his mistress, a beautiful woman who lived in Amarna, a few hours ride away.

"Too fond." He frowned. "Remember Ramses, those days are past. You must be faithful when you marry." Queb touched Ramses's right arm. "Your sacred totem will show you the way to your destiny. The tiger is fierce and courageous, but rushes into danger. Beware of this trait."

"I will not fail you Queb, or you, Father," Ramses promised. "I will be true to my vow to honor my bride. My body, and spirit, will remain pure for her." He gave him a level look.

Seti's amber eyes shone with obvious pride. Ramses felt moved to tears to see his father had regained his stately bearing. "I am deeply proud of you, my son."

The look in his father's eyes erased his pain. He would honor his vow to his bride and marry her, despite all his personal misgivings. No matter what, he would carry through his sacred oath and honor his father.

A golden-eyed warrior took her small, hesitant hand into his large one and dragged her into his black tent. He loomed over her, pressing her shoulders against the bed with his powerful hands. "Confess," the deep, husky voice commanded. "Tell me who you are." Sensual lips neared, closer still until they were a bare breath from her own mouth. Her veil lifted as he plucked it away. Ramses would kiss her until she became senseless and all her secrets would tumble out. Then he would reveal the greatest secret . . . as he stared at her scar . . .

Katherine awoke with a start. Darkness enveloped her in a thick cloak. Thin moonlight flowing in from a small hole in the ceiling pierced the inky blackness. She tilted her head and saw not the familiar ceiling of her hotel room, but rock. Now she remembered. A cave, deep in the Arabian Desert.

"My daughter of the desert, what is the matter?"

From across the cave echoed the reassuring voice of Ahmed, her cousin's shaman. She heard steel striking flint, then a candle's soft glow filled the small cave.

Ahmed's aging face was at her bedside. She had known him since first visiting Egypt at age five. He had never lost his mysterious air or his gentle manner.

"A dream. Nothing more. I'm sorry for disturbing you."

He sat down on her bed's edge as he held the candle. "You did not disturb me. I was not asleep. I was meditating."

"I think you stay awake all night just to watch over me." Her gaze flicked to the cave's entrance. Outside camped the four Egyptians working for Burrells. They feared the powerful shaman more than any loaded pistol.

He said nothing, but studied her left cheek. "Do you remember when the tiger cub gave you this?"

Pain twisted her insides. "How could I forget? I'm reminded of it every time I look in the mirror."

Ahmed touched her scar with a gentle finger. "Long ago, the tiger placed its mark upon you. It is your destiny, this mark. For a tiger shall call you his, my child. That day is coming. You must not be frightened, but trust in him. He will give you his protection, guard your life more fiercely than he guards his own and keep you from all harm."

His cryptic words scared her a little. Ahmed regarded her quietly with his dark eyes.

"I don't need a protector. I can take care of myself," she asserted. "Papa taught me how to use the crossbow."

Ahmed smiled. "You are a true daughter of the desert."

"If I were, I wouldn't be living like this. Cousin Jamal insisted I stay comfortable," Katherine said wryly. Two large, folding beds had been provided for her and

Ahmed. A collapsible table and two chairs faced the cave's back entrance. Persian rugs lay scattered on the sandy ground. She had mountains of supplies from dried food to stacks of fresh linens. More luxuries than she'd have than when she married Nazim.

"Ahmed, when will you tell me about my husband?"

"Soon," he told her.

She sighed. "Why must everything remain a secret?"

"It is tradition," he replied.

"A tradition to prevent women from running away when they discover they marry into a family of smelly, spineless goatherds," she grumbled.

His rollicking laughter bounced off the cave's walls. "What's so funny?" she asked.

"How you describe your husband's tribe is most amusing. You will see how wrong you are." His face grew serious. "Katherine, you bring with you information they need. Your knowledge of medicine and the herbal arts will serve them well."

"All I did was nurse patients when the doctor visited tenants on the estate. I can't help that much."

"Perhaps that will change in the near future. Trust me. You have nothing to fear when it comes to this marriage."

Her reluctant smile hid her true feelings. She had much to fear. After a lifetime of riding on Rotten Row and drinking afternoon tea, she would now ride camels and drink goat's milk.

Ahmed, as usual, sensed her distress. "Do not fret. I will teach you the ways of your betrothed's people, though I wish your father had sent you to Egypt earlier."

"Papa couldn't return. Not after we lost Mama to fever when we were last visiting Cairo. He was too upset. He only marries me to this goatherd to keep a deathbed promise to her."

"It is a sacred promise. I tell you this, my child. You are more Egyptian than you realize. You have long denied this part of yourself, but you cannot hide from it. The man you will marry also struggles with a deep inner torment. He fights within himself. With you beside him, the two halves that wrestle inside him will be made whole."

Katherine suppressed a yawn. "You talk in riddles, Ahmed."

He gave another mysterious smile. "Go back to sleep, Katherine. I will protect you. I will not leave you."

As she settled back into bed and closed her eyes, Katherine thought she heard him add softly, "Not until another comes to claim my place."

Chapter Six

A few days after his journey began, Ramses reached his destination. Golden sand spilled down a series of dunes. Ropes of small rocky hills ran north to south, topped with rich, gleaming black rock. Ramses let his camel's reins drangle as he secured items from his saddlebag.

He spread out a blanket in the lee of a small dune, and unwound the indigo turban from his head. Ramses prepared to perform an ancient ritual. He fetched soap from his bag and water from a nearby well. Like other Guardians who had made the pre-wedding trek into the deep desert, he shaved off his beard to honor his ancestors. Ancient Egyptians had regarded beards as unsanitary.

Ramses removed his weapons and sat, straightened his spine and set his hands upon his knees. He listened to the sounds of his own breathing. The deep silence of the desert. He allowed the desert's energy to flow into his heart. Let his soul drink in the tranquility of the dunes. Let his heart dance to the music in the shifting sands.

Breathing deeply, he smelled the heat of the bare sands. The sun coated him, gathered him into its burning embrace and sent tiny trickles of sweat rolling down his temples.

So alone. He poured his spirit out upon the sands like a stream of water. Felt the utter desolation of the desert stretch out before him, stripping him down to his naked soul, forcing him to bare all before his Creator. As he continued to meditate, Ramses felt something leak out of the corners of his eyes.

He let the wind dry the tears rolling down his cheeks.

After two days of meditation, he sought out the cave. Ramses dressed and packed his things, traveling south.

Long ago, his ancestors had discovered a hollowed section of mountain near the mine. Calling the cave sacred, they carved a small second exit. Then they used the cave as the Guardians' secret place of meditation after taking their betrothal vows.

The section of Arabian Desert containing the cave and mine lay halfway between the Nile and the Red Sea coast. Jagged, black mountains and several outcroppings of smaller hills dissected a wadi, a wide, flat area of golden sand created by an ancient river. Scattered wells lay at the foot of the mountains. It was an inhospitable climate, harsh and unforgiving to those who made mistakes. Ruins of ancient settlements were scattered along the wadi, their former occupants long vanished into memory.

Ramses saw camels standing outside the cave entrance. Four large, white tents had been erected on the sands. He jumped off his camel, then hid his mount behind the rocks. He crept closer, slipping among the rocks. When he was close enough, he slid onto the sand behind a boulder's jagged edges.

Four men in long *thobes* laughed as they passed a bottle. He noted the scimitars strapped to their waists. Armed, but at least not with pistols. Desert wind blew in his direction. He sniffed the air. They were inebriated, or soon would be, judging from the cloying scent of alcohol drifting on the breeze. They vanished inside the cave.

A sense of delicious anticipation filled his warrior's soul. He had expected this and had come prepared to administer justice to the prospective tomb robbers. Ramses remembered the rifle secured to his camel and frowned. Men of honor fought with blades. He gripped his scimitar's hilt, prepared to drive them off.

A high-pitched scream distracted him. Ramses gazed up, horrified to see a woman run from the cave. Sunlight gleamed in the folds of her deep blue trousers and shirt. She fled the four men who tripped after her.

He trembled with violent anger as one grabbed her sleeve. The woman whirled, slapped her assailant in the face, then kicked him and wriggled away. Admiration for her warrior spirit mingled with concern. Ramses draped the trailing end of his turban across his face, grabbed his dagger with his left hand, and performed the traditional hand-to-heart-to lips gesture of a Khamsin warrior about to engage in battle.

Another scream of terror pierced the air as two of the men caught her, tumbled her to the ground. Ramses charged, holding his weapons in a practiced stance and let out the Khamsin war cry. A wild, undulating yell rolled through the silent heat. As he raced forward, he saw the men rise off the woman. She fled back into the cave. The men withdrew long swords. As they charged, he attacked with his totem's fierceness. The tiger unleashed.

Metal met metal. Ramses whirled, dodged, thrust. He fought in a wild frenzy. Four against one. A small challenge. His blade slashed one man's arm, and an outraged cry rose up. His familiar cockiness in battle surfaced. *I could do this with my eyes closed.* Again, he let loose the blood-curdling scream of battle his tribe used to attack.

"I know that war cry! He's a Khamsin warrior."

The men withdrew a bit. Then one advanced. The man smiled, showing two nubs of yellowing teeth.

"A Khamsin warrior. Today I add a true warrior of the wind to the list of men I slay!" he sneered.

"I think not," Ramses retorted.

As he charged, one flung sand into his face, blinding him. Ramses staggered. His eyes gushed water. He thrust and felt his sword strike on the mark. The man screamed. Another kicked Ramses in his kidneys. Ramses grunted in pain and resisted dropping to the sand. He squinted, willing his eyes to open and slashed again. A blade scraped across his trousers. He ignored it and whirled. Another slice to his chest. Warmth dripped down to his belly. A well-placed kick sent him tumbling down.

He struggled to his feet, still blinded. They were playing with him, taunting him, and anger replaced the calm coolness needed in battle. As they raced toward him, Ramses slashed. His scimitar struck something deep. A scream followed. Struggling to focus, he saw one man run from the direction of a tent, something long and metallic held in his hand.

The sharp crack of a pistol shot split the air. His breath was sucked out of him as his right shoulder filled with white-hot pain. Instinctively he jerked back, biting back gasps of shock and agony. Forcing his eyes to focus, he saw his assailant spring forward to raise the pistol. Ramses ducked, rolled forward, then slashed blindly at his assailant's legs as he sprang up. Something hard connected to his temple with a blow that made his ears sing. He held on to consciousness by sheer force of will as he toppled to the sand, falling on his knees, the dagger dropping from his left hand.

Immediately, they landed on him like jackals on carrion. They panted eagerly as they took his scimitar, pinned him to the sand, flipping him onto his back. One sat on his legs, the other on his chest, squeezing breath from his lungs. The wounded man pinned Ramses's sword arm down. He bit his lip against the squeezing agony of the bullet wound. Ramses lay as helpless as downed prey. He struggled for air and control.

A stench of their liquored breath and unwashed bodies mingled with the rising smell of his fear. He swallowed it down, striving for calm. Fear paralyzed the senses as much as his anger had. No more mistakes. He could not afford them.

"Shoot him and let's be done with it. I'm hurting something bad," the severely wounded one whined.

"I have something better in mind. Hold him and don't move," the voice said quietly as a foot squeezed his left wrist into the hot sand. Tiny grains ground into his hand. Ramses struggled.

"This is what we do to desert scum. We chop them up, until nothing is left, but for the vultures."

He had a sharp, pointed face, all angles like the edges of a pyramid, but unlike those structures, he possessed no honor. The man lifted Ramses's scimitar and swished it through the air. A mirthless smile split his face into more sharp curves. The sword cut the wind with a whoosh, slicing through Ramses' heart. His beloved sword, his friend. Now in the hands of another, it became his worst enemy.

He felt no fear, only a raging, howling anger as the man bent down, forcing Ramses's right hand out. It pointed toward the black mounds of rocky mountains. Ramses bit his lip, steeling himself for the pain. His right hand. His sword arm. The arm he vowed to defend Jabari with. His head ached with dizziness, but he forced calm to think of a plan.

Even as he prayed for strength, he heard the scream. It roared in his ears like the rushing of the desert wind sweeping across the plain. It echoed over the sand in a wild, frenzied shriek as fierce as his own tribe's war call. Ramses turned his head toward the cave and saw such an incredible sight he knew the blow to his head had caused a hallucination.

The woman. She raised a crossbow to her chest. He closed his eyes, afraid to open them and discover she was an illusion he had conjured to feed him courage for the inevitable.

Something whistled through the air. A shriek followed. Pressure eased off his legs as the arrow's target fell to the sand. Now was the time. He focused on the man straddling his chest, who was groping for the pistol to point at the woman.

The fist he curled into a tight ball was directly on the mark, into the man's kidneys. His captor wheezed, falling off him. Ramses grabbed the gun from him and fired. The man fell like a stone to the sand. The wounded man holding his arm stood and fled as if demons unleashed from hell were on his heels. The tormentor holding his scimitar barely had time to lift the sword before Ramses rolled beneath him, raised the gun directly beneath his breastbone and fired. The man fell, a surprised look on his face. Ramses sprang to his feet and fired at the wounded man. He fell with a choking gasp. Shot in the back. Not very honorable, but he had no choice.

As if his body realized it was over, his legs gave way. The pistol dropped as Ramses tore off his turban, pressing it against his shoulder wound. He felt the warmth flowing down his arm like dark wine. Pain latched onto his shoulder, gnawing on it. He was too weak to stanch the flow of blood. Ramses had been wounded enough in battle, and had attended enough wounded men after such battles, to know that his injury was life-threatening unless he received immediate medical aid.

He collapsed on the sand, fighting unconsciousness. A small smile curved his lips. To die for a simple bullet wound! Not an honorable death. No warrior's victory for him, no glory, no stories sung about his courage around the crackling campfires at night. He lay there dully for a minute, regretting the inevitable. He mourned all that he would never have. Never father a son to be a Guardian to continue in his line. And then echoing in his mind was a soft, musical voice.

"Surely one of your good deeds, such as rescuing a lady in distress, will merit you the joys of Paradise."

Today I will find out if that is so. He felt a sharp pain, nearly as agonizing as the one his wounds caused, at the thought of never seeing her again. Maybe in another lifetime.

He wanted only to succumb to the pain and dizziness claiming him and let his spirit go. But instinct refused to let him do so. He would not die like a dog. He was a Khamsin warrior of the wind. Ramses struggled to rise and collapsed. Knives of agony dug into his flesh. A startled gasp roused his attention. Through his half-closed eyes he saw the woman. Gentle hands cradled the back of his head and lifted it. Ramses felt thankful that a woman's soft hands would be the last thing he felt.

"Oh, no," she cried out. Ramses's lips curled into a weak smile. Such a beautiful velvet voice would be the last thing he heard. He forced his eyes open.

As he felt his life's blood gush from him, he stared into a pair of luminous green eyes. A humorless smile spread over his lips. He would die with an enchanting vision ushering him out of this world into the next.

"Hello, my lovely little thief. All I ask is that you do not leave my body for the vultures, but give me a warrior's burial." Then he let the enveloping darkness drag him under.

Chapter Seven

Katherine roused herself from shock as she cradled
Ramses's head in her hands. Sand as fine as talcum
powdered the pale clean-shaven cheeks, clung with
greedy hunger to his clothing. She gently set down his
head. Katherine hurried inside the cave then ran back
to Ramses, covering him with a thick blanket and
pressing a folded cloth to his bleeding wound. Hearing
footsteps, she whirled. Her shoulders sagged with relief.

"Ahmed! I need your help, quick!"

Ahmed, bless him, wasted no time asking for expla-
nations. He lifted the blanket off Ramses, unfastened
his belt, then his robe and pulled it off. Ahmed withdrew his dagger and cut the shirt off. Katherine
flinched at the ugly bullet wound.

"This is all my fault," she said in a shaky voice. "If
I had gone with you to meditate as you asked. . . . He
just charged at them to protect me. I know it's all my
fault."

"Do not blame yourself. If you want to save him,

you must help me." Ahmed glanced around and saw the fire. He withdrew his dagger. "Here, take this and cut bandages. Get water, salt and soap, then cleanse his wounds."

Fear gave her speed as she again ran into the cave. Katherine shredded her Egyptian cotton sheets with the dagger. When she returned, Ahmed had retrieved another dagger from the sand and thrust it into the campfire to sterilize it. Her mouth went dry.

Katherine knelt by Ramses. He was half-conscious, breathing heavily. Despite the cloth over his wound, blood flowed in a steady stream, staining the ground. He had not passed out. But she wished he had, for what Ahmed must do to save his life would be agonizing.

After washing her hands, she poured the salt water over his wound. He moved about and moaned. Katherine's hand shook as she cleaned his shoulder, scrubbing it with soap and rinsing.

"The bullet is still embedded in his flesh. If you do not remove it, he will bleed to death," Ahmed said in an encouraging tone as he handed her the dagger.

"I can't." She panicked, tried to return the knife.

"I have not the knowledge. You have done this before."

"Not me! The doctor did it!"

"I will hold him down while you do it." Ahmed straddled Ramses, sitting on his waist, pressing upon his chest and arms.

The knife hovered above his wound, the heat warming her palm. She gave Ahmed a pleading look. "I can't do this."

He gave her a gentle smile. "You must. Or he will die."

Katherine gazed down at Ramses, growing pale from blood loss. If he died, part of her would die. She sucked in her breath and began working.

Ramses screamed in agony. He writhed, but Ahmed's grip was steady. Katherine focused only on her task as she dug the bullet out, then cleaned the wound. Blood streamed past her fingers. She pressed a bandage against the incision, but it reddened quickly. Ahmed took the knife, rinsed it and then squatted by the campfire, heating it.

"Hurry," she begged him. "I can't stop the bleeding."

He withdrew the glowing blade and handed it to her to cauterize the wound. She set her jaw and pressed the knife against Ramses while Ahmed held him down. Ramses cried out, thrashed and, to her immense relief, fell unconscious. Through a veil of tears she saw the bleeding stop. Releasing the knife, she tossed it aside.

Ahmed gave an approving nod. "You did well, Katherine."

Katherine gently mopped his wound, then cleaned her hands. Bandaging his shoulder a trifle clumsily, she tended to his other injuries and checked his thigh, ripping the trouser leg. Ahmed followed the direction of her gaze.

"Remove his trousers and cleanse it," he suggested mildly.

Remove the man's trousers? Katherine felt a blush creep up from her chest to her hairline. "In a minute," she mumbled. It wasn't deep. Katherine tenderly adjusted the blanket over him.

The shaman frowned. "He has lost some blood. But he will live, unlike those he dealt with." He gazed at the bodies on the sand. His dark eyes widened, seeing an arrow pointing from one man's chest. His gaze fell to the crossbow lying on the sand.

"I see he had some help," he commented.

She shrugged, her worry for Ramses turning aside his questions. "I need to get him inside, Ahmed. Help me."

Katherine unfurled the blanket lengthwise next to Ramses. Gently as they could, they rolled him over onto it. Then they stood, each grabbing one end.

It felt lifting a blanket filled with marble. The man was fashioned from solid muscle. Katherine wheezed as they struggled to carry Ramses inside.

"Put him down here, while I ready the bed," she told Ahmed. She layered the bed with several clean sheets, then they laid Ramses on it. Katherine tugged off his soft leather boots and the stockings on his feet.

Ahmed looked at Ramses. "Tend to him, Katherine. I will go . . . bury the others before the desert animals get to them. There must be no trace of them or the scavengers will come." He strode off, leaving her wondering if he meant human scavengers as well.

Panting for breath, she rested on the bed, gazing down at him. He had shaved years off his now hairless face. His chin now revealed a deep cleft. Despite the masculinity of his chiseled jaw line, he looked boyish, as threatening as an adorable kitten. Glancing at the odd tattoo on his left arm, Katherine realized what a deadly mistake it would be to deem this warrior vulnerable. Even in unconsciousness, an aura of muscled power clung to him. She remembered the tiger cub's deceptive cuteness. A clean-shaven Ramses could prove equally dangerous. She placed a quivering hand over her scar.

Katherine turned to more practical matters of nursing. She slipped a feather pillow under his head and checked his pulse. His deeply tanned throat was warm under her fingers and the pulse weak, but steady.

She pulled up a chair and stayed by his side, watching until Ahmed returned. He began carting items into the cave. Katherine's eyes met his as he laid the pistol and four oiled rifles in a corner, covering them with the tent fabric. Then he brought in a camel saddle and some large, hand-woven bags and a rifle. Ramses's, she presumed. Ahmed checked Ramses's pulse. Pulling back the blanket, he bent down and lifted up the muscled left arm bearing the strange tattoo.

The shaman stared at the tattoo as if spellbound. Then he examined the blue-inked tattoo of a falcon on Ramses's other arm. Ahmed nodded and crossed over to the table. To her astonishment, he began packing two small bags.

"What are you doing?" she cried out.

He glanced at her calmly. "I am going to get help."

Katherine looked at Ramses lying still and pale. If her cousin sent help back, she risked her father's life. Torn with indecision, she bit her lip.

"You are not here looking for artifacts, are you, my child?"

"No," she said, letting out a loud whoosh of relief that he knew. "I can't tell you what's going on."

Ahmed regarded her thoughtfully. "You are in trouble."

"I can't tell. Please don't make me," she begged.

"I know who he is," he said quietly. His dark eyes searched hers. "He is a Khamsin warrior of the wind. This is his desert."

Katherine rubbed her aching temples. A desert warrior protecting a treasure-filled tomb scared her, but not half as much as what would happen if Burrells returned and found her gone. She put her father's life in jeopardy.

"I must go inform his people what happened to him."

Filled with agitation, she shook her head. "Please, don't tell anyone! I can't have a tribe of angry warriors here! Give me at least two months. He'll be recovered by then. I have to stay here. Someone . . . is coming for me."

He nodded. "As you wish. I will tell them what happened, but that he is safe. I will not say where you are. The men are buried. There is no sign they were ever here. I will take their camels."

Katherine's fear doubled as he stood, pulling her with him, and kissed her on both cheeks. "Make certain to clean his thigh wound to prevent infection. Use honey afterward to kill germs. Now I must leave, daughter of the desert."

"Ahmed, you can't leave me here alone with him!"

He gave her an enigmatic smile. "Do not be frightened. You will be quite safe. I have seen your kismet. Trust me."

Katherine smiled uneasily. "I suppose we'll have to wait for you to teach me about my husband's tribe."

He gave a deep chuckle. "You will learn." Ahmed picked up his bags and left.

Katherine glanced at Ramses. Honey on his thigh wound would seal it and prevent bacteria from entering. In just a minute. She curled onto the other bed. Just a little rest. She was so exhausted. . . .

Chapter Eight

She woke at dawn the next day.

Katherine sat up with a start, struggling for a minute to remember her surroundings. Light spilled into the cave from the back entrance. Ramses! She lit a lamp, ran to him. He slept the deep sleep of unconsciousness.

Worried, she murmured soothingly and ran a hand over his flushed brow. Her palm came away damp with sweat. She cursed herself for being too squeamish to cleanse his thigh wound. His fever indicated infection had set in.

She stripped off the blanket and surveyed his body, trying to see him as a physician would. Tried. Dark hair dusted his broad, firm chest. Sweat glistened in tiny beads on his golden skin. Katherine placed the lamp on the chair next to the bed. Two vertical knife wounds slashed his belly and chest. They did not bleed, but looked an angry red. Her gaze traveled farther down. His indigo cotton trousers concealed the thigh wound. To inspect it, she'd have to remove them.

Pretend you are a man and this is your patient. The only difference is your gender!

Remembering talk in her cousin's harem, she reassured herself. Ramses probably wore a loincloth. This gave her confidence. She undid the strings tied at the trouser ankles. Taking a deep breath, Katherine unfastened the drawstring around his waist, tugged the trousers down and yanked them off.

No loincloth. She felt herself go scarlet with embarrassment. His most private parts were boldly displayed before her, his body naked to her exploring eyes.

Such a handsome man. A broad chest tapered into a narrow waist and hips. Legs tautly muscled and dusted with thick, dark hair were strong and straight. Katherine winced at the oblong bruises darkening his stomach and legs. Then her gaze shot upward to the area between his legs.

She gulped. Katherine had never seen a naked man, but had heard talk in her cousin Jamal's harem about what defined a man of "largeness," as the women called it.

Ramses certainly looked like a man of largeness. Fascinated, she stared at the largeness surrounded by a thick nest of dark, curling hair. She recalled when the bored women had made up names for men's private parts, comparing them to common objects. These names zipped through her imagination.

"King's potent scepter." "Warrior's immense lance." "Thick cucumber of passion." "Immense date palm." "Mighty snake of the night." Or, as one woman had giggled, "wrinkled little grape."

Katherine felt a heated flush burn her cheeks as she

looked again, tore her gaze away, then peeked again. No wrinkled little grape here. Nor a cucumber. No, more like a mushroom with a long stem. Very long. Somehow, she had the feeling Ramses would deeply resent his manhood being compared to a fungus.

Cucumber. Mushroom. All inappropriate metaphors for a proud warrior who saved her with his steel sword. Warrior. Yes. Warrior's lance. An apt description for such a proud, courageous fighter.

A soft smile curled Katherine's lips as she gazed upon Ramses. "Ramses, if you will not mind, I'm going to cover your mighty lance for modesty's sake to attend to your wound."

Katherine laid his trousers across said object and concentrated on cleaning his thigh wound. Now and then she stole a peek at his lance and smiled. It was indeed, aptly named.

For three days, Katherine tended Ramses, applying fresh poultices, sponging his body, keeping him clean, and changing his dressings and bed sheets. Three days of hovering on the edge of hell, worrying his spirit would quietly give in and pass on.

His fevered sleep was restless, fitful; and sometimes he cried out in delirium. He shivered despite the blankets she heaped upon him, and soaked them with his sweat. Once he grabbed her arm and his eyes opened, bright with fever, as he asked in a hoarse voice, "Where is she? I must find her!" Then he collapsed back onto the bed before she could utter a sound.

His fever finally broke on the fourth day. She returned from hanging laundry to dry and passed him, seeing his eyes closed and thinking he slept. With her back to him, she picked up her book on herbal remedies and began studying.

A dry, racking cough interrupted her.

Katherine's shoulders grew rigid with shocked joy. She groped for the black veil lying around her neck and attached it. She turned to see Ramses's golden eyes watching her.

"Praise God, you are awake and alive." She knelt by his side and pressed a gentle hand to his forehead. Cool, but no longer clammy. A brilliant smile formed beneath the veil.

"How long have I been sick?"

"Three days. You had a fever from infection. I feared . . . I would lose you." She checked the poultice. Blackened blood crusted the long, ugly scar. But it was healing. Her lower lip trembled with relief.

He raised his head slightly and peered at her, golden eyes still glazed from fever. "I dreamt a lovely thief with hands as soft as lotus petals rescued me." His right fingertips brushed her hand. "I see I was correct."

Katherine looked away as she replaced the poultice, distressed at his bitter tone. He was a proud man and resented being helpless, especially before the one woman who had stolen from him. She turned to more practical matters.

"You must be hungry."

Ramses looked away. "I smell garlic. Are you stewing me for your next meal, little thief? Did you save me only to marinate me for dinner?"

Distress gave way to annoyance. "It's herbs to heal your shoulder. I'm certain you wouldn't make a good meal. I'd crack several teeth on your tough hide."

Katherine gnawed on her lip. Arguing with him did

not help. Ramses was very weak and in the worst position for a strong warrior. "I will get you food," she offered in a gentler tone. "Soup, I think, for now."

Ramses gave her a sullen look, but nodded. "Thank you," he said in a barely audible voice, dropping his head. Her heart ached at the paleness of his face against the pillow's snowy whiteness.

"Are you in much pain?" Katherine took his left hand into hers. The large, broad palm felt rough and cool. She slid her thumb gently over dark hair dusting the back.

His eyes followed her thumb's trek. "It is nothing," he managed, those amber eyes darkening with pain he refused to admit existed.

"I will make you something," she said softly, trying to reassure him. His jaw clenched as he looked away.

"I can manage it," he stated through gritted teeth.

She started the fire near the smoke hole and put a copper pot over it, filling it with herbs and broth. Next she gave a hearty stir to her fever medication. Katherine stole a peek at Ramses. His face constricted as he closed his eyes. He would struggle with his pain, this proud warrior. She added a dose of valerian root, a sedative herb that acted as a pain reliever.

Propping a few pillows behind his back, Katherine raised him to a semi-sitting position. She held a cup of the medication to his lips. Ramses wrinkled his nose. "What is this? It does not smell like soup."

"Herbs to prevent another fever. First medicine, then food."

His curved lower lip jutted out like a pouting child's. "No. I will taste none of your strange potions."

"Yes, you will. I'm not going to nurse you through another fever," she said firmly, holding the cup to his mouth and giving him a sip. He scrunched his face as if she had forced castor oil down his throat. "This smells and tastes like camel dung!"

"It's good for you. Now stop being a child and drink."

Ramses's lips curved into a challenging smile. "Make me."

Men! They were all such babes. She returned the smile and said in a pleasant tone, "Very well." Katherine pinched his nose in a viselike grip. When he gasped for air, she poured the medication into his mouth, then closed his jaw and tickled his throat. He gave a mighty swallow.

"That's how my cousin's shaman administers medicine to sick goats. I thought it would come in useful one day," she said proudly.

"Sick goats," he sputtered in indignant outrage. "You compare me to a sick goat?"

Katherine cocked her head at him, considering the idea. "No, I believe you're more like my cousin's three-year-old son when he's told it's bedtime."

She set down the cup and patted his good shoulder. "Stop complaining. Or have you changed your mind about the soup?" She fetched the bowl and let the delicious odor of spices, vegetables and dried meat tempt him. Ramses sniffed and looked with longing at the meal.

"I will not complain any longer," he said in a sulky voice.

"Good." She began feeding him hot soup. His face lost the petulant look and relaxed into pure pleasure.

"It is delicious. Sweet."

"That's the angelica root. I flavored the soup with

it because it is a good herb for fever." She held the spoon to his lips again.

He sipped, his dark gold eyes never leaving her face. "You must know much of herbs to use them in your cooking."

Katherine lifted her shoulders. "I have some knowledge. I'm happy I could put it to good use."

When he finished, she wiped his stubbled chin. She gave him a critical look. "Your beard's grown back. Why did you shave it?"

Ramses made no reply. He studied her face so intently she started wishing he would fall back asleep again. Then he reached up and brushed his fingertips against her veil's edge.

"Why do you wear this?"

Katherine jerked away from his threatening silky touch and groped for a lie. "I'm a woman and you're a man, and it's my people's custom. Women seldom remove their veils before men. Is it so odd to you?"

"Not as a custom. But sometimes customs are shields people hide behind in order to guard secrets," he observed. Those clear golden eyes pierced hers. Katherine felt a flush fill her covered cheeks. Even lying in a sickbed, the man possessed a sharp instinct that missed little.

She thought rapidly. "You veiled your face before you attacked the men, I noticed. So I could say the same of you. Do your women also hide behind veils?"

His jaw muscles tightened. "Our warriors always veil themselves before engaging in battle. Our identities, especially those of our sheikhs, must remain guarded. Our women have nothing to hide. They go unveiled."

A cynical smile curved his lips. "Can you make the same claim, little thief?"

Katherine glowered at him, wanting to dump the soup over his head. "You act as if I'm the enemy. If so, why would I bother saving your life?"

He looked a trifle shamefaced. "You did save my life and I thank you for it," he said quietly.

"You saved mine," she reminded him, guilt striking her as she remembered how he had charged to her defense.

"I planned to deal with those men. You merely caused me to take action sooner. I knew they would follow the map to the cave."

"This cave?" Realization dawned. "The map was a fake!"

"Do you think I would be so foolish as to walk about such a dangerous city with a valuable map?" Ramses's eyes narrowed. "You did, for why else are you here?"

Katherine remained quiet. Silence offered a better defense than truth.

"I asked you a question."

Even from a position of weakness on the sickbed, his voice radiated quiet authority. Katherine laced her fingers together. "I was brought here to find the mine. I have some knowledge of the desert." She could admit nothing more.

He continued regarding her with his steady gaze, although his eyelids fluttered. The valerian root was starting to make him sleepy.

"You should rest now," she told him.

"How did you remove the bullet?"

Katherine stared. "Don't you remember? I operated on you."

Ramses nodded. "Excellent."

94

She felt her lower lip quiver. "I didn't want to hurt you like that."

His expression softened. Ramses touched her hand lightly. "Khamsin warriors are taught to manage discomfort."

Discomfort was stubbing one's toe, not what she had done. Katherine marveled at his self-discipline. Ramses started to move his right shoulder and winced.

"Lie still," Katherine scolded him. She crossed the room, put the dishes on the table and picked up the crossbow, examining the arrow. She needed fresh meat so he could regain his strength. "Tonight I shall hunt for real food. No more soup or dried rations. Perhaps a hare would do."

The incredulous look upon his face galled her. "You hunt?"

"Yes," she shot back, irritated. "I may not defend myself effectively against four attacking men, but I think I can handle the terrifying Arabian Desert hares."

"A woman hunter," he said in a marveling tone, settling back against the pillows. "You have many talents. Healing, herbs, cooking, and now hunting . . . and . . . steal . . ."

He fell quiet as Katherine pointed the crossbow at him. She set it back on the table with a regretful sigh.

"I can easily hunt hare, but I wish I had used it earlier on the men. I could have spared you this," she murmured.

He said quietly, "You did enough. You saved my life."

"Barely. You saved yourself. My crossbow only hit one man. And I ran into the cave like a coward before attacking them." Her lower lip trembled beneath the concealing veil.

Lines furrowed his smooth brow. Ramses gave her a bewildered look as if she talked nonsense.

"Women are to be protected, not act as warriors. Had you tried attacking them when they were not distracted with me, those four would have injured you."

She glanced at him. "They were no match for you. I say four against one is fair play for such a strong warrior."

Ramses smiled ruefully at the compliment, sagging back against the pillows. "Not so strong now," he said, sighing. "I am as weak as a babe."

"Of course you're weak. You were wounded and very ill. But you'll regain your strength," she said in an encouraging tone.

"I wish I could regain it now," he complained.

Katherine bit back a smile. How typical of a man! He hated being bedridden. Her biggest challenge now would be to keep him occupied and prevent him from overexerting himself.

"If you rest, you will be on your feet in no time."

"I had best recover my strength before more men come to claim you," Ramses responded with what she recognized was his protective growl. "Someone else is coming, am I not correct?"

Katherine struggled to not reveal information while being as truthful as possible. "The men. . . . were expected to be here for two months. Someone is coming to get them after that."

"Strange to only have four men. The desert is filled with dangers, such as warriors who do not trifle with those trespassing on their lands," Ramses observed.

"Four men with guns and a supply of ammunition,"

she corrected. "They were rather arrogant about their ability to ward off an attack, if one came."

"Where are these weapons now?"

She said nothing, but her eyes shot over to the corner where Ahmed had hidden the rifles. A small, satisfied smile jerked his lips upward.

"I know how to use a gun," she asserted, folding her arms.

"So you told me in the *souks*. But you will not handle these. Women should not handle firearms."

His arrogance annoyed her. "Who put you in charge?"

"I am always in charge. I am a Guardian of the Ages, sworn to defend and protect."

He stated this quietly, authority riding on his broad shoulders even in his weakened state. Katherine had the uneasy feeling she shouldn't underestimate this man. He had made no more references to her treachery, but it hung between them like fabric dividing a tent. Once Ramses regained his strength, what would he do? Punish her for stealing the map? Torture her for answers? Katherine remembered his broad palms roaming over her body and suppressed a shiver of pleasure. Certain forms of torture could undo her more than others. While he remained weak, she could control him. But Katherine suspected Ramses would recover more quickly than she wanted.

For now, he remained vulnerable, naked in bed. Her confidence returned.

He looked down at his naked chest and frowned. "Where are my clothes?"

Oh dear. So much for keeping him vulnerable. Katherine glanced away. Of course he would notice his state of undress.

"I had to remove them. I laundered them and I'll return them to you . . . when you're well enough to get out of bed."

"But I am not fully undressed. Something is binding me," he grumbled. Ramses lifted the blanket and peeked down below. His eyebrows shot up. "A loincloth?"

"I had to use . . . quite a lot of fabric," she admitted, feeling a burning blush spread to her hairline as he chuckled.

"So I see," he said in a teasing tone. "I regret that I had to deplete your stock of linens. You did a fine job."

"I had to practice. I could not get the correct fit because of the immense size of your warrior's lance," she confessed and then to her horror, realized what she had said.

" 'Warrior's lance'!" he shouted in delighted mirth.

" 'Mighty snake of the night' seemed too inadequate," she stammered, fire burning her cheeks.

He threw back his head and laughed. Katherine's jaw dropped. She thanked the veil for hiding it. "I need to bring in the laundry. If you need anything, just yell," she stammered, and ran outside, accompanied by a stream of proud male laughter.

As soon as she fled, Ramses threw back the blanket. He glanced at the white linen loincloth and shook his head, still chuckling. Immense warrior's lance. Ramses felt proud as a stallion at the compliment.

Then he sobered, feeling guilty for embarrassing her. She had saved his life. And he still didn't know her name! Well, that would soon change. After he got out of this bed.

He gritted his teeth, feeling the ache of bruises and

the bullet wound. The pain was manageable, even though he still felt weak. But he would be blasted if he were staying in bed another minute!

With all his strength he sat up, then stood. Ramses sucked in his breath, wheezing. Maybe his beautiful thief was right. He should stay in bed. Ramses felt a familiar pressure in his groin and groaned. No, business outside first. She would not care for him like a babe any longer.

Ramses glanced down at the loincloth and chuckled again. With his left hand, he ripped off the fabric.

Completely naked, he grabbed the sheet and draped it around his waist for modesty. Fighting dizziness, he walked on unsteady feet, then went outside. A few minutes later he returned and gratefully sank onto a chair at the table. He adjusted the sheet around his waist awkwardly with his left hand. Ramses winced at the fresh pain in his shoulder. He lifted the dressing and peered at the wound, admiring her bandaging job. An ugly red slash ran just below his shoulder. Thank God the lout had no sense of aim. Ramses shuddered, thinking of how his attacker could have easily hit his heart.

His nurse returned, carrying several folded sheets. Ramses gave a guilty start and then a chagrined smile. She set down the sheets on the table and scowled.

"What are you doing? Get back into bed now!" she scolded.

"Not until you tell me one thing," he said.

"What?" She gathered the sheets upon the bed and tossed them aside, then laid down fresh ones. They smelled like sunshine and he realized how much he'd missed the outdoors.

"Your name."

His green-eyed princess stopped smoothing the sheets and glanced up, her eyes huge. She looked frightened.

"My name?" She put a hand to her left cheek.

"Yes, your name," he repeated in his sternest voice.

"It is . . ." she seemed to struggle for an answer, then replied. "Kalila."

He studied her downcast eyes, the obvious fluster at his interrogation. Ramses decided to change tactics to see if a compliment would cause her to spill secrets. "It is a beautiful name," he said softly, watching her eyes widen. It *was* a beautiful name, he admitted, and matched her beauty.

Kalila seemed tense as she continued making the bed, but she did not reply. Ramses leaned his tired head upon his left hand and gazed at her. Such a shapely form beneath the loose-fitting trousers. The yellow shirt did little to disguise the rounded curves of well-formed breasts. Her hair tumbled past her waist in a thick cascade of ebony curls. If he ran his fingers through it, he'd caress silk.

But her face. . . . It was hidden to him, a mystery. The veil revealed only huge green eyes fringed by long dark lashes, highly arched brows, and a forehead lightly feathered with raven bangs. Her grace, nurturing nature, gentle mannerisms and soft, musical voice contrasted sharply with her caustic wit, intelligence and self-sufficiency. And deceitful, slippery ways. Kalila. She had evaded his grasp twice. Now he remained trapped in her lair, yet that would change, he promised himself. He would recover and find the answers he sought.

Ramses would coax truth from her unseen lips and have all her secrets spill out. His mystery princess was as exotic as a jewel, as fragrant as myrrh and graceful as a gazelle. Still, an ethereal air clung to her dainty shoulders, a wispy dream-like cloud of mysticism as if she would vanish in a puff of smoke . . .

"You are like a dream," he said softly.

"A dream?" She looked up from her task.

Ramses's eyelids fluttered with fatigue. "Yes, my dream, my vision. For you are as fragile and soft as one, and I fear you will melt away should I close my eyes, slipping once more from my grasp, and I shall be alone with only my dreams," he mumbled.

"You fear needlessly. I'm as solid as the rock in this cave. I promise, Ramses, I won't leave you. Not when you're this ill."

Exhaustion wrapped around him as demands of sleep pulled him down, and his eyelids half-closed. Ramses felt the gentle pressure of his vision's arms around his left shoulder.

"Come Ramses, lie down again. If you fall asleep at the table, you'll regret it."

He struggled to his feet, allowing her to support his weight with her slender frame. He could not trust her, but until he grew stronger, he needed her help. She held him around the waist and as he climbed into bed. Kalila covered him with a blanket and settled a pillow beneath his head.

"Sweet dreams, Ramses. Sleep well."

He forced his eyes open to gaze into the depths of her green ones as she knelt beside him. "Will you still be here when I awake? Or are you an enchantress who will vanish as I slumber? And steal something else of mine?" Like my heart, he thought.

She laid two gentle fingers upon his lids, forcing them closed. "Fear not, Ramses. You can't lose me that easily. I'm here to care for you. To give, not take. Now sleep."

Reassured, he drifted into sleep, but not before he swore he felt the softness of velvet lips brushing against his cheek.

Chapter Nine

At dusk, Katherine went hunting.

Taking the crossbow, she walked among the black rocks nestling against the mountain. Dull yellow and green plants, shrubs and trees dotted the area, perfect covering for small game. Hares liked eating during this cooler time of day. Settling on a rock to wait, she watched the desert come alive. A shiny black dung beetle scuttled through the sand. Poking its head from beneath a rock, a spiny-tailed yellowish-brown lizard regarded the beetle, then vanished again into the shade.

Ramses had not stirred since afternoon. Katherine wanted to surprise him with the savory odor of freshly roasting meat when he awoke. Show him a woman could hunt as well as a man, too.

She settled the crossbow upon her knees and sighed. The setting sun cast brilliant hues of crimson, violet and rose in the sky. Katherine stared out at the sea of sand, feeling peace and tranquility sooth her soul. She touched her cheek, realizing now that she could no longer remain uncovered.

Closing her eyes, she recalled receiving the scar eight years ago. The tiger had fascinated her with its exotic grace as it roamed its cage at her cousin's house. The cub was a gift from her father, who collected wild cats from across the globe. Intrigued, she had approached the cage, not realizing the restless pacing meant danger. She only desired to touch its soft fur, stroke the rich golden colors and ebony stripes. As she brought her face close to the bars, it attacked, raking a claw across her cheek. She screamed and cried out for her father, but the damage had been done.

A small movement in the bushy undergrowth caught her eye. Katherine took the crossbow and crouched down. A flash of gray. The arrow let loose with a sharp flip and sailed into the hare. It shuddered once and died. Triumphant, she scrambled down from the rocks and claimed her prize.

As she grabbed the dead animal by its feet, an uneasy thought shadowed her. She claimed skill with the crossbow and could hunt prey. But Ramses with his mesmerizing tiger eyes and instinctive hunter's skill was a far more deadly predator. She must watch him, and take care to avoid his sharp claws that had the ability to slash her heart in two. Drawn to Ramses as she had been to the tiger's cage so long ago, Katherine wondered if this tiger would carve a greater mark upon her heart.

A delicious odor of roasting meat woke Ramses. He stretched and yawned, blinking at the flickering campfire. He felt disoriented and even more tired than when he'd slept.

And very hungry. The smell of cooking drove him mad as he became more awake. He breathed heavily and rubbed his eyes with his left fist.

"Good, you are awake. Just in time for dinner." Kalila's soft, cheerful voice greeted him. She lit the lamp and its golden glow cast shadows on the walls.

"I believe you should stand and walk a bit, if you have sufficient strength. Lying down that much will cause your shoulder to stiffen and your lungs to weaken. She moved to his feet, and held out his trousers. Her eyes swept downward, looking embarrassed. Then she assumed a brisk manner.

"I'll help you. If I put these on your ankles, all you need to do is raise your legs."

She pulled aside the blanket, sat on the bed at his feet, slid the trousers on, bunching them at the ankles and gave him a questioning look. Ramses cursed his weakness. He was a Khamsin warrior of the wind. A man who could slay enemies with a whisk of his blade. Yet he could not even dress himself. Ramses bent his knees and let her slide the trousers up. He grit his teeth and moved very slowly, feeling sweat bead his forehead as he raised his hips. She tied the trousers at the ankles as he fastened them at the waist.

She continued sitting at his feet, gently rubbing the tops. Ramses enjoyed the sensation of her soft fingers against his skin. His stomach uttered a loud, rude growl.

"Now for this. It's chilly. I don't want you catching cold."

Kalila held out a shirt he recognized as one he had packed. Ramses tucked, rolled and sat, grimacing at the pain in his shoulder. He rested a minute, staring at the garment, then glanced at his shoulder.

Bonnie Vanak

"I will help you. Hold up your left arm."

He sighed and obeyed. She slipped the loose garment over his head easily. But his right arm hung limply at his side. He glanced down at it, and up at her, brows raised in a question.

"This will not do." She shook her head and squinted at him, and tugged the shirt off again. "I have a much better idea. Can you lift your arm a bit? Just raise it?"

Ramses huffed. "Of course I can." He tried. Pain stabbed him with knifelike precision. Sweat poured from his forehead. He grunted. She slipped the sleeve up his right arm. He lifted his left arm as she eased on the garment.

She went to slip an arm around him. Ramses pushed her hand away with rude impatience. "I can do it myself," he snapped. "Must you coddle me as if I were a child?"

Kalila watched him quietly. He struggled to rise, feeling shame at his rudeness, and shamed to admit he needed help. Ramses walked to the table, collapsed onto the chair. She knelt by the fire and ladled stew onto a plate, then set it before him with silverware. Picking up the fork, he examined it carefully. Usually he used utensils only when dining with business prospects at the Shepheard's. Seeing them in the sacred cave seemed as odd as the beds, table and chairs. A princess's life required much more luxury than the simple needs of a desert warrior, he thought with amusement.

He looked down at the plate, his stomach screaming with hunger. But she continued fussing by the fire. Finally, after a few minutes, she looked up, her eyes squinting in puzzlement.

"Why aren't you eating?"

106

"I am waiting for you," he replied. "Are you not eating?"

Kalila dished out a plate for herself and brought it to the table. Silently she began to eat, lifting her veil with her hand. Her eyes focused on the plate as she nibbled at her meal.

He pushed the thick bits of meat and vegetables around on his plate and brought a forkful to his mouth. Ramses chewed slowly. It tasted like nectar. He ate some more, watching her. With spine straight and shoulders rigid, she kept her eyes lowered, not meeting his. Suddenly the delicious meal stuck in his throat. Ramses lowered his fork and swallowed.

"Kalila, I am sorry for being so gruff." He struggled with his pride. "I am . . . not used to being this helpless."

Finally she raised her eyes. They shimmered with moisture. "It's all right. I'm sure it's difficult. Perhaps it's best you do as much as you can alone, and ask when you need help."

Ramses ate some more of the delicious stew, sighing with pleasure. "I taste fresh meat. Is it hare?"

She lifted her head, a hint of pride in her voice. "I killed it myself this afternoon."

"You are quite skilled as a huntress with the crossbow."

The compliment relaxed her shoulders and she nodded. Then an impish light shone in her green eyes. "I did not kill it with the crossbow."

"No?" He sat back a minute.

"No. I cast a spell upon it and the hare gave up its spirit. I told it that you needed fresh meat. It was more than willing to oblige."

"I could almost believe it," he muttered. She had an

air of enchantment about her, this woman who had the ability to make his head fuzzy and then vanish into thin air. He chewed another mouthful and swallowed.

"How does a woman learn to handle a crossbow as effectively as a man?"

She speared a slice of meat. "By learning from a man. My father taught me. I think he felt guilty over the accident and spoiled me."

"Accident? What accident?"

To his surprise, her hand flew to her left cheek, then touched her nose as if checking her veil. "Ah . . . nothing. It was nothing but a small accident."

She lied. Ramses studied her bent head. He had interrogated men expertly and knew the signs. Why did she hide her face? Surely it could not be for mere modesty's sake. "Is it your mother who gave you your jewel eyes?"

She touched her face again. "Yes. Papa met her in Alexandria. She died a few years ago," came the curt reply.

"I'm sorry," he said gently. "So you live with your father?"

Kalila shrugged. "If you persist in asking questions, your meal will grow cold."

He bit back an amused grin. She noticed, his little thief.

"What of you, Ramses? Where do you make your home?"

Very clever, turning his interrogation around. "In the sand," he said briefly.

"Oh. You and your tribe burrow into it like a snake?"

Raising his head, he studied her sparkling green eyes. "How do you know I have a tribe?"

Those lovely green eyes darted to one side. "Obviously, you have a tribe. Your . . . clothing. Your turban and robe . . ."

"Our people call it a *binish*."

"*Binish*. It's an easy guess you're from a warrior tribe because of how you fight and your protective manner."

"As our warriors are taught to protect and guard women. Although some women seem to use that to their advantage," he responded, a reminder he had protected her at the *souks*, and she used that concern to steal the map.

"Some women have no choice in what they must do." Her voice caught as if on the verge of tears. Ramses steeled himself. Kalila was a clever woman and pity would soften his resolve to uncloak her secrets.

"God gave us wisdom to deal with the circumstances we are given. We must listen for guidance in choosing the right path to follow. The easiest way is not always the correct way."

Two orbs of hard green ice glittered at him. "It's easy to judge what you don't know . . . or understand."

Ramses leaned forward, setting down his fork. "Then enlighten me. I wish to understand."

Even as he made the motion, she shrank back. He didn't mean to scold, but she dropped her chin. He must not be as rough with her as he would be with a man. This required more delicate treatment. He had time to secure answers from those unseen lips.

Silence fell between them as he finished eating, wiped his mouth and glanced around with interest.

"Did you move into the cave because the men were camping outside?"

A slow nod. "Ahmed thought it best after . . . well, he said the cave was sacred. He sensed it as we approached and when we saw the garlic strewn about. We knew someone had inhabited it."

"Garlic is an ancient deterrent against scorpions," he said absently. "Why were you alone with the men if they frightened you?"

She dropped her gaze. "My shaman wanted me to go with him to meditate . . . I thought it would be safe enough, because they had gone off . . . And then I heard them outside, drinking and then they came and . . ."

Anger soured his stomach as he listened to her trembling voice. An aging shaman provided little protection against cutthroats like those he had slain. Who dared to leave her with those men? They were the sort he'd expected to find looking for the mine. But Kalila had a touching innocence about her. If so, someone had forced her into a very dangerous, very unpredictable situation. But why?

"You should never have been left alone with them. They were unscrupulous, the worst sort of desert jackal," he said, struggling with his temper. He caught her look of alarm and softened his remark with a smile.

She reached across the table and touched his hand. "You charged them single-handedly, mindless of the danger. You saved me. Why did you rescue me, after . . . what I did to you?"

He caressed the hand resting on his right hand with his left thumb. "Precious jewels such as you should be

protected," he murmured, his feelings rising to the surface.

She looked down and he let her hand go. Ramses
deliberately moved his right shoulder, biting his lip.
The pain reminded him of the tattoo and his vow. He
glanced at her body's lovely curves and cursed silently.
What had he told his sheikh? What women would he
meet in a desert inhabited by jinn?

Beautiful, green-eyed thieves. His left hand snaked
to his hair, cringing as he envisioned Jabari's wide grin
as he took a dagger to Ramses's long locks. . . .

No. He would not lose control. Just because he was
alone with the one woman who threatened to set the
beast loose from its cage . . . he would not violate his
vow.

Ramses splayed his left hand upon the table, staring
at his fingers. He flexed them. Then he looked at her
with a penetrating stare. "Kalila, why are you after the
gold?" The question came across as pointed. Direct.
Authoritative.

Green eyes avoided his. Another sign of lying or
discomfort. Ramses leaned forward.

"I didn't say I was," she answered.

"Yet you are here."

"So are you."

"I am here to honor a sacred custom of meditation."

"What if I told you I was here to do the same?"

"You and I know that is not the truth," he said
softly.

Her eyes narrowed. "We do?"

He gestured around the cavern. "You obviously de-
ciphered the hieroglyphics. This is the cave depicted
on the papyrus you stole. That is why you are here."

"Things are not always as they seem. You aren't here just to pray in the desert, either!"

Anger spiked her tone. Ramses realized he had pressed too far. Time enough later to find out. He changed tactics to soften his questioning with a compliment.

"It is most unusual for a woman to enjoy the deep desert. Then again, you are a most unique woman."

Green eyes sparkled with life. Kalila heaved a deep sigh and pushed back her plate. "I adore it out here. There is something about the desert that is soothing. It is honest and raw and does not lie, cheat, steal or belittle. You can bare your soul and find out who you truly are."

He studied her shining eyes, the wistfulness in them. "The desert requires honesty. It has great spaces where one can strip down the soul until there is nothing left but the divine spark that created it." Ramses wondered if she would catch his statement's double meaning. Honesty. He hoped to evoke some from her.

Now he could see a smile beneath that veil, for the corners of her beautiful eyes creased. "Yes! That is what Ahmed said."

"Where is this shaman of yours now?"

Her emerald eyes clouded. "He said he had to leave."

Ramses knew shamans came and went with the wind, so her answer satisfied him. He asked the one question that had burned in his mind since meeting her. "Did you meet me at the Shepheard's to steal the map? And if so, why did you not take it when I kissed you? You had the chance."

She dropped her gaze to her plate and toyed with the food, pushing it around the plate.

"Kalila. Why?" he asked in a sharp tone requiring answers.

"I . . . had never been kissed before. When you kissed me . . . I could not think, I mean, you were so . . . I lost my breath. I'd never felt like that before."

Touched by her shyness, Ramses swore a blush tinted her hidden cheeks. Her awkward kiss had not been faked. He could tell she was inexperienced. Kalila had an innocent air clouded by the graveness of her crime.

She glanced at him. He smiled gently. "Kissing you was a most pleasurable experience."

"I had no idea a kiss had such . . . power to it," she confessed, toying with her fork. "I should have expected as much. When I saw you, proud as a tiger, you had the bearing and manner of a warrior."

A tiger? Ramses felt a sudden chill rush through him, as if a cold wind whistled through the cave. Despite the deep throb that hummed in his right shoulder, he felt his body stiffen with accustomed pride. "I am a Khamsin warrior of the wind."

Now those lovely green eyes widened. He felt a flush of masculine satisfaction at the awe flickering there. "I've heard of the famous Khamsin warriors and how they rule the desert sands. I'm not surprised you are a Khamsin warrior. You fight as fiercely as one."

Her gaze dropped. "Of course, I imagine you've had many women tell you things like this," she said, studying her hands. He looked at those hands, soft and frail as the lotus blossom.

"Yes," he admitted, not wanting to sound as if he were bragging. "But none as eloquently as you."

She rose and fetched a pitcher of water and two cups, pouring drinks. Ramses accepted his with a nod of thanks and drank deeply. Kalila glanced at him with those incredible eyes.

"I imagine you have many women who . . . kiss you."

Ramses settled his left arm upon the table, feeling uneasy with this twist of conversation. "A few," he conceded.

"Do you ever kiss women from your tribe?"

From his tribe? Ramses drew back at such a thought with a scowl. "The women of my tribe are honorable and I would never pursue them with my . . . ah . . . intentions."

"Oh." She wrapped a lock of hair around one finger and toyed with it, considering. "So you kiss women in the city?"

He shifted in his chair. "Yes."

"Many women?" A child's curiosity colored her voice. Kalila acted intrigued, like a schoolgirl wishing to learn about a taboo subject.

He started feeling uncomfortable. Recollections of Queb's remonstration nagged him. "Not all that many," he protested.

"But those that you do, where do you kiss them? Or do they all follow you into dark meeting rooms and kiss you?"

Ramses caught the teasing note that poked fun at herself. He gave her a long, thoughtful look before answering.

"In their rooms."

"Their rooms?"

Ramses gazed at her kindly. "Their bedrooms."

"Their bedrooms? Oh!" Suddenly it was as if a brilliant light flashed in her eyes. She looked down at the ground.

"It isn't just kisses then."

"No," he said softly. "It is much more than that." Now he knew she was but an innocent maid. Her chest rose and fell with each deep breath. She rubbed her small, delicate hands. He stared at those slender fingers, so skilled in caring for him, supporting his neck as she adjusted the pillows. How would they feel caressing the muscles in his back during lovemaking? He had taken her tentative kiss and showed her a man's deep-seated desire. But she met that desire. Beneath that virginal exterior—and he was certain she was a virgin—burned a fire as intense as the desert heat.

"These women, do you like their kisses better than mine?" she asked in such a low voice he barely heard her.

An uncomfortable crush of unexpected desire flared. Her kiss had inflamed him in a way no other woman's had. Ramses saw brittle hope flicker in her eyes.

"Your kiss enchanted me," he admitted, reaching across the table to stroke her soft fingertips.

"But these other women, you do things . . . in their bedrooms." Her gaze flicked away. Flicked back. "You prefer what you do with them, don't you?"

Ramses licked his bottom lip, feeling the temperature rise, despite the night chill. He put a hand to his brow. Was his fever returning? Such a thing to ask him! He suddenly wished they had stuck to simpler, safer dinner conversation, such as how best to cook a houbara bustard.

With her lithe, slender form, graceful movements and lovely sparkling eyes as clear as a crystal oasis, how could Kalila not realize how deeply she aroused him? Bad enough her body tempted him, but her questions brought many delicious images to mind. Ramses shifted in his seat. He could show her such pleasures, starting with . . . His eyes drifted to the gentle slope of her breasts. They were perfectly formed, delectable and round. The chilly air had caused a natural female reaction, for they were tipped with hardness much like two pearls he had seen in the *souks*. These rounded nubs pressed against her thin shirt. Ramses felt a familiar stirring in his groin.

Remembering his vow, he bit back a deep groan. But he could not prevent imagining her delighted shudders as he removed Kalila's shirt as gently as she had helped him dress, and bared her breasts to his hungry gaze. Ramses closed his eyes, thinking of her pretty sighs as he lowered his mouth to one delicate pearl, making her whimper with pleasure and cry out his name . . .

Scowling, he opened his eyes, grabbed his cup and drank deeply, then slammed it down. "May I have . . . more water please?" he asked in a croaking voice . . .

She filled the glass. Glad of the distraction, he drank some more. Good. At least now he could think normally and she'd ask no more . . .

"Ramses? You didn't answer my question. You prefer what you do with the women, don't you?"

She would not give up. Honesty was best.

"Yes," he said quietly.

He watched her reaction. Sadness clouded her green gaze. Absently her hand drifted to her left cheek, then jerked away. He wondered if she thought he preferred the women to her. This insight gave him pause.

"What I do with them," he added, studying her. "Not who they are. They mean little to me."

A deep vee formed between her brows. "What do you mean?"

He sought his next words with care. "There are certain . . . pleasures a man seeks from a woman. But that does not mean it is more than physical."

"Can a woman experience these pleasures as well as a man?"

He inhaled sharply. Ramses tried controlling his active imagination, tortured with the delights he could show her.

"It is like our kiss at the hotel. I felt you respond to me. Did it do something to you?"

Dropping her head, she peeped up from beneath her long black lashes. "Yes," she admitted. "It did."

"Do not be ashamed," he gently told her. "Indeed, I was quite pleased you enjoyed it."

"You were?" She gazed at him with wide-eyed awe.

"Yes." Ramses dared to reach across the table and brush his fingers against hers. "It is not enough for a man to experience pleasure. The woman should respond as well. A man should always strive to do this."

"I think I am beginning to understand." Kalila's perfectly formed breasts shifted upward as she lifted her long, slender arms in a languid stretch. It was a simple movement, but it filled him with raging desire.

Deliberately, he moved his right arm to impede the growing hardness between his legs. This woman was driving him mad and she did not even guess! Ramses bit back a yelp of pain. He peered down at his lap. His "warrior's lance," as she called it, cheerfully nodded at him like an old friend waving a greeting.

Ramses pushed back from the table. "I think I . . . need to go outside . . . for a minute. Fresh air."

"Of course." She nodded, not realizing the reason

for seeking fresh air was her. How could a woman be so unaware of her own attractiveness? Ramses shook his head. All the women he had bedded deftly used the power of their sensuality. But not this enchantress. She acted as if they discussed camel prices, not sex. He marveled. Never had he met a woman so innocent of her effect on men.

With great effort, he stood and turned his back. Ramses wiped sweat from his forehead and glanced down. His warrior's lance bobbed outward, leading the way like the divining rod Queb used for seeking water.

"But you had best wear your robe. The night is so cold!"

"Good," he snapped as he strode off.

Nighttime. He could not sleep.

Ramses tossed, wincing from his aching shoulder. She had offered a sleeping potion. Pride made him refuse. He lay in the dark, listening to Kalila's steady, even breathing.

Who was she? A princess of high rank and importance used to gain access to the Khamsin secret mine. Who made her steal the map? The tomb-raider Burrells? How could the man have known Ramses was in Cairo? His thoughts flicked back to the gold seller. The gold seller said shopkeepers selling gold knew the mine existed. Perhaps Kalila stole the map for them.

Then he remembered meeting his father-in-law and showing him the map. A chill raced through him. Could she be his bride?

Ramses dismissed the thought as quickly as it came. For one, Kalila looked Egyptian with her plump breasts, slender waist, rounded hips, long masses of black hair and dark-tinted skin. His bride was probably white as a sheet and bone-thin.

He would find out. For now, a more demanding question nagged him. What was she hiding beneath that veil?

Ramses knew enough about women to realize vanity hid her face, not modesty. He was no fool. Not after she had seen his naked body. No, she hid a secret. Her identity.

He must find out what she looked like. Quietly, he slid the covers off and sat up. His pupils adjusted to the dimness of the cavern. Silvery moonlight shone through the cave's back entrance. Enough to light the way.

After a few minutes, he stood. Bare-chested he padded over to the candles. He lit one. Its soft glow danced over the cavern. Quickly he glanced over at her. She still slumbered. He suspected it was her first real sleep in days, for she probably had stayed awake nights tending to him.

Decency demanded he blow out the candle, leave her dignity intact. Seeing her face would provide no answers. Guilt surged through him. Ramses shrugged it off. Impulsive curiosity won.

With great caution, he crept over to her bed. Kalila lay curled on her side. She slept as blissfully as a child. A sweep of thick ebony lashes brushed against the veil, which rose and lowered with the soft force of her breath.

Placing the candle on the floor, Ramses knelt, enchanted by the vision of her sleeping. Gently, he lifted the cloth from her face. A heart-shaped mouth greeted him, as pouting and full as the lips he remembered touching his. The bottom lip blossomed with promise.

Her soft, rounded right cheek boasted a high cheek-bone, suggesting an aristocratic lineage. Her pert nose swept up at the tip. Her hair, tousled in a silken tangle of curls, spilled across her slender shoulders.

Ramses moistened dry lips, staring at her beauty. He marveled at her silky skin, the dewy freshness of youth. He wondered why she hid her face. Surely not to dampen his lust, for he was too weak to exercise any masculine desires.

And then she gave a pretty little sigh in her sleep, and turned, baring her left cheek to his probing sight.

Candlelight exposed an angry slash across her left cheek. He drew back a minute, shocked, and then leaned closer. A wide gash, as if an animal had torn her soft skin with agonizing precision. Automatically, he glanced down at his own chest, marred and scarred from several old battle wounds.

"Oh, little lotus blossom, is this why you hide yourself behind a veil, cloaking yourself from those who taunt you? How I wish you would bare yourself to me. I would show you all the beauty that I see when I gaze upon your face," he whispered in awe.

Ramses's heart ached with pity. He knew too well the probable cruelties she had suffered. Men revered women for their beauty. Scars such as this tainted her, while his scars were badges of esteem and honor.

He gazed upon the mark with tenderness. He longed to kiss it and ease the pain it still caused years after she received it. Softly, he settled the veil back on her face. Ramses kissed her forehead.

"Sleep well, little thief. I will not reveal your secret. But I will discover who sent you to find the tomb."

He blew out the candle, replaced it and went back to bed. As Ramses closed his eyes, he vowed he wouldn't pressure her to unveil. But he must use whatever means available to discover who sent her.

Whatever means. Even seduction? The question rippled through his drowsy mind. His kiss had bewitched her. She had admitted as much. If one kiss made her vulnerable, what would a seduction accomplish? Would she spill her secrets if he bedded her? If he did, he broke his vow of fidelity to his bride.

For a long time, he remained awake, thinking of Lady Katherine and his vow to remain celibate for her, and Kalila, the woman tempting enough to force him to break his resolve.

Chapter Ten

Ramses grunted as he strained to lift his arm. A Khamsin warrior trained to accept pain. Wind fluttered the folds of his indigo *binish*. Muscles unused for weeks protested at the force used against them.

He flexed his arm, elbow to wrist up and down very slowly. Then lifted his right arm toward the sky. Ramses summoned images of his tribe's namesake, the fierce Khamsin wind, and concentrated, using the breathing method used in meditation to control the dull ache.

Each day brought more strength. Wary of her intentions, he hid this from Kalila. Instead of resenting her insistence on providing for him until he grew stronger, he took advantage of it. They had reached an uneasy living arrangement. She hunted and cooked dinner each night. He ate it. He bombarded her with questions. She skillfully deflected each one. She probed him with inquiries about his tribe's ownership of gold mines dating back to pharaonic times. He sidestepped this by grilling her about her own origins. The cat-and-mouse game must end. He would wring the answers from her pouty little mouth. But how?

Absently, he scratched his head. He had left his turban off, for tying it around his head had proved too strenuous. His hair felt tangled and needed washing. Dark bristles shadowed his jaw. He needed a shave, as well.

With a bounce to his step, he walked up the path, singing a bawdy tune. Walking into the cave, he saw Kalila examining his scimitar's handle, the tip of the sword dangerously near her leg. The song died on his lips.

Instinctively, he called out a warning. As Kalila turned and gave a startled cry, the blade's tip raked across her calf. She stared with wide eyes at her torn silk trousers. A small scarlet stain flowered on the yellow fabric. Ramses rushed over, took the sword and sheathed it. He knelt down and examined her leg, tearing the cloth apart to her knee. Relieved, he saw the wound was slight. Removing the sash from his belt, he padded it against the cut. His temper flared. The scimitar could cut silk in midair. Kalila could have seriously hurt herself.

"What were you doing with my scimitar?" he snapped.

She stared at him, her brows knitting together. "I just wanted to see it. It's got such a pretty handle."

Ramses gave her an incredulous look. His beloved *Shukran*, which had lopped off the heads of treacherous enemies, saved his life, had been handed down to him through a successive line of Guardians? Pretty?

"It is a warrior's weapon," he said, struggling with his temper. "It is a sword of honor and valor, not a trinket!"

Removing the padding, he examined her wound, which already had ceased bleeding. His bad mood evaporated as he studied the lovely curve of her leg. A wicked idea came to mind.

"I believe you will live. But this requires immediate attention," he announced in a voice filled with dead seriousness. His wink signaled the true nature of her injury. "I shall have to administer aid to it."

She protested, but he ignored her. Ramses fetched water, salt, and another cloth. He raised her injured leg onto a nearby rock.

Kalila squinted at him. "What are you doing?"

"Hush," he ordered, using his dagger to cut bandages. "I have much experience . . . in tending to injuries such as these. I have been in battle and bandaged many wounds."

Dipping the cloth in water, he added salt. She drew away. "Ramses, it is but a scratch, you do not need to . . . ow!" she yelped again as he swabbed her injury.

"Now, now," he admonished. "I must prevent infection."

She rolled her beautiful eyes up as if imploring help from heaven. "Your nursing methods leave much room for improvement."

"That is what Jabari always tells me," he said, beaming. Ramses started to wrap a bandage around her leg, then stopped.

"And now, something to ensure it will heal quickly and you will not suffer much pain." Ramses kissed her calf. Skin soft as lotus petals met his lips. He drew in a ragged breath and looked up. "Does that . . . feel better now?" he asked in a hoarse voice.

Passion danced in her eyes, darkening the emerald to smoky green. The damned veil billowed as her breathing grew uneven. She tried wrenching her calf away, but his unyielding grip held it fast. Ramses decided he needed to further demonstrate his medical skills and kissed her leg again.

"Now, how does that feel? Better?"

"Almost," she whispered. "I do believe . . . I need more medical attention."

And, as he always liked to do for a lady, Ramses gladly obliged her.

Katherine had drowned in pleasure when Ramses kissed her at the Shepheard's. Now, as his silky lips pressed against her bare leg, she sank into that welcoming pool once more.

Pleasure sang through her veins as his strong hands cradled her calf. Ramses tickled the back of her knee. He raised his head and regarded her with those huge tiger eyes, as lazy and sleepy as a purring cat's.

Warm, soft lips brushed teasingly against her leg. Katherine stuffed a fist against her mouth to stifle a moan. Glancing down at his dark head, she felt something deliciously warm and velvety slide over her bare flesh.

He was licking her leg with slow, deliberate pleasure. This time, she couldn't suppress a low moan. This must end before he decided to explore further. Like beneath her veil. Katherine bit her lips and frantically struggled for reason.

"Ramses, please . . . don't let your . . ." She took a deep breath and continued, "warrior's lance control you!"

He raised his head, giving her a dangerous smile that indicated it already did. Then his gaze dropped to the ground.

"Snake," he murmured, staring at her leg.

A hot blush flooded her cheeks. Snake, warrior's lance, what was the difference? Men were so vain about their male members!

"Please Ramses," she begged. "Can't you tame your snake and tell it to stay in place?"

His dark brows knit together in total bewilderment. "What?"

"Your snake," she repeated. "I know a man has . . . urges . . ."

Ramses rose to his feet and grabbed his dagger. "Not my snake," he said in a deadly serious voice, pointing to a spot beyond her leg. "That snake." Ramses shifted the dagger in his hand. "Do not move. It is poisonous. An asp. I will kill it."

She followed the direction of his intense gaze. A black asp slithered with deadly grace toward the rock where she rested her foot. Ramses looked like a cat stalking prey as he crept toward it, knife raised in attack stance.

Katherine came to her senses and cried out, "No!" She dashed in front of him. "Put the knife down!"

"Why?" Ramses's face twisted in bewilderment.

With a downward swipe of her hand, Katherine motioned him to retreat. Dropping to her knees, she stared with fascination at the asp, longing to stroke its black smoothness.

"An asp," she said, marveling. "They're very sacred in Egypt. In ancient times, they symbolized royal immortality. Cleopatra killed herself with the bite of an asp upon her breast. It was thought the snake's venom made her live forever."

Mesmerized, she crawled toward the snake, drawn by its sleek power and dark beauty. Suddenly it stopped and raised its head, the long forked tongue licking the air. Katherine reached out to touch it. Faster than the serpent, Ramses's hand shot out and gripped her wrist. The asp turned its head, ready to strike. Paralyzed with fear, she could not move.

"Do not move," he said in a low voice. "Keep absolutely still. I know the asp is sacred, but I can assure you, you will not live forever if it bites you."

It watched them for a minute, then lowered its head and slithered past the boulder, through the cave entrance and into the sunshine.

Shaking deeply, she collapsed on the ground. Ramses slowly released her wrist and sat beside her.

He shook his head with an expression of frank bemusement as he sheathed his dagger. "I have never met a woman who likes to play with snakes. At least not that kind of snake."

Katherine wrapped her arms around herself. Once more she had forgotten caution, approached a beautiful, wild animal and nearly suffered the consequences. Never again would she trust such creatures unless she was absolutely certain they would not hurt her.

"An asp is a very powerful totem. I did not wish to play with it, but bond with its power," she told him in a rigid, formal voice. "It symbolizes healing, change and spiritual initiation. Ahmed said when a snake crosses your path, expect sudden changes that kill old fears and birth power and wisdom. Snakes guard sacred places and hidden knowledge."

Ramses tucked a loose strand of hair behind her ear. "I know. I did not mean to mock you."

"You know?" How could he know about totems? Weren't they reserved for shamans, alone?

Glancing down at his hands, he flexed them. "Khamsin men are given totems when we are initiated as warriors. It is . . . a sacred ceremony. The tribal shaman sinks into a deep trance and whispers the totem's name to each warrior."

Katherine's lips parted in pure delight and surprise. "It is?" She leaned closer, eager to have him divulge more Khamsin secrets. "What is your totem?"

He smiled indulgently. "It is a secret." Ramses pressed a finger against her veiled lips.

She leaned back, disappointed.

"But . . ." he hesitated. "I suppose I may tell you, if I whisper it into your ear."

Nodding eagerly, Katherine leaned forward. Ramses gently grasped her shoulders and bent his head as though longing for a kiss. Then he lifted a thick tangle of her hair, and lowered his lips to her ear, tickling it with his warm breath.

"A tiger," he whispered.

Katherine recoiled, her eyes widening in astonishment. Against her chest, her heart galloped in a frightening cadence. Sheer mysticism made her light-headed. Ahmed's words echoed in her spinning head: "Long ago, the tiger placed its mark upon you, daughter of the desert. It is your destiny, this mark you bear. For a tiger shall call you his, my child. That day is coming. You must not be frightened, but trust in him. He will give you his protection and will keep you from all harm."

Before her sat the proud, striped beast who would stalk her heart and capture it as the great jungle cat trapped prey. Her skin went clammy. Fate had steered Ramses directly into her path with determined hands, even at the hotel before she had kissed him. Her shocked eyes swept up and down his powerful frame, sitting with a tiger's lazy grace. Ramses had an elegant charm all enfolded into one firmly muscled male body.

He watched with half-closed eyes if gauging her reaction. Ramses lightly brushed his fingertips against the veil. His touch made her raging nerves flame into an inferno of passion. Touching her left cheek, Katherine stomped out the flames, remembering past hurts from sneering men.

"Kalila, what is wrong? Why do you look like that?"

"Like . . . what?" she stammered.

"As if you are frightened of me. Do not be afraid. The tiger is only my totem. I will not bare my fangs and eat you." He offered her a charming smile, but it only heightened her fear.

"A t-t-iger," she stuttered, seeking to break the sweet, cloying tension between them. "The wisdom of power, endurance, courage and strength in the face of adversity," she babbled.

"Yes," he nodded, giving her a thoughtful look with his amber eyes.

"Action without thought or consideration of the consequences . . ." she finished, staring at him.

Ramses gave her a rueful look and scratched his bristled chin. "Yes, quite true. I am often reminded of how rashly I charge into life, blinded, and without thinking of the consequences of my behavior."

He caught her startled look. "But not with the most important things in life."

She licked her lips, wondering if he could read minds. "What do you mean? You do not make sense, Ramses."

"Not when it comes to . . . pleasing a woman." Ramses rubbed her hand with his thumbs. Then he pressed a kiss deep into her palm. Her senses reeled crazily.

"You forget the other meanings of my totem," he murmured, leaning toward her. Closer he came, with his deadly tiger eyes and tiger's grace, his powerful body coiled and ready to spring, muscles tensed beneath the bronzed skin.

Katherine tilted away, alarmed at the blazing desire lighting his eyes. "What?" she asked, trembling.

"Devotion . . . and sensuality," he replied in a husky whisper. Ramses touched her veil's edge.

"Those, those are good ones," she stammered, captivated by the intimate intensity of his hypnotic stare. Like the other time when the tiger enchanted her with its beguiling looks, entreating her to indulge every tactile sensation by running her fingers across its warm fur, Ramses' taut, muscled body beckoned to her. A lovely melody of longing filled her ears. This siren song contained a different command. *Touch me. Taste me. Kiss me.*

Ramses brought his face closer. She focused on his sensual, firm lips. Warm breath billowed her veil. He was going to kiss her. Fear of his claws raking over her heart dissolved into warm wanting. No harm in one small kiss. Her lips ached to touch his. Katherine parted her mouth in anticipation of their kiss, that delicious tongue teasing and licking . . .

"And passion." His playful wink as he touched the tip of her nose threw her off guard. Under the veil, her lower lip jutted out in frustrated longing. A burning ache left her strangely unsatisfied. *I need. I want.* Why did she long for his kiss? Kissing this man presented more danger than teasing a tiger by poking a stick through its cage.

He sprang to his feet with sudden grace, paced to where she had stored his bags and began digging in them.

Her heart resumed a normal rhythm. Tigers, totems and omens. Charming warriors who made feel as addle-headed as if she swallowed all Papa's brandy. Silly nonsense. She was a modern British woman who had her feet firmly planted on the earth. Katherine clapped a lid on the mystical Egyptian side of her longing to explore the mysteries of this sand- and sun-drenched world.

She should be grateful Ramses hadn't engaged in any love play. But although her mind accepted the rationalization, her body would not cease its painful, odd yearning for something she could not identify.

No mistaking the sullenness clouding her clear green eyes. Kalila expected him to kiss her. Passion smoked the swirls of her enchanting green irises. Her head angled as if to grant him full access to her mouth. Such a beautiful, pouty little mouth, too. Shame not to kiss it. He pulled back at the last minute, feeling the heat of her longing engulf him. Teasing dropped her veil of natural shyness. She needed to be gently coaxed, her own arousal flamed enough to bring about quiet acceptance of the truth.

Against him, she didn't stand a chance. She had danced away from his grilling questions. Skirted his attempts to uncloak her secrets. Ramses had tired of playing with her and aimed straight for the throat. Or in this case, her leg.

He was in charge and dammit, it was time he showed her. Kalila thought she could control a Khamsin warrior who could slay women with one look as easily as his scimitar slew enemies. She'd find out how wrong she was.

If aroused enough, Kalila would not only quietly accept his fevered kisses, but beg for more. As he had feasted on her leg's soft smoothness, she had become as pliable as clay in his expert hands. His lips had ripped away her caul of sharp intelligence. Kalila had become as flustered as a shy mare introduced to an eager stallion.

Women found him irresistible. This fact never inflated his ego, for he accepted his exotic good looks with honest modesty as much as he accepted being born with superior strength. One suggestive smile and women puddled into dazed confusion at his boots. He counted on Kalila doing the same. Especially when she saw exactly what he had to offer. Swallowing a smile, Ramses resumed searching through his belongings.

Kalila had assisted him with his injuries. If he pretended he could not wash his hair, she would offer to do it. Hair washing would lead to other things . . . Then she'd drop that natural caution. Secrets would spill from those lush lips in a torrent.

"What are you doing?"

"I am going to bathe and shave." He withdrew a small mirror, soap, towel and an alabaster jar. Ramses stole a glance out of the corner of his eye. She was smart. Not too eager, he cautioned himself. He must pretend he resented her help.

She retrieved a bucket and handed it to him. "Try this. It's much better for you."

Instead of peering inside the bucket, Ramses gazed at her in a moment of doubt. She was too innocent. He took in those large, exotic eyes, the sweet, unlined brow; and he noticed how her long lashes swept her cheeks when she dropped her gaze. Then she raised her gaze to meet his. He saw no childish innocence there, but adult resilience. She was a thief. He must wrench information from her any way he could.

A glass bottle sat inside the bucket. He uncorked it and sniffed a familiar fragrance. Jojoba. The Khamsin used it to wash their hair. Hiding a knowing smile, he decided to tease her.

"This smells like perfume. You expect me to use this?"

"The shampoo?" She gave him an exasperated look. "I made it myself from sesame oil, jojoba oil and rosemary and other herbs and flowers. It's good for your hair."

His left hand flew to his long locks in pretend alarm. "Flowers in my hair? I am not a girl!"

Slender shoulders merely shrugged in answer. Kalila scampered after him as he marched outside. Placing his supplies near a flat rock shaded by a date palm, he headed for the well. Kalila wrapped a hand around a long pole supporting the rope pulley, watching him intently as he hauled up water.

He splashed water into the bucket sitting by the well, then returned to the rock. Kalila hounded his heels like an eager puppy. She placed the bucket containing the shampoo down and gave him a shy glance as he shrugged off his *binish*.

"Can you manage on your own?"

A subtle reminder he'd needed help. Excellent.

"No," he said gruffly. He glanced at his shirt. "I would appreciate you helping me with this," he said brusquely, as if hating his dependency on her.

As before, she eased the shirt off. "Thank you," he said.

133

Kalila leaned close, examining the puckered shoulder wound. She frowned. You're healed enough."

Desire sang in his veins as her soft hands gently touched him. Ramses tracked her admiring gaze as it darted downward to his trousers. A sense of devilment came over him. Ramses reached for the drawstring.

"Care to help remove these as well?" he inquired in a teasing voice.

Kalila backed away. Her eyes widened as if a giant snake had suddenly appeared. He grinned again. Well, considering the size of what was concealed beneath the trousers . . .

"No, uh . . . I'm certain you can handle that yourself. I'll leave you alone." She turned and nearly tripped over a rock.

Ramses chuckled. She scrambled to put as much distance between them as fast as those lovely legs could carry her. Cupping water into his palms, he splashed his face, then lathered his chin. Ramses grabbed his dagger and perched the mirror on a nearby rock. As he began to scrape off his beard, his trusty instincts warned him she would watch from the rocks. Good. Ramses rinsed soap off his blade. He planned to give her an eyeful for her efforts.

Some time later, she peered at him from behind the rocks. Worried that Ramses would overwork his shoulder, she excused her spying as clinical observation of how he managed on his own.

Clinical observation soon collapsed. Fascinated by the flex of hard muscles in his back, she watched as he shaved. He finished, rinsed and stood. Ramses bent down. He undid the trousers at the ankles. Back toward her, he straightened, tugged at the drawstring and let his trousers slide past lean hips to the ground. He tossed them aside.

Magnificent. Her fascinated eyes traced the lines of his warrior's body, past sinew and hard muscles cording his shoulders and arms, down to his lean, narrow hips and firm buttocks. Limbs straight and long. Each warm, bulging muscle and taut limb seemed sculpted by a master artisan's chisel.

Katherine struggled to gulp air past the lump in her throat. Ramses's bronzed male beauty filled her eyes with burning tears. She was a scarred woman—conniving thief, in his amber eyes. Her most secret self dreamed Ramses desired her. The silly fantasy of a lonely woman who had shut herself away from the world. How could anyone so perfect and whole want someone so imperfect and broken?

Squeezing her eyes shut, she choked down a silent sob. Katherine stalked into the cave, knowing she must confront reality. With a vicious tug, she yanked down her veil, then retrieved a hidden mirror. In the looking glass, her scar expanded until it twisted her face into a grotesque mask.

Fool. What man could ever feel attraction for this? Replacing the mirror, she allowed herself a few tears, dried them and took a deep breath. Katherine attached the veil, went outside and hid again. Ramses would never want her, but she would not deny herself the pleasure of gazing at his superb form. He sat on the flat boulder, back toward her. Foam puddled at his feet, sucked in by thirsty sand.

Droplets sheening his body winked like tiny diamonds. She watched with curiosity as Ramses dipped his hand into an alabaster jar and began scrubbing his body with a gluey substance. After rinsing, he fingered his thick curling locks. She ached, knowing what was wrong.

Easy enough to bathe himself. But how to shampoo his hair? She would do it. Katherine gulped at performing such an intimate task on a naked man. But if his essential parts were covered . . . She returned to the cave, resolutely fetched a small bottle of lemon juice, another towel and strode toward his back, humming as she approached to warn him of her presence.

Those broad, square shoulders stiffened. Katherine stared with longing fascination at the firm, muscled expanse of his back, nicked with scars and old injuries. Marks of a warrior who had seen many battles and who had fought bravely.

Approaching from behind, she kept her gaze trained downward and fingered his hair.

"I know you have no wish to smell like a girl, but I worked hard to make that shampoo. Besides it isn't perfume, but herbs, and I'm going to wash your hair with it."

He started to turn and she dropped the towel on his lap to cover his private parts. Ramses looked at the towel with the same bemused look as when he had spotted the loincloth.

"What is this for?"

Katherine glanced away. "It's important to stay covered when you're in the desert. To protect yourself."

"From what?"

She shifted her weight. "Things. The sun. Animals. Yes, animals. The desert has many dangerous animals."

"Such as snakes? Snakes are dangerous only if you

rouse them from their resting places. Be not afraid of my snake, Kalila. It will not harm you. It is rather friendly to women."

He winked. Flustered, she fetched a bucket of water from the well. Katherine glanced back. A naughty grin spread over his face as Ramses reached down and fingered the towel.

She gulped. "You would not . . . do that . . ."

"If you put that shampoo upon my head I will," he threatened in a deep, seductive voice.

Bringing the bucket over, Katherine stood before him. He blinked, frowning.

"That shampoo is my best recipe. I won't have you insulting it, and I *will* wash your hair with it."

With a smirk, he reached down and, just as the towel threatened to fly off, baring all, she dumped the water onto his lap. Ramses yelled.

"That water is cold!"

She said in a smug tone, "I know." Katherine fetched more water and marched back, dumping it over his head. Ramses sputtered. Long brown hair hung in thick wet strands about his face. Shimmering droplets clung to his long, spiky black lashes. He looked like an indignant, sopping wet tiger cub. And just as adorable.

"Woman, are you trying to drown me?" he roared.

"Not yet," she replied. Katherine uncorked the shampoo bottle, poured a generous amount into his wet hair and began rubbing with vigor. "Close your eyes," she ordered. "The shampoo will sting them if you don't."

He grunted, but complied. Her nimble fingers massaged the shampoo into his scalp, lathering and working little circles with her thumbs. She lathered the long locks, rubbing his neck as she did so, delighting in the feel of hard muscles. A long, low purr of pleasure spilled from his lips.

For several minutes, Katherine continued massaging his scalp with shampoo. Warmth saturated her as she gazed at Ramses's magnificent body. The objectivity with which she had nursed him through his illness had vanished. No longer could she view him as a helpless patient. Now she noticed what nursing had forced her to dismiss: the long limbs curved with muscle and dusted with dark hair, his lean, narrow waist; and the odd tattoos on the powerful muscles of both right and left arms. Despite his injury, Ramses sat before her as proud and commanding as an ancient god. She was a mere mortal compared to his golden beauty. A trembling raged through her fingers as they glided over his silky hair.

Standing before him, she poured water over his head, watching soap streams float down his chiseled muscles. A river of bubbles gushed downward. Her senses perched on one, enjoying the ride. It slid with capricious abandonment down his neck, lingered in the curling hairs of his muscular chest, dripped past his navel's deep slash, where a triangle of hair stopped short of the concealing towel.

If washing his hair sent shivers of pleasure rippling through her, what did it do to him? She saw his mouth relax into a wide, lazy smile. And then it widened.

Peering down his front, she gulped. Something beneath the wet towel poked insistently upward, like a snake itching to free itself from a trap. Katherine gasped.

His firm, sensual lips parted slightly as if in invitation. Golden eyes fluttered open, met green ones. Hot embarrassment raged through her as she stared in disbelief.

"Kalila, I am sorry for . . . making you uncomfortable, but I cannot prevent the effect your touch has on me," he said softly. "I would pluck a thousand lotus blossoms from the surface of the Nile for just one caress from the soft petals of your hands."

Ramses's husky voice enchanted her with the deep richness of his poetic confession. Swallowing hard, she dropped her gaze shyly. Never before had a man praised her hands. Warmth sang in her veins. Small wonder ladies flocked to him when Ramses visited Cairo . . .

That thought jolted her with the abruptness of a swift slap. Ramses. Cairo. Women. That lethal charm women found irresistible, dazzling them into following him blindly into their bedrooms.

Infuriated at her gullible foolishness, she glared. He tilted his head, a soft look of concern wrinkling his brow.

She'd show him he couldn't fool her with his powerful charisma and seductive murmurs. How cruel to deceive her into thinking he was attracted to her!

"Kalila, what is wrong?"

Katherine retrieved another bucket of water. She tossed the refreshing liquid straight onto the towel. Indignant sputtering laced with muttered curses filled the air.

"The soft petals of my hands are equally effective at killing snakes as they are at washing hair," she replied primly.

The snake wiggled no more. She fetched more water, added a few drops of lemon and poured it over his head. Katherine swallowed hard as she stared at the chestnut highlights in his dark locks.

Ramses broke into her thoughts as he picked up the soapy cloth and handed it to her over his shoulder.

"Would you mind washing my back?"

She faced a difficult dilemma. She had washed his hair because his injury hampered him from doing it. This request presented a greater intimacy. Touching his naked skin filled her with trepidation. Hard enough to resist his poetic words. But running her hands over those rippling muscles . . .

His head turned. Two amber eyes looked up with a question lingering in their depths. Ramses glanced away with an air of stiff pride.

"Never mind, Kalila. Thank you for washing my hair. It is more than enough. I can take care of myself."

Again, that damnable pride. Shyness evaporated like the water. Ramses hated requesting help. To ask such a simple task took tremendous humility. For him, anyway.

"You can't reach, not with your shoulder still healing." Katherine reasoned she could objectively see him as a patient. She fetched more water and gingerly began washing his back.

"Kalila, you may use more force than that. I am a warrior. I can take it," he joked.

You can, but I don't know if I can. Objective nursing faded to fascination with his sun-darkened skin. Katherine gnawed on her lower lip as she stroked his back. His shoulders eased their rigidness and he uttered a sigh of contentment. With every circular sweep of the cloth, her hand grew bolder. Contours of his muscled back showed odd patterns of puckered scars, some jagged, some a straight vertical slash. Knife or sword wounds. Mesmerized, she traced the scars with one finger.

"Where did you get these scars? Are some from battle?"

"All of them," he replied with arrogant self-assurance.

Odd heat rushed through her lower torso. His body boasted the honor of a warrior's. His broad back rippled with strength as her trembling fingers explored each contour. She imagined those powerful muscles bulging as Ramses swung his mighty scimitar at enemies.

As she rinsed soap off his back, Katherine noticed a scar with ragged edges. Curious, she rubbed it. Textured with puckered tissue, much like her wound, it looked like an animal bite. Did he perhaps wrestle with a fierce beast? Was Ramses also marked by a tiger? She asked him about it.

Ramses threw back his head and laughed. "Ah that is my worst injury! The bravest battle of all fought with ferocity!"

"And that battle was?" She leaned forward, eager to bear the tale of chivalry and male strength.

"When I was eight and fought with my sister. She bit me."

Katherine giggled. "Such a fierce warrior you were . . . to carry her teeth marks upon you. You wear it with pride."

"I do, indeed," he said, turning his head to grin at her.

The charming boyishness of his smile contrasted sharply with the hard strength of his warrior's body. The smile shifted into something more dangerous and compelling. Lazy swirls of gold danced in his amber eyes. Long ebony lashes blinked once, then his golden gaze caught hers with a smoldering intensity so jarring she dropped the cloth.

With one look, he issued an invitation. *Come hither,* it beckoned, mesmerizing her, as if Ramses was a sorcerer enfolding her body with a spell cast by his magnetic charm. Befuddled, Katherine remembered the power of his kiss, the hard demand of his lips against hers. A shiver of preternatural anticipation coursed up her spine. Attracted to the chiseled firmness of his masculine beauty, Katherine drew closer, much as she had that other time long ago, when another beauty beckoned with deadly intent. A feline, graceful charm luring her toward the cage, only to rasp a sharp claw across her face . . .

Touching her veil, she remembered her scar. The tiger's mark. Never again would beast, or man, weave magic around her. Hadn't one lesson from the tiger's claw been enough? Hadn't she almost been bitten by the asp?

She forced a chilled blankness to her eyes. "Dry yourself and put on your clothes. I'll get my brush to tame all those tangles. I think you're strong enough to dress yourself."

Softness fled his face and was replaced by a guarded look, as if Ramses had become a fortress of impenetrable rock. If her curtness hurt him, it didn't show. At least he dropped the seductive smile.

A few minutes later, she untangled his hair with her silver hairbrush as he sat. Ramses closed his eyes and sang an uplifting tune about the desert. He had a lush voice that rippled over her like raw silk. She sensed it was as much a natural part of him as the scars he bore. Never had she met a man so comfortable with himself. Katherine began stroking his hair in rhythm to the words.

"You have a beautiful voice, Ramses. Do you always sing?" she asked as he finished.

"Thank you. In my tribe, we frequently sing songs around the night fires. It is common to sing on long trips across the desert. It breaks up the time, makes it pass faster."

The long curls that tumbled well past his shoulders felt luxurious and thick as satin. Katherine ran her fingers through them. Setting the hairbrush down, she gave Ramses a fastidious examination as she crossed in front of him.

"Is it your tribe's custom not to cut your hair?"

He frowned. "Yes and no. Our warriors all have long hair. Mine is . . . somewhat longer than others.' "

"Why do you wear it so long?"

He gave her a steady look as his mouth tilted upward in a mysterious smile. "It is a sign of man's virility."

"Oh!" She put hands on her flaming cheeks.

Ramses chuckled, scratched his head. "I am playing with you, Kalila. I believe it started as a competition with Jabari to see which of us could grow our hair longer. I won."

"Who is this Jabari? Your brother?"

Shadows crossed his face, like clouds chasing away sunshine. Ramses suddenly looked as if she asked a private secret. Katherine licked her lips, again reminded of her tenuous relationship with this man. He

143

could not trust her. Even though she had saved his life, he viewed her as the enemy for stealing the papyrus map.

His golden eyes surveyed the craggy mountains surrounding them. Ramses's chest rose and fell as if he struggled with a decision.

"Jabari calls me such, but we are not blood brothers. He is my best friend, our tribe's sheikh. I am his second in command and his Guardian of the Ages, sworn to protect and defend him unto death. Jabari is fearless in battle, as are all our warriors, and a strong, wise ruler. Although he is very compassionate and kind, like me, he does not take kindly to those who cross him."

Katherine had a feeling Ramses shared this information not to answer her question, but as a subtle warning of the dangers she faced in taking what belonged to the Khamsin. Was this a hint to avoid looking for the tomb? Even so, she had to risk it. For weeks she put off searching while tending to Ramses's injuries. She had to resume the search, and soon . . . for time slipped away like sand spilling from an hourglass. Katherine glanced up to see Ramses studying her.

"I am certain all your warriors are quite brave," she replied, toying with a lock of hair, glad the veil hid her expression. "What is a Guardian of the Ages?"

His golden eyes filled with a strange, reverent light. He drew himself up and she saw his manner change from cautious reserve to proud dignity. Again, she was reminded that he was no docile cat, but a fierce tiger who fought with might.

"Guardians are warriors from ancient times who take an oath at manhood to defend their rulers. Our lineage began in ancient Egypt when the Khamsin

144

ruler called for the fiercest warrior to be his right arm. He engaged all his warriors in duels. The one who defeated the Khamsin sheikh was selected and pledged his vow. That was my ancestor, and since then, the first-born sons in my family have always been Guardians."

Fascinated, she lowered herself to his feet, like a child eager for a story. "The fiercest warrior. Did you ever engage Jabari in a battle to prove you could defeat him?"

The corners of his mouth twitched with mischief. She steeled herself against his charm. "No, that would dishonor him. However, I have dueled with him . . . and let him win."

"Of course, for in addition to being a fierce, brave warrior, you are also a true diplomat," she murmured.

"Not much of a warrior now," he replied, rotating his right arm. "My sword arm has not the strength it once had."

Katherine felt moved by his woebegone expression. "It will return, this strength of yours. And you have these." She grasped his broad hands, feeling the rough calluses and strong fingers. "And you have a warrior's most valuable weapon. Your mind. It is sharper than any sword and will serve you better than a sword. And your brave spirit. For what use is a sword in the hands of a fool?"

"You are quite wise," he said softly. He looked down and suddenly enfolded her hands in his. Her heart thundered as he rubbed her skin with small circling motions.

"You have weapons of your own. These are quite lethal and could well disarm a man in a heartbeat, no matter how many swords, daggers or guns he carried."

Her "weapons" began trembling under his assured strokes, betraying the intense emotions wrought by his touch. Katherine yanked her hands away. Probably something he told all women. He was a handsome man accustomed to seducing women with verbal, as well as physical, caresses.

Looking for a distraction, she picked up the alabaster jar and sniffed. A delicious scent of the myrrh she used to anoint her hair teased her nostrils. Scooping out a smidgen, she rubbed the coarse material between her fingers.

"What's this?"

Ramses studied her. "Natron. Salt. A natural preservative. My people have used it for thousands of years. We combine it with oil to keep the skin healthy and cleanse it."

"Even the men?" Katherine giggled, picturing a circle of fierce Khamsin warriors, passing the sticky substance among them and chattering about its marvelous effects.

He gave her an exasperated look that withered her hilarity. "Yes, indeed the men. Especially the warriors. Natron is used for spiritual cleansing as well as physical. It is our tradition passed down from ancient times, to protect our skin against the sun. They used it in mummification to prevent decay."

Her smile faded. "Mummies? You're bathing with salt used for dead people?"

Ramses frowned. "Kalila, you're Egyptian. Surely you have heard of natron."

She hastily swerved around that comment. "Why the spiritual cleansing?"

"To purify oneself. The Old Ones believed that one must bathe frequently because an unclean body attracted evil spirits. Our Khamsin priests cleansed themselves several times a day and the tradition has continued, but it has dwindled down to daily bathing."

"In the desert?"

"Our tribe has a cave with a spring. Our southern tribe members are true Bedu, and their water sources are more limited."

"Why is this purification so important to you?" she asked.

"Khamsin warriors believe, as our ancestors did, that cleanliness is holy. It uplifts the *ba*, the person's soul, and the purification makes one pleasing to God."

"The same reason why you perform ablutions before prayers. But that's a Muslim custom, not an Egyptian one."

"Indeed. As our people are. The Khamsin revere our honored ancestors and many of their traditions. But we worship only the one true God, our Creator. The purification is to allow us to open ourselves up to his will."

"So you don't romp around naked worshipping alabaster replicas of Egyptian gods?"

"Romping around naked is something we do, but only in the privacy of our tents when we worship the beauty of a wife's curved backside." The playful wink he gave her caused a blush to flame her cheeks.

"But your tattoo . . . it's rather . . ."

Ramses clapped a hand over his left arm as if hiding the mark. "A tradition passed down through generations of Guardians. It is a symbolic icon that signifies my acceptance and my vow."

"Vow to what?"

He rubbed the natron between thumb and forefinger. "A private vow I made," he answered, studying the sheltering blackness of the mountains. He seemed distant. She wondered why mentioning the vow caused such a distressful reaction.

"I have some chores to attend to," she said, not looking at him. "Maybe you should stay here and try to exercise your arm."

He stretched his right arm and gave a leisurely, cat-like yawn. She watched, fascinated, as his biceps bulged, extending the smooth tautness of his deeply tanned skin.

"Perhaps I shall take a short rest. The sun is hot this time of day." Ramses's golden eyes stroked her body slowly. He gave her a lazy, diabolical smile and patted the length of the boulder. "Care to join me?"

Katherine glanced at the rock and then at the man perched upon it. Her chest tightened as desire heated her core.

"It's too hot," she murmured. "I'm going inside."

Lifting his hand to his smooth forehead, he shaded his eyes. "The heat is intense. I shall join you."

Her dismay doubled as he sprang off the rock with lithe grace and accompanied her back into the cave. Inside, Katherine fussed with her herbal recipe book, glancing at the pages. Warm breath heated her cheek as he leaned over her shoulder, peering with frank interest at her scribblings.

"What is this?"

"My book of herbal recipes. I'm writing down all my shaman's cures. It's a hobby."

"Useful recipes." His voice held a note of respect, then deepened with seductive intent. "However, I have a special recipe for making something far more enjoyable."

His hard body pressed against her backside. Katherine moved forward until she hit the table. A glass jar rattled and shook with the impact. She reached out to prevent its fall, but it slipped and crashed to the ground. Katherine knelt down, began gathering shards as scattered as her wits. Ramses squatted beside her, selecting the largest ones.

"Careful you do not cut yourself again," he warned.

In the confines of the cave, she felt trapped, as if caged with a large, predatory animal. The hard muscles of his thighs brushed against her as he picked up broken pieces. Her hand enclosed a sliver. Pain speared her palm. She yelped, dropped the glass and clutched her hand.

"Let me see," he ordered.

"No, don't," she protested as he took her palm, unfurled her fingertips one by one. A miniscule droplet of red beaded the skin. As his lips hovered over the injury, she snatched her hand away. Katherine stood, fetched a broom and swept the glass into a corner, brushing a dust cloud into Ramses's coughing face. He stood, arched his brows at the fury of her whisking.

"Do you always clean with this kind of energy?"

Her nervousness escalated as his palm enclosed over hers, gently tugging the broomstick from her sweaty grasp. He propped it up against the table. Warmth radiated from his body as he stepped near. Katherine sidestepped, went to pass and tripped over the broom. Ramses caught her by the waist. Gravity, or circumstance, pulled them to the carpeted ground. Ramses landed on her with so little impact, she swore he did it on purpose.

His broad chest pressed against Katherine's torso. Ramses flashed her an impish grin. She tried wriggling away, but his muscled weight pinned her down. Pressure released as he lifted off, but only for a moment as he slid up to bring his face close to hers.

"Interesting position we find ourselves in." His husky voice brushed across her overly sensitive skin like thin silk. Katherine wriggled, but Ramses refused to give ground. A dark, intent look came into his amber eyes.

Suddenly he gracefully rolled off and sat, pulling her with him, settling her into the cradle of his opened thighs.

"You are too tense," he scolded. "I will help you relax."

Strong hands began skillfully kneading her stiff shoulders, warming her skin through the shirt's thin silk as if the sun danced upon it. Ramses slipped the shirt from one shoulder, pressed warm lips upon her collarbone. She gasped with shock as his hands drifted down to her breasts and began gently kneading them.

Katherine's head buzzed and she struggled to find breath. His slow, pleasuring caresses whisked away good sense. She closed her eyes to the sensual magic his hands made.

"Do you know how much you tempt me, little lotus blossom? Your skin is softer than flower petals, your body made for love. How did you come into my life? You are more precious than the gold of the pharaohs. What strange destiny has brought you out here to the deep desert, to madden me with your sweet innocence?" He blew a hot breath against her neck.

"I didn't want to come here," she gasped, as his hand found a nipple. Ramses teased it to a hardened peak. Warmth flooded her, searing heat that scorched the juncture between her legs. No man ever made her feel like this. He was the Aten, the god of the sun, filling the darkness in her life with golden sunshine that chased away lonely shadows and other men's cold rejections.

"But you are here now. Why did you come here? To steal away my heart and capture it as you stole the map?" he murmured, massaging her breasts. The roughness of his warrior-callused palms inflamed her skin with every stroke.

"I never wanted to steal the map. I had to . . . the mine . . . if I don't find the gold he . . ."

"Who?" Ramses asked softly.

Katherine turned her head and found two orbs of hardened steel gazing down at her. Not golden eyes filled with passion, but purpose. Sudden understanding kicked her passion-drenched brain with a swift, cruel awareness. She pushed his hands away.

"Ali Baba and his forty thieves. Is that the answer you want? You can stop trying to seduce me. You'll get no more answers!"

Katherine twisted away and landed on her back. She was trapped beneath him in a minute. Ramses pinned her wrists on either side of her head. She'd discovered his ruse, and judging from the anger hardening his features, he didn't like it. A galloping tempo replaced her normal heartbeat. Hooking his legs around hers, he spread them apart. Power play. He fully intended to demonstrate his superior strength and show he could do as he pleased. Katherine felt as helpless as the hares she hunted with the crossbow.

"Ramses, let me go. Now," she ordered in a shaky voice.

He rolled off and lay on his side, that damned guarded expression replacing the tenderness she'd glimpsed earlier. Katherine recognized the predatory look as one Osiris had eyeing a mouse he wanted to seize. If Ramses had a long tail, it would be swishing against the ground as he anticipated the best way to pounce and conquer.

Fresh grief filled her. Burrells threatened to kill Osiris, Papa as well. She was no mouse. Anger flooded her body much as sensual warmth had minutes ago. Katherine shook her head to knock sense back into it. No more charming words or sexy smiles. This man was more dangerous than the asp that nearly struck her. One slip to him and Papa was dead. She glanced around, as if Burrells had spies lurking in the cave.

"Go away Ramses. I'm not one of your women to use and you'll get no information from me this way!"

Katherine sprang to her feet and stormed from the cave. Outside, she gulped air in several breaths.

Ramses sought only information. Why else would he try seducing her? With her flawed features, she offered nothing. No, he uttered those poetic words and turned her into jelly to get answers. How utterly clever. He felt nothing for her. Old insecurities skated to the surface. Ramses used her vulnerability toward his charm as a weapon, as if he held the scimitar at her throat. Katherine almost preferred the blade's honed edge, for it would feel less painful than the agony ripping through her heart.

She had to put distance between them. With his injuries, Ramses had already distracted her from finding the mine. He would not do so now with the sultry feel of his heated caresses.

For the first time, he failed in a simple seduction. Ramses examined his actions. Truly this woman vexed him. Her intelligence proved he could not win her with the usual methods. A charming smile here, a few flattering words there and women capitulated. Not Kalila. He admired her wariness even as he cursed it. His body's unleashed needs boiled. Once again, he had inserted the key to the cage, threatening to free the beast of his lust. This time, it came too close to escaping. Pouting anger of failing to secure answers from Kalila capitulated to the howling rage of unfilled need. No more attempts. He could not risk it, this torture of pressing against her soft body, savoring the rounded plumpness of her breasts in his hands.

Heated fingertips that stroked her body to awareness now touched his shoulder wound. Each day brought more healing for his body, but tripped his heart closer toward a dangerous cliff. He must find the mine without Kalila tagging along.

Ramses sprang to his feet, remembering the medication that lulled him into sleep. The Khamsin cultivated many herbs, using them for both medicine and flavoring. His mother used an herb to treat pain. It acted as a sedative. Valerian root. There must be some in the cave. Ramses lit a candle and pawed through a stack of small boxes identifying each herb. He opened the box labeled "valerian root," inhaled and recoiled from the noxious odor. A pinch added to the sweet tea Kalila loved to drink and she'd slumber like a babe. He went outside prepared to deliver a charming apology and a cup of tea.

"Forgive me, Kalila. I forgot myself and your sweet innocence. Please, accept my apology."

The words, murmured in a deep lilt, sent new warmth flooding her body. She turned, remembering how he used her for his own purposes. Prickly spikes

153

of caution rose as Katherine eyed him with suspicion. Shadows lingered beneath his eyes. Gone was the guarded look, replaced by two lines funneling his brows.

Still, he'd have to do better. Her back turned toward him signaled what she thought of his apology.

Tension stiffened Katherine's body as he sat beside her. Ramses wrapped a lock of her hair around one finger and tugged gently. "It was not such a terrible interrogation, was it?"

"Oh, for heaven's sake," she snapped, "Have you no decency? Is that how you treat your enemies?"

His hand captured her chin as he tilted it up, his smoky amber gaze meeting hers. Ramses's thumb lazily brushed her knuckles. Katherine resisted a shudder of pleasure and set her jaw in obdurate resolve.

"Khamsin warriors have other means for dealing with our enemies. Hot irons are much more effective against them. They have skins as hard and leathery as camel hides. Not like yours."

A hot iron would be less deadly than the blazing inferno of his touch. Her tongue skimmed against her teeth.

Ramses tapped her nose and smiled. "Truce then? I have brewed tea to make up for my poor behavior."

His lower lip pulled outward. Ramses looked as adorably contrite as a child confessing to stealing gumdrops. He knew she had discovered his seductive ways. What harm could come from a simple cup of tea?

Some time later, he watched her eyes close. He took away the cup and lifted Kalila easily. She felt light as air. Laying her on the bed, he tugged off her sandals.

Sitting on the bed's edge, he stroked her brow. With an impatient tug, he released the curtain hiding her face. Kalila relaxed in the innocence of sleep. Ramses smiled. He liked watching her like this, relaxed and stripped of all defenses, as vulnerable as a child. Need coursed through him as he stroked a finger against her mouth's rosebud curve. Forget the gold, for here lay a treasure worthy of the richest pharaoh. A succulent temptation stretched on the bed like a rare fruit, his to tenderly sample. Ramses fought his desire, slammed the beast back into its cage. He attached the veil, brushed a soft kiss against her forehead, gathered his things and left.

Chapter Eleven

Veiling his face, Ramses rode his camel past the squat, fallen ruins of a Roman fortress. Impassive rock sentries of the past looked on in indifferent silence as he scanned the area. Kalila and the men had searched for an entrance dug deep into the mountains. Had the jackals accompanying her any knowledge of ancient Egypt, they would have known the Old Ones tunneled under the mountains. Vertical or diagonal shafts sunk deep into the ground were preferred over tunneling horizontally into hard granite mountains.

His camel's hoofs disturbed rocky sand as he pressed deeper into the desert. A short while later, he dismounted near a rock display arranged pyramid-style. Ramses surveyed each stone and spotted a tiny, faint hieroglyph on one. The Udjat, similar to the tattoo on his left arm. Boyish glee surged through him. As fond as he was of his sheikh's wife, he had never understood Elizabeth's passion for unearthing ancient ruins. Ramses was grateful the archaeology team at Amarna had brought her into Jabari's life, but he despised the reason why. Old bones and old memories best lay forgotten under the sands. Now he empathized with Elizabeth's love of uncloaking the past. A mystery as old as his own lineage lay waiting to be solved.

A clump of scrub caught his eye. Treading with caution, he crouched down and saw a rock pile. A thrill surged through him as he parted the scrub and saw a dark shadow yawning open. The gold mine. He began pulling aside the rocks, glad to work muscles that had atrophied.

When he had cleared the stones, he gazed down into the tunnel. An almost vertical opening cut into the dusky earth. Remains of an old stone wall reinforced the shaft entrance. No steps. The Old Ones had lowered men, tools and baskets down by rope. Ramses fetched a heavy rope and supplies from his camel. Hooking one end of the rope to a nearby rock, he let it fall into the mine's depths. Then he tugged his veil free, grasped a torch, hoisted his pack over his left shoulder and clutched the rope. Steeling himself for the darkness, he controlled his breathing as he slowly climbed down. Walls closed around him, reaching out with eager, jagged fingertips for his *binish*. Tongues of darkness licked his body. Ramses sucked in a lungful of stale air as his trembling feet connected with solid ground. Sunshine pooled at his ankles. Rock dust undisturbed for centuries floated lazily on the rays. He gazed up with longing at the warmth and then back down into the chilled darkness stretching beyond him. Another deep breath and he felt enough confidence to light the torch without panicking.

Acrid smoke filled his nostrils, tempering the rancid smell of his own terror. Caves and dark, small spaces had tortured him since he was a child. Meditation helped garrote his fear, wrench it into a tight space of its own. He squeezed his eyes shut, breathing deeply, dispelling terror with images of sunshine.

Calmer now, he proceeded into the ebony stillness. Ramses navigated over pebbles as old as time itself, his boot heels crunching them like dried beetle shells. Shadows danced across the rock's surface as his torch caressed the blackness. Metal wall sconces set a few feet apart were ghostly reminders this had been a working mine. He came to a fork. Remembering the markings for the correct passageway, he examined the walls and spotted a small ankh painted on the wall of the right tunnel.

Walls narrowed as he pressed deeper into the passage. Ramses swallowed convulsively. He let the fear rise, envelop him much like the damp chill seeping into his bones. Riding the waves until they crested, he breathed deeply. The tunnel's narrow ceiling descended until the passageway thinned to a point, and then stopped altogether.

Nodding, Ramses placed his torch in a wall sconce and took two additional torches from his bag. Those he lit and placed in wall holders as well. He removed a pick from his bag, then raked his fingertips over rough rock, examining it for clues.

Sedation and seduction. She had been a victim of both and now her anger shook free the drowsiness.

Ramses's camel tracks stood out like red flags. Katherine clucked to her dromedary as she guided the stubborn beast past mountain and stone. One hand held her pounding head. Before she had recognized the faint, foul odor of the tea, she had greedily taken a huge swallow. The dreamless sleep that stole over her didn't last, for Ramses had failed to administer enough of the herb.

She spotted Ramses's camel, sandwiched between the mountains on the flat, sandy plain. Katherine urged her mount to a rollicking gallop that made her head pound harder. She stopped, urged the camel to its knees, and jumped off the rigid wooden saddle. Katherine's gaze followed the rope sliding down into an ominous dark hole, barely large enough to admit a man's body. Her dry tongue snaked over even drier lips. She fumbled in her bag for a candle, lit it and peered down.

Curiosity poked her like an inquisitive child. What lay beyond the depths? She had to know. One small peek couldn't hurt, Katherine reasoned. She grabbed the rope and prepared to enter the darkness.

A scattering of pebbles, no louder than falling grains of sand, froze him in place. Ramses knew if the solid rock mirrored his expression, it would show flared nostrils, a tightened jaw and a body stiffer than stone. Someone was coming. Ramses unsheathed his sword. Doing battle in this confined space would test his rusty skills in addition to straining his shoulder. But he had no choice. He extinguished the torches and waited in the dark. Cold sweat broke out on his brow. A rapid thrumming echoed in his ears and he realized with grim amusement his heartbeat had cracked the silence.

A thin ribbon of light rounded the corner. Ramses tensed into a warrior's stance. He sniffed and smelled nothing but the dampness, pungent smoke and the cave's dank musk. The light paused, then turned and began progressing back the way it had started. Ramses sucked in a breath and sprang into action. No war cries, no veiled face, but stealth and silence as he sped forward, then lunged at the shape silhouetted by the candle. Even as one arm seized her waist and the other brought his scimitar against his captive's throat, he knew. Even before smelling the exotic fragrance of myrrh and the dankness of her terror, he knew. Kalila. Tension eased, replaced by sheer fury. Ramses released her, took the candle from her hand and lit the torches. Then he yanked Kalila back against his chest, uttering a growl filled with relief, anger and frustration.

"Your attempts at herbal tea leave much to be desired," she managed to say. "I could smell the valerian root after one sip. If you didn't wish me to follow you, why didn't you say so? You didn't have to drug me."

She tried jerking free, but he pinned her against his chest. Ramses held her as if clutching nothing more substantial than Cairo's morning newspaper. Katherine writhed, struggled and kicked his shin.

"Stop that," he said in a mild tone, as if she did nothing more than tickle him.

She tried aiming for his foot, but when her heel descended, it hit rock as he deftly maneuvered his foot away. Katherine bit back a cry as her sole dug into sharp stone.

"You will hurt yourself," Ramses said quietly. "I know all your tricks by now, Kalila. They will not work."

"Perhaps it's time to try new ones then," she half-joked.

"What are you doing here!"

"What are *you* doing here?" she challenged him.

"This is my tribe's property. As I told you before, I do not tolerate others taking what is mine, or what belongs to my people. Are you here to steal again, princess?"

The rock-hard arm imprisoning her felt as unyielding as the mine's walls. Recognizing the quiet threat, Katherine fought panic.

"I came to see what you were doing." True enough, she reasoned. Katherine swallowed hard, aware that her heartbeat pounded in triple cadence. She didn't belong in this cave of ancients, where his ancestors had sweated to lift the earth's minerals from its core.

Torchlight caught the gold in his eyes, made them glisten like the soft metal they both sought as he turned her around.

"Ramses, stop holding me prisoner. You have no right."

"Do I not? And what gives you the right to trespass on my people's land? Do you know what Khamsin warriors do to trespassers?" Katherine's breath caught as his steely grip on her shoulders tightened. His eyes glittered with deadly intent. The mine's damp chill soaked into her bones as fear squeezed her heart. He backed her against the dead-end wall.

Not waiting for the answer, she set her foot against the rock for purchase and shoved against him. Her foot slipped against the rock wall, dislodging a shower of pebbles.

Fear melted into bewilderment. A solid sheet of earth shouldn't be this pliable. Pressure against her shoulders eased as he let go. Ramses's expression changed from menacing anger to distress. She stared at his widening eyes as he glanced down past her feet.

"What was that?" she asked. He did not answer, but bent down to examine the wall.

Katherine noticed a pick lying on the ground. Grabbing it, she swung hard at the rock. Stone crumbled and spilled down. She gasped at what the pick had exposed—a man-made wall.

Her eyes locked with his over the torch's glow. Excited hope shot through her.

"There's . . . something beyond this dead end," she whispered.

A muscle jumped in his tightened jaw. "Perhaps."

Gooseflesh rose on her arms. The secret burial chamber. Where better to hide treasure than behind a false wall in an old mine? Tombs were always robbed, even as cleverly as they were hidden. Judging from Ramses's distraught look, he knew this. And hated that she had figured it out as well.

Ramses gave her a speculative look as though she were a gold nugget. Katherine took a deep breath. She began combing the wall for clues, digging at the rock with the pick.

"Kalila, it is best you leave now."

"Not until I find out what's behind here. You can't drug me or drag me out of here. You can either help or stand and watch."

"If you do not leave now, you may regret the consequences."

"If I leave here now, I'll regret it more than anything you can do to me," she replied with spirit. His hand descended on her shoulder. Katherine twisted away and stood, surveying the rock for a hidden crevice indicating a door opening. She spotted a tiny mark resembling an eye with a long, curled lash. Katherine located an indentation that felt like a latch.

"I think I have something here!" She triggered the latch. The door began to swing open. Katherine and Ramses jumped back. When the door was fully opened, she started inside.

His hand shot out, seized her arm.

"The tomb is cursed. Those who enter the tomb to seek its treasures will die." Ramses's deep voice rumbled eerily in the hollows, echoing the beggar girl's warning in Cairo.

Katherine swallowed hard, peeking past dancing shadows cast by the torchlight. Her superstitious Egyptian side balked at setting one toe inside. But if she failed to retrieve proof of the gold Burrells wanted, Papa remained jailed. She thought of how Burrells had nearly killed Osiris and choked back a sob.

"Some things are worse than ancient curses," Katherine whispered.

"Wait!"

Ignoring his warning, Katherine started through. Barely inside the tomb, the ground crumbled beneath her right foot. Dropping the torch, she shrieked in panic as the earth collapsed beneath her. The torch plummeted down as two arms grabbed her waist. Ramses pulled her back with such force, they both fell backward.

Her heart drummed furiously. She gasped for air. Katherine rolled off him, glanced at her rescuer. His bronzed face had gone uncharacteristically pale.

"I told you to wait," he scolded her gently.

"I thought it was because you wanted to hide what was inside. I didn't think about a trap."

"The ancient ones used tricks to capture greedy robbers who would plunder their riches." Ramses's voice trembled slightly as he gazed at the black pit that had nearly claimed her life. Kneeling, they both crept to the well's lip. Darkness had eaten her dropped torch. Ramses dropped a rock into the ominous ebony depths. Katherine listened and counted. She gave up counting after one hundred.

"That could have been me," she said, dread snaking up her spine. "If you hadn't caught me . . ."

His confident tone filled her with reassuring calm. "But I did. I will always catch you, Kalila."

She peered into the tomb's dark depths as they stood. "Is there a way to get inside without encountering more traps?"

A loud whoosh of air escaped his lips. "No. You stay here." His curt tone indicated he would not tolerate a challenge.

But she had too much at stake to obey. Katherine grabbed another torch and sidestepped the pit. A hand shot out, seizing her arm.

"Stubborn woman," he growled. "I cannot let you go in."

"I'm going."

"And risking your life?"

Ramses pulled her back and took the torch. He took out his scimitar. Stepping past the well, he sliced the air before him with the sharp blade. "The Old Ones used many traps to guard their chambers. The hidden well is one. Another favorite is the locking door that closes behind the intruder, sealing him inside. And then there is the famous trick of shooting . . ."

A terrifying rush of wind interrupted him. She watched, stupefied as he dropped with graceful ease, tucking and rolling on the ground.

"Arrows," he finished, standing up. Ramses studied

the barbs that bounced off the wall, narrowly missing his body.

"You go in first," Katherine suggested in a shaky voice.

She slipped behind him even as he roamed the whole chamber. Sealing the well with a stone tablet, he placed the torch in a wall sconce. Katherine's curious eyes scanned the tomb. Her jaw dropped in shock.

"Oh my," she croaked.

Darkness had melted into shimmering, golden light. Torchlight cast gleaming reflections as sparkling as sunshine upon a crystalline sea. But no sea washed before her dazzled eyes. Only gold.

Her hands shook as she tried counting statues, jewelry, goblets and plates piled near a large rectangular stone sarcophagus. Superior disdain emanated from the carved features of a small golden cat sitting regally on the coffin. She fingered a gold scarab inlaid with lapis lazuli. Foster Burrells would shoot his way through an army of warriors to get his greedy hands on one statue. A shiver snaked up her rigid spine. She was no expert in metallurgy, but guessed the hidden chamber contained at least a million pounds worth of gold.

Ramses approached the sarcophagus, falling to one knee. Placing his scimitar's point on the ground, he rested his hands on the carved sword hilt. As he bowed his head, Ramses began reciting ritualistic words that sounded like ancient Egyptian. She backed away, wishing not to intrude on this very private, sacred ritual. Should she do something to show respect as well? Katherine did not want to offend him, or whatever spirits lingered here. With great quietness, she sank to her knees.

Ramses finished praying, stood and sheathed his weapon. He turned to see Kalila kneeling, head bent, her face hidden by a thick curtain of silk curls. Such respect deeply touched him. Surely a woman who showed reverence for the ancient ones could not be a tomb robber. No, she was a pawn in an evil game. The thought raised his protective instincts at the same time it raised his natural caution. She had found the tomb. Such knowledge would destroy the sacred resting place. If she were a man, his scimitar would end her life with ruthless precision. Honor stayed his blade. Ramses had sworn an oath at manhood to protect women. No choice existed but to take her prisoner, return to his people and let Jabari and the council determine her fate. They would scare Kalila into keeping the tomb's secret locked inside her pouty little mouth. But they would not harm her. Ramses's hand rested atop his scimitar's hilt.

Katherine's mind glowed with the shining display of riches before them. "Gold. The skin of the gods," she croaked, rising to her feet.

Ramses remained quiet, studying her. She reeled from the narrowed eyes, the tight slash of his mouth.

She'd discovered his tribe's secret. She alone, besides Ramses, knew the tomb's exact location. Katherine began backing away, fear rising in small, steady waves. She'd heard whispers of how the Khamsin dealt with enemies and recalled how they had slain the Al-Hajid at the Amarna dig site, leaving not one drop of blood, only questions about the missing men.

An even bigger question lingered. Would he let her walk out of here with her life?

NAME: _____

ADDRESS: _____

_____

_____

TELEPHONE: _____

E-MAIL: _____

_____ I want to pay by credit card.

__ Visa   __ MasterCard   __ Discover

Account Number: _____

Expiration date: _____

SIGNATURE: _____

*Send this form, along with $2.00 shipping
and handling for your FREE books, to:*

Historical Romance Book Club
20 Academy Street
Norwalk, CT 06850-4032

*Or fax (must include credit card
information!) to:* 610.995.9274.
*You can also sign up on the Web
at www.dorchesterpub.com.*

Offer open to residents of the U.S. and
Canada only. Canadian residents, please
call 1.800.481.9191 for pricing information.

If under 18, a parent or guardian must sign. Terms, prices and conditions
subject to change. Subscription subject to acceptance. Dorchester
Publishing reserves the right to reject any order or cancel any subscription.

The answer proved too horrible to contemplate. Katherine stepped away from Ramses, the man who had fought off her attackers, who had kept her from tumbling into the well. Fear twisted a huge knot in her stomach. She retreated until a wall stopped her. Her sweaty palm encountered a small protrusion. Katherine immediately let go. The chamber door began closing with a shuddering sigh. A shrill scream spilled from her lips as she raced frantically forward. Two firm hands caught her waist. Katherine struggled to break free.

"No, Kalila."

She wriggled, despairing as the door shut with an ominous groan. Panic gushed through her veins.

"We're sealed in!"

"Yes. And no. You forget something Kalila."

"What?" Surely he must be joking, for even his immense strength could not move that impenetrable sheet of stone.

"This is my ancestor's tomb. Khamsin Guardians pass down the knowledge, generation to generation, of a secret escape in the tombs we built. Watch."

He approached the huge sarcophagus and knelt with reverence, crossing his arms across his chest and bowing his head. Ramses pressed a hieroglyph on the wall beside the coffin, opening a small door. Sand spilled out, puddling on the ground with a sibilant hiss.

"When the sand runs out, the door will open."

Not exactly what she wanted. "When?"

"About a half hour, I think. The air in here will maintain us for that long."

"Half an hour! Why so long?"

"I expect to remind those foolish enough to seal

themselves in to take time to pray for wisdom," he remarked in a dry voice.

He acted so placid she wanted to scream at him. Her nerves felt scraped open. Sealed inside the tomb of the dead? And Ramses exhibited no signs of distress. He crossed over to a statue of Horus, and sat cross-legged next to it. His palm patted the ground beside him.

"Sit Kalila. No use pacing, for there is no other way out."

"There has to be another means out . . . you can't expect me to stay here for half an hour!" She shivered violently. Thin silk provided little protection against the damp chill or clammy fear seeping deep into her bones.

"There is not." He beckoned her with a crook of his finger. Sinking beside him, she cradled herself with her arms, rocking back and forth. Ramses uttered a deep sigh, placed palms upon his knees and closed his eyes. Deep, even breaths eased in and out in a steady rhythm. He was actually going to meditate. Here, in a closed tomb? She grasped for humor, anything to ease her body's quivering terror.

"I'm grateful I'm trapped in here with you and not a tomb robber. At least I know you won't kill me to get all this gold."

Mistake. The joke backfired. She reminded him of her own treachery, for his eyelids flew open. Ramses accorded her the same steady, burning look as before. She turned with a shiver. But what else could she expect? To him, she was as guilty as the tomb robbers he despised. An inner instinct to excuse the inexcusable overcame her. Katherine glanced at the length of steel at his waist. A good enough reason to try.

"I know what you think of me, Ramses. A thief. I know I have no right to be here . . . I know this place is sacred to you." Katherine gazed at the sacrophagus. "But I had no choice."

Rising, she slunk away to the farthest corner. A shadow crossed in front of her. Ramses blocked her path with his muscled, impassive body.

"Kalila. Please. I want you to see something."

She allowed his large hand to enfold her small one as he went to the sarcophagus. He stood silently for a moment, looking at the coffin.

"I want you to understand. This is more than treasure to me. The Khamsin do not value gold or money. We value honor, courage, fidelity and steadfastness. This," he rested one palm on the coffin, "is my heritage. This contains the mummy of one who walked before me, centuries ago. My lineage, and the traditions he set down are worth more than all the gold of Egypt. It is the code that guided my grandfather's life, my father's life and mine, as it will my sons' lives after me. Do you understand? When strangers come here to plunder the riches, they despoil not only the tomb, but the sacred memories that we Guardians have honored for centuries."

"Yes," she whispered brokenly. "I understand, Ramses." Katherine struggled to keep burning tears from scalding her throat and eyes. "I understand more than you realize. It's not my choice. I would gladly walk away from all this and never look back, for money and gold mean nothing to me. Nothing!"

Chapter Twelve

He believed her. God help him, but he did. Truth
shone in the emerald depths of her large eyes. He had
learned to read emotions there. Crackling with spitting
anger. Wide emerald orbs signaling surprise. Tiny
lines crinkling the corners as she laughed.

But never the sheen of tears as he glimpsed now.
Her lips might hide the truth, but oh those beautiful
jewel eyes could not lie. They blurted out secrets her
veiled lips concealed.

Kalila had no desire to steal the gold that had lain
here for thousands of years. Something else held her
here. Something evil and foul as greedy men's
thoughts. He wished he could lift the spell weaving
her into this sticky web of deceit.

With the veil curtaining her face, soft silk trousers
of indigo and matching shirt, Kalila looked as exotic
as a princess from ancient times. Thick ebony curls as
lustrous as heavy satin spilled down to her slender
waist. Her diminutive figure bragged of curves and her

melodious voice whispered to him like sand singing in the dunes.

He could not have her. Ramses wrapped his fingers around his hidden tattoo. It burned through his *binish* as if heated from within, reminding him of his oath of fidelity.

Questioning her might yield some answers. Better to converse and keep his shattering nerves from further unraveling. When the door had sealed the tomb shut, he'd forced a scream down his throat. Only years of self-discipline and control allowed calm to shoulder aside pure panic.

"If the gold means nothing to you, why did you steal the map?"

She sank to the ground, sitting with her head buried into trembling palms. "I had no choice," came the muffled reply.

He lifted her chin with a finger. "We always have choices," Ramses said softly.

"Not always. Sometimes we have to do things against our will, even though we know they are wrong, for a greater purpose."

Her words made no sense. "Evil deeds only bring a greater purpose of evil. The Old Ones always stressed this. Indeed, they lived in fear of failing at the judging in the afterlife."

"The afterlife isn't what I fear," she murmured, staring at her hands.

He grasped one, pulled her up as he stood and went over to the coffin. "My ancestors did. Look."

The sarcophagus was inlaid with the eye of Horus and other markings of his tattoo. Kalila bent over it,

171

long ebony curls hiding her face as she examined the markings.

"Why is it so important?" She pointed to the eye.

The eye of Horus? She did not know? Every Egyptian knew the eye's protective powers. The pieces of mystery surrounding Kalila began forming a mosaic that distressed him. She knew of totems from her shaman, yet remained ignorant of the Udjat's protective powers. Myrrh scented her hair, yet she untangled it with a brush stamped with a foreign crest. Ramses did not want her to be foreign. He wanted Kalila as comfortable and familiar as his own heritage, as Egyptian as the tomb imprisoning them. Dismissing the nagging instinct as quickly as it surfaced, he rationalized there must be another reason for her ignorance.

"It is the Udjat, the symbol for Horus's eye. Horus fought with Set, his father's evil brother, and Set gouged out his eye. The eye was restored by Thoth, the god of wisdom. It symbolizes protection." He uttered the last note in a forlorn tone and caught himself, cursing silently. His jaw tightened as he struggled with his emotions.

"The same symbol is on your arm." She frowned. "Except for that odd, roundish shape and the line running through it."

Kalila pressed a hand against his upper left arm. "May I see it again?"

Ramses obliged, rolling up his sleeves. Kalila traced the markings, resting a fingertip against Min's flail. Green eyes asked the question her lips did not as she tapped the symbol.

He released the breath he'd been holding. "The tattoo on my arm is the Udjat and the Ieb. The Ieb is the heart, the center of consciousness."

"This?"

"Min's flail," he said shortly, rolling down his sleeves.

"Which god is Min?"

He glanced down at the sarcophagus and began exploring the symbols. When he located the glyph for Min, his finger rested upon the god. Amusement filled him as her emerald eyes widened in shocked disbelief. A small gasp sucked the veil inward.

"This same symbol is what this figure is holding, but he's . . . He's . . ." Ramses swore Kalila's cheeks pinkened beneath the veil. He crouched down and examined the figure.

"Yes, he is," Ramses agreed, admiring the glyph of Min holding a flail in his left hand. Unlike the other glyphs on the coffin, this god featured a very impressive, very erect penis.

"Quite." He chuckled as her eyes darted away from the fertility god.

"What's that stick he's holding that's on your tattoo?"

Ramses suppressed another chuckle. "His flail. Better the flail than the other symbol of his power. I have no desire to go through life tattooed with an erect . . ."

A hand clapped over his mouth cut the sentence short. Ramses had a sudden inclination tempted to lick the warm, soft palm pressed against his lips. The god of fertility must be working his magic, he thought, grinning against her hand's gentle pressure.

"What is he? This Min? What does it mean for you?"

His amusement fled as his stomach churned. Ramses removed her hand, desire soured as if he sucked on a raw lemon.

"Min is an ancient god of fertility. He guards the Arabian Desert and protected the miners."

"But why is he on your tattoo?"

"The Ieb and the Udjat mean that I am sworn to protect the one to whom I pledge my heart. Min's marking bestows me with fertility to father a son to become a Guardian of the Ages after me," he said quietly. A son mothered by a woman he could never love because of her culture. English ancestors tainted his pedigree. He treasured his tribe's ancient Egyptian heritage more than any other Khamsin warrior. Khamsin culture provided a life raft in his blood's polluted whirlpool. But marriage further diluted his children's bloodlines.

He would share his body and make babies with his bride, but never share the deepest part of him. His heart. His Ieb would remain locked in a tomb as dusty and old as this one.

Her heart skipped a beat. Huge dimples of gooseflesh pricked her arms as if a cold wind swept through the tomb. Ramses appeared dejected as his hand covered the odd tattoo.

"Pledge your heart? You mean when you marry?"

"Yes," he said quietly.

Katherine wished that she could be the chosen bride Ramses cherished and protected.

"When are you getting married? Who is this woman?"

"Do not ask me any more questions regarding this, Kalila. I will not discuss it." Iron wove through his husky voice.

"I'm getting married. An old Bedouin goatherd," she admitted. The truth entombed her heart as if someone shoved her into the sarcophagus' confines and slammed the lid shut.

Ramses shot her a sympathetic look. Unhappiness clouded his handsome features. They were two souls tied to fates of marrying those they did not love.

"Have you met him?" he asked, and jealousy laced his voice.

She nodded, thinking of seeing Nazim. "I saw him in the hotel going to meet my father. He looks like an old goatherd," she mused. "But I won't marry him. I'll find a way out. I can control my fate."

Ramses's mouth twisted as if in amusement. "What, you don't believe me?" she asked, hurt at his reaction.

"I believe there is a reason for everything that happens in our lives. God chooses to show us signs. There are signs all over the desert, if you choose to look for them."

She thought of the flat, sandy plain, the jagged, unsympathetic black granite mountains. Such signs were not revealed to her.

"Do you believe in signs? What do you believe in?"

"I don't know," she said, ruminating over the question.

"Everyone has to believe in something," Ramses pointed out.

"I believe in taking charge of my own destiny." Her lip jutted out in stubborn protest.

"That is not always possible. Sometimes when we force a path through life, it is blocked," he said gently. "Destiny then calls us to follow a different way."

"You sound as mystical as Ahmed," she complained. "Stop lecturing as if I'm a five-year-old."

"You are stubborn," Ramses said, shaking his head. "But God wears down even the strongest rock by water. You will learn that you cannot always control your fate, little one."

His mild scolding raised her resolve that she could control her fate. "That theory isn't applicable in the desert."

"Ah, but you are wrong. Flood waters carved their way through the mountains and created the wadi enclosing this tomb."

Annoyed at his knowing smile, she knew he was right. Ramses reminded Katherine of the helplessness flooding her life, others who forced her to do their will. Controlled by Burrells to steal a map. Even Papa making her marry a Bedouin goatherd.

Not if I do something about it first. If she lost her virginity, the Bedouin would reject her. The insight came as quickly as a summer storm. She considered, knowing her bridegroom prized her maiden state as much as he probably prized his camel. If she lost her virginity, she violated the marriage contract. The idea sounded tantalizing.

"I won't marry him," she stated with bold defiance. "I'll do anything. Cut my hair. Better yet, I'll deprive him of my virginity."

Two black brows arched. Amber eyes regarded her with a thoughtful look. "You would do this, Kalila, and shame your father?"

"Papa wouldn't be shamed. He doesn't want this any more than I do," she asserted weakly.

Not true, for the marriage honored her mother's dying wish. Katherine swallowed a lump in her throat as she recalled her mother's laughing green eyes, soft smile and exotic grace. Papa had loved her fiercely and would deny her nothing. As she lay in her coffin, he had lovingly placed the Bast amulet around her mother's neck to "guard her in the next life." The same amulet that choked him with grief when he saw it in the Giza Museum. The amulet that provided evidence to imprison him for years if she didn't do what Burrells ordered.

Katherine bent over the sarcophagus, hiding tears burning her eyes. A colorful illustration showed an ebony-haired man in a white gown, led by a figure with a jackal's head. Her fingers rasped over the surface.

"What's this?"

Ramses peered down. "Anubis, the god of the dead. It is the ritual of the afterlife. My ancestor is being judged for his deeds on earth. Anubis leads him to the scale to weigh his deeds. His heart, his Ieb, is placed on it and measured against the feather of Ma'at, the goddess of truth. His Ieb is not heavier than the feather, so he is worthy."

Katherine leaned over the painting. "What happens if he was judged unworthy?"

"Ammit, the god with the crocodile head, devours the Ieb, sealing the deceased into oblivion for all eternity. Ammit is the eater of the dead."

"The eater of the dead," she whispered, wrapping her arms around her for comfort. Katherine glanced at the darkened corners of the tomb. Such creatures would dwell here, ready to leap out of the dancing shadows with their razor-sharp teeth.

He nodded. "In this scene, Horus presents the deceased before Osiris, the god of the afterlife, who grants him access to the next world. Thoth, the ibis-headed god of wisdom, records his deeds."

"But why all the gold?"

"The Old Ones believed the departed would continue the same life he led in this world, thus the reason for the riches."

She traced the coffin's glyphs with a hesitant finger. "So your ancestor is buried inside. Is he a mummy?"

"Yes. Do you know how they mummify a body?"

"No," she whispered, uncertain that she wanted to know.

Ramses's gaze flicked to the coffin. "The internal organs are removed and placed in four canopic jars with lids. Each lid bears one head: human, baboon, falcon and jackal, representing the four protective spirits, the four sons of Horus. The Ieb is removed to be weighed against Ma'at's feather of truth. The brain is taken out through the nasal passages and thrown away. The brain was the most difficult organ to preserve. Then the ritual opening the mouth, to allow the dead to speak."

Katherine shuddered. All this talk of death while sealed inside a tomb spooked her. She searched around for another topic of conversation.

"What do these hieroglyphs mean? Can you read them?"

He gave her an amused look. "Khamsin warriors learn to read glyphs before we read Arabic. This," he pointed to what looked like a bird with a human head and arms, "is the symbol for *ba*. And this," his finger rested on a cross with a looped top, "is an ankh. It means life."

"What is this?" Katherine traced the edges of what looked like an upside down English "u" with a flat bottom.

"That is very important. That is *ka*, or life force."

"I don't understand. You mean a person's soul."

"Not exactly. The *ba* is the soul. The *ka* is also part

of the soul, but the life force, the spirit. The Old Ones believed the *ka* was the person's twin that united with the body once death claimed it. When a person is born, his *ka* is born as well. The *ka* waits for the soul to leave this world and reunites to live in peace forever."

Fascinated, she stared at the symbols that marked his world. "Can you translate this?"

Ramses nodded, furrowing his brow. He gave her a boyish grin. "It has been . . . some time since I read glyphs. I am out of practice." His index finger rested on the symbols as he outlined each one, reading aloud.

"Greetings to you, honored Glorious One who rules for all eternity. My *ka* is washed clean, my soul pure and prepared to . . ." he frowned at one symbol, then smiled. "Eateth bread with thee for all eternity. My son after me will guard the steps of the honored one. Guard his steps and looketh upon his soul with favor. Protect him from the one who swallows the Spirit-souls."

He straightened. A shiver scampered up her tense spine. As beautiful as the sentiment was, it had an ominous note.

"Who is the one who swallows the Spirit-souls?" she asked.

Ramses's broad shoulders stiffened. His hand shot to his scimitar's hilt, an automatic move she sensed he was unaware of. The move of a man protecting himself against danger.

"Ammit, the eater of the dead," he replied, looking around the tomb. "The Khamsin termed certain humans eaters of the dead. They are the desert jackals who do not sleep, but prowl the sands looking for weak prey. These evil ones steal to satisfy their greed. They devour others' hopes and dreams for pleasure.

They sell their own souls for paltry sums, such as gold."

He locked gazes with her, letting the silence drop between them like a stone wall. Sell their souls for gold. Another reminder of the glittering treasure before them.

"What was your ancestor's name?"

"Rastau. Rastau was a great Khamsin Guardian who protected the mine during the reign of Pharaoh Tutankhamun."

"So the mine is quite old!" Despite her inner shivering, an odd excitement gripped her.

"This mine is unlike many others, for the pharaoh bequeathed it to my ancestor. The gold vein had thinned out and other mines were yielding more," Ramses explained.

"And Rastau used it as his tomb." Katherine shuddered. "But where did all the treasure come from? I thought only pharaohs were permitted to own gold."

Ramses's smile seemed as cryptic as the mystery surrounding them. "You thought."

"If you knew it was here, why did you come? Why not just send an army of warriors to kill us and stop us from exploring?"

"Us?" Ramses repeated. "Who is us, Kalila? Whom are you working for?"

Katherine pretended ignorance with an elegant shrug. "The men you killed could have easily been forty instead of four."

"I doubt it," he said softly. "Whoever sent you could not find more than four to unseal this tomb, for the curse is well known. This desert is haunted by jinn. Few dare to venture here and brave the curse."

"But you're here."

He frowned. "For good reason," Ramses said guardedly.

Katherine toyed with her veil's hem. A dreadful thought seized her. He acted calm about her discovering the tomb. Could it be because the secret would lie here forever with her?

Perhaps Ramses planned to leave the tomb when the door opened. Alone. Sealing her inside forever, only her screams and dead men's dreams echoing in the lonely darkness.

"Ramses," she asked slowly, "What are you going to do with me? I'm the only one, besides you, who knows where the tomb is. Aren't you afraid I'll take the knowledge with me?"

Torchlight caught the golden flecks of his eyes, making them gleam with fierce intensity. "I am not afraid, Kalila. For you are not going anywhere at all."

A determined look, the look of the hunter, came over him. Ramses advanced toward her on silent feet. Intense fear sent adrenaline surging through her veins. She could not escape him. With his powerful strength, he could easily overcome her.

Katherine backed away from Ramses, looked at the glow of the single torch on the wall. The one chance. An eerie calmness blanked her mind, allowed her to think. Throw the tomb into total darkness and she could claim a small advantage. He was large and strong, but she was fast and clever. Maybe even head him off and reach the door before he did.

Her next move came so quickly it surprised even her. Katherine sprang forward, grabbed the torch and darted to hide among the statues, peering out between Isis's shoulder and Horus's beaked mouth. Ramses's expression tightened.

"Kalila, give me the torch. Stop this."

"Stay away from me. I'm warning you, Ramses. I'll not have you leave me in here with, with . . ." She pointed at the coffin. "Your dead relative."

He recoiled, drawing his brows together. His smooth forehead sported rows of lines. "Leave you here?" Ramses sounded incredulous. "Kalila, do not be silly. I would not leave you. Now come, be a good girl and give me that torch."

In answer, she wriggled back against the wall until the cold stone pressed against her spine. Katherine held out the torch as if offering a sacrifice. With one sudden move, she thrust it into the sand, extinguishing it and plunging the tomb into inky darkness.

Memories surged back with a vengeance, taunting him with their voices. A child's fear wrapped around him. Suddenly he was no longer a grown man, a warrior who had slain many and feared none. Ramses became as helpless as that long ago six-year-old who had been tied up and left alone in a dark cave.

He tried anything. Breathing. Closing his eyes. Nothing worked. Prayers and petitions to God, to his ancestor. Terror gripped him with icy tentacles, wrapping around his arms, paralyzing him with exacting precision. He could not move, think or speak. All he could do was stand, frozen to the sand like a statue left here to honor the ancient Khamsin Guardian.

Breath escaped his lungs in darting pants. His hands grew chilled and clammy. He heard a rapid thrumming and knew his heart beat as furiously as his hands did on his beloved *darrubuka*. Thoughts of Kalila faded. All he could think of was how he could escape this tomb before he went stark, raving mad.

A scraping sounded near the wall. Ramses's eyes flew open. No use. Adjusting his eyes to darkness brought no relief from the ebony blackness. No light shone in this stone prison. His nostrils whistled with the tune of panicked breathing.

Katherine slid along the wall toward the door and stopped, her desperation to flee diverted by a low, barely perceptible moan. Like that an animal would make if caught in a trap.

Ramses. He sounded . . . scared? The fearless, mighty Khamsin warrior, afraid?

She inched along the wall, but kept listening. There, again. The unmistakable sounds of ragged breaths, as if he tried frantically to control, and conceal, his fear. Katherine wavered, hesitating, torn between the instinct to escape and a blossoming need to comfort. Perhaps it was a ruse. Clever Ramses pretending fear to disarm her, toss her off guard. No, ridiculous. She recognized the honest sounds of genuine terror. How many times in the past few weeks had she felt caught in its nasty grip when she thought of her father dying in jail?

Fear for herself evaporated, replaced with need to nurture, just as she had nursed Ramses back to health. Katherine licked her lips. "Ramses?" she called out hesitantly.

No answer. Then a small, hoarse half-plea, half-command in the dark that shattered her heart.

"Do not leave me, Kalila."

The words sounded strained, forced, as if it took all his strength to say them. His raw need of her was evident. Katherine remembered Ramses asking in a wistful, almost little-boy voice as he lay drugged with the valerian root back at the cave, "Will you still be here when I wake?"

Leaving him alone in the tomb with fears he would not admit filled her with guilt. Ramses had a part of him he hated, just as she did. Not all scars were visible in the mirror. Compassion flooded her. Still, she had to make sure of his intentions.

When she spoke, her voice was strong and controlled. "Ramses, I have to protect myself. I know your tribe's secret. A secret you would prevent me from telling."

"I would not harm you," he rasped.

"You said I wasn't going anywhere. You were going to leave me here to die, sealed here forever with that . . . mummy."

A sharp intake of air came from across the tomb. "I said you were not going anywhere. You are not. Not without me. I must bring you back to my people. I am a Khamsin Guardian of the Ages, sworn to honor and protect women. I swear to you on my oath as a warrior and a Guardian, I will not cause you injury."

Another deep inhalation. "Please," he said hoarsely. "Trust me."

A wash of deep tenderness for him mixed with helpless frustration. How could she leave him like this? Damn Burrells for putting her in this situation. Even her father was at fault, taking the amulet and admiring it, mourning her mother.

Ramses curled his hands into tight fists. He felt exposed, vulnerable, and inwardly cursed his weakness. A Khamsin warrior, the bravest fighter of his tribe, brought to his knees by a childish fear of the dark. He tried to move his limbs. They remained frozen to the ground as if sealed there.

A small rustling neared him. Fear kicked up a notch. Ramses thrust out his hands groping the air and bit back a startled yell as his fingertips brushed against something soft. He jerked back and nearly fell down.

"Ramses," came her soft, reassuring voice, like velvet brushing against his raw nerves. "I trust you. Now trust me. Take my hand."

He could smell her warmth and it cleaved the chill in his heart. He fought his fear, reached out in the dark, trusting. Warm alive flesh brushed against his trembling fingertips, then a velvet soft hand curled tightly around his. She stepped closer and pressed against his body. Ramses eased out another trembling breath as he wrapped his arms around her, his anchor. Katherine snuggled against his chest. He held her as if she were the sun, wrapping himself in her light and warmth. His heart eased its excruciating cadence. Slowly, calm settled over him. And then a frustrated, bitter voice in English sent him reeling back on his booted heels with fresh shock.

"I never wanted this to happen to you or me. It's not my fault. I hate tombs. I hate gold. I wish Papa had never seen the gold amulet and longed for it. And I don't want to get married. I just want to go home! Oh, I wish Papa had never left England and Smithfield!"

Chapter Thirteen

Smithfield? England?

If darkness made his heart beat triple time, those two words made it stand absolutely still.

Ramses spoke fluent English. So did she.

The woman pressed against his chest was not Egyptian, or exotic, or a tomb robber, but his bride.

Ramses's mouth went drier than sun-baked sand. Awkwardly he settled one arm around her waist. Lady Katherine Smithfield. The woman he wanted to seduce was none other than his intended wife. He would have laughed if he hadn't been so shocked.

Possessive tenderness flooded him, washing away all other emotions. His bride. The unknown English woman he thought he could never love. His little lotus blossom. His thief.

Anger wrestled inside him. Lord Smithfield, who knew the mine and map existed, and probably the secret tomb as well, forced Katherine to steal for him. His future father-in-law lusted after a gold amulet and wanted more. Katherine's hysterical words told him as much.

Not a good way to start off a relationship, he thought with grim humor. Could the earl, with his vast wealth, have more greed than good sense? He thought of Lord Smithfield, a man who bore little resemblance to his daughter but for his ebony hair. Ramses thought he could never love an English bride because she'd be formal and overbearing. Katherine was not. But her crime indicated a despicable English trait. She stole from his people, just as the British ruling his country stole from Egypt.

The mosaic fitted into place. Ramses swore silently.

Katherine's slender shoulders shook. He stroked her satin tresses gently, murmuring comforting words. She snuggled against him. He recognized her determined courage. She did all this for her father. What was he going to do with her? Honor bound him to marry her, despite her treacherous father's deceit. A promise made by a Khamsin warrior could not be broken.

The one woman who denied him, defied him, escaped him, and tantalized him with her intelligence matched his own intelligence and fierce family loyalty. As he recalled his vow to protect her, Ramses felt a rush of tenderness so piercing, the rock walls surrounding his heart crumbled. Then he remembered her defiant promise to escape marriage by losing her virginity. Possessive rage darkened him. She is mine, he thought with savage, primitive jealousy. No other man will have her. But no vows sealed their union to make her legally his.

His hand tangled in her long curls. Her softness

pressed against his hard body began arousing a different hardness. Ramses felt a desperate need to forge a tender bond in the flesh with Katherine. If he claimed her, she'd have to marry him. He'd sweep her away from that treacherous English father to his people. Once estranged from Lord Smithfield, Katherine would be safe. He'd separate her deceitful English half from her Egyptian half by fully immersing Katherine into his Egyptian culture.

The idea made him smile. With loving words, he'd gently coax Katherine into surrendering what she wished to sacrifice to escape marriage. Then he would marry her. Husbands had more rights than fathers.

Ramses's body tightened in hungry anticipation. He wanted her with a dark and deep passion. Warmth flooded him as he prepared to deliver a soul-searing kiss that would banish everything but him from her mind.

His deep tones murmuring endearments swept aside her frustrated resentment. Katherine relaxed into his protective, sheltering embrace. He stroked her hair with gentle caresses. How could she ever fear this man? He risked all to save her. Ramses would not abandon her to mummies and cold stone tombs. He was a Khamsin Guardian, an honorable man who did not harm women. Even women who defied him by stealing ancient maps. She pressed deeper into his robe, burying herself in his rich, spicy scent of sandalwood and cloves.

She sensed a change as he stopped caressing her hair. No more gentle murmurs. Fingertips callused by sun, steel and fighting grazed her veil, then tugged off the cloth barrier. Katherine drew back, afraid of his

THE TIGER AND THE TOMB

intent, but he pulled her closer with a determined arm snaked about her waist. Ramses lowered his mouth and captured hers.

At first, his lips felt gentle, warm and inviting. Then he pounced, claiming her mouth with hard, hot fury. Katherine's mind reeled with shock. Ramses molded her body to his, his grip implacable and dominating. Bursting shafts of heated desire dispelled the tomb's darkness as his mouth devoured hers. Swirling tongues of flames licked her body with erotic pleasure. His tongue traced the seam of her lower lip, finding the slight parting and slipping inside. Ramses growled into her mouth, nipping, coaxing her to open to him. Katherine curled her arms around his neck, surrendering to his demands. He cupped her bottom, kneading it gently, pressing her against his rigid arousal. Her breasts tingled as she rubbed their softness against his hard chest. She wanted to purr from the delicious feel of his muscled body.

Ramses uttered a groan and gave small, thrusts with his tongue. He could have been making love to her mouth in the cloudless, joyful sunshine instead of deep beneath the earth, cradled in its womb. Hunger birthed from desperate need arose. Her fingers curled around the sculpted muscles of his shoulders. Katherine moaned into his mouth as he gently prodded her tongue with his, urging her to taste him.

His persistent ravaging of her mouth tore away all coherent thought. Katherine struggled to remember to breathe as white-hot passion engulfed her. She sagged against him in the inky blackness, using other senses to replace sight. The delicious smell of spices, the slightly salty taste of him mingling with the sweet tea he'd consumed, the feel of his callused palm heating her nape as he cradled it, the sound of her own low moans as he deepened the kiss and awakened her desire.

Ramses swept her into his strong arms, gently laying her upon the sand. His lips scraped along the column of her throat, igniting the skin there with bursts of heat. Katherine clung to him as if drowning. She caressed his hair, toying with the thickness of his curls, lost in remembrance of the other kiss, the other time and place.

For days she had nursed him as a weak, helpless man. And controllable. Now she became aware of his enormous power, his body's solid strength firmly trapping her beneath him. Katherine felt as helpless as a gazelle held under the paw of a predator—a golden-eyed tiger who punished not with cruel claws, but hot kisses. Ramses wasn't a man with a meager appetite satisfied by a few chaste kisses, but a warrior with a deep, driving hunger determined to possess every inch of her.

His raging desire swept her into a tumultuous sandstorm. Newly awakened senses spun with pleasure as he sought her mouth again. Katherine opened herself fully to him as she shyly met his tongue's insistent thrusts with one of her own. She allowed everything to vanish but the scent and feel and taste of this desert warrior. Her body strained with anticipation as he rubbed against her, creating a delicious friction. She would let him do anything and wondered if it would come to that, after all.

Just as she entertained the thought, it happened. The hush of sand spilling to the ground ceased. With a strangled groan, the door opened, equaling the frustrated groan she suppressed. Flickering torchlight from the mine flooded the inky darkness. Ramses tore his mouth from hers and looked down.

He saw her face.

With a startled cry, she clapped a hand to her scar. Ramses recoiled with a startled look. Katherine shoved at his chest and as he rolled off her, she scrambled away, searching for the veil. The veil, the damn veil, where did he put it? Finally she spotted it lying on the ground like a crumpled black flower. Katherine grabbed it and attached it. A tremendous lump clogged her throat. Memories hooked cruel claws into her heart. Other men's repulsed expressions upon seeing the scar. Ramses had looked stunned when the faithless light revealed her flaw. She'd cherish their passionate kisses in the dark, for she knew his lips would never seek hers again.

Ramses swallowed past the thickness in his throat as he watched Katherine desperately scramble for her veil. He cursed silently. Hands curled into tight fists he longed to smash into mocking mouths that had taunted her. Who had hurt Katherine this badly? She was so sweet, so soft and pretty, with her generous curves and teasing masses of hair, delectable plump breasts aching to be touched. When light had pierced the tomb, he looked into her face. Passion darkened her eyes to smoky emerald. Her pouty little mouth parted, swollen from his fevered kisses. His breath had caught as he stared down at her in wondrous incredulity. The rapt pleasure captured in her expression cracked all his carefully mounted defenses. He had never seen a woman more beautiful. And then her expression had shifted into horrified shame. He heard the unspoken cry rising from her protesting lips. Men had taunted Katherine because of her scar and he saw that pain as if she stood bleeding before him.

Tension radiated off her in waves. Katherine acted like a puppy kicked too many times. Ramses reached out to trace the mark, to claim her as his own. He ached to draw her into his arms and kiss her scar from tip to top. But as he moved forward, she whirled, presenting her back.

"Please Ramses. Leave me alone a minute. Please."

Drawing in a deep breath, he left the tomb, knowing she wanted to hide what he'd already seen. Muscles tensed as he waited for her. Finally she emerged from the tomb looking as drawn and pale as death. When she failed to meet his eyes, Ramses enclosed her soft, small hand in his. It felt swallowed by his immense palm, as if he clutched something as fragile as a lotus petal.

"Come Kalila," he said gently, tugging her toward the mine's entrance.

He climbed out first and hauled her and the rope up. Judging from her bent head, she preferred being left in the mine's sheltering darkness. Ramses gulped in several delicious breaths. Night had fallen, but this darkness he could handle as long as he had his beloved open desert.

Ramses looked at Katherine, who refused to meet his gaze. His hand caught her chin, turned her toward him.

"Kalila," he began.

As she had at the Shepheard's, Katherine pressed a finger to his lips. The sob she choked down sliced his heart in two.

"No Ramses. Please, say nothing. It was glorious. I don't want to spoil it," she said in a broken whisper.

He stepped forward to offer comfort, an embrace, words to soothe away tears. She jerked away, holding out her hands.

"Please, leave me alone," she told him.

As they walked toward their camels, the desert sky blazed with the fire of stars set against a midnight black sky like brilliant jewels on display in the *souks*. A pale of silvery moonlight washed down on them. Ramses tethered her camel to his, and lifted Katherine onto his saddle. Moonlight caught moisture shimmering in the emerald depths of her eyes. His finger reached up to wipe away a lingering tear threatening to spill out. Katherine went rigid. She had stated before she despised tears. Any gesture to offer comfort she'd interpret as pity.

Ramses tucked his body behind her and settled his arms around Katherine's waist. His heart ached with each sniffle she suppressed. He began singing softly, wanting to erase her pain, yet knowing she desired privacy to weep. When something warm and wet splashed onto his hand, he pretended it was a raindrop in the dry, clear air and ignored it.

Much later that night, when she heard the deep, even breathing indicating Ramses had fallen asleep, Katherine eased out of bed. Guided by moonlight spilling into the cave, she tiptoed over to her bag. Hidden between her breasts nestled the little gold cat she'd swiped from the tomb. Proof she needed to show Foster Burrells she'd found the gold. When he arrived at the cave, she'd show it to him and free her father. She stuffed the feline deep inside the bag, then crept back to bed.

Chapter Fourteen

Katherine studiously avoided him the next morning. He watched her with guarded anxiety as she scrubbed laundry outside, slapping wet sheets on the rocks. Ramses studied the luscious sweep of her rounded bottom as it wiggled with the furious energy she expended. Sweet, impassioned words would not convince her how beautiful she was. Only action would. Tonight. Tonight with tender words and even more tender caresses, he would show her.

Shame from last night's revelation of her scar turned to puzzled speculation at Ramses's odd behavior. He said little, but she caught him casting her intent looks. Ramses had a graceful restlessness. He paced the cave during the day. Prowled the sands like a hunter. He reminded her of the tiger that struck with vicious precision. Like that long-ago tiger, would Ramses carve a mark? Only this time, an invisible one on her heart? Last night, the paw had been raised to strike when his face twisted with shock as he looked at the scar. Had she not retreated so quickly, his claws would have lacerated her already injured heart.

She had retreated to bed early, murmuring excuses. He kept staring as if he were hungry. Then the impartial blank look descended. He mentioned taking a short stroll and left.

He returned a short while later while she pretended sleep. She heard him settle into the other bed. When his even breathing filled the cave, she slipped out of bed. As she had previous nights when he slept, Katherine went outside to bathe.

Ramses heard her leave. He lay in bed, debating whether to follow her. Finally he shrugged into his *binish* and sandals and stole outside. Hearing splashing, he followed the sounds to the well, gawking in disbelief.

Katherine stood like a raven-haired vision in the moonlight. His own skin puckered in sympathized gooseflesh at the chilled well water beading her naked skin. Ramses's eyes traced the curve of her spine down to the lovely rounded bottom and long, graceful limbs. Moonlight shimmered in the black silk of her wet hair. Proud shoulders quivered as she dried her face. She was shivering, he realized with dismay. Ramses unbuttoned his *binish* and slipped it off, approaching from behind. Her body tensed as pebbles crunched beneath his steps. Ramses gently draped the *binish* over Katherine's shaking body. It swallowed her nakedness whole.

"Come inside and I will make you something hot to drink. If you stay out here, you will become sick," he said softly.

Ramses returned to the cave, lighting a fire, then set

the copper pot to boil water. Kicking off his sandals, he padded through the cave barefoot. He fetched a cup, leaves and set them down, then retrieved his *darrubuka*. Sitting before the fire, he thumped the drum's surface. The conical-shaped instrument had a goatskin head and a rattan weaving framing the edges.

He needed to play the drum tonight and rid his body of tension. Ramses glanced up as Katherine approached. She draped his damp *binish* over a chair, then sat beside him.

"Thank you," she said quietly. She brushed her hair, pausing a few times to stretch her hands to the crackling flames. He added boiling water to the cup, stirred, then set it down. Ramses sat down behind Katherine, opened his legs and settled her into the cradle of his thighs.

"Body heat is the best way to keep warm in the desert," he said, easing her against his chest. She stiffened, then relaxed, drinking her tea.

"Nothing like a good cup of tea on a cold night," he murmured. A small sigh told him she agreed.

Ramses settled the drum into Katherine's lap. "It goes well with a *darrubuka* to warm one's blood," he added, reaching around her to thump on the surface.

Katherine stroked the drum's head, evoking a shudder from him when her soft fingers brushed against his.

"What is this?" Her melodious voice rippled over his raging nerves, heating his blood fiercely.

"My *darrubuka*. A drum. The Khamsin use it for many reasons; celebrations, war councils. I use it to sing. I play this all the time at home. It is a tribal tradition around the campfire,"

The firm strength of his body against hers created a

delicious tension. Katherine rose, stretching. She hugged herself, glancing at Ramses sitting bare-chested and cross-legged, cradling the drum between his thighs. He leaned the instrument toward the fire.

Suddenly his hands beat a wild polyrhythmic beat. Ramses closed his eyes as if surrendering his spirit to the melody. Her lids fluttered shut as she swayed, called by the drum's haunting pattern. She heard his world with each beat, the desert sands he called home, the deep rich secrets of the Bedu tribes hidden within those golden dunes, battles fought with fierce courage and love tucked behind black tents where a man showed a woman the secrets of passion.

"Your dance is quite enchanting." Ramses's voice startled her. Her eyes flew open. She had danced around the fire, reacting naturally to the thrilling cadence of the drum's beat. Tiny beads of sweat studded her temple. She rotated hips and arms, teasing the air, coaxing it toward her.

Immediately she stopped, flustered. Although she had seen belly dances in her cousin's harem, Katherine felt more comfortable with the traditional waltzes of England. Belly dancing seemed too exotic, too sensual for her English side. What was Ramses doing to her? He suppressed her rigid, proper English side and un-locked her Egyptian side much as he unlocked rhythm from the drum. She was no longer half-Egyptian. Now she was a true daughter of the desert, much as any Bedouin bride.

"Do not stop, Kalila, for you dance most beautifully. I find your movements extremely pleasing."

"I would rather hear you play the drum," she pro-tested.

"A fine instrument." His deep voice massaged her

overly sensitive skin. Ramses caressed the drum's surface like a lover. "Always play a *darrubuka* toward the fire. The heat from the fire's surface stretches the skin and makes for a tighter surface and better rhythm."

Ramses glanced at her, a smile playing on his sensual lips. "A man who is skilled enough can coax excellent rhythm from many things with tight surfaces."

Her cheeks flamed at his suggestive remark. Katherine raised her chin and replied coolly, "It is easy to brag about being skilled enough when the instrument offers no resistance. But some are not so readily played. No matter how close to the fire it is set."

Passion sparkled within the swirls of those golden irises. "Ah, but such resistance is part of the challenge, my little Kalila. The more stubborn it is, the more I am determined to conquer it. As my hands coax life from the object, it becomes one with me, for I set the rhythm, and eventually it reacts to my touch and responds back with a life and beat of its own."

Now she did avert her gaze, unable to meet his penetrating scrutiny. Ramses eyed her like a tiger that had captured her and waited to dine. A naughty recollection surfaced; his warm lips licking her leg. Her cheeks flamed.

A soft, amused chuckle turned her attention back to the man commanding all the cave's space. The intent look in his dark gold irises scared her. Katherine moistened her lips, suddenly aware the heat filling the cavern wasn't from the fire.

"Please sing me a song," she asked, needing to ease her nervousness.

Ramses leaned upon the drum, seemingly deep in thought. "A song," he said softly. "Not just any song for you, Kalila. But a special one I shall compose. A song especially for you, sweet lotus blossom of the desert." He put a finger on his lower lip, rubbing it. "Ah, I have it." Ramses smiled softly.

He cleared his throat and began pounding out a slow, steady beat. The rhythm was seductive and she wanted to sway with it. Heat warmed her body as he sang the words, his eyes locking with hers. Tension hung in the air, sweet and cloying, as he sang his intimate proposal, the words a tender caress.

"My heart beats only to the sweet rhythm of
   yours.
Let our hearts blend as one
As the sands melt together on the golden dunes.
As I touch my lips to yours
Let our bodies join together as earth meets sky.
Give in to your deepest desires.
Let me take you to that deep place on the
   golden dunes,
And teach you all there is to know about pas-
   sion in the desert.
Your sweet lips are nectar for my starving soul.
Little lotus blossom that opens its petals,
To the sun in the day,
And sinks below the Nile at night,
Do not hide from me.
Open yourself to me.
Let me nestle within your sweetness.
And together we shall sink below the water,
Drowning in pleasure as our bodies become
   one."

He stopped singing and drumming on the *darru-buka*. Katherine felt her heart thrum. Ramses stood the drum upright, away from the fire. His golden eyes captured her gaze and held it captive. Ramses's song clearly signaled his intent. He wanted them to be lovers. Katherine felt as if she breathed in his deep, blazing desire.

Ramses abandoned the drum and stood. She stepped back, filled with a nervous excitement bordering on anticipation. Flexing his muscular body, he advanced, stalking her like a predator. She retreated until her spine pressed against unyielding rock. Ramses's large form trapped Katherine against the wall as he braced his palms on either side of her.

"I need you, my darling Kalila," he said softly.

His voice brushed against her in a velvet caress. She felt her resistance waver, hearing its deep, hypnotic tones. Ramses tugged on a strand of her hair. Wrapping it around his finger, he lifted it up, as if admiring its sheen. "I adore touching your hair. It feels softer than a cloud of silk," he murmured.

Katherine's pulse drummed out a heated beat fiercer than Ramses's drumming on the *darrubuka*. Longing to touch him mingled with fear of the unknown. He brushed his lips against her forehead. She laid restless hands upon his shoulders. The taut golden skin rippled with warm muscles. Hot, fierce feelings swept through her, pooling an odd heat between her thighs.

One strong hand lifted her chin to his. She looked into his eyes and saw not lust, but deep tenderness.

Katherine looked away, unable to bear the piercing intensity of his gaze. "Please, Ramses, leave me alone." Her voice cracked.

Ramses ran a thumb where veil met cheek. His deft touch barely made contact, but she shivered. How could she find any strength to resist him? Katherine drew in a shaky breath.

"What is it, Kalila? Why do you fear me?" he asked in a softer tone.

"You'll act just like the others."

"What others?"

"It's not your fault. I can't blame you."

He drew her closer. Ramses brushed back a tangle of hair spilling over her face. "Have I done something to frighten you?"

"No," she protested weakly. "It's not anything you did. It's how you look."

A muscle tightened in his jaw. "How do I look?"

"Like a perfect sun god," she whispered. "When I first saw you in the hotel, I couldn't take my eyes from you. And I knew it was all a dream, because someone as beautiful as you could never be with someone like me."

"Kalila . . ." he began.

"Someone as ugly as me." She jerked out of his sheltering embrace. "Look at me, Ramses. Look at how marred I am. Look at what you saw in the tomb."

With that statement, she tore off the veil. "Go ahead, I've hidden it too long from you. With this face of mine, you'd never kiss me like you did before!"

Chapter Fifteen

As her soft hands ripped the veil from her face, Ramses felt his heart splinter. Courage and desperation drove Katherine to unveil. Instead of arousing passion, his seductive words scared her. She thought he'd act like those who had hurt her. But Ramses uttered an awed gasp. Her face in the tomb paled beside the stark beauty now exposed. His fingertips brushed her lips, full and ripe as a fresh pomegranate. Katherine's cheeks were round and soft as he stroked their velvet smoothness. Her small nose had a slight upward tilt. Like an exclamation mark upon her beauty, it accented it. Ramses felt as if he gazed upon a beautiful mirage that would vanish if he blinked.

Then his gaze shot over to the scar. The white slash contrasted with her skin's faint golden tint. He looked at the mark scarring her heart. Then he focused deep into those green eyes. Now he was lost, drowning in a whirlpool of passion dragging him down into a bottomless oasis.

"I am looking at you, Kalila. And what I see is beauty."

Katherine jerked away as he reached out to touch her face. "Don't lie. I'm not a freak of nature, Ramses. I'm a woman. I know I'm ugly. But don't mock me," she cried out.

"I would not do that," he asserted quietly. But her wounds ran too deep. Words would not help. Only a demonstration would.

He gathered Katherine into his arms. Cupping her chin, he tilted her face up. Gently, he brushed his mouth against hers. Giving himself over to her honeyed lips, Ramses felt all control slip. He eagerly sampled her sweetness like a starving man hungering for fruit. Tugging on her glorious masses of hair, he gently prodded her lips, seeking entry. When her tongue shyly met his insistent thrusts, Ramses uttered a deep groan and released her.

His hooded gaze caught hers. "My beautiful Kalila, do you believe me now?" he asked in a voice thick with passion.

She did. Despite her flaws, Ramses thought her beautiful. Katherine's heart beat with love for this man, who rained soft kisses across her scar, dousing heated shame with cooling tenderness. Ramses shone light into her soul's darkest corners and illuminated the beauty she hid deep inside. His shining amber eyes reflected the beautiful woman she longed to be.

His hands curled around her shoulders. "Kalila, I cannot promise much. Not now. But I promise you this. I am your protector. I will protect you always and guard your life as my own. I promise I will keep you safe from all danger."

She puzzled over his enigmatic statement as Ramses's strong hands cradled her face.

"Kalila," he said softly, "You are so beautiful. Give in to your passion and let me love you as you are meant to be loved."

Katherine pulled away, torn by regret. She wanted him, but couldn't go through with this.

"No, Ramses. This is wrong." She struggled against his powerful sensuality, drugging her with need.

Stubble from his cheek abrased her skin as he kissed the corner of her mouth, rubbing against it. "How could it be wrong, little one? Do you want me?"

His fingers laced into her hair, forcing Katherine's head back as he gained access to her throat, nuzzling the slender column with tiny kisses. She bit back a whimper of pleasure. "I can't do this."

"You said you wanted to lose your virginity to prevent marrying your Bedouin," he whispered in her ear. His teeth nipped at the lobe, then he gave it a delicate lick.

"I do. I would do anything to stop the marriage."

Ramses stopped and raised his head. His eyes blazed with possessiveness so intense she shivered. A smile touched his mouth. "Then allow me . . . the supreme honor of being your first," he murmured.

Before she answered, he deftly unbuttoned her shirt, tugging it down. His fingertips brushed naked skin, edging her collarbone's curve. Ramses's touch felt so warm her skin threatened to ignite. She trembled with desire.

Katherine thought about her encounter with the asp and her vow never to trust beautiful, wild creatures unless she was absolutely certain they would not hurt her. Ramses would never hurt her, she realized. She trusted him and longed to surrender to passion.

Her nose wrinkled as she remembered Nazim's long, skinny body and the stringy black hair beneath his white turban. The Bedouin would not inflame her as Ramses did. She craved Ramses and the powerful mystery he promised to unveil with his heated kisses.

Shadows danced across his face. His thumb stroked a gentle caress across her lips, as if seeking answers. When he spoke, his voice rubbed across her sensitive skin like a purring cat. "Show me you want me to love you, sweet Kalila. Take off your clothing."

Taking a deep breath, she showed him by shedding the silk garments. Air caressed her naked skin. Shielding her breasts with trembling hands, Katherine stood before him, praying he'd approve.

"Do not hide yourself, sweet Kalila, for I wish to see all your beauty." Ramses removed her slender wrists, exposing her breasts to his hungry gaze. Amber eyes locked with green ones.

"If I am the Aten, my Kalila, then your beauty is the fire that ignites my core, for you are more radiant than the light of one thousand burning suns."

He kissed her hands with such reverence, she felt like an ancient Egyptian goddess honored by masses of worshippers. But Katherine needed no adoring crowds paying homage. All she needed was Ramses and the stark approval in his amber eyes.

Gentle kisses skipped along her skin as he nuzzled the slender column of her throat. Ramses stopped, giving her a smile filled with seductive promise as he stripped off his trousers. Katherine gulped as her gaze traveled down to the hardness standing straight and proud between his legs. She had seen him naked while nursing him. But that was as a weak, helpless man.

Not weak any longer. Immense warrior's lance no longer suited him. He was . . . magnificent.

She blushed furiously, feeling shy and awkward. "Ramses, I don't know . . . what to do."

He tugged her over to the bed and sat her down. "My darling, I do. I will show you."

A desire to reveal the truth wrestled inside him. *You are mine. I claim you as my bride, sweet Katherine. There will never be anyone else but the two of us, pledged to each other for all eternity.* Ramses longed to open the tomb encasing his heart. But instinct kept it slammed shut. Would she flee if he told her? Ties binding her to Lord Smithfield remained strong. When he claimed Katherine as his, those ties would loosen. Expectation shone in her emerald eyes. He cupped a breast in his palm. His thumb circled the rosy peak of a nipple as it tautened. Katherine flushed as passion darkened her green eyes. Her excitement sent the lusty beast inside him howling.

"Slow," he breathed, removing his hand. "We will go very slow, my little lotus blossom. There is no need to rush."

He wanted Katherine to release the passion he'd sensed when she kissed him at the Shepheard's. His body tightened with anticipation. Aching need flooded him to meld his body into hers, to bury himself deep inside her warm, welcoming heat. Ramses took a controlling breath, concentrating on arousing her. For when he took her, she must be fully prepared to receive him.

Nuzzling her lips, he spoke into her mouth. "You are so sweet, so innocent. Let me teach you about passion, and your body."

His hands slid over her skin like hot velvet, trailing

fire in their wake. Ramses settled them upon her rounded hips, squeezing them gently. "A woman's body is far different from a man's. We were made different, but fashioned to fit perfectly when we come together in love." He guided her hands to his hips. She stroked them, then touched the muscled flatness of his rippled stomach.

"They're much larger than yours," she mused aloud.

"They are meant to be," he said gently. "Your body is designed for bringing forth new life. There is a purpose to the lovely curves of your hips, my darling. Do you see how you are made, how beautiful your body is to me?"

Ramses lifted her hair, kissing her neck nape. "I adore this spot, for it feels like down upon my lips."

As he caressed every inch, her body sparked with warmth. Katherine felt awkward, but instinct directed her to explore. One fingertip traced the deep cleft in his chin. She skimmed his jaw line, then trailed his tanned throat to collarbone and shoulder. She touched the oblong, ugly slash where the bullet had pierced his flesh. Katherine laid her lips against it and tasted the slight salt of his skin. Tears pricked her eyes as she remembered how he almost died. Ramses stroked her hair as she kissed his scar.

Katherine pressed a palm against the silk furring his chest. So different. Hard, like the rock surrounding them. Firm in places she had softness.

"Yes," he purred, "Touch me, Kalila. Are you not curious?"

"Yes," she admitted, running her hands over the gleaming, thick muscles in his arms and shoulders. Such strength, yet he touched her with astounding gentleness. Fire jumped down her body as he cupped

Bonnie Vanak

her breasts. Capturing her mouth, he licked the bottom lip, then bit gently. Katherine whimpered with aching need as his thumbs lazily swirled around her nipples. Her gaze dropped downward to his lap, then up as she met his amused glance. Ramses chuckled softly.

"You have never touched a man there before, have you, little one?"

Ramses guided her hand to the throbbing hardness between his legs. Her fingers curled around the steely thickness. Like his scimitar sheathed in velvet, she thought hazily, stroking its long length. A strangled sound arose from his throat. He removed her hand, kissed the fingertips. His golden eyes filled with a feverish intensity.

"No more, sweet Kalila, for I will surely lose control."

His amber gaze pierced hers with tender regard. As if this was their wedding night. Katherine wished she were his bride. Even though the dawn brought reality, she could dream that tonight he would be hers, forever.

His bride. He would be the first to touch her, to sample her sweetness. Ramses wanted Katherine more than he'd ever wanted the women whose beds he had sought with insouciant abandon. His secret wish during the tattooing rushed back at him. *If only I had my emerald-eyed thief as their mother, I would gladly father sons more numerous than the stars.*

The thought flushed him with possessive tenderness. He gazed at her abdomen's slight curve, imagining it round with his child. A baby, conceived in heated passion. She would be marked as his.

Her voice cut through his heated thoughts, startling him.

"Ramses, what is it? What are you thinking about?"

"You," he answered truthfully.

She had a body suited for love . . . and bearing children. Ramses kissed her, feeling her lips part slightly under the gentle pressure of his. Her sensuality enchanted him. Pushing Katherine gently down on the bed, Ramses stroked her silky skin, working his way down. She arched against him as he caressed the soft thatch of dark curls, and pressed lower. Delicately he slipped one finger inside her woman's passage, delighting in its dewy moistness. Katherine whimpered as he stroked the tender flesh.

A wide smile curved his face. Oh yes, she was most ready. She was wet and tight against him. The thought of burying himself deep inside her drove him crazy with desire. Ramses looked down.

"Your body was fashioned to receive mine, little one. Does this give you pleasure?"

"Yes," she gasped as he stroked, heightening her arousal.

Katherine's excited little cries filled the air with each skillful pass of his fingers. As she arched and thrust her hips up in response to the hot wetness he created, a primitive, male instinct urged him to take her now. He stopped, drew in a controlling breath. Ramses lowered his mouth upon hers, crushing it with a hard, hungry kiss.

Aching with newly awakened need, Katherine slipped her hands behind his neck and surrendered herself to him. He growled as her hands explored the muscles at his nape. Molten heat rushed through her as their tongues coupled in an exotic dance as wild as the one she had performed for him.

He tore his mouth away and trailed fiery kisses upon the most sensitive part of her throat. Katherine whimpered as Ramses's lips danced over her bare flesh, igniting it as if the sun god kissed her skin. His lips settled upon one breast. She felt something warm and deliciously velvet encase the bud as his tongue swirled around it, then he suckled deeply. Katherine whimpered.

"Ramses," she moaned, "I never knew . . . are these the pleasures that a man may give a woman?"

Raising his head, he possessively hooked his hands through her hair and blew a soft breath against her mouth. "A few. I have many more to show you. Warriors of my tribe have a ritual. We call it the secret of one hundred kisses."

Ramses began to demonstrate. He ran the tip of his tongue against her lip's lower curve. Catching it between his teeth, he nipped playfully. The tiger had trapped her with his passion, but she willingly walked into the cage. Katherine entangled her fingers in his long satin locks, wanting only to ensnare herself further in his embrace.

"The secret of one hundred kisses is well known among our warriors," he whispered, kissing the corner of her mouth. "It is a display of a warrior's true prowess."

She gasped as he licked and kissed the valley between her breasts with possessive intent. His touch was light, assured and burned like the searing sun. Katherine's fingers tightened around his marbled shoulders as his mouth claimed her. Ribs, belly, the soft underside of her breasts did not escape his fevered kisses, chased by swirls of his tongue. Ramses did not know much about coaxing rhythm from surfaces. He played her like the drum, every beat in cadence to her heart's rhythm, forcing her to meet his pace.

She arched her back as he licked the edges of her navel, and threatened to dip lower. Katherine managed to connect vocal cords to thought.

"And, uh, what is the secret of the one hundredth kiss?"

He lifted his head and gave that dangerous smile of his. Fire blazed in his golden eyes. His hands caressed her soft thighs, easing them wide open. Ramses gazed at her sex with an intent look that exhilarated and scared her. She drew back, a little afraid. His expression softened. "Do not be afraid, little lotus blossom, it will not hurt you."

Then he lowered his head to that hidden place no man ever touched before and claimed it for his own with the one hundredth kiss.

Katherine's fingers gripped the sheets tightly as scorching heat raged through her. Ramses was wrong, for his tugging lips and tongue's skilled swirls filled her with the exquisite agony of molten pleasure. Straining with need, she writhed as he licked and kissed and loved her with his mouth. Hot velvet rasped across her feminine softness, faster and firmer as she thrust her hips up in response. Katherine moaned from the sweet torment inflicted by his ravaging mouth. The pleasure was so intense, it felt almost painful.

"Please, Ramses . . ."

He lifted his head and chuckled. "Do not fight it, sweet Kalila. Relax, let this sun god worship you as you so richly deserve."

*   *   *

She was so slight, fragile and delicate. So small, like a dream. He drank deeply from the fountain of her sweet innocence. Thirst ravaged his soul as he sampled her, as pure and refreshing as the crystalline waters of a bubbling spring. Ramses's tongue swirled around her tender, rosy skin. He felt her satin thighs move upward as his hands compressed them into the bed. Not yet. Determined to bring her to passion's peak before claiming his full possession of her, he continued. His lovely Kalila responded to his teasing touch, the sweet juices flowing like thick, succulent syrup.

The sweet intensity increased. Pleasure mounted, the throbbing in her loins drumming much as Ramses had drummed upon the *darrubuka*. Her body tensed, and she grew stiff as the taut skin on the drum. Fire swept throughout her body with such intensity she didn't know if she could bear it. She gasped, feeling the smoldering flames build.

"Ramses," she grasped his shoulders, "Oh, oh . . ." Katherine cried out his name, bucking and writhing as the inferno consumed her. Ramses gave one last soothing kiss, staying with her, then raised his head and planted one tiny kiss on each parted thigh. He slid up and drew her into his arms, kissing her deeply. Katherine tasted the nectar of her own desire upon his lips. Then his big body covered her. She welcomed his weight as he stretched her arms above her head.

This was the moment he had waited for since she innocently kissed him in the hotel. His loins, brought to a heightened state, cried for release. Ramses felt a flush of possessive pride that he would be her first.

In a husky voice trembling with passion, he uttered

the Guardian wedding night vows in ancient Egyptian. "My beloved wife, I can no longer wait to make you mine. My love, let us join together now and become as one body, our spirits mating together, for all eternity."

Though she didn't understand what he said, Katherine sensed the ritualistic words were more than a lover's whispered ardor. As Ramses positioned himself between her parted thighs, a finger of fear stroked her spine. He pressed into her, easing partly inside. She gasped at the thick fullness of him. He slowly moved forward again, withdrew. Her fingers curled tightly around his. Ramses whispered a command to look at him. As she locked her emerald gaze to his amber one, he thrust forward. Burning pain shot through her as he breached the barrier of innocence. He captured her cry with his mouth.

"Relax, little one," he whispered against her mouth. "Lie still. It is done." He showered gentle kisses down her left cheek.

Katherine saw Ramses looking down with tender concern. Veins in his neck bulged as his muscles tensed. His nostrils flared as if he exerted tremendous physical restraint. Awe spilled through her, diminishing physical discomfort. Judging from his intent look, Katherine sensed this was not mere lovemaking to Ramses. Her spirit felt merged with his as their bodies joined. She had melted into him so that they entangled so closely, she could not tell where one began and the other ended. Overcome with the intensity of the moment, she began to weep.

Ramses kissed a tear trickling from the corner of her eye. Masculine pride that he claimed her as his own mingled with aching regret at causing her pain.

He murmured soothing endearments, gently licking salt water from her cheeks. Her feminine passage clenched around him, encasing him with hot wetness. He controlled his breathing, feeling the beast in him wanting to thrust deep inside. But her fingers curling tightly around his cautioned him to go slowly.

In all his lovemaking with women, he had never felt such overwhelming tenderness mixed with raging passion. It was as if his Ieb, his heart, had left his body and twined with hers, mating as their bodies now mated. A primitive, possessive instinct filled him to begin a new life in her womb.

He withdrew slowly and slid into her again. Releasing her hands, he braced his palms on either side of her. Katherine's muscles lost their tension. Holding her gaze with his, he eased slowly out, then penetrated her inch by slow inch. The tight warmth of her felt incredible. She raised her hips to meet him in inexperienced, instinctive thrusts. Soft hands pressed into his buttocks, urging him deeper inside. Ramses wanted to howl with triumph as he pumped his hips forward in deep, penetrating thrusts. The beast, freed at last, ran into the night, panting with the pleasure of unrestrained freedom. He could take Katherine again and again and never sate his raging hunger for her.

As her tiny muscles stretched to meet his deep thrusts, his movements took on a new urgency. He increased the pace, surging into her with raging need.

"Beautiful mate of my heart," he said softly in ancient Egyptian. "I am your Guardian of the Ages, sworn to protect and defend you unto my dying days. We are one now, my flesh joined to yours. My spirit mated to yours for all eternity. My heart melting into yours. Nothing will ever separate us."

With a mighty roar, like that of a imprisoned tiger freed at last, Ramses raised his head, crying out, "Kal-ila, my beloved!" as his passion came to fulfillment and he filled her with his seed.

Chapter Sixteen

Never had he experienced such utter satisfaction, a feeling leaving him languid and relaxed, easing his warrior's awareness. He had finally found his spring of life, drunk from it and slaked the nagging, relentless thirst. Ramses felt as if he had finished wandering in the arid desert and discovered his oasis of eternal refreshment.

His beloved Katherine left him full and content. Ramses stirred, stretching with languid ease, relishing the feel of his powerful muscles returning to normal strength. He felt content to lie beside her, feel her plump softness curve into his body.

"You are mine now, Kalila. I will never let you go," he said quietly in ancient Egyptian.

He gently pulled her into the protective embrace of his sheltering arms. Ramses massaged her scalp, relishing the silkiness of her long curls.

She was destined to be his, body and soul, for eternity, mated to his heart. Aching tenderness and fierce protectiveness for her flooded his senses. He only wanted to shield Katherine from the world, guard her from all the cruelties and pain others had inflicted. If he could, he would tuck her away in this cave, like a precious amulet of purest gold, away from those who harmed her.

Splaying one hand against her belly, he thought of how they shared their bodies. He kissed the skin there tenderly. What would a child of theirs be like? A son, of course, he'd want a son to follow in his footsteps and take the Guardian oath. But a little girl as well, one like his Kalila who giggled and had haunting green eyes. He closed his eyes, envisioning singing stories of the desert, tucking her into bed and kissing her forehead.

He could not decide which one he wanted. Perhaps they had conceived him or her tonight. The thought filled Ramses with so much tenderness his heart wanted to burst. He settled his mouth against the slight rise of her abdomen and began to sing.

"Ramses, what are you doing?" Katherine sounded amused.

I am singing to our baby. He continued crooning against her sweet skin.

He had lost his heart to Katherine. He came to the deep desert to cleanse his soul and prepare his spirit for his marriage. And here he had discovered his Ieb, his heart, hidden away in a cave, like a jewel discovered deep within the earth.

He would fall on his sword to protect and defend her. And Katherine could use that sword to cut him to ribbons, for she had already stated a desire to lose her bridegroom. Would she love him as he loved her if she knew he was her "old, Bedouin goatherd." Was she so deeply entrenched in English culture that she would reject him and everything Egyptian?

Ramses felt deep sorrow at this. He stopped singing, envisioning her eyes hardening to chips of green ice when he swept Katherine away to his people. But he could not think that tonight. Tonight was for magic, woven by his enchanting little lotus blossom. Tonight was for dreams, to dream of the babe they might have created. Tonight was for love, even if he had to pretend she shared it with him.

Katherine listened to the beautiful melody her lover sang against her skin. Never had she met a man so virile and masculine, yet so gentle. Her heart flooded with love. He stopped his song, shimmied up the bed and settled her head against his furred chest. She snuggled against him, listening to the steady, reassuring beat of Ramses's heart. In his strong, protective embrace, she could forget all worry and fear. Katherine smiled and shifted her legs, giving a small, involuntary yelp as the soreness between them stung.

She felt him stir. "You are still in pain . . . I have almost forgotten something. Stay here."

A protest rose from her lips, but he laid a finger across them as he left the bed. Bringing a small bowl of water and a clean soft cloth, he knelt at her side. He wet the cloth, wrung it and then parted her thighs. Shocked, she felt cool, wetness caress her flesh as her lover bathed the blood from her with a gentle, loving hand.

"Ramses, this is . . . too intimate!" she protested.

"Shhhh, it is not. Let me care for you. This is a tradition among my people. Only we use herbs to ease the pain. But I cannot find the herbs I need."

He stopped his tender ministrations, then laid next

to her, gathering her into his arms. Ramses kissed her and began softly singing. His soothing melody and the protective strength of his sheltering arms lulled her into drowsiness. He ceased singing, kissed her hair and buried his face into it.

Her eyes fluttered shut and images of their shared passion danced before her. They shifted. Darker images emerged.

A tomb, sinister and deep, waiting to claim her.

Katherine stirred in her sleep, pressing against the sarcophagus's lid as it closed over her screaming face.

Chapter Seventeen

The murky tomb enclosing her body shattered into bits as Katherine awoke with a start. Trembling, she rubbed her eyes, brushing away sticky cobwebs of fear-ridden sleep. Rose-gold ribbons of daylight threaded their way into the cave. She raised herself on her elbows to regard Ramses, desperate for the comfort of his big, solid body. He still slept, his left arm hooked above his head, cradling his face. Sensual lips that had created such rivers of delight parted slightly as he breathed. Her eyes focused on the dimple clefting his strong chin. Katherine stroked his thick hair, marveling at its satin texture. He looked so defenseless and adorable. The sheet lay tangled about his hips, showing the broad expanse of his chest and the assorted scars carved there. One foot poked out from beneath the sheet. She curled her body to the firm contours of his, wanting to bury herself into him.

She needed him awake, his strong arms wrapped around her to soothe away the terrifying dream of being buried alive. Mischief coursed through her. Katherine eased out of bed and knelt at the edge. She rubbed her forefinger across his exposed foot. He rolled over, groaned. She frowned. Tickled some more.

"Wake up, my darling. This is your early morning wake-up tickle," she murmured.

Ramses thrashed, kicked out, but she playfully bent down and lightly bit his ankle. Sheets flew aside with lightning speed. Naked, he scrambled down the length of the bed and hooked his hands around her waist. She felt herself lifted up as if in the clutches of a powerful bird of prey. As he turned her over his knees, she squealed and wriggled, but he held fast. He lightly swatted her round bottom. Katherine giggled and writhed.

"Let me go!" she protested with a laugh.

"Not until I punish you for waking me," he growled back, delivering another gentle smack. Then she felt his mouth administer a soft kiss there instead.

"Ramses!" she said, laughing.

He answered with another growl, and lightly bit her, chasing it with a delicious swirl of his tongue.

His arms lifted her once more and tumbled her on her back onto the bed. Ramses searched her face. "I am awake now. And hungry. But not for food," he purred in a predatory voice. Gold flecks in his eyes darkened. Dark eyebrows wiggled impishly with the implied threat of pleasure.

Shivering with anticipation, Katherine tried wriggling away but he pounced and straddled her. Capturing her wrists above her head, he brushed kisses against her breast, rousing her with delicate caresses of his tongue.

Katherine melted into a puddle of sheer longing.

She squirmed as the pleasure mounted. Her hips responded to his call, thrusting up as he sought her breast. Ramses suckled and tugged gently, teasing her with expert little flicks of his tongue. She whimpered, needing him inside her. Releasing her wrists, he kneaded her breasts in gentle squeezes. A soft smile touched her lips at his ragged breaths. Ramses was equally affected by their lovemaking.

He nuzzled the curve of her throat, kissing each inch slowly as if savoring her. His touch became a luminescent dance chasing away the nightmare's frightening darkness. Katherine snaked arms around his neck, relishing the musky scent of their passion, clutching him as if he were a marbled column of strength.

"Ramses. Please don't let go of me," she whispered.

The soft, hot kisses stopped. His hands cupped her face, bringing it close to his. "What is wrong?"

Memories of the nightmare surfaced. She shuddered, unable to express the dread snaking through her. His touch on her cheeks felt soothing, as though he could press the evil shadows away with his heated fingertips.

"A bad dream, little one?"

Katherine nodded. Ramses sat up, looking concerned. The hard muscles of his arms bunched as he flexed his biceps as if to duel with the forces inhabiting her subconscious. He looked so strong and powerful and protective she believed he could defeat his enemies with one single blow. Then she remembered. Her trembling palm touched his arm. She was his enemy, the one who committed a crime against his people. How could she possibly expect this man to protect her?

* * *

Ramses ran a thumb across his lower lip. He wanted her now. His body pounded with need, but he contained his arousal with rigid self-discipline. Other matters took precedence. Something had frightened her in the depths of sleep. An urgent desire to protect her overwhelmed him so much he trembled inside. Ramses flexed his powerful muscles, wishing for a physical enemy to battle. Far easier to defeat them than the unseen demons torturing Kalila. She was so small and fragile, his heart ached to hold her and never let go.

His natural inclination to fight for her struggled with caution about unanswered questions. He swore an oath to guard Katherine, but how could he protect her when she refused to reveal the threat? A low growl of frustration rose deep in his throat. He needed her under his complete control to keep her safe and that meant getting answers.

If he gained her confidence, she might open up. Ramses raked a hand through his hair, thinking hard. He had awakened her sensuality by introducing her to the pleasures a man and woman shared. Perhaps the same could convince her to trust him. Implicitly. Katherine had bared the most painful part of her soul when she uncloaked her scar. He wondered if he could take it one step further. Ramses traced her lips with a forefinger.

"Kalila, if you let fear rule your emotions, it can paralyze you. I know this from experience," he asserted.

"I can't help how I feel," she protested.

"But you can control it. Trust me. I know how to do this. Would you like me to teach you?"

She shot him a sideways glance. "I am not a warrior, Ramses. I can't be as brave as you are."

His short bark of laughter made her brow furrow. "You think because I am a Khamsin warrior, my birthright gives me courage?" His gaze flicked away, then met hers again. He drew a deep breath and she sensed he was about to reveal something of great importance. A secret of his own.

"Kalila, when we were sealed in the tomb and you extinguished the torch, I asked you not to leave." His hands fisted until she could see the knuckles whiten. "I asked you not to leave not because I needed your silence about the tomb. I did so because . . . because I was afraid."

Katherine watched him, deeply moved at his courage to confess what must be a painful admission.

"When I was six, I was left tied up in my tribe's sacred cave that hides our water source. For six hours . . . with the body of one of our warriors who had just died. When I finally emerged, I was paralyzed with fear of all dark, enclosed spaces. Especially tombs."

"Oh Ramses! Who would do this to you?"

He studied her narrowed eyes, immensely relieved she did not laugh at him. The protective anger in her voice filled him with tenderness. "Only my best friend, Jabari. Our tribe has an ancient tradition honoring warriors who die bravely by bringing their bodies to the sacred cave to lie in state for a full day. My people believe the warrior's spirit lingers and blesses the cave before going on to Paradise. Jabari's mother was giving birth. I kept bragging to Jabari about how Khamsin Guardians are born in the cave to endow us with the power of these courageous warriors. Jabari brought me there and tied me up, taunting that I needed more of the special powers and I should receive them directly from the source."

She stared at him with wide eyes. "He left you alone for six hours with a dead man in the dark? How cruel!"

He gave an indifferent shrug. "He did not mean to leave me there, but forgot when he visited his mother and the new baby. But fear restricted me. Khamsin Guardians are taught to sequester themselves in caves for short periods of time for meditation. I knew if I did not at least learn to control my fear of caves, I would fail in my duty."

"How did you do this?"

Ramses touched her nose, pleased with the interest she displayed. "Meditation and breathing. By controlling my breathing, I learned to harness my fear. I can sink into a deep, meditative trance and lower my respiration to the point where I require little air."

"That's why you were meditating in the tomb?"

"Yes." A wry grin touched his lips. "I had it fully controlled until you put out the torch."

Her large green eyes widened. "I'm sorry," she told him.

"Do not apologize. It was an excellent tactic to escape. A warrior's move. I would have done the same," he said, smiling.

Ramses patted the space next to him. "Sit up. I will show you how to meditate." For the next several minutes, he taught her to inhale through the nostrils, listening to the sound her lungs made emptying and filling. Then he grasped her delicate wrists.

"Kalila," he said softly, "I want to try something different. Do not be alarmed. It means you must trust me."

225

Doubt blossomed in her face. Throat muscles clenched as she swallowed convulsively. Katherine gave him a brave smile and nodded. Unable to prevent touching her, he swept a hand through her hair, massaging the scalp. "Are you certain?"

Another nod, this one more vehement.

He touched her lips to his, then drew back. Ramses fetched five silk scarves. He brought them back to the bed and instructed her to lie back. Katherine obeyed. Ramses put two gentle fingertips on her eyelids, forcing them closed. He kissed her tenderly, then fixed a scarf over her eyes, then looped scarves around her wrists. He tied the scarves to the bed's metal legs. Not a tremble flickered across her body as he repeated the same with her ankles.

"Are you all right?"

"Fine." Her voice quivered, but she smiled. He hesitated. Perhaps this proved too much. Again he asked if she wanted this. She nodded. He gathered the necessary items, talking to her in soothing tones all the while.

"Khamsin warriors undergo initiation at age thirteen. One of the tests is to trust our brethren. Initiates are blindfolded and led through the tunnel of scimitars. They must rely on the hand that guides them lest they stumble against the sharp blades," he said softly as he settled onto the bed.

She drew in a quivering breath. Fear touched her heart, despite intuition that he only wanted to help. "Does this mean you're going to wave a sword in front of my face?"

His light laugh chased away fear. "I have something much more pleasurable in mind for you," he murmured. "Open your mouth."

Her mouth parted. Something wrinkled and soft slipped inside. She felt the rough pads of his fingertips brush against her bottom lip as he closed it.

"Taste this, my darling, for it is sweet as the freshness of rain, but it sours next to the nectar of your lips."

Her tongue probed the strange object, recognizing it as a date. Katherine ate it. As her tongue eased out to lick her lips, he touched it with his, then drew it into his mouth. Ramses deepened the kiss, drinking her, consuming her with thoughts of nothing but his sheer power.

He tore his lips from hers. Her skin felt like soft lotus petals as his hands explored each curve of her body. Burning heat filled him as he tightened with need to claim her once again. He wanted her, but Ramses drew a deep breath and controlled himself. Drizzling honey over his tongue, he lowered his mouth to hers. His tongue probed the closed seam of her lips. As they parted in invitation, he licked her tongue. She suckled on him with demanding insistence, tasting him.

Deprived of sight, she used other senses to explore. His scent filled her, spices and musky skin. Hot breath warmed her cheek as Ramses's lips touched her earlobe, whispering delightful promises of what he planned to do. A soft gasp escaped her as he began to demonstrate. Katherine moaned as his teeth skimmed the surface of her neck, seeking her pulse. Ramses nibbled and kissed, then gave a delicate lick. He cupped a breast possessively, thumbing the nipple, teasing it to tautness.

She felt his hands leave her body and tilted her head to hear what he planned next. A drop of warm stickiness fell upon the hollow of her neck. Warm lips fastened to that spot in a heated kiss. Then his tongue swept the honey away in swirls that made her pulse pound. Katherine arched her back in an unspoken plea. Another dollop dribbled onto her shoulder. More caresses with his tongue followed. When the honey landed with sticky softness on her breast, Katherine writhed against the bonds holding her, filled with sweet anticipation. Her body grew rigid with fiery pleasure as he kissed and licked, swirling his tongue around her nipple, then suckled deeply. He trailed every inch of her skin in scorching kisses and warm honey until her body screamed for release and her breath came in ragged pants.

"Please," she begged.

"Please what? Do you want me to stop?" he asked softly, nuzzling her earlobe.

Numb, she whispered for him to continue. A light laugh caressed her ears as he slid a hand up her leg, then retreated in a teasing caress. Drizzling honey over the inside of her thighs, he licked it off with slow, deliberate strokes. Katherine strained, desperate for his touch as his mouth ventured near that place she longed for him to kiss. When he finally landed on the soft petals of her feminine core, pleasure exploded all around her. Katherine cried out as she shook from the force of it, her heart beating wildly.

She sensed a dark, dangerous might to him, a breathless eagerness and burning need as he suddenly untied her bonds. Ramses lifted her into his arms and placed her on the floor. Katherine gripped his arms as her knees threatened to buckle.

"Bend over the mattress." His voice was gentle and reassuring, but she sensed the power and command emanating from him. Katherine hesitated, a shaft of natural fear slicing through need. Ramses lifted her hair and dropped a kiss on her neck nape.

"Do not be afraid," he reassured her as she obeyed. His hands roamed over her bottom, kneading gently, then dipping into her cleft, massaging her. Katherine whimpered with need. Ramses grasped her hips and she cried out as he thrust into her with sudden force. He was so huge, hot and throbbing, stretching her to the limits of endurance. Wrapping an arm around her, he caressed her tender bud. Katherine cried out as her fingers curled around the bed sheets. Ramses and his golden warrior's might flooded every pore as he penetrated deeply. Lifting her hair, he nuzzled her neck, then nipped the soft flesh like a tiger claiming its mate. Erotic pleasure shot through her as he suckled her skin.

His hips pumped into her, the mattress cushioning her against the force of his powerful thrusts. She felt the waves of hard, hot desire crest once more and smash down into explosive ecstasy as her cries of release mingled with his.

Several minutes later, her heart finally settled into a normal cadence. Still blindfolded, Katherine lay in languid ease on the bed. The bed sagged beside her. His hand captured her chin, tilting it up.

"Do you trust me, Kalila? Do you know now I will never hurt you?"

"Yes," she told him, unsure of his intent.

"Then tell me who is threatening you."

Katherine jerked up, yanked off the blindfold, now damp with sweat. "I can't," she whimpered. "I just can't. Stop asking me. Just stop asking me!"

A mixture of disappointment and pity flickered over

his face. Sweat glistened on the hard curves of his muscles. Ramses captured her face in his hands. Worry clouded his amber irises, along with some dark emotion she couldn't read.

"Kalila, please tell me why are you so scared." His quiet voice brushed across her raw nerves, soothing them.

Her face paled. Dark shadows pooled beneath her beautiful green eyes. Ramses swore under his breath, ready to take his scimitar and slay those who endangered her. He could not. Not unless she told him what threatened her.

"My darling, I am your protector. I need you to trust me with all your heart and soul, for I have something to tell you. But I need answers. Who is terrifying my beautiful Kalila?"

"Please," she whimpered, pulling him down to her. "No more questions. I'm scared, Ramses, and I need you."

Her soft plea shredded his heart into ragged strips. Ramses swallowed frustration and gathered Katherine into his arms, as if his embrace could erase her fear.

She thought of how Burrells threatened to kill her sweet Osiris. He would do the same to Papa. The thought became too much to bear and she started to cry. Katherine buried her face into his chest. Once she had told Ramses on a busy Cairo street she had no use for a woman's tears. Now she proved herself weak.

He knew her pride and exactly how much it cost her to weep in his arms. Katherine laid her head on his chest and sobbed pitifully. Saying nothing, he continued stroking her thick, silky hair, humming a soothing tune. He loved her, his Katherine. Sobs finally died down to quiet hiccups. Ramses fetched a clean linen cloth. Handing it over, he caressed her hair as she wiped away tears.

Sitting her up, Ramses drew Katherine against him. With gentle hands he worked tension from her slender shoulders. He could tell his massage would work its soothing magic. Laying her down, he yanked the blanket up and kissed her lips. Gentle fingertips brushed against Katherine's eyelids.

"No more bad dreams, little one. Sleep and I will watch over you."

Chapter Eighteen

Silence shrouded her heart. Katherine shut her book of herbal recipes. Days had drifted by, filled with heated lovemaking and thin silence. He asked no more questions about what terrified her. She offered no answers. Ramses was tender and passionate, yet the stone barrier of secrets between them never dropped. Katherine went outside, wishing she could confide in her lover. But she didn't dare.

Ramses sat on a shady patch of sand. A basket of dried figs, a jar of honey and flatbread she had baked sat before him on a blanket. His brow furrowed with concentration as he carved a beautiful piece of olive wood. She sat, silently watching his nimble fingers create a sculpture from the red, pigmented grain. He glanced up, smiled and murmured good morning.

Transfixed by his intent look, she touched his lips, tracing their fullness, feeling the warm velvet surface part. His eyes not leaving hers, Ramses opened his mouth further. That delicious tongue slowly flicked over her finger. Then he smiled and offered a dried fig. She nibbled on one.

"Do you carve often?"

Ramses gave her a sideways glance. "Often I carve trinkets for friends and family. Olive wood is the best." He held up the shapeless round object. "Such an exotic wood, it possesses a life of its own, breathing like a living animal. The wood's pattern is hidden deep within the tree's heart. Olive wood is fluid like the Nile and just as deep and mysterious."

Smiling, he continued carving.

"What are you making?"

A gentle finger tapped her nose. "You will see. Do not be so impatient, little lotus blossom. Works of art take time."

Katherine finished the fig and licked her lips. He watched, setting down the dagger. Hunger dawned deep in those dark amber irises. A shiver of anticipation inched up her spine.

He wanted her again. Her gaze swept up the long length of him. She wanted him, too.

"Have you practiced your meditation, Kalila?"

She nodded. He touched her nose again.

"Perhaps we should test it to make sure you are doing the breathing method correctly." The flash of impish mischief warned her the test might involve something other than breathing. Ramses stood and led her inside the cave.

They sat on the bed as he instructed her to begin. When she became fully absorbed in the pattern of long, deep inhalations, he gently pushed her backward, tugging off her clothing, then his own. Ramses kissed the long curve of her throat, then drifted down to a breast. As his mouth teased the tender bud to pearl-like rigidness, her breathing quickened. Ramses lifted his head, spoke softly.

"No, sweet Kalila. Keep concentrating. Do not interrupt the pattern of your breathing."

She nodded, and resumed the rhythm. Satin curls slipped through his fingers as he tangled them in the long masses of her hair. Ramses straddled her body and continued delivering hot, hungry kisses to her tender flesh, relishing the salty taste of her skin. Once or twice, her breathing quickened, but she quickly resumed the pattern. His hands cupped her rounded bottom, squeezing and kneading. Katherine's thigh muscles bunched as she spread her legs open for him. Ramses murmured a tender order to relax and let him love her. He angled himself between her legs. Her breathing pattern changed into low gasps of pleasure as he teased, stroked and caressed her. Low moans rose from deep in her throat. But he had no intention of fulfilling her pleasure now.

"Breathe, sweet lotus blossom, continue to follow the sounds of your own breaths," he instructed.

As she complied, he angled his throbbing shaft at her entrance. His mouth descended on hers in a consuming kiss, swallowing her breath as he slid into her. Ramses broke the kiss and lavished her with a tender smile as her eyes widened with surprised pleasure. She opened to him like a tender lotus blossom greeting the sun, her warm wetness tightly sheathing him. He withdrew and slid back again, creating a pattern to match the slow, deep inhalations she took. Deliberately he positioned himself to rub against the most sensitive part of her feminine core. Katherine's eyes darkened and a rosy flush lit her cheeks. A vein pulsed wildly in her neck, but she controlled her breathing.

Katherine focused on breathing as scorching pleasure flamed her body. As he thrust deeply into her, flames laved her body. His heated gaze captured hers as he laced his fingers through her hands. Sweat glistened on his brow. Bronzed muscles of his shoulders bunched and rippled as Ramses drove into her with deep, hard strokes. This was true magic, an enchantment never imagined, a spell he wove with every movement against him. The pleasure mounted into a roaring crescendo. Katherine forgot to breathe as it splintered her, exploding like thousands of crystal shards. And she heard her own name called out in wild cries of ecstasy as his heat matched hers and the magic burst into thousands of points of sunlight inside the cave.

He fell atop her, gasping for air. Ramses buried his face into her hair then raised his head. Two large emerald jewels held his gaze. Worried about the shimmering of moisture in her eyes, Ramses dropped a kiss on her cheek. "My little lotus blossom, did I hurt you?"

"No, Ramses. I'm crying because I'm so happy." She gave a choked whisper, smiling through a veil of tears. Katherine grasped his neck and dragged his head down to meet her hungry lips. When she released him, her emerald eyes sparked with mischief.

"But I can't be certain I have my breathing right. Maybe we should try it again?"

Hot blood surged through his veins at the hope in her eyes. Ramses sought Katherine's lips with fierce hunger, eager to comply with her wish.

Chapter Nineteen

Tomorrow he must take her back to his people.

Katherine snuggled into his arms. Her loveliness radiated through the cave with glowing warmth. Closing his eyes, he remembered others were returning for her. They must leave tomorrow, before those who would harm her returned. Alone, he could not defend her against men desiring the tomb's gold. And her father? Anger tore his insides with ragged claws. He presented the greatest danger, for Katherine would feel compelled to obey him. Although he had bound her to him by joining their bodies, he needed to legalize the union. Once they married, her father had no claim on her.

They would have to travel by day, but Katherine was young and strong. She had much to learn about becoming a Khamsin wife. He would teach her. Ramses thought about this. He would be gentle but firm with his lovely Katherine. He sighed. She would not go quietly. He anticipated a fight.

* * *

Katherine's stubborn streak surfaced like a rearing stallion when he told her he was leaving and taking her with him.

Burrells probably was already on his way. Rivulets of fear ran down her spine as she thought of the curator's angry reaction when he found she'd left. He might even hire someone to kill her father. Katherine knew she must show him the gold taken from the tomb as proof she'd found it.

"I do not wish to go." She thrust out her chin. Let him try to drag her from here. Ramses cared only to whisk her away and take the tomb's secret with him.

Now his eyes became hard chips of gold. "I must return to my camp and I will not leave you here with my tribe's secrets to spill to those who would steal from the Khamsin," he said. She recognized that quiet tone laced with decisive command, but ignored it.

"You would force a woman?"

He eyed her red silk trousers and flimsy yellow shirt. Ramses dug into the bag containing her clothing and withdrew a cotton shirt, trousers and an ankle-length navy *kuftan* with slits up to the thigh. Next he removed a length of white cotton.

"We shall cross the desert during the day. You will need to change. The thin shirt is tight and worn first to keep perspiration close to your body, for if you lose too much moisture, you will dehydrate. The dark *kuftan* draws up the heat from the ground and allows it to escape through the top. The white cloth is wrapped around your head against the sun."

"I'm not wearing that," she stated, folding her arms.

He smiled slowly and set the garments down. She backed away from the calculating look of that smile. Ramses stepped forward and withdrew his dagger. Before her astonished eyes, he easily cut her clothing off, leaving her totally nude.

"This is how Khamsin warriors make stubborn women obey," he said in a mocking tone, reminding her of how she'd poured the medicine down his throat. "Now you have no choice, except if you want to ride across the desert naked. I do not recommend it."

Glaring, she picked up the clothing and dressed, watching as he packed several items. She could hold out until Burrells arrived. Ramses could not force her, even though he was bigger than she was. . . .

Ramses advanced. "Will you go willingly, Kalila?"

"I will not go at all," she declared.

She shrieked as he scooped her over his shoulder and went outside. Katherine beat at the broad, impassive back that seemed impenetrable to blows rained upon it. He was much too strong, and her feeble struggles seemed like the impotent protests of a mouse caught in a cat's paws. Setting her on her feet, he fashioned a turban around her head from the white linen, draped the trailing end across her face, and lifted her onto the camel.

Ramses veiled his face with his turban's edge, showing only his eyes, fringed by long, dark lashes and arched black brows. Somehow it made him look mysterious, dangerous and exotic. She wondered if her own veil did the same.

Two cool amber eyes met hers as he grasped her chin and peered at her. "Will you sit here quietly or do I have to tie you to the saddle?"

No answer but a baleful glare. Ramses lifted his brows. He took a slim cord from his belt and went to loop it around her waist. Katherine recognized defeat.

"You don't have to tie me," she mumbled.

A curt nod greeted her words. Ramses took a charcoal pencil and Katherine's small hand mirror. He outlined his eyes with the kohl, making the amber irises stand out against the black. Now his eyes appeared larger and even more predatory.

"The kohl cuts the sun's glare this time of year when crossing the desert for long distances. Our ancestors used it." He beckoned to her.

"Close your eyes." When she refused, he heaved a deep sigh. "Kalila, you will regret it if I do not use the kohl. Trust me."

Trust him? He was a man of the desert and knew such things. She obeyed, closing her eyes. Ramses gently traced the lids with the pencil. When he told her to open them, he held up the mirror. The green irises were huge. She looked as Egyptian as an ancient princess.

He put the mirror and pencil away, climbed on in back of her, clucked to the camel as it stood. Tied to the back of the beast was her camel, carrying supplies.

Katherine willed her turbulent rage and frustration to calm while she thought of a plan. They would stop. And when they did, she would run away. Remains of an old Roman fortress sat impassively as they passed.

"Where are we going?" she asked, hopeful he'd clue her on their direction.

"My tribe's camp," came the short answer.

Katherine peered at the ground, mentally gauging landmarks so she would remember the return route. "How far is that?"

"From here, a few days' journey."

"Are we headed west?" she asked hopefully.

"North."

Her distress mounted. North. Not crossing the desert, but traveling its length. At least five days or more in this heat? Could she manage the return voyage? Katherine wasn't even certain she wouldn't shrivel into a crisp for the initial journey. Determined to keep her spirits up, she fell silent, eyeing every rock, looking desperately for marks to distinguish them.

After riding a while, Ramses executed a series of maneuvers. He rode a short distance down one canyon, reversed his tracks so he came out the same way, then took another route. The third time he traveled a short distance and then jumped off, leaving Katherine and taking her camel. He returned a while later.

She eyed him with suspicion. "What were you doing?"

"Covering our tracks. Now if anyone tries to follow us, there is a broken trail." He grinned at the disappointment in her eyes. His move also eliminated tracks Katherine could trace back to the cave if she escaped. Not that he'd allow that, he amended as he mounted the camel and settled Katherine firmly before him.

Ramses hummed a tune as they set off. He wrapped one arm around her waist. The camel's gentle swaying back and forth soothed him. Mounds of black rock passed by as they pressed north. Sun hammered down at them with pounding fists. After an hour, he reached up and placed a hand on Katherine's throat, checking her pulse. It beat with a steady rhythm. Excellent. Hopes soared, along with his spirit. Perhaps the journey wouldn't tax her that much. Ramses let his hand rest on the lovely curve of her throat. The big vein throbbed beneath the pads of his fingertips. He gently squeezed her waist and rubbed the underside of one breast, enjoying the sensation. Now her pulse beat faster.

He swallowed, removed his hand. Enough heat existed in the desert without him adding more. He could only pray that she proved as sturdy as her spirit and would make the trek without any undue stress. Strong men died here. He vowed he would do all he could to protect her. But his Katherine possessed a stubborn determination. Ramses had no doubt she'd flee as soon as the opportunity presented itself.

Katherine's throat ached with thirst as they stopped for a short rest. Ramses had given her a goatskin bag filled with water. She pretended to drink as he did, but swallowed little. Sweat soaked her clothing, but true to Ramses's word, layers next to her body kept perspiration close. Katherine closed her eyes against the burning sun.

Conserving water, even in this heat, was more important, for she needed a supply for the escape back. Although he stopped at wells scattered here and there to fill extra water bags, she could not guarantee finding them. Katherine gazed at the jagged rocks sheltering them, the pebbled sand where he had stretched out a small blanket. She needed to escape and do whatever she could to save her father.

They traveled for three days, pressing onward in the burning sun at a pace that would test many warriors. Katherine made no complaint, sat quietly and said little. Ramses felt torn between needing to reach home as quickly as possible and giving her frequent rest stops from the relentless heat. When she tried escaping during one of those breaks, he decided to travel more at night to provide relief from the heat.

At night he spread out a bedroll on the sand to sleep.

Ramses curled his body protectively around Katherine. Sensing she would escape, he had removed the risk by using an old Khamsin warrior trick and tying her waist to his. During the day he had sung, hummed and even told her a story about his tribe, reasoning that she needed to learn these things when they married. Katherine did not respond. His warrior's instincts honed fully now, Ramses did not trust his betrothed. Something else equally disturbed him. Katherine began exhibiting signs of dehydration, despite the numerous sips of water she took. Ramses noticed she did not excuse herself to retreat to the rocks for privacy as frequently as she should. In fact, her trips to the rocks dwindled to twice a day. This, a classic sign of dehydration, worried him. Her body stored water instead of eliminating it.

He turned over on his back, staring up at the glittering stars coating the sky. Ramses glanced at the woman beside him whose beauty shone like a diamond and made the stars pale in comparison. He closed his eyes and cradled her body, wrapping one arm protectively around her. Her breathing was shallow and uneven. Lifting the thick curtain of her tangled hair, he pressed a kiss to her neck nape. Tomorrow he would watch her closely. Very closely.

The next day about midafternoon, Katherine nearly fell from the camel. Her body sagged beneath the tight grip of his right arm. Cursing softly, Ramses stopped and sat her on the ground. No shade existed, not a scrap of relief from the sun's merciless rays. He checked her pulse. The vein throbbed too fast for his liking. The dizziness alone was enough to alarm him.

Framed by the veil, her sparkling river-grass eyes

looked sunken and dull. He left her sitting, her head drooping on her chest, and fetched her goatskin water bag. He tested its weight and groaned. It was too full.

"Kalila, have you been drinking at all?"

"Some," she mumbled.

Ramses ground his temper down. Katherine was dehydrated. If she didn't replace her body's fluids soon, she could die. He poured water into a tin cup and raised it to her lips.

"Drink this. Now," he commanded in his sternest voice, but she reeled away. Either the effects of dehydration had taken their toll and confusion had set in, or her customary stubbornness rose up again. Ramses grit his teeth and pried her jaw open. He poured the water into her mouth, then closed it and tickled her throat. She swallowed.

He looked around. Home was at least two more days' journey. Closer still was the Khamsin southern camp where the tribe bred horses. They were constantly switching locations to keep the breeding grounds a secret. Only another Khamsin tribesman knew the hidden signs marking the way. He hoped she'd make it before losing more precious moisture. He'd packed salt, but he'd forgotten the sugar necessary to restore her body's proper balance of fluids. He cursed softly, wishing he hadn't been so eager to rush her from the cave.

Ramses placed both hands on her shoulders. His fingers curled around fragile bones that seemed even more delicate. "Kalila, you are dehydrated. Your body has lost fluids that must be replaced. I want you to drink as much water as possible."

He pressed more water to her lips, forcing her to drink. Her large eyes looked pleadingly at him. Her protector. Her Guardian, sworn to watch over her. He would save her, Ramses promised himself. His keen sight roved over the desert ground as he searched for a small pile of rocks shaped like a pyramid, the secret sign the Khamsin would have left behind.

Chapter Twenty

He found the camp and its familiar cluster of black tents dotting the dusky sands after only a few hours' ride. Unlike the main camp with more than one thousand warriors, this camp was kept deliberately small. Designed for mobility, the southern camp was home to three hundred warriors. A circular group of stones with three arched poles marked a well. Sheep and goats grazed on scant summer scrub. A group of children tending the flocks gawked with wide-eyed amazement. A large herd of beautiful Arabians, startled by the newcomers, shied away and moved off with fluid grace.

Ramses wasted no words as his camel trotted toward the first tent. Men shouted greetings, but he paid them no mind. He slid off the dromedary, and as his camel sank to the ground, Ramses lifted Katherine into his arms.

"She is dehydrated. Shade and fluids. Salt and sugar. And bring a fresh towel and clean water," he barked to the first warrior who reached him, recog-

Bonnie Vanak

nizing him as Salah, Kareem's father. Salah's cheerful expression turned serious. He led the way to a nearby tent, its flaps rolled up to allow the breeze to flow through. Ramses gently laid Katherine upon a thick sheepskin bedroll. Salah called for his son and ran out.

Ramses stuffed a pillow beneath her head and checked her pulse. Still too rapid. He surveyed her body. Dehydration combined with heat had ravaged her. Salah and Kareem scurried inside, bearing pitchers, a glass, a bowl of water and some cloth. "We keep the mixture handy in the summer," Kareem explained, handing the glass to Ramses. "Salt and sugar."

Ramses glanced over and gave a curt nod. The youth's smile faded upon seeing Katherine.

"Can you save her?"

"That is what I intend to do."

Katherine opened her eyes. Confusion clouded her clear green irises. Her gaze landed on Kareem, who hovered nearby. The boy learned over, apparently fascinated.

"Her eyes are as green as grasses in the wadi after a winter's rain," Kareem said in awe.

Ramses grunted. He understood the boy's curiosity, but had no time to indulge it. "I need to lower her body temperature." Ramses's eyes locked with Salah's. "Roll the tent flaps down."

Salah nodded to Kareem. When the tent flaps were fully lowered, the older man tugged his son outside. Ramses removed her veil and turban, then brought the cup to Katherine's lips. He cradled the back of her head with one hand, lifting her.

"Kalila, drink this. You are too dehydrated for mere water."

She began to sip and then gagged and coughed, spit-

246

ting it out. He forced more into her mouth, shutting her lips and watching as she swallowed in reflex. Katherine coughed again and looked at him with woebegone eyes.

"It tastes awful."

"Like your fever medication. And you will drink all of it," he said firmly.

Her hand wrapped around his as he lifted the glass to her mouth. This time she drank obediently, emptying the glass, then he gently lowered her head. Ramses began removing her clothing as she struggled weakly.

"Kalila," he murmured. "I must cool you down. Lie still. You have already expended too much precious energy."

She relaxed as he stripped off her kuftan and the underlying garments. When she was fully nude, he wet the cloth and began stroking her skin with it. Katherine watched him, her heavy-lidded gaze dull and listless, lacking its usual sparkle.

"Ramses, I feel awful. My head hurts something awful and I'm sick to my stomach." Her voice sounded frail and croaking, lacking the sassiness he loved so much.

He slid the cloth over her legs. "You are very weak, but as soon as you have enough fluids restoring your body's balance and you cool down, you will be fine."

He gave her a reassuring smile and continued his ministrations. Gratitude swept through him as she closed her eyes. She couldn't see how his hand trembled as he bathed her. The very thought of her dying in the open desert knotted his stomach with fear. Ramses sucked in a shaky breath, and dropped a kiss on her temple as he continued bathing her.

* * *

Some time later, he emerged, after pulling a thin sheet over her and rolling up the tent flaps. Ramses gazed around the Khamsin camp. An imposing man with threads of gray in his closely trimmed beard approached, accompanied by a few other men. Ramses embraced him in greeting.

"Hassan." He inclined his head in respect to the commander of the Khamsin southern camp.

"Ramses. It is good to see you, but I fear the reasons why you are here are not so pleasant." The older man gave him a respectful look. Jabari ruled the Khamsin, but Ramses's authority seconded the sheikh's.

Ramses nodded toward a nearby tent. As the men settled beneath its sheltering shade, he explained his journey, leaving out the part about Katherine being his betrothed.

"I need a scout to spy on the cave to see if the English have arrived yet. He should wait there until they do. As soon as they are there, I want to know immediately. Tell him to observe the men. Are they warriors? Or men with rifles?"

Hassan nodded, his dark eyes thoughtful. His sight roamed to Kareem talking with another warrior. Ramses glanced at him.

"Kareem will beg for the task. He has been edgy after his father demanded he return four weeks ago. His warrior's heart has the blood fever of battle brewing in his veins."

"Send him. Spying upon the *samak* will hone his warrior's edge. Stress to him how important this assignment is, how Kalila and I found the tomb and how it must be protected from discovery."

Hassan shot him a thoughtful look, which eased

into a sly grin. "She knows the tomb's location? Will you keep her as your prisoner as our sheikh did with his wife?"

Biting back a smile of amusement, Ramses eased out a long breath. Hassan assumed Ramses kidnapped her, much as Jabari took Elizabeth captive last year when he caught her trying to steal the sacred Almha. He glanced around, lowered his voice.

"Kalila is my bride. However, she . . . does not know this yet. I need to keep this knowledge from her for a while yet." His eyes locked with the commander's. "I trust you will help me."

"I will make my men vow silence. They will guess who she is, of course, knowing you have taken the Guardian oath." He paused. Amusement shone in his dark eyes. "Should I arrange to have you share a tent? Or do you want her to look like a guest?"

"A guest. If I desire, I will visit her tent as I please," he said arrogantly. Hassan laughed and slapped his knee.

"Kareem will make an excellent spy," Ramses added, changing the subject with ease. Shifting his weight, he nodded toward the teenager. He liked the boy's eagerness, and his prowling restlessness reminded Ramses of his own impulsive youth.

"What are your plans, Ramses?"

"Stay here until she recovers. Kalila has a vested interest in the tomb. She stole the map from me."

He caught the frown on Hassan's face. "But she is under my protection. She is to be treated with nothing but the best hospitality your camp has to offer."

Ramses said this all quietly, a hint of iron in his tone. The older man's frown eased as he nodded thoughtfully.

"We have another English lady arriving soon. Lady Dolores Fitzwilliam is coming here to purchase two colts."

Ramses accepted a glass of fruit juice from Hassan's wife with a nod of thanks and drank thirstily, back-handing his mouth. "You have the English coming here?" His brow wrinkled with bemusement. "And reveal our secret location?"

"She insisted upon seeing the colts in person. Two of my men are escorting her party here and then back. They are taking the long way. The very long way," he said smugly. His eyes twinkled. "The colts she intends to purchase are special. Lady Fitzwilliam promised she will pay much higher prices for them."

Ramses grinned, seeing a mischievous gleam in the older man's eyes. "How so?"

"One has four white stockings. Another is a yellow dun."

Laughter erupted from his throat. Four white stockings signified an evil omen; a yellow dun also brought bad luck. No Egyptian in his right mind would purchase such horses.

"You are a good horse trader, Hassan, and make our people proud," Ramses told him, still chuckling.

He smirked. "I will convince her she is getting a bargain."

Katherine woke up much later, exhausted. During her rest, Ramses kept waking her, forcing fluids down her throat, alternating between the disgusting salty/sweet mixture she didn't recognize and water. Her eyes felt sticky and gluey. But for the first time in days, the aching thirst and heat that had plagued her had evaporated. She glanced around the spacious tent. Several wood poles supported the structure. Quality hand-woven carpets had been set upon the sand, their red, blue and yellow patterns lending a soft air of comfort. Propping herself up on her elbows, she touched the one next to her bed.

Remembering the gold, she scanned the tent for her bag and saw it atop a low table. Katherine sighed with relief. Her secret remained safe. She shuddered, imagining Ramses's deadly fury if he found the little gold cat she'd stolen from the tomb.

The tent's interior proved surprisingly cool. Katherine felt grateful for shade. Glancing around for her clothing, she clutched the finely woven cotton sheet to her breasts. A few women passed, casting shy glances her way. Unveiled, they wore indigo kuftans, their heads covered with loose blue scarves. Two men strode by, wearing the same indigo *binish* as Ramses, swords and daggers dangling from their belts.

Indigo robes. Unveiled women. She had arrived in the camp of the Khamsin warriors of the wind. The tribe boasted a fearlessness and ruthlessness in dealing with its enemies. Enemies like women who stole maps and discovered their tomb filled with gold. Her heart thudded crazily. Dealing with Ramses was dangerous enough. But facing a whole tribe of warriors? Ramses had been protective and loving with her. She wondered if his attitude would change now. Did he bring her here to punish her, to demand restitution for her crime?

Katherine pressed fingers against her pounding temples. First, she had to regain strength. She would deal with the consequences as they arrived, and later, find a means to escape.

She glanced outside as a familiar pair of soft leather

boots appeared. Ramses tugged off his footwear and padded inside in his stockinged feet. He knelt beside the bed, placed a hand on her forehead. Layers of travel dust had vanished from his clothing, and he appeared scrubbed and clean.

"You look much better," he observed. "And your temperature has cooled. How do you feel?"

"Still shaky. And I am rather hungry, though. And . . ." her fingers tightened around the sheet. "I'm not wearing anything."

He removed his hand and sat back on his haunches, giving her a pondering look. "We will eat soon. I will ask the women to get you some fresh clothing after your bath."

Ramses stood and rolled the tent flaps down, then left. He returned carrying an odd folding contraption. Made of a dull gray canvas, it looked frightfully complicated. He set it down and opened it, then left again. She sat up, peering at it with curiosity. A real bathtub in the desert! The thought cheered her as he returned with two women who bore buckets of water and shy smiles. Long, light blue scarves covered their heads and shoulders. The delicate fabric circled their necks and was weighted down by lovely silver charms dangling from the ends. They poured buckets of water into the tub, carrying the water back and forth until the tub was half full. The women brought in towels, soap and a bottle of shampoo, then left, murmuring politely.

Alone now with Ramses. She sucked in a shaky breath as he knelt by the tub, stirring the water with one finger. "Excellent. Just the right temperature."

"Which is?"

"Cool enough. They keep water heated by the sun

in large containers, but I asked for water to be drawn from the well."

"A lot of work."

"They do not mind. It is part of our way, our hospitality."

Katherine felt heat creep into her cheeks.

"Come Kalila," he said gently, tugging back the sheet.

She let him pull her up, felt her knees buckle and started to sag. Immediately he lifted her into his arms. Without words he lowered her into the tub. Katherine sighed as cool water enveloped her body. She sat, hugging her knees.

Her breathing hitched as he squatted by her side. His face clouded with emotion as he took her hands, kissed them.

"My darling Kalila, I feared I would lose you in the desert. Never do that again. You gave me such a fright."

Ramses gave her a look so tender she felt her throat muscles tighten with emotion. Then she blinked, and the look vanished, replaced by formal politeness.

"I will leave you now. One of the women will be by shortly to help you. Dinner is at sundown."

He stood and strode out of the tent, a warrior in firm control, radiating such power and might she wondered if the sheen she had glimpsed in his eyes was a trick of the light.

Chapter Twenty-one

Two days later, her past returned to haunt her.

It arrived in a floppy straw hat, dun-colored skirts and shirt, and chattering madly. Lady Dolores Fitzwilliam and a party of eight friends and servants, with camels and trunks galore. Ramses told her the English visitors were purchasing Khamsin colts.

She hid behind her veil, grateful the cover concealed her identity. Katherine evaded her until that night, when the Khamsin prepared a feast to honor Ramses.

Ramses sat at the head circle in the position of highest esteem next to Hassan, the Khamsin commander, and Lady Fitzwilliam. Katherine sat in the next circle, watching her lover as he chatted with her friend. Jealousy knotted her stomach.

Thick, exotic carpets had been laid on the sand for seats. A large circular platter sat on the ground before them. Katherine watched the others, then followed suit, scooping up the mixture with her right hand, using the flatbread as her utensil. She savored the taste. Gamey, but delicious.

"What is this?" she asked the warrior to her right.

"Houbara bustard. I caught it this afternoon with the hunting party to honor Ramses. I am Kareem," Kareem bowed his head and smiled. His beard barely shadowed his jaw. He had warm brown eyes and a youthful, eager air, like a friendly puppy.

The warrior began bragging about his expertise in hunting the large bird, telling her extravagant tales of his prowess. She pretended interest. Her eyes kept drifting to her lover. Lady Fitzwilliam and others at the head circle hovered on every syllable that passed Ramses's lips as if the giant statue of Ramses II at Luxor deigned to speak. Power radiated from him. Every eye admired him as if the sun god had, indeed, descended into their midst. She sensed the tribe's tremendous pride in this warrior. They claimed him as a hero who came to visit. Yet he appeared unmoved by the praise.

She licked her lips, staring at the indigo robe hiding his smooth curved muscles, the easy way he sat, one knee bent, the other leg tucked beneath him. She did not belong here with these people and their worship of him.

Ribbons of chestnut in his long locks gleamed as they caught the flickering firelight. A tiger's feline grace and seamless movement accented every flex of his powerful body. Pride rode firmly on those broad shoulders. Grace stroked his every move as he mopped sauce with flatbread and ate it. A shiver coursed down her spine as she watched his tongue lick the corner of his mouth. That tongue had traced every curve and hollow of her body with consummate skill.

Katherine licked her own lips, feeling a hunger no food could ease. She craved the shining golden purity of him. He seemed as refined and elegant as she imagined the pharaoh's courts of his sloe-eyed ancestors must have been. She did not belong to this exotic world, to a people whose past intimately tangled with the present like two lovers sleepily curling their bodies together for comfort.

The two warring sides of her, Egyptian and English, clashed in a cacophony of confusion. Which ruled her? The mysterious, exotic past of ancient Egypt or the lush richness of practical England? She belonged to neither, a ship adrift in a turbulent sea of aching loneliness. She only wanted to cast anchor, unfurl her sails and settle down on one side. Her heart and soul longed to belong with Ramses. In his strong arms, she would never drift again into uncertainty. Oh, how she wanted Ramses to capture her heart and offer it back, wrapped in the protective shield of his love. But he did not love her. Like legions of women before her, she only eased his body's needs.

Her heart ached as Lady Fitzwilliam playfully touched Ramses's hand and cooed at him. Dolores's flawless skin, huge blue eyes and beguiling manner had smitten many men. Now she focused her pretty smile on the warrior of love. Her friend had gazed dreamily at him at Shepheard's. Would she coax Ramses into her tent tonight for "hysteria" treatments? Katherine pressed a hand to her left cheek. Beneath the veil, her scar seemed to burn. Why would Ramses want her anymore when he could have someone as beautiful and flawless as Dolores?

Kareem touched her bare wrist, then hastily removed his hand as if he'd touched a hot iron. Katherine watched his face redden. Nice boy. He seemed as intrigued by the shrouded portion of her face as many other Khamsin men appeared. She needed an ally in this unknown enemy camp. Kareem might fit the part.

Katherine looked over the flat, sand-covered valley and sharp granite mountains. If she were to escape and head back, she needed a guide. She, the huntress who killed game as easily as some women wove rugs, began showering him with flattery about his skills in killing their meal. Her questions shifted to innocent probes about navigating through deep desert.

Surely, Kareem could tell her a way back to the cave.

He watched her converse with Kareem, heard her gurgling laughter. Jealousy poured through him like a rush of heated water. Ramses examined this new emotion with as much detachment as possible. No woman ever had caused it before. He could easily bed one, then watch her walk into another man's arms a few minutes later. He guarded his heart and allowed his body to seek its ease without the interference of emotional attachments.

Not with Katherine. He had bonded with her, lain with her in the dark, taking her innocence as was his right. He longed for the sweet thrill of inhaling the exotic scent of her, tasting the honeyed cream of her soft skin.

Next to him, Lady Fitzwilliam pressed against him in a most impolite manner. Ramses swore silently at the forward English woman's behavior and leaned away.

"My Ramses, you have a huge weapon. Could you take it out and show it to me?" she gushed.

The English woman's Arabic was so bad he wondered if she wanted to see his scimitar or something much more personal.

"I think not," he replied as politely as he could.

His sight roved to Katherine. A startled gasp caught in his throat. Her sleeve had slid up her forearm, exposing a lovely length of naked skin. Kareem laid a hand on her bare wrist as he leaned close to murmur something. He immediately removed his hand, but Ramses uttered a low growl deep in his throat. He would not tolerate another warrior touching his woman.

Her veil created a tantalizing intrigue for the men. Khamsin males were accustomed to women baring their faces. The mystery of unseen territory drew men to Katherine as if she were a ripe pomegranate dangling just out of reach. Sidelong glances drifted in her direction with increasing abandon. Many pairs of dark eyes filled with admiring appreciation for the lovely sway of her curved hips. Her body's natural rhythm called them to her side, as if it were an unseen *darrubuka* playing an intoxicating tune. Men watched her covertly, waiting for the wind to lift the veil for a delectable peek at what lay beneath.

He wanted to stride up to her, rip off that damn veil, show off her beauty to all present. Make them gasp with wonder at the delicate curve of her high cheekbones, the lovely pouting lower lip, the adorable sweep of her upturned little nose.

Then he would proudly display the scar she hid, the tiger's mark that had branded her from childhood as one destined for him, to keep her pure and away from other men. Ramses viewed it as a symbol of honor similar to his own tattoo. It marked Katherine as his, just as the tattoo of the Ieb, the Udjat and Min's bolt marked him as exclusively hers.

He would allow the Khamsin males to see this and marvel. Then he would smile, knowing he possessed what they could never have. He would sweep her into his black tent and make passionate love to her until she begged for mercy. Until her cries of his name in release informed everyone exactly to whom she belonged.

He clenched his teeth and breathed through them. Lady Fitzwilliam touched his arm and murmured in bad Arabic something about feeling hysterical. He inched away. A loud rush of blood buzzed in his ears as he watched Katherine's eyes sparkle as she talked with Kareem.

Turning to Hassan, Ramses lowered his voice. "When does Kareem leave for the cave?"

Hassan shot him a questioning look. "I will send him tonight, if you wish. I told him about how you and Lady Katherine discovered the tomb and how important it is to find out how many English are there, for we must protect sacred Khamsin territory. He seems most eager to go."

Hiding a smile, Ramses nodded. He swallowed the flatbread with his jealousy. A sweet anticipation flowed through him. He savored it and glanced at the darkening sky. After dinner, after the songs and poetry were exchanged around the campfire, when all retired, the night would be his. To hunt, as his totem hunted. He would prowl toward her tent. And capture her in his arms and not let go until he satisfied his deep, feral need.

* * *

A steady breeze blew in through the partly rolled-up black tent as Katherine lay naked on her sheepskin bed. Accustomed now to the night sounds in the desert, the occasional call of jackals, sighs of the wind, she could not sleep. Loudest was the heavy pounding of her heart thudding against her chest. Her instincts warned her of approaching footsteps even before the tent flap lifted and a silent figure stole inside.

Katherine raised herself on her elbows, prepared to cry out when a familiar voice cut through the blackness.

"Kalila. So you are alone."

"What else would I be?" She could not keep a quivering note of joy from her voice. Ramses had come to her, not Lady Fitzwilliam, in the dark of night.

"From your improper behavior tonight, I would think that Kareem would be sharing your bed."

A tiny thrill surged through her. The thrill faded as he settled to the carpet beside her and tugged at a strand of her long hair, forcing her toward him. Ramses wove his strong hands into her hair, then laid his lips upon her neck and gently nipped her throat in a possessive manner as if staking his claim. She felt the raw hunger emanating from him in heated waves, cutting the night's chill.

"What is so improper about talking with a man?"

"The way he touched you was most unacceptable. Like this." Ramses slid a hand over her bare arm, evoking a shiver of anticipation mixed with fear at the husky threat in his voice.

She had never seen him like this, driven by some wild, primitive call. Savage. Ramses had been nothing but gentle, even amidst his deepest passion. Now the gentleness had fled. For the first time she could see the hint of the fierce warrior feared by all. He needed no scimitar to evoke respect. The dark promise of danger in the rippled tones of his deep voice did it all.

Katherine swallowed and backed away, half afraid, half terribly excited by this change in him.

He folded the tent flaps completely down. Ramses lit an oil lamp on a low table. He quickly undressed and flexed his arms. Tension coiled in the bunched muscles, like a tiger waiting to pounce and capture.

"Kalila, I will stay with you tonight."

"Go back to your tent," she said haughtily, praying he would not.

A soft, amused chuckle answered her. "I think not." His low voice held a hint of steel.

Her chin lifted in defiance. "From the improper way Lady Fitzwilliam was touching you tonight, I would think you wanted to be with her."

A short bark of laughter. "Her?" His voice held an incredulous note. Ramses's expression softened. He stroked her hair. "No one else, Kalila. No other woman but you, I will have in my arms tonight."

He pulled away and lifted his shoulders in a shrug. "If you want me to return to my tent . . ."

"No," she said in a trembling voice. "Stay."

A half smile touched his mouth. "If you insist . . ."

Ramses raked his gaze over her in a possessive sweep, his hunger for Katherine growing to fever pitch. Sweet anticipation rolled through him as he traced her lips with one finger. Katherine had no idea what pleasures he planned for her. Tonight he would fill the air with her cries of ecstasy for all to hear. He would make her scream with the pleasure only he could give her and not stop until she lay spent and weary in his arms.

He carried the lamp to the main portion of the tent where several camel saddles were stacked, then returned. He swept her into his arms. She felt light and airy as moonlight. Golden lamp light danced in the shimmering masses of her ebony hair. Lowering her gently to the carpet, he leaned her against the sturdy saddles. He pressed a finger against her slightly parted lips.

Anticipation filled those green eyes. Ramses lifted her by the rounded smoothness of her lovely bottom and positioned her more firmly against the camel saddles.

"Why did you light the lamp?" she whispered.

"I want to watch your face as I pleasure you."

She gave a pretty little shiver. Her luminous green eyes widened as he stroked the inside of her thighs, splaying them apart. "Ramses, what are you . . ."

"Shh." He laid a finger softly against her lips.

He knelt before her, and claimed her mouth with a hard kiss, his fingers grasping her arms. As she opened her mouth to admit him, he drank of her, delighting that she drew his tongue into her mouth with the same feverish heat. Ramses began touching her with savage, heated intensity and she responded in kind. He growled and nipped her breast, sucking the tender flesh there. She hissed and dug her nails into his back as she kissed his body with fevered lips. He roared and sank his teeth gently into her neck in a tiger's possessive gesture of dominance. A violent whirlwind eclipsed them, as ferocious as the Khamsin, so turbulent Ramses felt the air around them spin in a crazy maelstrom much like a sand tornado. Then it slowed as he pulled back.

Ramses began caressing the soft petals of her feminine core, massaging her with loving, gentle strokes. He leaned against her and heard her soft gasp as he eased one finger deep inside. Smiling, he dropped a kiss on her lips and glanced down at the part of her which awaited his pleasure. Watching her face, he positioned himself at her entrance, then plunged deep inside. She gasped as he thrust against her, fingers digging into her rounded hips. He increased the pace, feathering kisses on her lips, her neck, driving himself deep within her. Ramses watched with tender satisfaction as her beautiful green eyes grew smoky with passion. She hooked her hands around his neck, thrusting her hips up to meet his strokes, whimpering deep in her throat.

Ramses smiled gently as she stiffened with what he knew was to come. Surrender filled her beautiful green eyes. Her rosebud mouth parted.

Fire streamed through her as he filled her to the core. Her fingers dug into the firm muscles of his backside, urging him deeper inside her. She strained toward him, eager to melt into him. Heat pooled between her thighs, thrumming as if each nerve were Ramses's *darrubuka* and he pounded upon the drum. She tried fighting it. Could not. Would not. Katherine's body shook as she neared her release. She moaned, tossing her head back.

"Do it, Kalila." His voice rippled across her sensitive skin like heated satin. "Scream. Cry out my name. Now. Scream, little one."

She could not resist the iron command in that voice or her body's own searing heat. Her back arched from the mounting pleasure swallowing her whole. Katherine's lips opened and she let out a long scream as her body shook. She cried out his name to the silent night, to the indifferent sands, not caring if others heard, not caring if the stars in their velvet case of blackness listened. Over and over she cried out his name, clinging to him as if drowning.

Such was his pride in watching her achieve her pleasure, Ramses allowed desire to sweep him into a drowning tide of passion. Never before had having a woman writhe with pleasure beneath him felt so intoxicating. Blood fever of claiming his victory rode hard and fast in his veins. Ramses felt as wild and predatory as his totem, hunting in the dark night. Power surged up, inflaming him. Passion engulfed him as he claimed Katherine with one last powerful thrust, penetrating to her womb. He threw back his head, trembling with the force of his release, opened his mouth, and let loose the Khamsin war whoop in a loud, undulating cry that rippled through the tent and the camp.

Chapter Twenty-two

Still locked inside his beloved, Ramses froze. He looked down at Katherine, her eyes rounding to full moons. Soft lotus hands dug into the taut muscles of his buttocks.

"Ramses," she whispered. "What was that?"

"That," he said with grim irony, "was a very big mistake."

Footsteps thudded upon the sand. Voices cried out in alarm. He heard a shrill feminine voice call out in English, "Good heavens, what was that? Are we under attack?"

Sounds of warriors running, steel scimitars sliding out of metal sheaths. Khamsin warriors, even in the deepest sleep, were trained to awaken and respond to that call of a brother warrior. The pounding boots stilled outside her tent. A hesitant voice called out.

"Ramses. My friend, is all well?"

The delicate question, phrased in a tone indicating Hassan knew what had transpired, gave him enough time to gather his scattered wits. Ramses bowed his head, then raised it, assuming his firmest tone of command.

"It is. Go back to sleep and tell the others as well."

"Very well, then." The Khamsin southern commander assented, but before his footsteps fell away from the tent Ramses swore he heard a chuckle in the older man's voice.

Not daring to move until the last footstep had shuffled away, Ramses cocked his head, listening. Finally he looked down at Katherine, her green eyes huge and expressive. Ramses brushed her lips with a kiss and eased out of her with a groan of satisfaction and frustration.

He rolled off her, lay next to her body, stroking her belly with one hand. Her stomach muscles jumped beneath his touch. She turned toward him.

"What happened? Why did everyone come to the tent?"

Ramses sucked in a breath, shook his head. He didn't know whether to be embarrassed or amused. "Because, little one, you bring out feelings in me I've never had before during love. The yelling sound I made was the Khamsin war cry."

"War cry?"

"The call all warriors of my tribe make when we engage our enemies in battle. We use it to identify ourselves during the heat of battle, or as an alarm when something is amiss." Ramses looked at the smooth curves of her silky cheeks, the pouty little mouth and brushed a finger against her bottom lip. "Like this." He uttered the cry again. It rose and fell in a soft purr between his lips.

"Oh! So that is what you think of me? As engaging the enemy."

He caught the teasing tone of her voice as she smiled. "No," he said honestly. "Khamsin warriors do not only use the cry for war. On rare occasions, we also use it when . . ." Ramses looked at how she curled her body trustingly close to him. His finger traced her lips. "We use it when our hearts are so filled with joy, we feel so victorious that there is no other means of expressing our emotions."

He said all this very slowly, not wanting to rush the words, for he had never uttered them before. But he had to let her know the feelings she brought out in him. Once he had despised the fact he would be married to an Englishwoman. He thought of Katherine's gentle, healing touch. Medical skills she'd acquired in England had saved him. Prejudice had soured his view of the British. Not all were tomb robbers. Certainly not Katherine, who respected his ancestor's grave with as much reverence as he did. A weight lifted from his chest. Ramses hid a smile. His heart had begun healing from the lacerations of his fractured past.

Katherine sat up, took his hand and placed it on her chest, where he felt the rapid thrumming of her heart. "You are not the only one, for if I were Khamsin, I would also yell this war cry. I have never felt this way before."

He felt deeply roused by the throaty note catching in her voice. Her honesty moved him and joy filled his heart. Still, instinct urged caution.

"When I make love with you, you mean." Deliberately, he kept his voice casual.

"It is more than that," she said, her teeth catching her lower lip and nibbling on them. "As lovely as it is."

Katherine lowered her eyes in a shy gesture that

charmed and touched him. "I feel as if my soul has blended with yours. It is as if we are so close, our bodies have merged with our spirits. We are as one."

Ramses marveled at the honest beauty of her, this woman chosen to become his wife. Her courage and spirit, her passion and drive. Then Katherine looked away and he was troubled by the pain crossing her features. Her lower lip trembled violently.

"I am being silly, for how could such a thing happen? You have probably heard this many times before from other women."

He grasped her shoulders and turned her to face him. "No," he said quietly. "No, Kalila. You are right. It is more than making love. I feel the same."

She stroked his cheek with a shaky hand. Ramses dropped a kiss on her lips.

"I will stay here from now on," he finally managed to say. "It is for the best."

"But—" she protested.

He laid a hand upon her lips. "Hush. Let us go to sleep." Ramses stood, lifted her into his arms and went back to the wide sheepskin bed, settling her upon it. He crawled beneath the sheet and blanket with her, feeling the smooth satin of her sweat-slicked skin as he curled up against her, then kissed her scarred cheek.

Chapter Twenty-three

Life in the Khamsin camp fascinated Katherine. She was awed by the women's exotic beauty and their talent as they wove intricate, colorful patterns on their looms. They had clear, fresh-faced looks that belied the harsh desert life, and floated through the camp with inbred elegance. The men scared her a little with the deadly scimitars and sharp daggers dangling from their belts. But unlike the Egyptian men in her cousin's household, who considered public displays of affection impolite, Khamsin warriors did not. Their fierce expressions always softened when they greeted their wives, and they had no qualms about holding hands or bestowing kisses. They adored their children with the same single-minded devotion they showed to their wives. The life here was peaceful, serene and she regretted that she'd never share it with Ramses.

To her relief, Lady Fitzwilliam stayed only two days, then left, triumphantly hauling two Khamsin colts. Hassan and Ramses had roared with laughter after her party left. Ramses said Hassan had coaxed her to pay twice the original asking price because of the "rare beauty" of the colts. Then he explained how the colts were unsaleable because of their markings. Katherine laughed with him.

She had regained her strength, but an odd queasiness squeezed her stomach. The Khamsin women treated her like a guest, but Katherine stood for none of that. She helped them with laundry, learned to make yogurt from goat's milk and weave fabric on the wood looms while chatting about which routes the warriors took when they traveled south. But they only offered gentle smiles, not answers.

Katherine watched Ramses prowl gracefully past as she sat with Hassan's wife, churning milk into cheese by swinging a goatskin bag back and forth. The milk in the bag, suspended from an arch formed by three long poles, sloshed as much as her churning stomach.

Ramses stopped, turned and watched her with an amused smile. A wily one, his Katherine. He had heard her questions regarding the desert. He knew what she planned. But there would be no escape for her.

A sudden shout caught his attention. Ramses frowned, squinted and shaded his eyes, looking as three camels approached on the horizon. His heart beat wildly with joy. He grinned, recognizing the cheers that rolled through the camp. He had expected this and was glad he had waited to return to his camp. His gaze roamed back to Katherine, looking confused at all the rushing bodies racing past.

Jabari had arrived.

He steeled himself for what he knew he must do. The time had come. Although there was no shaman to perform the ritual ceremony, the sheikh had the power in his absence.

Ramses flexed his muscles and watched Katherine quietly. *Prepare yourself, my love. Today is your wedding day.*

She heard all the fuss and asked one of the women why everyone rushed toward the new arrivals. "Our sheikh is here with his wife and new son," the woman explained, dusting off her hands and rushing over to join the crowd.

Sheikh. Oh, dear. Ramses's friend. An idea burgeoned. Katherine eyed the deserted camp. Everyone had gathered around the newcomers. Now would be a perfect opportunity to slip away.

Katherine scrambled to her feet and started for her tent to secure provisions. Barely had she reached it when a familiar grip enclosed her wrist.

"Kalila, where are you going?"

She gulped. "Just to my tent."

"Later. My father has arrived with our sheikh and his wife, and I must introduce you. Listen carefully, Kalila. When women are presented before the Khamsin sheikh, they must show respect. Do not look him in the eye and you must bow."

Resentment stirred the ashes of her rebellion at his strict tone. The assembled crowd parted respectfully to make way for Ramses. He steered her toward the center of attention and released her elbow. A wide smile split Ramses's face as an older version of himself stepped forward and engulfed him in an enormous hug. Ramses hugged his father back with equal intensity. His face clouded with emotion; then he regained his dignity.

"I see you have found something in the deep desert,

my son." Amber eyes, much like Ramses's, twinkled at Katherine.

Next to him stood a tall, dark-eyed man, his arm hooked protectively around the waist of a lovely woman in an indigo *kuftan*. Like the other Khamsin women, a long scarf was draped around her head and was weighted with lovely, jingling silver charms, but the difference ended there. Hair the color of corn silk spilled from beneath the head covering. The woman's blue-eyed gaze held hers and she offered a friendly smile. Katherine gawked, the queasiness in her stomach trebling. She looked American or British. The woman gazed at a small, blanketed form cuddled by another Khamsin woman. Clusters of doting women clucked with adoration at the bundle.

Ramses laid a possessive hand on her shoulder. The tight, dark smile on his face warned her he planned something chilling. But nothing could have prepared her for the icy dousing his next words brought.

"Father, Jabari, Elizabeth, may I present Lady Katherine Smithfield? My betrothed."

Katherine's gaze riveted to him in horrified astonishment and denial. "No! My bridegroom's name is Nazim."

"Nazim Ramses bin Seti Sharif," he corrected.

Her stomach pitched and rolled. "It can't be! I saw him knock on Papa's door, the day the marriage contract was signed."

Ramses frowned, then smiled. "Wearing a white turban and a white *thobe*?" At her nod, he continued. "You saw the Khamsin attorney. He arrived at your father's room before I did."

His amber eyes pierced hers with burning intent. Grim triumph radiated from his proud, commanding stance. He had the satisfied look of a tiger clenching a plump, tasty gazelle.

Nausea boiled inside her. Her stomach twisted into tiny knots. His bride. The truth hit her full force: Ramses was her unknown Bedouin bridegroom. She had stolen the map from him. Saved his life, then slept with him . . . just to avoid marriage . . .

To him. Katherine put a hand to her spinning head. He knew, all this time. And he played with her, toyed with her like a tiger swatting its helpless prey with a giant paw before downing it in a hungry gulp. Had his tongue traced those firm lips in a slow, contented lick, it wouldn't have surprised her.

"Katherine, bow before the sheikh to show your respect to the Khamsin leader," Ramses ordered sternly.

She could not hold it any longer. A tremendous rumbling wrenched her stomach as it spasmed. Katherine tore off her veil, lowered her eyes and head. She jerked forward in a hasty bow, then showed her respect by vomiting her breakfast all over the dark blue boots of the Khamsin sheikh.

Shocked murmurs raced through the assembled crowd. Tears burned in her eyes from the violence of her retching. Trembling hands clutched her stomach, willing it to calm. Katherine wiped her face with the scarf and then veiled herself again. She straightened and met the sheikh's dark eyes. He gave her a long, thoughtful look before dragging his gaze down to his soiled footwear.

"These were new," the sheikh mused almost to himself.

"This is all your fault. You made the poor girl ill,

forcing her to bow to you like a puppet," the sheikh's young wife accused her husband.

"My fault? Blame Ramses. He is the one enforcing that tradition. I tried to stop it, as you asked," Jabari protested.

"Katherine, are you all right?" No longer the smug captor, Ramses's voice filled with sharp concern.

She turned her back, fell to her knees as the nausea took hold again. Katherine clutched her stomach, willing it to calm. Never had she wanted privacy as much as she needed it now. Dimly she wondered if presenting her back to the sheikh constituted bad manners. Certainly, it was not as rude as what she did to his feet.

She felt Ramses's hand clutch her shoulder, then the gentle pressure of a softer, feminine hand take her arm.

"Leave her alone. I'll take care of her. You two are enough to make anyone nervous. Come, Katherine." Elizabeth snapped an order for water and towels, gently guided her toward the shelter of a nearby tent.

Inside, Katherine sank onto the carpets. She removed her veil and pressed quivering hands to her throbbing temples. Elizabeth took the bowl of water and cloth the Khamsin women had scurried to fetch and began bathing her face. The woman's touch felt soothing and gentle. She poured a glass of water. With a nod of thanks, Katherine drank and handed it back.

Her stomach had quieted more than the truth reeling with fiendish glee inside her head. Ironic cruelty hit home with the force of a Khamsin wind. The very man who took her virginity was the man destined to become her bridegroom. He knew, she screamed silently. How could he play with her feelings like that when she had given herself body and soul to him?

Elizabeth patted her hand. "The sun can be quite intense."

"I'm so sorry," she whispered. "I feel so embarrassed."

The blond woman waved an indifferent hand. "Don't worry. Jabari won't cut off your head. He only does that to men who throw up on his boots."

When Katherine stared at her with wide eyes, she added, "That's a joke."

A tremulous smile tugged her lips upwards. "Cutting off my head might be a good thing, if I could stop feeling like this."

A deep blue gaze held hers. Elizabeth scrutinized her appearance. "How long has this been going on?"

"A few days. It comes and goes. Mostly in the morning, like now."

"Any feelings like you're dizzy and want to pass out?"

"Oh, yes," Katherine said, glad someone understood.

"Do you feel very upset all the time, like you want to cry or scream and you have no idea why?"

"Well, yes." Of course she had a perfect reason. Ramses held her prisoner and her father's life remained at risk.

"Interesting," she murmured. Katherine didn't care for the speculative gleam in her eyes. "I daresay you won't be wanting any dinner. They're slaughtering some lambs in our honor."

The thought of eating meat made her stomach pitch and roll again. Katherine shook her head.

"Tea then. And flatbread. How does that sound?"

She nodded, something in her chest easing at the

compassionate look in the woman's face.

"I was the same way. But it will pass in a couple of months. That you have to look forward to."

The other woman's smile made her queasiness return. Sudden understanding dawned. Katherine clutched her stomach. She blamed her sickness on the sudden shock that the lover she took to escape her Bedouin bridegroom was her Bedouin bridegroom.

"You mean . . ."

"I know exactly what's wrong with you. The very same thing happened to me. You're going to have a baby."

Chapter Twenty-four

"A baby!" Katherine felt her stomach lurch more as she stared at Elizabeth in shock.

"Katherine, I'm certain. How long have you been ill? Have you missed your monthly courses?"

She did some rapid calculations and groaned. "I'm late."

"Well, there you are," Elizabeth said comfortably as if that settled everything.

"But I can't be pregnant! Because I can't marry Ramses!" she burst out, as if denying it out loud would erase the reality. Their child, conceived in love in the dark cave.

"Pregnancy brings all your emotions rushing to the surface. I nearly bit Jabari's head off several times. And I cried at the silliest things."

Elizabeth put her hand on Katherine's shoulder in commiseration as she gnawed on her lower lip. The thought of carrying Ramses's child filled her with pride and love as much as it grieved her. More complications.

"You'll have to tell him," Elizabeth said gently.

"I can't."

"Why?"

Saying nothing, she fingered her scar. Elizabeth touched her cheek. "How did this happen?"

Katherine studied her. "My cousin's pet tiger cub, when I was ten. I stuck my head too close to the cage. It was so pretty, I just wanted to pet it." Like another tiger she dared to approach. *Your warrior, Ramses, is a far deadlier beast.*

"Ramses is my husband's fiercest warrior, a brave and honorable man. He would defend those entrusted to him to the death. Don't you want to marry him?"

Katherine hesitated, her insecurities surfacing. He was a perfect specimen of manhood with his sculptured body rippling with strength and cords of muscle. Practically speaking, Ramses should want a beautiful bride to compliment his own looks.

She buried her head in her hands, thinking of a knife sinking into her father by Burrells's command if she revealed the truth. Burrells said he had spies, maybe even here. She must bring him the gold she had stolen and rescue her father.

"With all my heart, I want to marry him," she whispered. "But I can't."

"Do you love him?"

Katherine wiped her streaming eyes. *More than life itself.* The unspoken words hovered on her lips. She managed a shaky nod.

"But I don't know if I could fit in. I'm more English than Egyptian."

"I was more American than Egyptian when I married Jabari," Elizabeth said with a wry smile. "I adjusted. You will as well. I love my husband, and I've grown to love this life. But sometimes I get lonely for someone from a culture similar to the way I was raised. Just to share things, like English books . . ."

"And a good cup of English tea," Katherine added.

Elizabeth smiled and winked at her. "But I must confess I don't miss my corset. Not one bit."

The sheikh's young wife gave her a conspiratorial smile, but it failed to evoke one in response. Shot down by the reality of her predicament, hope fell like a dead bird to the earth. Her first obligation was to her father, not Ramses. If she didn't help him obtain the gold, she might as well have killed him.

Blue eyes held hers with compassion. "There's something else, isn't there?"

Katherine glanced down. "I can't tell anyone."

A soft palm settled over hers. Elizabeth looked worried as she began toying with a strand of long blond hair. She switched to English. "Katherine, is something threatening you?"

Her gaze darted away. Hearing that question in English from a woman seemed less dangerous than hearing it posed in Arabic by the Khamsin warrior from whom she had stolen the map.

"Ahmed warned us someone was."

Shock rolled through her at Elizabeth's words. "Ahmed?"

The sheikh's wife nodded. "He arrived a few weeks ago in our camp and told us what happened. He wasn't worried, though, because he said Ramses would protect you."

Despite her churning emotions, light amusement rippled through her. "That's why he said I would learn about my husband's tribe. Ahmed knew Ramses was my betrothed. He left me alone with him, as my protector."

Elizabeth smiled, then her lovely face tightened with anger. She squeezed Katherine's hand. "Someone is threatening you, Katherine. That's why you must trust Ramses. Don't hold back on him. He needs to know. Ramses is a Guardian of the Ages. He swore a sacred oath to protect you. He can defeat whoever is scaring you."

"It's not that. I can't tell him. If it were just my life at stake . . . but he threatened to hurt Papa." She bit her tongue, trembling, realizing she had already revealed too much. Talking to the sheikh's kind wife lowered her natural defenses.

Concern darkened Elizabeth's blue eyes. "Katherine, why are you so frightened? Have faith in Ramses. A Khamsin warrior can defeat whatever scares you. They are men of honor who would fall on their scimitars to protect the women they love." A soft smile touched her lips. "I know. Jabari nearly gave his life for me, just as I know Ramses would give his life for you."

An image of Burrells tapping her nose with the knife he used to threaten Osiris with surfaced. Katherine pressed her lips together. "It's not that. I know Ramses would . . . you don't understand. Please, don't tell Ramses what you know. Please promise me you won't breathe a word to anyone."

Elizabeth's lips twisted, but she nodded. "I think you're making a huge mistake, but I'll respect your wishes."

"Thank you," she whispered.

"I know Ramses. He would never admit this, not even to Jabari, his best friend. But I've seen it in his eyes. He's lonely. He hides behind a smile and his fierce warrior's might. I saw the way he looked at you, like a man deeply in love. Trust him. Love him. You both deserve it."

Katherine could not speak for the lump in her throat as the sheikh's wife rose to leave her alone.

His concern over Katherine being ill turned to concern for his own physical well-being when he saw his best friend's wide grin. Jabari's smile made his heart drop to his stomach. He tugged his jeweled dagger from its sheath and held it up, admiring the blade.

Ramses cringed and backed away. "No, Jabari."

"A bet is a bet, my friend."

"But how do you know that I. . . ."

"Well? Did you not?" His sheikh arched a brow.

Ramses gazed at the tent sheltering Katherine. His hand reached up, pulled a sheaf of long hair. He released a long, slow sigh. "You win," he muttered.

Mirth twinkled in his friend's dark eyes. He clapped a hand on his shoulder. "Come, Ramses, this will hurt less than all the times you attended to my battle wounds."

"You have longed for this day," he accused him, unable to drag his eyes away from the knife's wicked gleam.

Jabari chuckled. "And so I have."

Standing outside the tent, Katherine stared at her bridegroom marching toward her. Satin curls fell just below his shoulder blades. Ramses looked miserable. The sheikh looked triumphant. In his right hand he carried something that resembled an animal's tail. She squinted and looked again. Ramses's hair. Stopping before a campfire, the sheikh handed the long locks to his Guardian with a flourish. Ramses looked at them morosely for a moment, then tossed them into the flames. He looked up, saw her and headed toward her, determination carved on his face. She ducked inside, wishing for a door to slam, but the sides were rolled up, not even giving her the satisfaction of privacy.

Even this new twist of events would not make her spill secrets. Ramses would think Papa forced her to steal the map for his own gain. But how could she confess the truth? Indecision clouded her. Telling Ramses the truth endangered her father.

Ramses stalked inside the tent. He solved the privacy problem by rolling the tent flaps down. She turned from him. Two strong hands settled on her shoulders. Flinching as if his touch burned, she lifted her chin and stared at the wall. When he spoke, solicitous concern rippled from his deep voice. She braced herself against it.

"I am worried about you, Katherine. You have not eaten properly as of late and now you are sick. Is it the heat?"

Katherine turned, staring at him. How could he not guess? After all the times they had made love? She resisted the impulse to put a hand on her still-flat abdomen.

"Why wouldn't I be ill, finding out how you played me for a fool?" she snapped. "You knew all this time and you kept the truth from me. You seduced me Ramses, knowing I was your bride!"

His hands lightly squeezed her shoulders. "You seemed determined to lose your virginity to escape marriage to me. I could not let another man take what was mine," he said softly.

A pained whisper escaped her lips. "How could you toy with me like that? You knew how I felt about you!" She shook off his hands. "You could have told me who you really were."

"I did not dare risk telling you, for I was uncertain of the motives driving you to steal the map and find the tomb." His jaw tightened. "Or who drove you to it."

Ramses had bedded her, knowing she was to be his bride. He must have thought her an impulsive fool. Her emotions raged to the surface. She had given her body, and her love, to a dashing warrior who used her for his own purpose.

"So you made love to me, knowing we were to marry. Why Ramses? So you could change your mind if I didn't prove satisfactory?"

His lips curled into a half smile. Ramses laid a hand atop hers, stroking the skin with his thumb. "You are mine, sweet Kalila. You were destined for me as I was destined for you." He took her hand and placed it over his upper left arm. "This tattoo symbolizes what must be. I belong to you, body and soul, just as you belong to me. There can be no other way. Jabari has the legal authority to marry us, Katherine. I am asking him to do so today."

"There can be no marriage. You can't keep me here," she cried out. "You don't understand. So much is at risk."

"Does this risk concern your reasons for stealing the map?" Ramses peered into her face, searching for answers. "This has to do with your father, am I correct? He is returning for you, with others?"

Katherine remained silent. He reached out, cradled her cheek with his hand. One thumb brushed the corner of her eye where a tear threatened to make its traitorous appearance.

She could not chance it. Not with the spy who knew Ramses's every move. Her promised silence kept Papa alive.

"Never mind. We shall talk of it later. Jabari and Elizabeth insist on us dining alone with them tonight. Rest now. You look too pale." His solicitous look filled her with guilt.

"Ramses, I can't marry you," she whispered.

He gave her a smile filled with arrogant self-assurance. "Katherine, we will be married. Tonight, after the evening meal." Swallowing her small hands in his large ones, he gave them a quick squeeze.

Katherine stared after him as he left. Settling a hand on her belly, she began using Ramses's breathing method to calm herself. Her eyes roved around the tent. A goatskin water bag hung from a nail on a tent pole. On a low table sat a bowl of fruit. She went to her bag and dug into it and took out the stolen artifact. Katherine stared at the regal expression on the cat's golden face. If the Khamsin discovered her theft . . . She shuddered and dropped it into the bag. Ramses said he didn't tolerate anyone taking what was his. She imagined how angry and hurt his reaction would be upon discovering her theft. But without the gold, her father remained imprisoned.

Katherine knew she must find the cave. By riding straight south, she could do it. Desperation and the risks fought inside her. Desperation won. She began gathering supplies.

Few people were about when she headed for the grassy area where the Khamsin kept their Arabians. Soon she came upon thatches of yellow and green scrub and a herd of grazing horses. Katherine noticed a beautiful, sleek black mare tossing her head. Saddles and a bitless bridle sat nearby. Some minutes later, the docile mare was saddled and ready. Katherine mounted and began riding south in the cave's direction.

She had barely congratulated herself on escaping when grunting sounds of men and metal clashing against metal greeted her ears. Katherine stopped the horse and dismounted. Weaving her way through boulders, she rounded a corner, ducked behind a rock and watched.

Ramses and Jabari. Fighting. Her hands flew to her mouth in panic. No, training. Clad only in trousers, they swung and feinted, ducked and parried, each with a distinct rhythm and elegance unique to his own style.

Fascinated, she drew back, wondering how she could sneak past them. Large clouds of dust rode the wind in lazy swirls as the men fought. Jagged, dry mountains provided a rugged backdrop to their fierce dueling. The unforgiving harsh desert terrain seemed as brutal as the men tangling with each other in a wild battle of steel and might. They fought with animal grace, two large predators snarling with dauntless energy.

Her gaze followed the bareheaded men. Both were firmly muscled. Jabari was taller, but Ramses had a dangerous catlike elegance and feisty determination that made him a fierce opponent to Jabari's long, lean form and skillful maneuvers. Her lover's powerful arms, rippling with firm, sleek muscles that flexed with mighty strength, twirled the sword with poetic speed. Coated with a fine sheen of sweat, his body glistened in the sunshine. Desire coursed through her veins as she studied Ramses's naked torso.

He made a humorous face at Jabari and beckoned to him with his sword, taunting him to attack. Jabari scowled and feinted. Ramses sidestepped easily and threw his hands into the air, cocking his head.

"Are you slowing down in your old age, sire?"

"Not as much as I will make you slow down in yours," Jabari grunted back good-naturedly.

Ramses's grace and boyish playfulness reminded her of a cat amusing itself with prey, teasing it before pouncing for the final kill. He thrust forward, a clean move executed with powerful speed that caught Jabari off-guard and nicked him. Ramses raised his eyebrows at the thin trickle of blood flowing down the sheikh's arm.

"I must practice my medical skills on my leader again. I cannot have you bleed to death. Elizabeth will have my head!"

"If you touch my wound with those foul treatments of yours you will not have to wait for my wife to remove your head, for I shall do it myself!" Jabari grunted, twirling his sword. He reached into his belt and withdrew a long silver dagger with his left hand.

"Let us see how healed you truly are," he said, gesturing with the knife.

"Oh, you are finally deciding to get serious now and stop fighting like a girl?" Ramses crouched down and narrowed his eyes. A deadly smile graced his sensuous lips. He withdrew his own dagger. The two men circled each other, focusing on each other's faces. Then Jabari rushed and attacked with surprising speed. But Ramses was equally fast. He rushed forward, dove into a roll, then hooked one foot around Jabari's leg, tripping him. Ramses sprang up, knocking Jabari's dagger away and then thrusting forward with his own dagger, deliberately missing the Khamsin sheikh's lower torso.

Jabari sheathed his scimitar, then bent over and retrieved his dagger, breathing heavily and laughing. He replaced the blade in his belt, then gave Ramses a hearty clap on the back. "You are almost back to your old form, my friend!"

"Almost?" Ramses bent over, panting and raised his head, flashing a cocky grin filled with charm. That smile made her heart ache with longing. "I would say I am there right now."

She shifted her handhold on the boulder, sending a shower of pebbles tumbling down. The sudden noise made both men whirl around. Katherine froze. She gazed at Ramses. And this time could not prevent her shudder at the icy look he gave her.

Katherine! Ramses checked his anger and surprise to see his bride. Khamsin training grounds were forbidden to women. His hand automatically flew to his uncovered head. Both he and Jabari had shed their turbans and tied back their hair with leather thongs. A woman viewing them like this outside the privacy of their tents was disgraceful.

He gripped the handle of his scimitar with white-knuckled intensity, then sheathed the blade. She wore the customary indigo *kuftan* all Khamsin women wore. Katherine had wrapped her head in a fringed blue scarf, similar to the one Elizabeth always wore. Unlike Jabari's wife, she had draped one edge of the scarf around her face to veil it.

Seeing this evoked more frustration. When would Katherine ever work up the courage to uncloak her face? How could she assimilate into his world of unveiled women if she did not see herself as he did, as a beautiful woman who didn't need to hide behind a cloth? Knowing she still harbored deep pain about her scar filled him with grief. His temper rose to the surface.

"What are you doing here?" he snapped.

"I, I, didn't mean . . . to intrude," she stammered.

The stricken look in her eyes lowered his temperature. Ramses advanced toward her, his jaw tensing as his gaze locked with hers. She held her ground. He kept walking until he could count every one of those long, lustrous lashes. Training with Jabari had worked his emotions into a lather. He felt the lusty, raging beast rattle the cage, demanding release.

When he was a breath away, Katherine reached out, touched his right shoulder. He recoiled in surprise as she probed the bullet wound. Her touch felt like the brush of flower petals against his aching muscles. Two lines furrowed her brow as she examined the scar.

"This has healed nicely for you to have executed such powerful moves. But you were badly wounded. Don't strain the muscle too much. It still needs to mend or you'll cause further damage by tearing it."

Her gaze met his. "Your shoulder should hurt after working it so furiously."

"I can manage. It is nothing," he stated.

"Pain is your body's way of saying you must slow down," she said, refusing to look away.

Again, she proved correct, for a sharp ache rolled through his shoulder. Ramses took a deep, controlling breath, glancing at his sheikh. Jabari lifted one eyebrow. He saw the question in his friend's eyes and sought to reassure him.

"I am a Khamsin warrior. I know my body's limits," he growled, watching her expression.

Katherine acted nervous. Her gaze kept darting to behind the rocks. Ramses inhaled the air, smelling the familiar scent of horses. Narrowing his eyes, he strode past her, beckoning to his sheikh. She scurried to keep up and hung back as they rounded the corner. Jabari's eyes met his as Ramses reached out a hand and stroked his beloved mare's muzzle. The Khamsin sheikh lifted a thoughtful brow as Ramses folded his arms on his chest, looking to Katherine for an explanation.

Katherine paused and petted Fayla's muzzle with affection.

"Your horses are beautiful," she explained as if that excused everything. "I wanted to take one for a ride."

Those large, emerald eyes held a hint of guile. Ramses felt his body tense as he examined Fayla. Saddled and with supplies. He should have known Katherine would try to escape.

"Our horses serve us well enough," he said guardedly.

"Oh, no, I would not say that. Well enough does not do the horse justice! I grew up riding the finest Thoroughbreds in London and they cannot compare to the elegance of your horses."

Jabari looked interested as Katherine stroked Fayla's withers. "They are short, but have amazing lung capacity and can ride for miles! It is simple to pick them out with their beautiful faces. Look at these ears, always alert!"

Katherine gestured toward Fayla's ears. The mare pricked them forward, as if she knew she was the object of discussion. "Your horses are well-suited to a desert life."

A murmur of surprised approval drifted from his sheikh's lips. Ramses watched Katherine with suspicion as she ambled over to Fayla's side. She might charm his sheikh into thinking all this praise meant only that she wished to study his beloved mare, but he knew better. Katherine wanted only to deflect their attention away from her real purpose. Ramses lifted the goatskin water bag, tested its weight, and dropped it.

"Well-suited for a desert life and for crossing long stretches of sand, for women who try running away?" he suggested.

Katherine swung into the stirrup and mounted the mare, startling both men into leaping back as she dug her heels into Fayla's sides and rode off in a cloud of dust.

Ramses swore under his breath and looked frantically back at the herd of placid, grazing horses. He raced toward one mare, gave a running leap and grabbed the mane, swinging up onto her bare back. Digging his boot heels into her sides, he galloped off after Katherine. Fayla was swift and he urged the horse faster to catch up. Ramses caught sight of Katherine. She rode as if one with the horse, woman and mare blending into one shape. Long, silky black curls trailed behind her in the wind created by her ride. Despite his rage, he admired her grace and expert style. She could ride as well as any Khamsin warrior galloping into battle. Her grace was like watching a beautiful dancer sway to the beat of unheard music.

Katherine heard the pounding echo of hoof beats drawing up close behind her. Tossing a hasty glance over her shoulder, she saw Ramses gaining on her. He rode with the powerful speed of his totem—the tiger. His firmly muscled, handsome frame bent over the horse, handling her with confident assurance. Her heart tripped frantically as she rode faster.

A shrill, loud whistle sliced the air. As if she had jerked on the reins, the noise made her mare slow and then stop in perfect obedience. Katherine did not kick the horse to urge her on. She loved animals, and knew when she was beaten.

Ramses pulled up and stopped short by expertly digging into his horse's sides with his knees. He slid off with ease and ran to her side.

"Are you quite mad?" he roared. "Fayla is pregnant! She could have tripped and injured herself. She must not be ridden hard. And what would have happened to you, riding like a mad woman in this heat?" He drew in a shuddering breath and stroked the mare's quivering nose with affection. More affection and consideration than he showed her, Katherine thought bitterly.

"Get off now. You will ride back with me and I will walk her. She is dangerously overheated."

Her temper dangerously overheating, as well, Katherine ignored his hand as she dismounted. His eyes seared her as Ramses removed Fayla's saddle and placed it on his own horse, tying Fayla's reins behind. When she had mounted, he swung up behind Katherine, encircling her waist with his arms. They rode in silence. When he finally spoke, his concerned voice startled her.

"Katherine, do not attempt this again. It is far too dangerous. What would you have done if you ran out of water? You could have died out there."

He gently squeezed her waist. She thought he murmured, "I would die if I lost you, for I cannot live without my Kalila." His protective concern brought all emotions rushing to the surface. Leaning against his hard body, Katherine wished she could confide in him.

"Ramses, I wouldn't do this if I didn't have to," she mumbled, fighting an urge to confess all. Hysterics laced her tone. "I have no choice. You keep saying we have choices. I don't. Why can't you just let me go! I have no choices!"

"Kalila, stop it. Calm down." He stopped the horse, gently twisted Katherine toward him. He looked deeply troubled.

"Please trust me. Tell me now how your father is involved in this. Tell me, so we may know what to do."

Agitation eased at the soothing, deep tones of his voice. Golden eyes searched hers, so piercing and intense. If she trusted Ramses, what if Burrells found out? Burrells had a spy who knew everything Ramses did. One word from the spy to Burrells and she jeopardized Papa's life.

Memories of Osiris surfaced. Tears pricked her eyelids. She had nearly lost her beloved cat, only to find the tiger she loved with her whole heart. Agonized indecision ripped her heart in half. Wetness slid down her cheeks as tears finally spilled out.

"I can't," she whispered. "Osiris. Oh, my poor Osiris!"

Ramses's gaze clouded with concern. He wiped the corner of her eye with his thumb. "Osiris? The god of the afterlife? What does an ancient Egyptian god have to do with this?"

Her veiled lips trembled on the verge of telling him. Katherine pressed a hand to them.

"Please, Ramses. Stop questioning me."

His attitude changed into tender concern. He kissed her forehead. When they reached the herd of Arabians, Jabari had vanished like a silent wind. Ramses dismounted and helped her off.

"Katherine, my love. Come. You are so tired. I can see it in your beautiful eyes. I will bring you to your tent so you may rest."

Exhausted, she let him take her arm. His kindness pierced her guilty conscience like a sharp sword. How would he react if he discovered the gold sitting at the bottom of her woven bag?

Katherine didn't dare think about that.

Chapter Twenty-five

Katherine's stomach constricted with anxiety at dinner as she sat on a colorful carpet in the sheikh's tent. Jabari, who previously treated her with utmost kindness, aimed his piercing dark gaze at her. Shards of obsidian chipped her composure. She had no idea what had soured his mood.

She was afraid to find out.

The sheikh radiated a regal presence with his neatly trimmed black beard and long hair curling beneath his indigo turban. Her hands went cold and clammy as she eyed the deadly scimitar at his waist, a duplicate of Ramses's, but for the ivory handle.

As Ramses tossed puzzled glances at his silent friend, his jaw hardened beneath his dark beard. Since arriving at the Khamsin camp, his beard and mustache had grown back, accenting his strong jawline and cheeks. It served as a reminder that this man who had been inside her body was a virtual stranger. He belonged to these people of sand and dust and ancient Egypt. She did not.

An air of dominating strength and power radiated from him, masking the playful grace she'd seen in the desert. Katherine realized it was the natural aura of a man with many responsibilities at home in his world.

Set on a low table before them, a platter containing thick, rich lamb stew failed to stimulate her appetite. She nibbled on the flatbread as Jabari, Ramses and Elizabeth dipped wedges of it into the food, then drank sweet tea from small, handleless cups.

Elizabeth handed her a teacup filled with English tea. She smiled her thanks, grateful for her thoughtfulness. She raised her veil and sipped, feeling the warmth slide down into her churning stomach.

Elizabeth chattered about Egyptian archaeological sites as if the thick tension fogging the air didn't exist. The sheikh's wife failed to notice the guarded look her husband aimed at Ramses. A deep flush skated up Katherine's throat to her face. She felt as helpless as the lamb sacrificed for the evening meal.

"Do you ride, Katherine? I never felt comfortable on a horse. Still don't, despite my husband's attempts to mold me into a rider." She threw the sheikh an exasperated look, to which he responded with a gentle smile.

"She rides," Ramses's short reply answered.

Katherine swallowed, determined to return the young woman's friendliness. Elizabeth's attitude helped thaw the chill. Surely, she could add to the continued defrosting. "In England I rode in Hyde Park, the London park where all the gentry ride. I was practically raised on a horse."

Jabari dipped a wedge of flatbread into the sticky mixture of rice and roast lamb and ate it. "The gentry would find riding in Khamsin territory more challenging than on the soft grass of an English park," he observed.

"Or Khamsin mares too spirited, compared to their docile mounts," Ramses added, wrinkling his brow at his sheikh.

"English horses could never win a race with our mares," Jabari stated.

"Ignore them, Katherine. They think only Khamsin Arabians are worthy of their attention," Elizabeth remarked.

"Khamsin Arabians are," Ramses said with pride. His broad shoulders stiffened as if he had personally bred the entire herd. "Our mares are of the purest bloodlines, the finest stock. We never dilute our line with impure, foreign blood."

Katherine's English half bristled as she set down her teacup and locked eyes with him.

"Sounds to me as if your Arabians are too inbred, which can make for short-tempered, problematic horses. If you breed too much among your own stock, you fail to incorporate the quality traits of others."

Both Jabari and Ramses threw her the exact same withering look. The twin intensity caused a chill to race up her spine. But she didn't drop her gaze.

"Our horses are prized among the royal families of Europe as being the fastest, strongest, most spirited Arabians. Mixing the breed only taints the bloodlines," Ramses said tightly. He drank and backhanded his mouth.

"Not tainting the bloodlines. I see it as strengthening them with traits that perhaps your own horses lack."

Elizabeth threw her an admiring glance. "I've often thought that of our son. He is the combination of two different cultures. Tarik will have the best of us."

The sheikh's expression softened as he looked at his wife. "Your brains and my beauty," Jabari teased.

"I was thinking more about blending our two cultures," she said seriously. "Our people will need a sheikh with appreciation for Western technology and your leadership skills to keep pace with the world's changes."

The loving way the Khamsin chieftain lifted his wife's hand and grazed her knuckles with a tender kiss moved Katherine. "Tarik will have the best, only because he has you as a mother," he said quietly.

Elizabeth gave her husband a serene smile. Katherine ached to share the same intimacy with Ramses, one loving glance, one slow smile that said everything.

A whimper sounded in the corner where the baby slept. Elizabeth rose, gathered him into her arms and sat again. She soothed her son, and then opened her *kuftan*, discreetly hiding him from view as she tucked him against her breast. Listening to her coo softly to the baby filled Katherine with sad longing. She would bear Ramses's child alone. Her son or daughter would be dutifully raised to drink English tea, attend Cambridge and wear starched neck ties, not gallop through the dusky plains, sleeping under the stars. English life sounded awfully stuffy compared to the exotic thrills the Khamsin experienced.

"Let's talk about the gold mine. It has such a fascinating history. I love discovering Khamsin history. Would you like to hear its secret, Katherine?" Elizabeth asked cheerfully, ignoring the furious glances both men cast in her direction.

The other woman gave her a quick, conspiratorial wink. She hid a smile. Elizabeth was well aware her husband and his Guardian wanted to keep quiet about that topic. In that moment, the sheikh's wife became an ally.

Katherine smiled. "I'd love to hear it."

"Do you know that Pharaoh Tutankhamun bequeathed it to the Khamsin warriors of the wind for a very special reason?"

"Elizabeth," Jabari's voice rose on a warning note. But the sheikh's wife bent her head and cooed to her nursing son.

"Many Egyptologists theorize that King Tutankhamun was the son of Queen Kiya, Akhetaten's minor wife, and the pharaoh."

"And?"

Elizabeth grinned impishly at her husband. "Tutankhamun bequeathed the mine to the Khamsin because of his real father. Queen Kiya's lover, Ranefer, the Khamsin leader."

Katherine nearly dropped her teacup.

A muscle worked in Ramses's jaw. His body stiffened with this revelation. Secrets Ramses kept from her. Secrets she shielded from him. Secrets layered the foundation of their relationship.

"This knowledge is not for anyone outside our tribe, Elizabeth," Jabari said, his face tightening with clear disapproval. But Elizabeth answered with a shrug.

"Katherine won't be outside our tribe when she marries Ramses, so stop fussing," she told him.

Hostility radiated off Jabari in waves. She was an outsider, not to be trusted. She saw it in his guarded expression, in the icy looks he directed at her.

The sheikh focused his chilled black gaze on her. "Tutankhamun cursed the tomb to outsiders before he sealed it." Jabari emphasized the word "cursed."

"Except for the Khamsin, all who dare to breach the sacred chamber will be haunted forever by Rastau's spirit," Ramses droned as if he were the pharaoh uttering the words.

"If a Khamsin blade does not catch them first," Jabari added. "Do you understand, Katherine?"

Two pairs of eyes, one black as pitch, one amber as gold, regarded her. Katherine swallowed, put a hand to her throat.

"Please," she begged, humiliated at her pleading tone of voice, but too scared to stop it. "Why are you acting like this?"

Ramses frowned at his sheikh, asking the same question with his eyes. Jabari unbuttoned his *binish* and reached inside. He withdrew the little gold cat she'd stolen from the tomb.

A shock of fear slammed into her. Her mouth went sand dry.

"One of my men dropped your bag while unloading it from Fayla. This spilled out." His jaw was set, his lips a tight slash. The sheikh's eyes narrowed to furious slits.

"Your bride, my friend, is a thief," he told Ramses.

The black-eyed sheikh directed his piercing glare at her. Katherine only had eyes for her love. Deep anguish twisted his face. Ramses looked stricken, as if she'd wounded him.

His jaw muscles jumped beneath his beard as he quietly regarded his sheikh. "If Katherine stole the cat, I am certain she had a good reason for it."

"Such as selling it? Her father wanted to partner with us to work the mine, Ramses. The English are greedy. You have stated so. And so are your bride and her father."

299

Two angry amber eyes locked with hard black ones. "Do not insult my future wife, Jabari. I will not tolerate it."

The sheikh's expression softened. "Ramses, I am only thinking of you. You did not want this marriage. I could see it in your eyes, my friend. I do not want to see you hurt." His gaze shot over to Katherine. "Or dishonored."

Ramses nodded curtly. "I appreciate your concern, but this is a matter between Katherine and myself." He turned to her, his voice low and urgent.

"Why Katherine? What possible reason could you have for stealing from the tomb?"

An undertone of grief threaded through Ramses's quiet voice. It lacerated her heart.

"I can't tell you," she whispered, clenching her hands.

A muscle jumped in his clenched jaw as he shut his eyes for a minute. When he opened them, his golden gaze had turned hard. "When did you do it, Katherine? When you asked me to leave the tomb so you could gather your composure?"

"Yes," she admitted, her shoulders slumping. Katherine studied the ground in miserable shame.

"This matter does not concern only you, Ramses. It concerns the tribe, as well. Show her what we do to tomb robbers." The sheikh's command filled her with terror.

Katherine backed away. She had seen the gentle Ramses, the lover who lavished tender kisses on her. The passionate Ramses whose teeth nipped her neck when they coupled like wildcats. Even the vengeful Ramses who cornered her in the Cairo alley.

But never had she seen the furious Khamsin warrior

who uncoiled his powerful body and swept them all with a razor sharp look. Ramses stepped a few feet away from the circle and withdrew his scimitar. In a series of graceful moves, he twirled it into the air. Her frightened eyes followed every motion. Not even a sheen of sweat beaded his brow from the magnificent, terrible display of a warrior's prowess.

Ramses turned suddenly. He plucked a fig from the table and tossed it into the air. The blade descended with lightning speed, splitting the fruit into two.

"That is what we do to tomb robbers," Jabari remarked with satisfaction.

"No, Jabari," he said quietly, sheathing his blade. "This is what I will do to the one who threatens my beloved Katherine and forced her to commit this atrocious act of theft."

Awed with tenderness for him, Katherine watched him resume his seat with proud dignity, those broad shoulders squared. Jabari gave his friend a thoughtful look.

"And what if that person forcing her is Lord Smithfield?"

Katherine's breath hitched. Anger darkened Ramses's face. "The English are treacherous," he admitted. "Perhaps the earl did not truly want to partner with us, but steal for himself."

"If so he will know the sharp end of a Khamsin blade," Jabari vowed.

Horror pulsed through Katherine. She gave Elizabeth a pleading look. The other woman frowned, stopped feeding the baby and covered herself. She sat him upright, patting his back.

"Stop it, Jabari. You're scaring her," she said sternly.

"Elizabeth, this is a most serious matter," Jabari warned her. "What Katherine has done jeopardizes our people's future."

"Lord Smithfield will know the tomb's location and reveal it to the *samak*. My ancestor's sacred resting place will become a tourist haven." Ramses growled.

"I never wanted that," Katherine protested.

Ramses locked a grief-stricken amber gaze on her. "Do you know what the English do with mummies, Katherine? They become spectacles for curious gawkers. Your people, the wealthy of England, purchase mummies. Not entire bodies. Heads, fingers, toes are all divided and placed neatly on English mantles as trophies!"

Katherine pressed her trembling hands against her belly. "But that's not me. I would never dishonor your ancestors that way," she whispered.

"How can we be certain, when the English are as cunning and treacherous as desert jackals?" Jabari demanded.

"They are Ramses's people, as well, Jabari," Elizabeth commented. "How can you insult your best friend?"

"Elizabeth, stop." Jabari admonished her, his dark brows drawing together like thunderclouds. He threw his Guardian a distressed look.

But his wife pressed on. "Jabari, how could you condemn the English when your own Guardian's grandfather was English?"

Her mild blue eyes held no recrimination, but Ramses reddened just the same. Katherine gawked at this revelation. Ramses was a product of mixed bloodlines, just as she was. No wonder he clung to his Egyptian ancestry. It was a desperate attempt to deny the part of himself he hated.

Sudden understanding filled her. Just as she struggled with her own dueling halves, a similar battle raged inside Ramses. His body tightened with pride, those muscled arms folded across the breadth of his enormous chest. An instinctive need to offer comfort filled her.

"The fiercest warrior possesses the best traits handed down through successive generations. That is the advantage of mixing bloodlines," Katherine said softly.

His glance was so filled with anguish her heart shrank inside her chest cavity. Ramses's jaw tightened.

"And the disadvantages are traits I despise, like the greediness that makes the English steal from our sacred tombs. How I wish my children would not be tainted by English blood," he commented tonelessly.

Katherine pressed a hand to her belly where the baby grew. Their child. Tainted in his eyes because she was English. Pride refused to let her shed the tears rising in her throat. Murmuring a polite thanks to Elizabeth, she stood and raced back to her tent, desperate for a warmer atmosphere than the one she fled.

Reaching her tent, she hesitated. A silver crescent moon hung low in the darkening sky. She stood for a minute, drinking in twilight and its chill, then walked slowly toward the camp's edge. When she reached the animal pens, only a small boy watching the sheep stood guard. She smiled at him, standing as if he guarded gold, not sheep. Katherine thought of her child and her breath hitched.

Ramses loved her. But he thought the English were all tomb robbers, and he thought her father was one, as well. Papa was one of the most noble men she'd ever known. He revered Egyptian culture as much as he honored his own. He'd gladly give his life, as Ramses would, for those he loved. Ramses didn't know her father's life was in danger. He thought her father was merely greedy and made her steal, which further sealed her betrothed's prejudice against the English.

She thought of how Ramses had hugged his father and knew he loved his father as dearly as she loved hers. Ramses was the father of her child. Her child deserved a father. A Khamsin warrior who could slay dozens of enemies with his scimitar. She struggled with her emotions. All the times in the cave, he talked of trust, soothed her fears. Tears scalded her eyes. He had to know, finally. Only by telling him the truth, could she erase the barriers between them. Ramses was a Khamsin warrior who possessed incredible strength and stealth. Surely, he could help find a way to release Papa.

Katherine realized she must step out in utter faith and trust in him. She simply couldn't go it alone any longer.

An approaching camel caught her attention. She watched as the beast sank to its knees, and then Kareem slid off. The young warrior went toward her, his step filled with purpose. Katherine put a hand to her belly, filled with a sudden, unknowing dread.

"Kareem, nice to see you," she managed to say.

"Lady Katherine. Just the person I need."

His hand snaked out so suddenly she had no time to react. She felt a heavy pinch to her neck, then darkness engulfed her.

*　　*　　*

Ramses stood to pursue Katherine. Elizabeth handed Tarik to Jabari. Then she rose and pulled on Ramses's arm with surprising strength. "Leave her alone. How can you insult her? What gives you the right?"

"Her father is a tomb robber," Ramses countered, guilt flushing him as her icy blue gaze met his.

"And Katherine is a pawn. She doesn't love gold." Elizabeth sank to the carpet and turned to her husband. "Just as I didn't. Remember, Jabari?"

His friend set his jaw like flint against his wife's soft pleas. "Elizabeth, this is different. You never intended to steal the Almha. You wanted to dig up the disk for the ancient remedies to try to save your grandmother. Katherine stole a priceless gold artifact from the tomb of Ramses's ancestor. You cannot compare the two."

"I can," she said stubbornly.

Ramses growled deep in his throat and looked away, fighting his own frustration. Katherine's act of thievery shed a dangerous light on their relationship. Katherine knew he despised tomb raiders. What possible reason could excuse her plundering?

He studied Elizabeth's narrowed eyes, her racing pulse. Insight came to him. Women sometimes talked, revealing secrets to each other they hid from men.

"Elizabeth, what did Katherine tell you?"

Jabari's gaze shifted to his wife. She glanced back.

"I promised not to tell anyone. I promised."

"Elizabeth, if Katherine gave you a clue as to why she stole the gold, we must know," Jabari said gently.

"My only desire is to help her," Ramses added.

Elizabeth twisted a strand of hair around her finger. "She didn't exactly say, but she's not the one being threatened. Her father is."

Bonnie Vanak

"She's protecting her father. Someone is endangering him," he thought aloud.

"You have to help her, Ramses," Elizabeth pleaded. "She needs you. Isn't Katherine more important than some old gold buried in a musty tomb for thousands of years? She's going to be your wife and the mother . . ." The blond woman bit her lip, then gave him a guilty look and rose, hastily clearing the meal.

Ramses looked after her thoughtfully, then at Jabari. He didn't like the sly grin curving the sheikh's lips.

"Ah, that explains why your bride soiled my boots. That hair of yours, Ramses. Perhaps I cut it too late, if it is the sign of virility you claim it is."

"What are you implying, Jabari?" But his racing heartbeat told him he already knew.

The Khamsin sheikh lifted his son up and clucked at him. Then he handed him over with aplomb to Ramses. Ramses held up the baby with growing wonder, staring up at his chubby face.

"You burp him. You will need the practice."

Tarik's large dark eyes held his as the truth slowly dawned. Practice. Burping babies. Because Katherine was carrying his child.

Just as the thought hit him, Tarik spit up over his *binish*. Sour milk stenched the air. Tarik gurgled. The delighted laugh of his proud father followed. "Now we are even, my friend, for what your bride did."

Ramses could only gaze at the baby with dawning awe. Oh, Katherine, he thought, why did you not tell me? The words he'd uttered about his children's tainted bloodlines haunted him. Again, he had acted impulsively.

His baby. Their baby, he corrected as he stared at Tarik thoughtfully. All his life he had despised his English side. He struggled to repress it. Yet Katherine made a valid point. His mixed blood gave him advantages other warriors never had. His strength and cunning resulted from it.

Tarik's delighted babbles as his father took him and lifted him into the air drew his attention. Like Tarik, their baby would be a perfect blending of cultures. English stubbornness and Egyptian impulsiveness. Ramses grinned as he removed his *binish* and tossed it next to Jabari.

"Washing it is the least you can do."

As he stalked off, a tender, fierce possessiveness stole over him. He wanted to enfold her in his arms and whisper his sheer joy at the news of their child. But he had wounded her deeply. He must make amends now.

Ramses went to her tent and pulled aside the flaps. It was empty.

Alarm raced through him. He took a shuddering breath, reassuring himself. She could not get far. But several minutes later, he combed the entire camp and saw no trace of her. He spotted a young boy tending sheep at the camp's edge. The child looked up as Ramses squatted down next to him, asking if he had seen anyone leave.

"Kareem was here and then he left with that lady."

Ramses's guts twisted. He bent down and spoke gently to the boy. "What lady?"

"The lady with the pretty green eyes. She was sitting on the camel funny, like she was asleep."

Standing, he could only stare at the empty horizon. Katherine was gone, taken by Kareem.

He'd lost her.

Chapter Twenty-six

An assembly of warriors gathered on the sand, discussing the latest twist of events. Flames from the glowing campfire cast eerie shadows on the men's solemn faces. Jabari assumed his rightful place at the circle's head as Ramses told them what had transpired. When he finished, Salah glared at Ramses.

"Kareem is young, but he is a warrior. I refuse to believe my son took your bride. Why would he act so foolishly? Perhaps the child was mistaken. Or perhaps your bride wished to run away and Kareem could not allow her to go alone."

Ramses leveled a look at him. "If so, Kareem's obligation was to return her to me, not leave. You make no sense, Salah."

The older man returned his steely look with a solicitous one. "You are upset, Ramses, and with good reason, for Lady Katherine was severely affected by the heat when you arrived. Hopefully, she will take care of herself, for the desert sun is hot and she is so small and delicate."

A distant memory tugged at his mind with nagging insistence. Lady Katherine. So small and delicate. And then the memory hit him with the power of a fist socketing into his jaw. The words Kareem had uttered long ago. Words he had glossed over, focusing on the boy's insulting him.

English women sometimes are beautiful. At least the ones who are so tiny and delicate, like Lady Katherine.

How did Kareem know Katherine was petite? He had never seen her. No Khamsin had. Not until Ramses met her.

Unless . . . Ramses concentrated on Salah, a man he trusted, beside whom he had fought many times.

"Salah, why did you want Kareem to return home so soon?"

The older man looked shamefaced. His gaze slid over to Jabari, who suddenly went still. "It was his mistress in Amarna. She gave him the pleasures of one thousand nights. I made inquiries and discovered Kareem had soiled himself with spoiled goods, for she was an Englishman's mistress. This man makes his living robbing the tombs of the honored dead."

Salah spat on the ground. "I warned Kareem, but he insisted she loved him. He said nothing could stop him from seeing her again. That is why I made him return home."

"Who was this Englishman?" Ramses demanded.

"He has an odd name. Burrows or Borrows . . ."

"Burrells," Ramses said quietly, thinking back to the tomb raider he'd injured—before.

Salah's eyes widened. "Yes. Burrells."

As if the mosaic suddenly shaped itself into a clear pattern, he saw the entire picture. Burrells pressured

Katherine into stealing the map. Perhaps he even held her father hostage and threatened to harm him. Burrells had discovered the tomb because a Khamsin warrior happened to tell his lover about it . . .

"Your son gave away the tomb's secret," Ramses said flatly.

Salah halfway rose to his feet, his face darkening with rage. "You insult my family!"

"Sit down, Salah," Jabari ordered, beckoning to the ground. He turned his attention to Ramses. "Why do you say this?"

Ramses explained the connection to Foster Burrells. "Lovers talk. Kareem mentioned he had a mistress."

Deep creases furrowed Salah's forehead. "Kareem did tell me he would find her again, and they would be together," he admitted, giving Ramses a stricken look.

His guts coiled into thousands of knots. His beloved was in the desert with an impulsive youth who put her in terrible danger. Ramses looked around the circle of sober warriors.

"I am leaving tonight to try to stop him before he reaches the cave. I need a few strong warriors with me, for I do not know what lies ahead."

As expected, several men, including his father, stood to show their support. But when the Khamsin sheikh rose as well, Ramses's jaw dropped.

"Jabari, not you," he protested. "I will not place you in jeopardy. Your place is here with Elizabeth and your son."

"My place is by your side, my friend. Ramses, you were the only one to stand with me to rescue Elizabeth last year. I will repay that favor and that loyalty."

He started to object when his father held up a hand.

"Jabari is right, my son. A favor must be repaid, for it is a matter of honor." He glanced at the Khamsin sheikh as he said this. Jabari's lips had tightened and his black eyes glittered fiercely. Ramses understood. Jabari's personal honor. His honor as a friend, not a sheikh.

"I will be most grateful for your help, sire," he stated.

His friend relaxed. "I am most happy to offer it," he said with equal formality.

Ramses nodded, too overcome with emotion to speak. His father gazed at him kindly, touched his sleeve.

"Do not fear, Ramses. We will find her."

Chapter Twenty-seven

For three days, she had talked, reasoned and argued with Kareem. From the time she had awoken, Kareem had treated her most gently. He shared provisions, took rest breaks, inquired about her health. But he refused to listen to her fervent warnings about the danger awaiting them. He rejected her story about Burrells threatening to kill her father. She coaxed information from him and discovered Kareem had gone to the cave and met up with Burrells and Lord Estes. When Kareem told the curator where she was, Burrells had instructed him to return with Katherine.

Kareem's dark eyes filled with a dreamy longing and his smile grew wistful when he talked about how the gold would give him and his love, Maia, a new start in life in Cairo. Burrells had the one spy whom no one would suspect—a Khamsin warrior so sick with love he would betray his tribe for money.

Long fingers of rose, lavender and gold stroked the tawny sand as they reached the cave's outskirts. Kareem captured Katherine's wrist in a solid grip as he dragged her inside the cave. A dull glow of lamplight sliced the darkness as he strode inside. Her eyes adjusted and caught sight of a small group of Egyptians armed with scimitars, a slender woman, Foster Burrells and Lord Estes. But when she saw her father, blindfolded, his hands tied in front as he sat, she yanked free and raced toward him.

"Papa!" she screamed. An armed guard scowled as she rushed to her father, embracing him tightly.

"Katherine," he whispered. "Thank God you're safe."

"Lady Katherine," Burrells droned in his cold, nasal voice. "So nice of you to drop by again."

Her joy evaporated as she regarded Lord Estes and the curator. "You released him from jail. Why? Does this mean you returned the amulet?"

"Of course," Lord Estes said briskly. "All charges have been dropped. When you didn't return to Cairo, I arranged to free your father. I knew he had partnered with the Khamsin and would know where the tomb was."

Her jaw dropped. "Return to Cairo? But I wasn't . . ."

Burrells interrupted her. "We knew you missed your dear papa, Katherine." She studied him, her suspicions growing. Something didn't add up.

A choking gasp drew her attention away from Burrells. Katherine turned as Kareem raced toward Maia. Her lovely sloe eyes shone like polished onyx as she cried out his name. Understanding flowed through Katherine, along with an intense pity so deep she wanted to cry. She released her tight grip on her father and watched the pair. The exotic beauty opened her arms and he tumbled into them. The young couple kissed with such fervent eagerness, she knew his heart was true, even if his intentions were misguided.

Kareem would do anything for love. She knew the feeling. She too, would do anything for love.

Finally, the lovers parted. "I have missed you," Maia said, her face soft with love as she clasped his hands. Suddenly, the woman didn't seem wicked or sultry, just a girl enthralled with her lover. Katherine's mouth quirked into a reluctant smile. She saw herself and Ramses standing there, their feelings clearly displayed for others to see.

The tenderness revealed in the young warrior's smile melted Katherine. He reached up to cup Maia's cheek. She pulled back with a wince. Kareem frowned and turned her face toward him. Even from her vantage point, Katherine could see the distinctive bruise marring the girl's perfect cheekbone.

Kareem dropped his hand. His lips curled into an ugly grimace. "Who did this to you?"

She said nothing, but darted a quick glance at Burrells. Katherine dragged her gaze over to the tomb robber. He stared at the pair with cold, dead eyes. Her pulse raced at the furious expression he directed at the young couple. He hated them. He hated their beauty, the beautiful simplicity of their love. He would destroy it.

"So, Maia, you lied to me. He *does* mean something to you, after all. Whore," the tomb raider said softly. He pulled a small pistol from his belt, cocked the trigger and pointed it.

One. Two. The sounds exploded in her eardrums with an earsplitting roar, but not half as deafening as the scream of anguish rippling from Kareem. Maia slumped to the floor, crimson flowering her pale blue shirt.

"There," Burrells said simply. For a moment an expression of grief crossed his face. Then it vanished.

"You fool," snapped Lord Estes, his rotund face paling. "Why did you kill her?"

Burrells remained silent. Kareem dropped to the ground, gathering the girl into his arms. Her lovely eyes stared sightlessly ahead. Long hair, black as a raven's wing, spilled over his trembling hands as he cradled his lover's head against his chest.

"Maia, my darling Maia, please, do not leave me," he whispered softly, but she did not respond. Kareem threw his head back and released an undulating shriek so piercing Katherine pressed fingers into her ears to shut out the agony.

"Oh, please," Burrells said, tucking the gun away.

Kareem placed a tender kiss on his lover's forehead. He set her down as gently as a mother laying down her baby to rest. Then he rose and his young, thin body seemed to gain years and stature. Dark eyes narrowed to enraged slits. The fierceness of his expression, the tight coils of anger as he unfolded his body, awed her. Burrells had made a very foolish mistake. He had plotted a dangerous trajectory straight toward the full-fledged fury of a Khamsin warrior of the wind.

Lethal silence fell over the cave as Kareem withdrew his scimitar. He touched his hand to his heart and then his lips. A thunderous, swelling cry, the same Ramses had made in love, rippled through the air. This time, she knew the piercing sound indicated war.

Sword held aloft, he rushed Burrells. The five armed Egyptians whipped out their scimitars and shielded the tomb raider with their bodies. Kareem became engulfed in a whirling ballet of sharp steel.

"Go, Lady Katherine, take your father and run!" Kareem screamed as his sword clashed against those of his attackers. Their eyes met for one brief second. She saw raging grief and dull acceptance. He knew what awaited him.

Frantically, she ripped the blindfold from her father's eyes and grappled with the tough knots binding his hands. She glanced at Kareem. Deep in her mind whispered the thought that someone needed to bear witness to Kareem's gallantry, to ease his father's pain and let him know his son had showed courage in the end. They fell on him like jackals, swords arcing and descending. One thrust the point of his scimitar through Kareem's chest. The warrior gasped, fell back, clutching his wound. But he did not drop his sword and dealt a crippling blow to one of his attackers. Kareem staggered back, and collapsed. He crawled toward Maia, then laid his head upon her breast. The young lovers lay side by side as if sleeping. Tears stung her eyes.

Katherine finally jerked the ropes from her father's hands. He sprang to his feet, taking her hand and racing for the entrance. They were going to make it, she thought frantically, but two men raced before her and blocked the way. They pointed their long blades at her. She swallowed convulsively.

"Now Lady Katherine, you will show me where the tomb is. And you'd better hurry," drawled Burrells.

Color drained from Lord Estes's face. "This is preposterous, Foster," he sputtered. "Everything is going wrong. You said all we needed to do was bring Landon here to find the tomb."

"Not exactly," Burrells corrected. A calculating

smile spread over his face. "I just told you that so you'd come with me. Did you really think I'd share the gold?"

The curator pointed his pistol at the nobleman and fired directly into Lord Estes's chest. He sagged against the wall, a look of surprise on his face as he collapsed.

Terror seized her as Burrells advanced, swung the gun toward her father, and fired. Her long scream equaled Kareem's anguish as scarlet spread across his white linen shirt. Her father wheezed and slumped to the ground, clutching his side. Burrells hard gaze met hers as she struggled to free herself from the man holding her back.

"The tomb, Lady Katherine. Take me to the tomb. Or stay here and watch him bleed to death. The faster you show me where the gold is, the faster you return here to treat him. The choice is yours."

Chapter Twenty-eight

The band of warriors rode at a breakneck pace. When they arrived at the cave, Ramses spotted a group of camels outside the entrance. Burrells and his men had returned.

Forgetting natural caution in his fear for Katherine, Ramses slid off his camel and unsheathed his scimitar, but his friend was quicker. Jabari dismounted and grabbed his arm. Seti held up a cautioning hand.

"Steady son, steady . . ." his father warned.

Ramses drew in a ragged breath. He nodded. The trio stalked toward the cave, followed by the remaining warriors. They tucked in their veils securely, withdrew their scimitars and touched their hands to hearts and lips.

As quiet as wraiths the men made their way to the cave. As they crept inside, Ramses forced himself to adjust to the dimness. Standing in the shadowed recesses, he saw where his love had saved his life. Where they had created a fire of passion and love.

Two men stood around in a circle, jeering as they

pointed at something. They stepped back and he saw what held their amusement. White-hot anguish raged through him, seeing the bodies lying on the ground, one clad in an indigo *binish*. Ramses gripped his weapon so tightly he could feel his nails digging into his palm. Slumped against the cave wall, Katherine's father gripped his side. Scarlet spread over Lord Smithfield's fingers. Badly wounded, the man looked as if he, too, would lose his life.

No emotions. Emotions meant danger. He could not lose his head to anger. Not this time. He felt Jabari's questioning tap upon his arm. Ramses signaled for the sheikh and his father to move forward. They nodded. He watched them cross over, creep along the opposite wall, silent as scorpions. Ramses advanced into the open.

Drawing in a deep breath, he arced his blade through the air in a deadly whoosh. He let his voice ring out, filling the entire cave with a resounding growl.

"Prepare to meet your maker, filthy dogs of the desert!"

He watched their faces crease into grins as swords snaked out of their sheaths. Having killed one Khamsin warrior, they thought he would prove equally easy to defeat. What an advantage this gave him!

"Say a prayer, jackals. Today you are flying into hell!"

As they charged, he attacked, slicing, feinting and dodging. He felt his body ease into its natural whirling dance of deadly steel, elegance and grace. It was over in minutes. They died with surprised looks on their faces. Ramses wiped his blade and rushed over to Jabari and his father, hunkering over the bodies on the ground.

He recognized the girl as his mistress's sister, who lived with her in Amarna. She had a pretty name, he remembered, staring at her with dull anger and grief. Maia. Ramses fell to one knee, checked the girl's pulse, even though he knew the vein would be still. With a heavy heart, he gently closed her eyes. Such a waste of life.

A hand seized his *binish*. Kareem grimaced with pain. His pale lips moved, trying to form words. Kareem's eyelids fluttered as he struggled to raise his head. Ramses bent closer to catch his whispered words.

"Lady Katherine. In the tomb. Save." Then he fell back and spoke no more.

Sounds of men rushing into the cave distracted him. Ramses looked up at Salah. Color drained from his sun-tinted face. His shoulders began to heave as if he suppressed his emotions.

"Your son died bravely." Ramses struggled with his own grief, but he knew he must address Salah, who had lost a precious son this day. Somehow, he had to restore the man's honor by assuring him Kareem had redeemed himself. As the older man knelt down to embrace his son's lifeless form, Ramses went to Lord Smithfield. He winced as he examined the earl. The bullet had exited, but he had lost much blood.

The earl opened his eyes and regarded Ramses with pain-glazed eyes. "Forget me. Save my daughter, Khamsin Guardian," he rasped. "Or my spirit will return and haunt you all your days."

Ramses's heart went still as Katherine's father slipped into unconsciousness. He rested his hand upon the earl's pulse, relieved to find it steady.

Leaving two other warriors to tend to the earl, Ramses left the cave, leading the way to the tomb.

With dull acceptance, Katherine guided Burrells and his accomplices through the mine to the burial chamber's secret entrance. When the fear-stricken Egyptians balked at entering the tomb, Burrells shoved one inside. Arrows peppered the man's chest. He dropped to the ground as the others ran off, but Burrells discharged his pistol, making them think twice. He ordered them back inside.

She saw their attitudes change when torchlight swept over the gold inside. Burrells's beady eyes glittered with greed. He shoved the torch into a wall sconce. Dropping the sacks slung over his shoulder, he squatted by a pile of treasure, sifting through it with trembling hands. The Egyptians crowded around it, kneeling like supplicants worshipping at an altar. Katherine edged back. Her heel connected with stone. She looked down over her shoulder and spotted the tablet covering the well. The men still occupied themselves with fondling the gold, exclaiming over it. Katherine bent over and struggled to push the rock aside. A dark pit yawned open like a round, ominous mouth.

Burrells finally stood, instructing the men to begin removing the gold. So eager were they, one nearly tripped, falling into the well. Burrells gave her a level look as she backed up against the sarcophagus, hugging herself as the men lugged out sacks brimming with treasure.

Then he turned to four men and snapped his fingers. Handing over a crowbar, Burrells ordered the sarcophagus opened as his fingers wrapped around Katherine's arm. The four struggled with it, set it on the ground, then removed the inside cover and balanced it against the wall. Burrells turned to her with a dark smile. Horror beat furious fists on her body.

"You told me I'd go free if I helped you find the gold," she whispered.

"I lied." He flashed an obscenely cheerful grin. "Bad habit of mine."

"The Khamsin won't let you get away with this."

"By the time they find out, I'll have sold the gold and left Egypt. Do you know why I sent you to find the tomb? Kareem told me you were marrying Nazim. I mean, Ramses." His laughter filled the air.

"What a fool I played you for! Sending you to steal a map from your own fiancé! Kareem told Maia *everything* and she told me. How you were marrying a Khamsin Guardian named Nazim Ramses bin Seti Sharif, but he was changing his name to Ramses with marriage. How he used the name Ramses in Cairo to seduce women. How neither you nor your father knew about the name change! I knew all about your father's business partnership with the Khamsin and how they made him keep silent about the tomb. Kareem even told Maia that Ramses kept the map on him at all times. I set you up."

She stared in thunderstruck horror as he gloated over his victory.

"That's why I framed your father: so you'd steal the map and the gold. It's a brilliant plan. If your desert fleabag caught you robbing the tomb, he'd think your father got greedy and sent you to do it. He'd seek revenge on your dear papa."

His face twisted with anger. "I hate that bastard Khamsin. Maia told me where the map was buried. I was just about to get it, too, when he surprised me in the tomb at Akhenaten. He nearly killed me."

Courage flickered. "I wish he had," she retorted.

Burrells narrowed his eyes. "Too late. I'm not the one who's going to die today."

Katherine's mind whirled. "Papa . . ." she whispered.

"Will be blamed for killing Lord Estes. By the time the Khamsin arrive, I'll be gone and they'll think your father and Estes shot each other over the gold. Now, Lady Katherine, come meet someone."

Her body went limp with fear. One hand drifted down her belly. She had to fight to save her baby. This fed her new strength. Katherine lashed out, kicking him. He grunted with surprise and twisted her arm. She cried out in pain.

My darling Ramses was right that day in the souks. *I am defenseless against a man! Oh, if only you were here, my love!*

Katherine fought, pummeling him with a tight fist as she screamed. She bent down and bit his wrist. He grunted and slapped her. Katherine reeled from the blow, but ducked her head and bit him again. Teeth were good weapons.

He slapped her again, more forcefully and she staggered backward, slipping to the ground. Pinpricks of light swam before her eyes. Someone jerked her ankles together and wound rope around them, then seized her hands and did the same. Awareness shot through her in a frantic torrent. They bound her like ancient Egyptians prepared a body . . . for burial. She writhed and screamed. Someone yanked a strip of cloth between her lips. Then they lifted her and carried toward the sarcophagus. Her screams died on her tongue as she saw what they planned. Katherine struggled to free herself, but they laid her in the coffin. She felt the mummy lying beneath her. Terror iced hysterics in her throat.

They were going to bury her alive with Rastau, Ramses's ancestor.

"No," she cried in a muffled voice through the choking gag. "Please, please don't do this!"

Scraping noises sounded as the lid descended toward her in a terrifying rush. The last pencil-thin beam of light faded as they adjusted the lid over the sarcophagus.

She was sealed in.

The musty smell of death and decay enveloped her. Katherine moaned. Tears trickled from her eyes. Her hands groped the coffin's smooth stone sides, then pressed against the heavy lid. She remembered the little girl's warning back in Cairo. "Those who enter the tomb to seek its treasures will die." Now she would pay the ultimate price for her thievery.

Her breaths came deep and frantic. She tried not thinking of the cold, prone form lying beneath her. Katherine closed her eyes and corralled her thoughts. She thought of Ramses and her breath hitched. Breathing. If she hypnotized herself into calmness, into a state where she used little air, she improved her chances of survival. The harder she breathed, the more air she used. Panic would decrease the length of her life.

Slow. In. Out. She summoned Ramses's smiling face, his gentle touch, his loving tenderness, and she focused. She must calm herself and stay alive for him and their baby. Katherine felt herself hover on the edge of consciousness. Then she slipped below, like dipping into a warm pool of quiet water.

Katherine dreamed. Or perhaps it was real. She couldn't be sure. She was outside the coffin, standing in the tomb. Blazing white light filled the chamber. Katherine blinked, looked around and noticed she was not alone.

Standing amid all the gold treasure, the statues, the jewels, was a man of medium height. Well-formed, he had muscled, bronzed shoulders and arms, a flat torso and long, chiseled legs. Sandals encased his feet. A white kilt slung low on narrow hips was his only clothing, but for a heavy gold and lapis collar around his neck. Her gaze shifted to his right arm, where a blue-inked falcon adorned the upper muscles, just below a golden circlet. He crossed powerful arms across his broad, gleaming chest. His head was shaved, as smooth as an egg's surface. The handsome stranger looked familiar, and the startling realization came to her that the person he resembled was Ramses. A bald Ramses. She wanted to giggle, but the stranger regarded her with such steady intensity she didn't dare.

Katherine feared breaking the silence. Her dream self reasoned that this man could not harm her; after all, he was a vision. And a strange, comforting feeling surrounded her, as if he were an old friend. Or family.

"Lady Katherine," the man said.

"Who are you? Where did you come from?"

"I have traveled through the mists of time to find you. I am Rastau, Guardian of the Ages."

Rastau, Ramses's ancestor. Katherine's dream self licked phantom lips, nervousness spilling through her.

"Listen to me, Katherine, and listen well. I have come to show you the future and you must heed it, for locked away in this tomb is the destiny of the people."

His severe expression softened into a fond smile, much as an uncle would bestow on a favorite niece. "For your children."

"My children?" Her hand automatically shot to her abdomen.

"The twins you carry in your womb."

Twins? She didn't know which shocked her more, the idea of carrying twins or the fact she was in a tomb talking to a man who had been dead for thousands of years.

"You're really a mummy?" she asked trying to keep from sounding nervous.

Rastau gave her a scrutinizing look, so much like Ramses she shivered. He waved a hand and her eyes automatically followed in that direction. There on the ground was the little gold cat she had stolen. Katherine felt horrible mortification and lowered her head, certain he chastised her for the theft.

"Look," he said softly.

Compelled to obey that deep voice, she lifted her chin. An amazing phenomenon took place. The little gold cat shifted shape, elongated and grew thick white fur. She stared dumbfounded as a beautiful Persian with large green eyes sat before her, meowing.

"Osiris!" She cried out with joy, rushing toward him.

"Follow him," Rastau instructed as the cat gracefully rose, arched his spine and padded on silent feet toward the wall.

Solid rock vanished into mist as she darted after her beloved friend. Osiris trotted forward through mists and shadows, then stopped, twitching his long tail as he sat. She bent down to pick him up and he sprang suddenly onto a rectangular table.

Katherine found herself in a large, wood-paneled room lined with shelves of books. It looked like an enormous library. Young people in Western dress moved back and forth among the volumes. It was an academic facility, she realized, a British college.

At the table, three young people pored over thick books. They looked vaguely familiar. One had hair the color of corn silk and an elegant, leanly muscled frame. He lifted his head and regarded the girl sitting across from him with a quiet, searching look. A gasp flitted from Katherine's lips as she recognized those dark, brooding eyes. He had his mother's grace and his father's regal air. Tarik, fully grown into manhood.

She dragged her gaze over to the dark-haired girl and boy sitting close together. Her heart stilled and she put a hand to her breast, gasping with delight. The boy had a firmly muscled form and sat with an aura of quietly controlled power, just like his father. He glanced up and smiled at the girl as she raised her head. The boy's square jaw contrasted to the girl's gently rounded one, but their green gazes were duplicates of her own. Her twins. A boy and a girl. Her throat clogged with emotion and pride as she gazed upon her children. Osiris meowed again, and suddenly he shape-shifted, turning back into a small gold cat. From deep in the shadows, the voice of Rastau spoke.

"The gold is naught but metal and brings no honor to the dead. Use it to educate the living and prepare generations for the world's changes. Through the strength of community, the foundation of family, the Khamsin will embrace the future. Never forget that."

Katherine moved closer to the table, tenderly gazing at her children, forgetting about everything but the love swelling in her heart for them.

* * *

At the mine's entrance, the Khamsin warriors caught the Egyptians struggling to load gold onto their camels. As Jabari, Seti and the others unsheathed their scimitars, the sheikh snapped a command for Ramses to rescue Katherine. Ramses paused, torn between the need to protect his leader and an urgency to save his bride. But Seti's blade whirled with righteous power and as one of the Egyptians lifted his scimitar to attack Jabari, his father roared with the strength of a lion. He struck down the attacker with graceful ease. Something deep inside Ramses eased, replaced by a calming peace. His father had restored his honor that day, and protected the Khamsin sheikh.

Ramses raced ahead, lowering himself by the rope into the mine. He followed the torches on the wall until he stood outside the tomb. There he waited, a shadow folded against the rock. Inside, three men grunted as they lifted small gold statues, stuffing them into burlap sacks. He recognized the thin, concave face of the tomb robber. Burrells. Ramses clapped a lid on his fury and quietly waited.

When their attention was fully focused on their task, he sprang into action, leaping forward. Burrells scrambled out of the way as Ramses's sword sliced down the men. They died reaching for their weapons. Turning for the Englishman, he raised his sword and struck. Burrells screamed in pain, and the pistol he had been reaching for flew out of his injured hand, landing near the open well. Burrells danced out of the way. Ramses's rage mingled with fear. Where was Katherine? He pivoted on his boot heels, his eyes frantically searching the tomb.

"Looking for your girlfriend? She's quite cozy. In

good hands, so to speak." Burrells snickered. The robber jerked a thumb toward the sarcophagus. The inner lid rested against the wall. Horror pulsed through Ramses's veins. The tomb robber had sealed his beloved inside Rastau's coffin. Katherine would suffocate and die, along with their unborn child.

As Ramses lifted his scimitar, Burrells rolled toward the well's lip and grabbed the pistol. He fired, grazing Ramses's arm. Instinctively the warrior dropped his blade as pain sliced through his skin. His heart froze in his chest.

Pointing the gun toward him, Burrells backed against the wall, depressing the hidden lever as his weight sank against it. The tomb's door began sliding shut. The robber screamed, grabbed the torch and raced for the door. Ramses darted after him, pouncing as he flung his weight against him. Both men sailed to the ground. Torch and gun flew from Burrells's hands, skidding toward the well, then tumbling downward, plunging the burial chamber into blackness as the tomb door closed.

Ramses's heart stilled with terror. The tomb robber kicked and thrashed, socking him in the jaw, then rolled away. He could hear the man's panted breaths, along with his own. He could not think or move. An icy chill coated his skin.

He stood on shaky feet. Too damn close to the well. One false move and he'd plunge to his death, entombed in darkness for eternity. Panic took hold as blood roared in his ears.

Ramses struggled for calm. Katherine. He must save her. A coffin entombed his bride. If he gave in to fear, she would die. Katherine had hammered at the stone tomb encasing his Ieb and captured his heart in her small, lotus-soft hands. She had freed it from an imaginary sarcophagus and cradled it with the nurturing tenderness of a mother with her newborn. He must free her from the very real sarcophagus imprisoning her. Responsibility to protect his bride and unborn baby weighted him down more than terror.

Dragging in several deep breaths, Ramses crossed his hands over his chest. Bowing his head, he prayed in ancient Egyptian to the spirit of the Guardian who walked before him.

"Most honored Rastau, Guardian of the Ages, your descendent, who carries your blood in my veins, stands before you. My heart is pure and my spirit strong. I beg you now for my beloved and my unborn child. Guide my steps so I may rescue them. Avenge yourself upon this evil one who violates the sanctity of your eternal resting place and harms my beloved. My life means nothing, but save Katherine and our baby. I would give my life a thousand times for them, if they should live."

Calmness took hold as he breathed deeply, willing his body to relax. Ramses heard ragged breaths and realized the tomb raider was equally scared. Insight came to him. He spoke in a low, booming voice.

"You have desecrated this sacred burial chamber and disturbed my ancestor's eternal rest," he intoned in a solemn voice. "Beware the curse. Those who seek the tomb for its treasures will die."

He heard Burrells stand, shuffle his feet in the sand as if testing the solidity of the ground. "Shut up," he squeaked. "I don't believe in curses."

Ramses summoned all his courage and sharpened his senses. He listened intently, calming his own breathing, following the sound of the robber's terrified pants. Footsteps away from the well, he'd plunge down to his death with one misstep. He must risk it. Ramses trusted. Smelled the fear pulsing from the man, the sour scent of horror. And then hurled himself toward him.

Burrells screamed as Ramses's full weight hit him sideways. The curator's arms beat wildly at him as the impact sent him falling backward, then hurling into the well. Ramses pulled away, rolling to safety. A loud shriek of terror followed for several minutes, growing fainter and fainter until it became a tiny whistle. And then nothing.

Stillness settled over the tomb. He stood, groped for the silk sash at his belt and bound his bleeding arm. Ramses carefully made his way toward the coffin. Bumping into the cold stone, he used every ounce of might to push the lid. Grunting with the pull on his muscles, he strained. But even his enormous strength barely moved it.

Hearing the stomp of feet outside the chamber, he yelled for help, instructing about the door's hidden lever and calling out a warning about the well. The door slid open. As his father and Jabari rushed into the tomb, carrying torches, Ramses gestured to the coffin.

"Help me! Katherine's trapped inside," he shouted. Wasting no time, the men sprinted to his side and struggled with him to slide the lid off. As it crashed down, he bent over the coffin to confront the still, colorless form of his beloved. Katherine lay atop Rastau's mummy as if clutched in a lover's embrace. Her beautiful, pouty mouth showed cracked lips between a dirty gag. Ropes trussed her hands and feet in the same style bodies were bound before the mummification process began.

Sliding his dagger out of its sheath, he cut her bonds and carefully slit the gag free. Her soft skin still held warmth, but she appeared as lost and dead as the ancient Guardian entombed with her. Ramses reached down, lifted her out. He gathered her into his arms and sat on the sand. Cradling her head with one hand, he pressed a kiss against her temple. Her body was so soft and round. So alive with her fierce spirit and gentle, healing touch. She had healed him. Saved his life. Now he couldn't do the same. Katherine had slipped through his frantically grasping fingers like grains of sand tumbling down.

"Ramses . . ." Jabari's voice cracked. "I am so sorry."

His friend sounded as if he called from a great distance. Ramses wrapped his arms around Katherine as if to give her his strength. Hot tears scalded his eyes as he rocked back and forth with her body in his arms. One droplet fell upon her brow, rolling down to catch in the smoky lashes feathering her cheeks. It glistened like a diamond.

"Please," he begged in a broken voice. "Please live."

A steel sword thrust through his heart. How could she be dead? He couldn't lose her. His Katherine, the keeper of his Ieb. He needed her. Without her love, life presented a cold, bitter possibility. His heart would retreat back inside the stone tomb, sealed forever. He thought of Kareem dying with Maia and knew a terrible jealousy, for at least they were together in death. He simply could not bear life without his Katherine. His wife. The mother of his son. Or daughter. Ramses's blurred vision dropped to Katherine's still flat abdomen. Would their baby have been born with rounded cheeks, a button nose and fat dimpled arms and legs? He imagined a raven-haired, green-eyed little girl shrieking with glee as he twirled her around. How could a life, newly created, vanish as swiftly as a gust of wind? He touched Katherine's belly.

"I am sorry, little one. I wanted you so very much. Please forgive me for not saving you," Ramses whispered.

He needed to trace every inch of her, burn it into memory. Ramses clutched her tighter. He could not release her. Not yet. One last kiss. Her lips under his still held warmth. He knew it was futile, but Ramses breathed into her mouth as if he could breathe into her his life force.

Nestled deep in the fascinating dream-illusion of watching her grown children, Katherine felt something yank at her with demanding insistence. A veneer of light spilled into her vision, tearing away the fabric of the dream. Strong arms settled around her. Caught between the dream world and the real one, she hovered, captivated by her vision, yet unable to ignore the nagging feeling she must leave this place.

Warmth touched her lips and a soft breath blew into her mouth. The dream world vanished like a ghost mist. Light pierced her eyelids. Her sluggish brain awakened. She drew from the breath flooding her lungs and answered back with one of her own.

Ramses jerked back, hope pulsing wildly through him at the rush of air returning to his mouth. He covered her mouth with his and blew air deeply into her lungs, then drew back. Now her chest rose and fell.

His own breath still now, Ramses stroked her cheek. Long, smoky lashes fluttered as she slowly opened her eyes. Her lips tugged up as she tried to smile.

"Ramses," she croaked weakly. Her hand rose, touched his lips. It felt like the kiss of an angel's silk wing. He traced her rounded chin with his finger. He could not speak, only buried his face into the masses of her satin hair.

Ramses lifted his head and gazed into her eyes, placing his hand to check her pulse. The vein pulsed with life.

Color began to bloom in her pale cheeks. It was like watching a lotus blossom unfurl its petals to the sun's warmth. Laying a gentle hand on her chest, he felt the reassuring rhythm of life. Ramses continued to embrace her, too choked to speak. If he had to stay frozen like this for a thousand years, he would, if only it meant having her heart beat beneath his trembling hand.

Chapter Twenty-nine

Katherine raised herself up on her elbows and peered into Ramses's sleeping face. His lips parted as he breathed. Unable to resist, she brushed back her husband's hair and kissed his earlobe.

He adored being kissed there. And there. Katherine nuzzled his throat. Since the wedding, she had made many delightful discoveries exploring her husband's erotic zones. For one week they had remained isolated in a tent away from the main Khamsin compound. Katherine cherished every single moment of their privacy. Rescued from death, she needed to seize life with both hands and never let go.

Every detail of her vision had been relayed. Her father met with Jabari, Ramses and the Khamsin council. In the end, they agreed with Papa's suggestion. Leave the mine alone. The gold in the tomb remained as future security for the tribe's children to attend school.

Impatient for Ramses to awaken, she jerked the sheet down and stared at his taut, rounded bottom.

Katherine nipped the muscled flesh. Her husband awoke with a startled grunt. He captured her in his arms, then affixed his mouth to hers in a passionate kiss. Warm lips glided over her throat as his tongue expertly delivered several sensuous flicks.

A soft meow interrupted their bliss. Ramses opened one eye as Osiris leapt onto the bed and settled atop Katherine's legs. The white cat regarded him with cool green eyes. She stifled a giggle as Ramses frowned.

"Osiris, stop watching us. Go find a nice mouse or chase the dogs." Ramses padded with languid grace to the tent's door, lifting it. "Now," he said sternly.

With a disdainful tail swish, Osiris stalked outside. Ramses grinned and returned to bed. They made love in a long, leisurely fashion. Afterward, they lay in each other's arms, purring with contentment.

"My warrior of love." She smiled into his chest, rubbing her cheek against the silky hair.

He stiffened and uttered a deep groan. "Do not call me that."

Katherine raised her head. "Why? Because the other women did?"

A sheepish blush crept into his bronzed cheeks. "You know about them?"

"My friends mentioned a thing or two." Katherine told him about the day at the Shepheard's lounge. Ramses's mouth twitched violently as if he fought to suppress a wide smile of male smugness.

"You think this is funny," she accused him.

His body quaked with restrained hilarity. "A manipulator?" his deep voice asked. Tears streamed down his cheeks as he let loose howls of laughter. Katherine punched his thickly muscled arm.

"Don't mock modern medicine. Dr. Taylor worked

long and hard to find a way to relieve women's hysteria." She chastised him, but her playful smirk belied the scolding tone.

"I know other long and hard ways to relieve hysteria," he pronounced, sealing her lips with a deep kiss. Ramses lifted his head and grinned. "Let your friends have their manipulators. You have me, Katherine. This warrior of love prowls no more. From now on, my weapon is sheathed permanently." *In you*, the glint in his dark gold eyes said.

A delighted smile curved her lips. Katherine touched his perfect cheek with a hand trembling with love for him. Her hand fell, then shot to her own marred cheek. Terrible doubts shook her self-confidence. Today they officially ended their seclusion. Ramses swore his people would love her, and she agreed to abandon her veil. But still, Katherine felt great trepidation.

He noticed and brushed back a lock of hair. "Katherine," he said quietly, "do you fear going unveiled?"

"I don't know if I can do it," she told him.

"You can," he said in an encouraging voice.

Katherine bit her lip. "Ramses, I can't. Because not everyone will see me the way you do. The world never has. For years, I suffered people mocking me because I am ugly."

He sat up, raking a hand through his hair. Her sorrowful expression tugged at his heart. "My beloved, you do not need to be afraid any longer."

Doubt filled her glittering green eyes. He struggled for kind, reassuring words to express the depth of his love.

His gaze took in her long slender neck, as graceful as a winged ibis taking flight. And her rose-red lips, a

Cupid's bow mouth that begged for kisses and returned passion for passion. And her pert nose and beautiful, expressive eyes.

Then the left cheek covered by her lotus-soft hand.

Crystalline tears shimmered in her jewel eyes. Katherine seemed to struggle for words. Perspiration sheened her brow.

"Look at me, Ramses. Look hard at this. I want you to truly see my scar. See how damaged I am. How can you keep denying it?" With that, she bared the nasty gash. A single tear chased a pathway down her left cheek, dampening the old wound with a silvery reflection.

Two warm hands cupped her face. Love and tender concern radiated from his amber eyes.

"Katherine, my love, I have always known of your injury."

Her lips parted in shock. "But how? I hid it from you!"

"During the day, your veil was most effective. But you forget my nature." A shy grin lit his face. "Like my totem, the tiger, I am quite curious. I lifted your veil the first night I recovered from my fever. And I saw."

"You saw?" She gaped at him.

"Yes, my love." Ramses softly stroked the scar, the wound that caused her so much pain.

"I love you, and no scar could ever stand between us." Then he dropped his hands to his chest.

"Look at this body, and all the old wounds marking it. What are these to you?" He took her hand and placed it against his chest. Silky hair passed beneath her palm as Ramses moved her hand over one scar, then another and yet another.

"They are marks of honor, of bravery, of nobility," she replied, not understanding.

"And how is your own scar anything less?" Ramses pressed a kiss against her marked left cheek. "When I see your scar I see all the beauty within you that it represents. I see you, my beloved. All of you. And I would have it no other way."

Katherine's lips trembled as her eyes filled with fresh tears. But they were tears of tremendous love and gratitude for the handsome, chivalrous man who professed his heart and soul.

He splayed his hand across her abdomen and she flushed from the warmth of his possessive gesture. Ramses looked at her with pride. "Our babies have a beautiful mother. I want them to look like you. I love you, my darling. You are a part of my heart now, and always will be."

A mysterious smile played about his lips as he stood and retrieved something from a colorful woven bag. Sitting down, he pressed two gentle fingertips against her eyelids, closing them. Warm hands slipped a thin chain around her neck.

"Open your eyes."

Katherine looked down. Attached to the silver necklace were two wooden hearts, no bigger than a walnut shell. Beautiful gold and red striations ran through the olive wood grain.

Ramses's hand gently encased the charm. "It is my heart and yours, my Kalila. I carved it for you. I wanted my heart to bond to yours, forever."

"Oh, Ramses, it's beautiful." Her heart swelled with love at his tender, thoughtful gift.

"My Kalila, long ago I vowed never to fall in love. I thought my heart was safe, sealed inside a tomb. Until

Bonnie Vanak

the day you kissed me. You stole my heart. You have my Ieb, my heart, my seat of consciousness. I give it to you freely for all eternity, my darling Kalila."

Ramses settled her head against his chest. Clutching the wooden heart charm, she listened to his Ieb's steady beat. The tiger had captured her heart, but instead of lacerating it with sharp claws as she had feared, Ramses had healed it.

Reluctantly, they scrambled from bed and dressed. Katherine draped a blue scarf around her head and neck, securing it so the silver charms weighed it down. Picking up her black veil, she shot him a questioning look.

"You can do it," he told her. "I will be with you."

Donning their footwear outside, they strolled toward the main camp. Women carrying clay jars of water smiled in passing. Someone had built a small cooking fire near one of the black tents. Curls of smoke wended upwards, beckoning with lazy grace.

Katherine started to throw her veil into the flames and stopped. She gnawed on her lower lip with mounting anxiety. It was so difficult giving up this security blanket. The veil had protected her from the world's cruel sneers. How could she muster the courage to do this?

As she hesitated, Ramses took her hand. He looked at her. She nodded. Together they tossed the veil into the fire and watched greedy tongues of flame devour the fabric.

A tremendous burden lifted from her shoulders as fire consumed the remains of her old life. Katherine touched the charm on her necklace. Their Iebs. Her heart and his, like the twin babies nestling in her womb, bound together forever. Ramses's Ieb now

340

wound around hers so securely, she could not tell where one ended and the other began. They had freed their hearts from a lifeless, dark tomb and planted them in a beautiful, sunlit garden, regenerating them with their tender love for each other. And there in that garden her heart, twined with his, would remain.